Unforgettable

Unforgettable

A COUNTRY ROADS NOVEL
BOOK 4

Shannon Richard

New York Boston

Forever Yours
Hachette Book Group
1290 Avenue of the Americas
New York, NY 10104
Hachettebookgroup.com
Twitter.com/foreverromance

First ebook and print on demand edition: January 2015

Forever Yours is an imprint of Grand Central Publishing.
The Forever Yours name and logo are trademarks of Hachette Book Group, Inc.

The publisher is not responsible for websites (or their content) that are not owned by the publisher.

The Hachette Speakers Bureau provides a wide range of authors for speaking events. To find out more, go to www.hachettespeakersbureau.com or call (866) 376-6591.

ISBN 978-1-4555-6099-8 (ebook edition)
ISBN 978-1-4555-8845-9 (print on demand edition)

To Kaitie Hotard
Who gets how a melody is a memory.
Our friendship started with a love of music
and has only grown from there.
Sometimes we do get to choose our family.
You are my sister in every way.

Acknowledgments

I must start with my work wife, Jessica Lemmon. You are a fantastic friend and I'm truly blessed to call you such. I cannot even begin to express how much you've helped me in the last year, especially with this book. Thank you for pushing me with the prologue. I don't think this book would be what it is without you. And, of course, I must also say thank you for introducing me to the wonder that is Charlie Hunnam.

To Nikki Rushbrook, I still thank my lucky stars that you happened upon *Undone*. It makes me beyond happy that you fell in love with Brendan King and the world of Mirabelle, Florida. You are amazing and I do so love talking to you about all things inappropriate. You've become an invaluable sounding board and your enthusiasm for these books is humbling. I must also thank the other women at Scandalicious Book Reviews. Nikki, you along with Donna, Lola, Teena, and Tania continually make me laugh on your podcasts and all forms of social media. The five of you are simply delightful.

To fellow authors Gina Conkle, Nicole Michaels, and Heather

Heyford, you all are beautiful women and I'm so glad we've become friends. It's remarkable the bonds that can be formed over a few drinks, a fancy dinner, and a meaningful conversation.

To Tony Silcox, who gave me insight and perspective when I needed it. You helped me talk out more than a few scenes, and I'm grateful for your time. Also, the support that you and your wife, Mindy, have given me, and my books, has meant so much to me.

To Katie Crandall, I don't think I would've been able get through these last couple of months on deadline without your constant help. Thank you for your grilled cheese, *Downton Abbey* Sundays, and our mutual love for all things Scottish. You spent more than a few hours going over plot points with me and listening to my constant ramblings. I don't know how you deal with my scattered trains of thought. God bless you.

To Amy Lipford and Katie Privett, fantastic neighbors and even better friends.

And for the people I'd be remiss if I didn't mention: my parents; my agent, Sarah E. Younger; my editor, Megha Parekh; my publicist, Julie Paulauski; everyone at Grand Central; Marina and David McCue; and Ronald Richard.

To Eric Church for the song "Springsteen." The first time I heard it, I knew it was the story behind Nathanial Shepherd and Hannah Sterling. It still gives me goose bumps when I hear it.

And to every person to whom I've posed a question about any and all of my books. There are many of you. Your thoughts and opinions are forever appreciated.

Unforgettable

Prologue

Forgotten

Thirteen years ago...

Hannah Sterling snapped her cell phone shut for the fourteenth time, hanging it up with a loud *thwack*. She was going to break the thing if she kept it up. At least this time she'd gotten to the last digit before she'd freaked out.

Her heart was pounding loudly in her ears, making it difficult to hear. Then there was the state of her throat, which seemed to keep getting smaller. Swallowing was becoming a feat unto itself.

She wiped her sweaty palms on her jeans and tried to take a deep, calming breath, but she couldn't get her lungs to expand. Maybe because she'd spent the last few days having more intense crying jags than she could count.

Hannah wasn't normally a crier. It just wasn't something that she did. Her parents had never really responded to any strong emotions, happy or sad. Kendra and Russ Sterling were about as warm as freezer burn and had perfected indifference in all manners of life.

Except for money. They loved money. That was what they threw at a problem to fix it. But no amount of money was going to fix this problem. No amount of money was going to reverse the miscarriage.

The baby was gone.

Her eyes started to burn at the corners, and she closed them tight. Somehow the tears still managed to leak through, trailing down her cheeks.

How the hell was she supposed to make them stop?

To say that her emotions were all over the place would be an understatement. The doctor had said something about how she'd heal physically within a couple of weeks. But emotionally? That could take much longer.

How long was much longer?

Her grandmother Gigi was the only person who knew about the miscarriage. Gigi was her best friend and was more of a parent to her than her mother and father had ever been. The woman had pretty much raised Hannah and was the only reason she'd had an ounce of affection growing up. She loved her dearly and told her everything... normally.

Before the miscarriage, no one had known about the pregnancy. The reason? She'd wanted to tell the father first. The problem? He lived more than a thousand miles away in Mirabelle, a tiny little town in the middle of nowhere, Florida.

Nathanial Shepherd.

Just thinking about him made her heart hurt. She'd never thought it was possible to miss someone so much. Because really, what did she know? She was barely eighteen, her birthday having been only a few weeks ago, so what in the world did she know about love?

Three months—that was the extent of their relationship.

She'd known it was going to end before it even started. She'd known there was an expiration date, but she'd gone and fallen in love with him anyway.

She hadn't had a choice. The first time he'd looked at her, all sense and logic had vanished. Her pragmatic brain was nowhere to be seen.

It had been two months since she'd left him, two months since her heart had broken right in two. But what other choice did she have? She'd been about to start her freshman year at Columbia University, and he had no intention of ever leaving Mirabelle.

It was a few weeks before she realized her period was late. She'd never been one to avoid reality, as it wasn't practical. But as she'd never been all that spot-on with this particular schedule, she'd chosen to ignore it.

By the second month, there was no more ignoring it.

The test had been positive. That was the only answer she knew; everything else had been entirely up in the air.

What in the world was she going to do? Drop out of school? Raise the child with Shep? Where would they live? Would she move down there? Or would he come up to Manhattan? Would he even want to raise this child with her? Would he want anything to do with either of them?

For two weeks she'd agonized about calling him, figuring out exactly what to say to him, thinking about what he'd say, what they'd decide to do. But none of that mattered anymore. There was nothing to figure out.

He still deserved to know, though. He still deserved to know that for a couple of months there had been a baby. *Their* baby. And she'd be lying if she told herself she wasn't desperate to hear his voice. That talking to him might make her feel human again for even a moment.

Hannah picked up the phone, her hand shaking so bad she thought she was going to drop it. Somehow she managed to hit all of the correct numbers with her fumbling finger. Somehow she managed to not hang up when it started to ring. Somehow she managed to not throw up when the phone clicked and his voice came through on the other end.

"Hello?" The deep Southern timber of Shep's voice was groggy.

"H-hi." Her eyes darted to the clock on the wall. It was six o'clock in the morning. Of course he'd been asleep. He was still in bed; she wanted to be there with him. Wanted him to put his arms around her and tell her that everything was going to be okay.

"Hannah."

He knew it was her. She sighed and closed her eyes in relief. *Thank God. He didn't forget me.*

"What's wrong?" There was so much concern in his voice. He still cared about her, and she wanted to wrap herself in it like a warm blanket. Wanted to wrap herself in him.

Her throat tightened, painfully so, but she managed to make it move. "Everything. I–I miss you."

Stone-cold silence came from the other end of the line.

"Shep?"

"Hannah…" His voice was no longer sleepy. It had dropped to a low whisper, and the concern had something else mixed in… regret?

"Sheppy, who is it?" A breathy female voice drifted through the speaker.

Hannah's eyes flew open and her stomach heaved. Yeah, now she *was* going to throw up.

Tears clogged her throat. She couldn't breathe. She couldn't think. It was too much. She snapped her phone shut for the fifteenth time and threw it against the wall.

This time it did break, and it wasn't the only thing in pieces on the floor.

She'd been wrong. Wrong about all of it. He had forgotten about her. He'd forgotten about everything.

And now she was going to have to do the same.

Chapter 1

Remembered

Present day...

Hannah Sterling had been back in Mirabelle, Florida, for exactly twenty-four hours before she was finally brave enough to venture out among the living and leave the dusty confines of her new—and temporary—residence.

There was a Seafood Festival down at the main part of Mirabelle Beach. The pier was loaded up with vendors selling their shrimp gumbo, sautéed scallops, and fried alligator on a stick. She was pretty sure that half of the five thousand people that populated the six hundred square miles were packed into the area.

But crowd or not, Mirabelle was a far cry from Manhattan. It would take some time for her to get used to it, more time than she was going to be spending there.

This was just a temporary thing. Three months, that was it. That was how long Hannah had to figure out what she was going to do with the Seaside Escape Inn, to possibly start to deal with the death of her grandmother, and to maybe figure out why her grandmother had left her said inn.

But within ten minutes of walking around the festival, she doubted her decision more than ever. She froze in her tracks as she stared at the first man she'd given her body to, the only man she'd given her heart to, and the one man who had ultimately broken it.

Hannah had immediately noticed Nathanial Shepherd the first time she'd seen him thirteen years ago. It had been at a distance, but there'd been no denying how good he looked. He'd worn his black hair long and shaggy, and even at eighteen his square, chiseled jaw had always been covered in five-o'clock shadow. As he'd been wearing sunglasses, she hadn't seen his eyes then, but later she'd discovered the deep blue color that reminded her of sapphires and how they were surrounded by thick, dark lashes women everywhere would covet.

He'd been without a doubt the most attractive guy she'd ever seen.

And now? Now he was thirty-one and about thirty-one times more attractive. His hair was a little bit shorter—though still tousled in an incredibly sexy way—but he must have just transferred the length to his jaw. He was sporting what could be described only as a ten-o'clock shadow. For just a second she let herself imagine that it was a little softer than the rough scruff she'd known in a previous life.

And then there was the not-so-small matter of the tattoos scattered across both of his arms. He'd already started the collection the summer she'd been here, but it appeared he'd added several. There were only a few on his left, but the right was covered all the way up to the sleeve of his T-shirt.

Hannah found the whole package so sexy she couldn't think for a second...or two...or ten.

And then she took in the rest of the scene and her entire body cringed.

The whole perfect little picture in front of her made her so unexpectedly sad she could barely see straight. He had a little boy in his arms, a little boy whom he was bouncing up into the air, and both of them were laughing. And then there was the woman at his side. She had legs all the way up to her ears and a wide smile. She tossed her dark brown hair over her shoulder as she looked at the duo with adoration and love.

Shep was married.

Married.

And his family...God. They were beautiful together. She'd known he'd moved on from her thirteen years ago, but not *on* on. There was something about seeing the happy little family in the flesh that literally ripped her in half.

It was the life that could've been hers. The life that would *never* be hers.

It wasn't like she'd come back here thinking there was a chance in hell at another shot with him. Not at all. She had much more sense than that. Otherwise she was screwed. Royally so.

Shep handed the little boy to his wife and pressed an affectionate kiss to her cheek. Then he looked up and scanned the crowd. Hannah had a heart-stopping moment where his eyes landed on her, and he hesitated for seconds that were more like an eternity. His mouth quirked to the side in question and his eyebrows lowered.

But then a guy with buzzed dark blond hair came up behind him, and his gaze left her. She immediately began to breathe again and quickly merged with the group of people next to her.

Why the hell am I hiding, anyway?

As he'd moved on about a second after she'd left, she doubted he would even remember her. And the odds were even less that he'd recognize her.

So she walked away and didn't look back, leaving Shep and the life that wasn't hers behind. She rubbed at her chest, an ache that she hadn't felt in a while blooming under the skin.

What the hell was she doing here? Had her grandmother really thought that coming back to Mirabelle was going to help? What was the purpose?

Gigi Sterling had been absent from this world for four months now. Hannah hadn't exactly grieved her beloved grandmother. She didn't know how a person was supposed to grieve the loss of a best friend. How she was supposed to cope with the death of the only person she'd ever thought of as a parent. Her only real family.

She'd avoided it, but there was no avoiding it now. That's why she was in Mirabelle. She thought this all might help in the grieving process, as it was the last thing Gigi had done for her. The last thing Gigi had wanted of her.

For years Gigi had talked to Hannah about unfinished business. Settling things before it was too late. The importance of closure. She knew her granddaughter better than anyone else, so she'd known that the miscarriage and things with Shep had always haunted Hannah.

And that was how the current adventure had come into play.

Gigi had learned long ago how to get exactly what she wanted. She put plans into place that guaranteed Hannah was going deal with things. About a year ago—and unbeknownst to Hannah—she'd bought a beach house in Mirabelle. The very same house Hannah had spent that summer in more than a decade ago.

Hannah was now the owner of the Seaside Escape Inn. When she'd come down, she'd had absolutely no idea what she was walking into; nor did she have any idea what she was going to do with it. But she did have a little time to figure it out.

Somehow everything fell into line perfectly. Right place, right time. Even in death Gigi was pulling strings.

Hannah was a partner at one of the biggest commercial law firms in Manhattan. She worked in the contracts department at McAvoy and Sutter, where there was more than plenty to keep her busy. They'd just finished working on a merger between Harrison and Bloom, two billion-dollar tech companies.

Harrison was their client, and it was the biggest and most important deal the firm had ever done. It consisted of months of work that had kept her and many of the other partners in the office for hours on end. It had been exhausting and a distraction from her personal life.

Shortly after the merger was finished, Gigi's will had been read and Hannah had found out about her inheritance. With no huge projects at work consuming her every thought, she'd had to start dealing with her loss, and it hadn't been pretty.

Allison McAvoy was more than just Hannah's boss; she was a mentor and the only person whom Hannah really considered a friend. Allison knew everything that was going on; she also knew exactly how hard Hannah had worked on the Harrison contract. So when Hannah had asked for the time off, Allison had given it without blinking.

It wasn't like Hannah wouldn't be working for the next three months; she was more than capable of drafting contracts and going over them from Mirabelle. So with the green light from work, she'd packed up some of her stuff and hit the road with her six-month-old kitten, Henry.

After two days of driving, she got into town in the early evening with gritty eyes and a need to hibernate. She was pretty sure it wasn't just the drive that had done her in but the last few months as a whole. Despite the rock-hard mattress, she'd passed out, though her back had been more than slightly sore when she'd woken up.

Henry had apparently needed rest, too; thus he'd let her sleep in that morning. The afternoon was spent taking stock of the massive three-story inn they now resided in. What with the eighteen bedrooms, most complete with their own private bath, they had a lot to explore.

Henry played shadow, following her around for hours, his little gray tail in the air, as anxious as she was to stretch his legs and check out the new digs.

Though they weren't that new.

The inn had gone through some changes since Hannah had been there last, none of them good. Two different sets of owners had taken a shot at entrepreneurship. Neither had been all that successful. Certain things had fallen into disrepair, while some changes had been horribly misguided.

Someone had thought that wallpapering the bathrooms was a good idea.

They'd been wrong.

Projects had been started and not finished, boxes of purchased supplies stored in one of the bedrooms upstairs. Almost every single wall was in need of a fresh coat of paint, and a lot of the lighting and plumbing fixtures needed to be replaced. The furniture was old and banged up and the linens, threadbare. It was a good thing she'd brought her own sheets, towels, and blankets.

At least the hardwood floors were still in fantastic condition. They might squeak when anyone walked on them, but she liked the noise. It invoked happy memories of when she'd been here before, every room occupied by vacationers. Sure Gigi could've rented a house for just the two of them, but she'd always done things differently. It was all about the experience, trying something new—the adventure of it all.

Hannah was pretty sure that Gigi had purposely picked out the inn as a stepping-stone for her first year of college—forcing Hannah to meet new people and open up, getting her used to a community-type living.

There was something about being in that house that was both comforting and disconcerting at the same time. Memories of that summer flooded Hannah's brain. Gigi in her big floppy hat, sunscreen smeared across her nose while she lay out on the beach reading a book. The two of them curled up on the couches while it rained outside, drinking mugs of tea and laughing. Shep coming over and eating dinner with them. Shep sneaking into her room late at night. Shep kissing her one last time before she got into the car and left him for good.

Seeing him again made everything that happened thirteen years ago open up like a fresh wound. Well, didn't it just go perfectly with the more recent wound that was the loss of Gigi?

For thirteen years Hannah had avoided pain at all costs, and now she was knee-deep in it.

* * *

Nathanial Shepherd never had a problem getting a girl into his bed. Too bad for the blonde at the bar he'd sworn off women.

"Get you anything else, Andrea?" he asked as he stopped in front of her.

"I'm thinking what I want isn't on the menu." Her eyes narrowed as she chewed on the end of her straw. She had very big lips that were coated with some shiny red gloss. It made him think about her lips wrapped around something else.

That wasn't happening, either. He'd used his dick as a coping mechanism for far too long. But not anymore.

Shep's sex life had cooled down of late. Way down. Like… glacial, and he had a damn good reason for it, too.

His grandfather had been his hero from as far back as he could remember. Hell, Owen had built the Sleepy Sheep, the family bar that Shep helped run and of which he was now a partial owner. He'd also built the house Shep lived in now.

So when Owen had said in no uncertain terms that he was disappointed with Shep, it had been a blow. But not nearly as big of a blow as the call Shep received five hours later. Nothing compared to the pain he'd felt when he'd found out Owen was gone. The heart attack had been sudden and swift. His grandfather never even made it to the hospital.

There were certain things that could set a man straight, and to have the person he respected most think that he was pissing his life away? Yeah, *that* was certainly one of them. All of Shep's life he'd wanted to live up to his grandfather's legacy, and he was nowhere near it.

Thus, Shep's *somewhat* calmed libido. But even though he wouldn't be sleeping with Andrea, it didn't mean he couldn't flirt with her. Tips were tips, and a guy had to pay the bills.

"I'm sure we can find you something." He grinned as he placed both hands on the counter and leaned in. "Wine? Beer? Sex on the Beach?" he asked with a wicked grin.

Andrea's eyes dilated and she licked her lips.

"Or I can whip up something special, just for you."

Her smile widened and she nodded. "I'll take the something special. Sweet and salty, preferably."

"Coming right up."

He headed to the middle of the bar and pulled out a bottle of gin before he eyed the juices stocked in the fridge. He was adding a splash of triple sec to the grapefruit juice and raspberry concoction he'd come up with when his little brother, Finn, came out of the back with a tray full of clean mugs.

Finn was a little bit buffer and just slightly shorter than Shep, coming out at about six foot two to Shep's six foot three. But they had the same blue eyes and easygoing grin. The only other visual difference, besides the tattoos that covered Shep's arms, was the fact that Finn wore glasses.

"I'm pretty sure the hot blonde in the corner wants to nail you to the wall," Finn said out of the side of his mouth.

"Of course she does."

"Might want to take her up on that."

It was a lot harder for Shep to conceal that he was on a self-imposed dry spell when he was currently living with his little brother. Finn had been back in Mirabelle for about four months now, ever since he'd passed his Veterinary Medical Exams and started working at the only animal doctor in Mirabelle.

While Finn got settled into his new life postschool, he was bunking it up with Shep. They had opposite schedules, so it wasn't all that bad, except when Finn ate everything in the fridge, which was fairly often. Shep had no idea how his little brother had made it through eight years at school, because the guy was physically incapable of going to the grocery store.

Doctor Dolittle worked at the bar only occasionally. And as one of the guys who was supposed to be on shift that night called out, he'd filled in. And now Shep was dealing with Finn poking him...with a very large stick.

He looked at his baby brother and raised an eyebrow. It was a move that would've intimidated the hell out of Finn a decade ago. But now it had absolutely no effect.

"Maybe you should mind your own business," Shep said as he grabbed a glass and salted the rim.

"All kidding aside, what the hell are you doing?"

"What do you mean?"

"Your new vow as a man of the cloth, Father Shepherd."

"Watch it."

"I'm not saying nail everything within a ten-mile radius like you used to, but maybe a date with Miss Bedroom Eyes over there would be good for you." Finn didn't even wait for a response from Shep before he walked away, which was good because the words out of Shep's mouth would probably have included a *fuck* and an *off*.

Finn was enjoying life after school, taking advantage of his freedom and spending more than a few evenings in the company of a variety of women. Though Shep suspected that had a little to do with the fact that his high school sweetheart, Becky Wright, wasn't really giving him the time of day since he'd come back.

So Shep really wasn't inclined to take his brother's advice to heart.

He returned his focus to his drink mixing and poured his creation into the glass. He turned around, snapping into work mode and replacing his scowl with a smile.

But there might've been a little something to Finn's words. What the hell *was* he doing? Okay, so maybe the one-eighty he'd pulled after Owen's death hadn't been the answer. And maybe sitting on his ass waiting for something to happen wasn't the best solution. Maybe he needed to step up and take some action, and Andrea would be some good action.

His dick was in agreement, but his brain hesitated. Why the hell wasn't that even remotely what he wanted to do?

* * *

Hannah stared up at the swinging sign above the Sleepy Sheep. The sign had two sheep sleeping in the corner, *Z*s trailing above their heads. There were large, pained windows on either side of the front door, giving a good view of the establishment within. The same mahogany wood was on the inside and out, giving the place a Scottish pub feel.

Maybe the longer she analyzed the outside, the longer she could delay walking inside.

That sounded like a good plan.

A perfect plan, in fact.

She'd never been in during business hours, as she'd been underage, but she'd spent plenty of time inside the building, playing pool and making out with Shep in the back office.

There was a war waging in her at the moment. One was to run away. It had been three days since she'd seen him at the Seafood Festival, and she wasn't sure she was quite over the shock of him settled with a family. There was no need to put herself in an uncomfortable situation.

But as Hannah was going to be here for the next three months, she felt like she needed to get this little meeting out of the way. It was a small town, and she was bound to run into him sooner or later. On the off chance that she'd made a lasting impact on Shep's memory, she figured that if she got it over and done with now, she'd be in complete control of the situation.

"So now it is." She opened the door and walked inside.

The place was packed. The tables out on the floor were crowded with occupied chairs. People were lined up all along the bar, waiting for drinks. Country music played through the speakers, keeping the couples out on the dance floor busy.

Hannah's eyes went to the bar, and she zeroed in on who she thought was Shep. She immediately realized it wasn't him, but she was a little taken aback by the resemblance. Finn was no longer a baby-faced thirteen-year-old. He was almost Shep in miniature...*almost*, but not quite.

She wasn't sure if Finn would remember her or not, but there was no point in hiding anymore. She was doing this thing. Ripping off the Band-Aid.

She went up to the bar and took one of the few empty seats. She settled in next to a guy who was sipping on his beer and staring up at some sporting event on TV. The game went to a commercial for a special report, and it took her only a moment to realize what it was.

There was a high-profile court case going on in Manhattan between basketball player Raymond Larson and his wife, actress Angel Hall. She'd tried to kill him—stabbed him fourteen times—and though he'd survived, his basketball career had not. The whole thing was being televised and hashed out and dissected every night by anyone who took a prelaw class.

The wife's lawyer, Jeffrey Phillips, was doing everything in his power to make her look like the victim. He was arguing self-defense, saying the wife had been abused for years, and he was doing a pretty damn good job at it. There was no doubt about the fact that the guy was a talented lawyer. He was charming, manipulative, and so good at lying it should be illegal. Hannah would know, as he was her ex-boyfriend.

Jeffrey appeared on the screen, gesturing with his hands as he talked to the jury, everything about him immaculate and groomed, from his three-thousand-dollar suit to his manicured fingernails. She couldn't stop the scoffing noise that erupted from her throat.

The guy sitting next to her turned in her direction. He reached up and pushed his sandy blond hair out of his eyes as he looked her over.

"You think it's a joke, too?" he asked, nodding up to the screen with his chin.

"I think she's guilty as sin, and she's going to get away with it."

"Yeah, the prosecutor can't tell his ass from his elbow. Sorry." He looked at her apologetically when he realized what he'd said.

"Don't worry about it." She waved him off. "It's true."

"The prosecution is going to lose, especially up against a shark like Jeffrey Phillips. That man has no soul."

He could say that again.

It was then that she took in the man's somewhat expensive attire—clothing that was not the norm in Mirabelle, where shirts were grease stained and jeans were torn. But this guy was wearing a light blue button-up shirt, no stains in sight, and what she assumed were fitted trousers. He'd rolled up his sleeves to his elbows and wasn't wearing a tie, the top button of his still-crisp shirt undone.

"Are you a lawyer?" Hannah asked.

"Guilty as charged. I hope to God I never have to deal with anything like that."

"Down here in Mayberry? I think you're safe."

"I don't know about that. We had a string of robberies last year. My friend Melanie was shot, and then my other friend Grace was held at gunpoint."

"Melanie O'Bryan and Grace King?" she asked, horrified.

Shep's best friends were Jaxson Anderson and Brendan King, Grace's older brother. Grace and Mel had been best friends. Hannah had spent plenty of time with the three guys and their friends and family. She distinctly remembered the two girls from that summer, Grace with blue eyes that looked at Jax with no small amount of adoration and Mel with her crazy curly blonde hair.

"You know Melanie and Grace?" He looked at her, confused.

"It was a long time ago."

"I was going to say...She's not Grace King anymore. It's Anderson now."

"Are you serious?" Hannah couldn't stop the wave of excitement at that news, or the smile that popped up on her mouth. "She married Jax? I always knew he'd figure that out."

The guy's eyebrows bunched together even more. "How did you know that and...who are you?"

"I'm Hannah. I spent a summer here years ago." She stuck out her hand toward the guy, but it took him a second to realize it as his jaw dropped and his eyes nearly bugged out of his head.

"You're Hannah Sterling?" He stared at her in shock for a second before he recovered and stuck out his hand, shaking hers firmly before he let go. "I'm Preston Matthews."

Now it was her turn to be baffled. "How do you know who I am?"

"You're the only girl who's ever broken Nathanial Shepherd's heart. Darling, you're a legend."

"Excuse me?" And just like that she went from baffled to stunned.

"Does he know you're here?" Now Preston was grinning as he glanced behind the bar, no doubt searching for Shep, who wasn't there.

"Not yet. I haven't seen him. What do you mean I'm the only one who ever broke his heart?" That couldn't be true; he didn't have a heart.

"Some theory Grace has as to why he hasn't settled down."

Hannah suddenly felt light-headed, and she wasn't exactly sure why. She chose to ignore it. "I thought he was married with a child."

"What? Not even close." Preston moved, turning his body to face her, and in the process he knocked over his beer on the bar. Most of it splashed onto the counter, but a good portion of the cold liquid landed on Hannah's arm and shirt.

"I'm so sorry." He apologized profusely, looking horrified. "Let me get you some napkins."

"It's okay." She shook her head. "Don't worry about it. Let me just run to the bathroom to wash the beer off." She slid off the bar stool and started making her way through the crowd.

It was a legit enough excuse to get away for a second and process. She wasn't even remotely upset about the spilled beer. Her mind was reeling from that little bit of information she'd just learned. She needed somewhere to think for a second without the staring eyes of a complete stranger.

But as she rounded the corner, she stopped dead in her tracks.

Shep was standing at the far end of the hallway, caging a woman in against the wall. He was just lowering his mouth to the woman's when a large someone ran into Hannah from behind, sending her sprawling toward the ground.

* * *

Shep pulled away from Andrea and turned in the direction of the commotion. There was a woman sitting on the floor, her light red hair spilling over her shoulders and covering her face. She was cradling her arm close to her chest while a hulking man Shep didn't recognize leaned over her.

"You okay? I didn't see you there," the man slurred as he swayed over the woman.

"I got this." Shep crossed the space and squatted down next to the woman. The drunk guy moved off, no longer concerned that he'd just knocked someone to the ground.

Asshole.

"Ma'am, are you—" but the words literally stopped in his throat when she looked up. He was lucky he didn't fall on *his* ass.

Holy. Shit.

Hannah.

Over the last thirteen years, anytime he'd seen a woman with even remotely red hair, he'd do a double take, thinking for a fleeting moment it was her. Then, when he realized it wasn't, he'd be filled with crushing disappointment.

He had one of these moments the other day at the pier. His heart had kicked up hard in his chest as he'd spotted a woman with strawberry-blonde hair across the way. His attention had been pulled from her for just a second, and when he'd turned back, she was gone.

It *had* been her.

There were certain things that Shep never expected to happen. Seeing Hannah Sterling again would've ranked higher on the impossibility chart than having Bruce Springsteen come strolling into his bar singing "Born in the USA."

What the hell is she doing here?

And the universe surely had to be screwing with him. Seriously, Hannah *literally* fell back into his life when he had his hands on another woman? Which was the first time in who knew how many months he'd done something like that?

There were tears swimming in her sea-glass-green eyes, and she was breathing unevenly. "My...glasses. They got knocked off."

He turned and looked behind him, spotting black plastic frames. Andrea moved, scooping them up as she crossed the space and bringing them over.

Andrea handed him the glasses, and he looked down at the lenses, making sure they were clean before he pushed Hannah's hair back. His fingers slipped through the strands, and he didn't quite understand why it felt like a punch to the gut. He slid the frames onto her face and balanced them on her slim little nose.

"Thank you," Hannah said shakily.

Why is she here? When did she get here? How long is she staying? His brain filtered through a hundred questions. But as she was sitting in front of him clearly in pain, and as they had an audience, it wasn't exactly the time. So he asked the most important question.

"Are you okay?"

"I–I heard something pop when I fell. I can't really move it."

"It might be broken," Andrea said.

"No." Hannah shook her head, horrified. "I'm sure it's fine. Really." She looked away from him as she made a move to get up, letting go of her injured hand. But she gasped in pain and immediately went back to cradling it.

"Can I see it?" Shep reached out, putting his hands on her arms to still her. His palms were on her bare skin.

She gasped again, this time not in pain so much as surprise from the contact, and her gaze returned to his. She didn't say anything as she held out her hand. He reached out, lightly touching her wrist. She winced as his fingers skimmed her skin. There were no protruding bones, which was a good thing, but if she'd heard something pop, she probably needed to go to the hospital. He'd played sports almost his entire life, and he'd had his fair share of sprains and broken bones. A lot of the time the only way to figure out the difference was with an X-ray.

"Andrea." Shep let go of Hannah's hand and looked over his shoulder at the woman behind him. "Can you go get my brother? He's the guy with glasses behind the bar. His name is Finn. Ask him to get a bag of ice and a clean towel, and then ask him to come here."

"Yeah." She nodded before she moved off down the hall.

"Your girlfriend doesn't know your brother?"

Shep returned his gaze to Hannah. If he didn't know any better, he thought there was a touch of jealousy there. "Not my girlfriend, babe."

"Well, I see nothing much has changed."

"I see nothing's changed with you, either. You're still tripping all over yourself when you're around me."

"I never tripped all over myself when I was around you." Color bloomed in her cheeks, and the pain in her eyes was quickly replaced with anger.

"I beg to differ. I distinctly remember you falling off the dock at the marina and straight into the water. It was right after I'd kissed you for the first time."

"It had just rained. The wood was slick. That had nothing to do with you...or your kiss."

"All right. Whatever you say." He shrugged his shoulders. "Your denial is no skin off my nose."

"I wasn't tripping all over myself."

"How is it that you're even more stubborn than I remember?" Not only that, she was absolutely more stunning as well. He took just a second to study her. Took a second to see all of the subtle, and not so subtle, differences from thirteen years ago.

Her strawberry-blonde hair was slightly redder. She wore it

shorter, around her shoulders as opposed to when it had stretched down her back. The waves running through it were messy and so sexy that his fingers itched to plunge into them. And those lips. Man had he ever missed that beautiful, full mouth of hers. He'd always taken advantage of every single opportunity to get her kisses.

He forced himself to stop the examination of her face, something he definitely didn't want to do, and dropped his gaze to her hand. It was again cradled between her breasts. Breasts he immediately noticed were fuller. Yeah, he needed to not examine those right this minute, either.

"Come on. Let's get you off the floor." He stood and walked around her, placing his hands on her hips and pulling her up. She fell back into him, losing her balance, and her entire body pressed against his.

Yeah, she definitely was no longer the seventeen-year-old girl from thirteen years ago. She was a full-blown woman now with all the curves to prove it. Her hair was in his face, and he was unable to stop himself from pressing his nose into it and inhaling deeply.

Nor was he able to stop his dick from going hard.

Not the time or the place, buddy.

His body still had an instantaneous reaction to hers. Apparently, some things never changed.

Hannah regained her balance, and Shep took a step back, letting go of her hips.

Finn rounded the corner, and the second he saw them, his step faltered. "Hannah, oh wow." His eyes went wide, but he quickly recovered. "What happened?"

"Some guy ran into her and she fell. Something is wrong with her wrist. Can you and Brand cover the rest of the night? I need to take her to the ER," Shep told his brother.

"It's not necessary." She shook her head. "I'm perfectly capable of taking myself."

"Yeah, that's not happening." He held his hand out to Finn, who handed him the ice and the towel.

"Really, this is ridiculous—"

He interrupted her. "I'm taking you. End of discussion." No way in hell was he going to send her on her merry little way when she couldn't move her wrist.

"Excuse me?" There was even more fire in her eyes now.

"Babe, we can either stand here and argue for ten minutes or you can concede now and let me take you."

"First of all, Nathanial Shepherd." She reached up with her good hand and poked him in the chest. "You can stop calling me *babe*. Second of all, stop acting like you still know me. Thirdly, you need to stop bossing me around like I'm your little woman. You lost that right thirteen years ago when you proved I didn't mean anything to you. And last, but certainly not least, I *never* concede. Not to you or to anyone. Not again. Not ever." She snatched the ice pack and towel out of his hand and marched away, rounding the corner past a surprised-looking Andrea and disappearing from view.

Shep stared down the hallway, unsure of what had just happened. Not only was Hannah back in town, but she'd handed his ass to him within five minutes of him seeing her.

And now Andrea was turning around and walking away as well.

Yeah, that's about right.

"Hannah seemed really excited to see you." Leave it to Finn to offer his very unwanted observation.

Shep shot a frown at his little brother, but all it did was cause the shit-eating grin plastered across his face to get bigger.

Chapter 2

Fantasy vs. Reality

Hannah stared at the can of cat food on the counter at a complete loss as to how to get it open with one hand. The little metal tab on the top had never proved a complication before. Of course, that was when she had two working hands, something that was not the case today.

Her wrist was surely sprained, and though she was pretty sure it wasn't broken, she wasn't sure if she'd torn anything. She couldn't move it at all without putting herself in pain, and there was a little bruising to go along with it, the purple a nice overlay of color to the swelling.

Not.

She was going to have to do something about it, but she couldn't leave the inn until the delivery guys got there. The horrible mattress situation had reached the max of what she could handle. They were cheap and had petrified over the last few years. No wonder no one rented from this place anymore. Sleeping here could put a person in traction.

She'd ordered a new one after that second night, and it was

going to be delivered within the hour. Until then, she was going to have to figure out what to do about her cat's breakfast.

She looked down at her feet, watching Henry as he wound his tiny little gray body through her legs, meowing as he impatiently waited for his breakfast. He didn't deal very well with being hungry, which wasn't all that surprising given how she'd come to adopt him.

She had never had a pet before Henry. Her parents hadn't allowed it when she was growing up, and she hadn't had the time or the space for one when she'd been in college. During her relationship with Jeffrey, he'd been anti taking care of anything besides himself. So it hadn't exactly been an option then, either.

Hannah and Jeffrey had had an on-again, off-again relationship for the past three years.

Five months ago she'd ended it for real. There was no going back after he'd cheated on her. Yup, she sure knew how to pick 'em. And Hannah had chosen to take it as a sign of the final demise of their relationship when Henry showed up the very next day.

She'd found him on the steps of her brownstone during a particularly cold night in December. He'd been starving and half frozen. She'd made the necessary calls just in case he belonged to someone, but no one had claimed him.

She'd done her best not to get attached to him…but she'd failed. Spectacularly so. He'd worked his way into her heart in about five seconds flat.

And now he was hers, the only man in her life who hadn't hurt her.

"All right, pal. Looks like it's dry food for you today." She went to the pantry and pulled out the bag she'd brought with her from New York. She unrolled the top and scooped some out, dumping it into his little bowl on the floor.

He stopped circling her and sat down. He looked at the bowl and then up at her. If it were possible for a cat to pout, he was pulling it off in spades.

"Meow."

"I'm sorry. I don't know what to tell you."

"Meeeeow."

"I promise I'll go to the store and get you something else I can open. Just as soon as I go to the doctor."

She said this only somewhat begrudgingly. It was more than just her hand that had gotten hurt last night. Her heart had been pretty mangled by the end of it, too. First she'd seen Shep with another woman. That had sucked. It had been the second sucker punch straight to the stomach she'd received since coming back to Mirabelle. Though as he apparently wasn't married with children, that first punch had been a false alarm.

Then she'd been up close and personal with him. He'd had his hands on her, and damn her traitorous body, because she'd missed his touch and had craved it immediately. She'd thought she'd be able to handle it. She'd been so unbelievably wrong it was ridiculous.

And last, but certainly not least, Shep had been right. She did need to go to the hospital. But she hadn't wanted to attempt it in the dark... driving one-handed.

So she'd taken some Advil, wrapped it with an Ace bandage she'd found in a first-aid kit stowed away in one of the bathrooms, and iced it before she went to sleep. She'd attempted to elevate it, sleeping on the very lumpy couch in the living room—which was only marginally more comfortable than the rock-hard mattresses in the house—with her wrist on the armrest behind her. But as to be expected, she'd moved it in her sleep.

She'd woken up to it throbbing.

The really big problem Hannah was facing was that she'd hurt her right hand. And as she was right-handed, like ninety percent of the world, things were about to get a hell of a lot more complicated than they'd been.

She'd had a hard time of it that morning washing her hair, and then there'd been the issue of trying to put on jeans. She'd vetoed that almost immediately. Doing a zipper one-handed was not a task she wanted to deal with all day. So she'd gone with a skirt instead.

But nothing compared to the process of putting on her bra. Hannah had a big enough chest where going braless wasn't a viable option. She'd had to shimmy out of her bra the night before, pulling it over her head like a sports bra. She was thankful she hadn't messed with the intact hooks, because she was able to do the process in reverse that morning.

It was somewhat of a miracle she was dressed presentably, and good thing, too, because there was a knock at the front door. She headed for it excitedly; at least she'd be somewhat comfortable tonight. Small favors, something that were few and far between these days.

She didn't even bother looking though the peephole. Who else would even be stopping by but the delivery guys with the new mattress? Thank the good Lord.

So one could only imagine her surprise when she opened the door to find Shep on her porch.

* * *

Hannah's entire body tensed, her good hand gripping the door and her knuckles going white. Shep was pretty sure she wanted to shut the door in his face. It was no small amount of relief when her hand loosened on the wood before it dropped to her side.

"What are you doing here?" She frowned at him.

He wasn't used to women directing looks of displeasure at him, and he definitely wasn't used to Hannah doing it. Sure, the two of them had bickered every once in a while that summer they'd spent together. But that had lasted for like...what? Five minutes before he'd push her into a corner and kiss every ounce of her irritation away. And when their relationship progressed... well, they'd done a whole hell of a lot more than kissing.

"I wanted to see how your hand was doing." His eyes dropped to her side, and he caught a glimpse of her swollen wrist before she shifted it behind her back.

"It's fine. How did you know where I was?"

So she was obviously lying to him. That was new and different. He didn't like it.

Not one. Fucking. Bit.

"New York license plates," he said, pointing to the white SUV parked in the driveway. "It wasn't exactly detective work. And I'm not leaving until you show me your hand."

She sighed and moved her arm, holding it up for him to see. The glimpse he'd caught a second ago hadn't given the damage justice. The whole area around her wrist was swollen, and there were a few dark purple splotches. He clinched his fists at his sides, trying to contain the anger running through him at seeing that color on her skin. If he ever crossed paths with that drunk jackass who'd knocked her down, he wouldn't be held accountable for his actions.

"It's fine," she repeated, pulling her hand away from him and resting it on her chest. He raised an eyebrow at her, challenging that statement. "Are you really going to keep saying that?"

"I'm going to the doctor today just as soon as I finish up here. Happy?"

"No. I'd be happy if you'd let me take you."

"Look, it's not necessary. You don't owe me anything."

"Owe you anything?" he said slowly. Was she joking? "Hannah, can you stop being so damn stubborn?"

"No." She shook her head. Her refusal was immediate. She hadn't hesitated for a second.

He switched gears. "What do you have to get taken care of here?" Distraction was the best policy. He wasn't ready for her to shut the door in his face, and if he had his way, he was taking her to the damn hospital.

Last night he'd had no idea how to respond to her speech, so he'd had no choice but to let her walk away while he regrouped. Then he'd spent the entire night trying to process the fact that she was back in town. He still hadn't quite wrapped his mind around it, even with her standing in front of him.

She sighed again. "I ordered a new mattress, because the ones here are horrible."

"Are you sleeping in the same room?" he asked. His mind flashed to images of them in that room together, their bodies tangled up in the sheets. But it wasn't images from the past. No, it was the two of them in the present, moving together, her hands holding onto his biceps, her fingers tracing the tattoos that hadn't been there before.

Pain flashed in her eyes, but it disappeared almost as quickly as it had appeared. "No. Henry picked one of the rooms downstairs."

And those images came crashing down and with them the floor beneath Shep's feet.

What the hell had he been expecting? That she was still single after all this time? Of course she had a man who was sharing her bed. But why hadn't the guy been at the bar last night? And why hadn't he taken her to the hospital this morning? What kind of a chump was she with anyway?

"*Henry?*" He tried not to choke on the name. *Please don't say* husband. *Please, please, please.*

But she didn't get a chance to respond before a loud clatter came from somewhere in the house. "Crap. What's he getting into?" She turned and hurried away, leaving Shep standing in the doorway.

He took advantage of the opportunity and walked in, closing the door behind him and following her down the hallway. He got a quick glimpse of the living room, the back wall of windows lighting the space entirely. The couch, love seat, and oversized chair were a bright turquoise. Then there was the peach and brown rug in the middle of the space. It had a truly awful pattern that made him somewhat dizzy on first glance. But the room was empty of Hannah, or this Henry guy, so he continued on to the kitchen.

"You are a pain in the ass, you know?" Hannah was kneeling on the floor, picking up little brown pieces of what he assumed to be food and putting them back into a bright blue bowl.

At first he wasn't sure who she was addressing—for all intents and purposes it could've been him—but then he spotted the little gray kitten to her left. He was batting around a can of cat food like it was a hockey puck.

Shep looked between the two of them and grinned, feeling happy beyond words again. He wasn't fond of 'em, but a cat he could deal with.

"I never pegged you for a cat lady." He squatted down next to her and started sweeping the food up with his hand.

Hannah looked at him and narrowed her eyes in what she probably thought was an intimidating stare. Yeah, not so much.

All she looked was adorable. "Hey, I just have the one, and besides, Henry picked me, so he's a lady cat…or a ladies' cat…or a…I don't know. But he was the one that adopted me," she rambled on.

Shep raised an eyebrow. "Is that so?"

"Yes. He showed up on my stoop this past winter. He was cold and pathetic and big enough to just fit in my hands."

"And I bet he was putty in those hands, just like the rest of the male population."

Hannah snorted, the intimidating look disappearing for just a second before she recovered. "I can assure you," she said seriously, and more than somewhat self-deprecatingly, as she looked back to the ground searching for stragglers, "that men are *not* putty in my hands."

"I was." His voice dropped low as he said it. *Was?* How about *is?* Yeah, that statement definitely wasn't a thing of the past.

Hannah looked up so fast that she lost her balance, falling backward on her butt. "Ouch! Dammit!"

"You okay?" He got to his feet and leaned over her, holding out his hand.

"Yes. I'm fine." She put her good hand in his and let him pull her up. But he went one step further, pulling her in to his body.

"Want me to check for bruises?" he asked.

She glared up at him, clearly not amused. "Can you be serious for a second?" She took a step away from him, her back hitting the counter.

He followed, taking a step toward her and caging her in, putting his hands on her hips. She gasped, startled.

"I *was* being serious." Serious as a fucking heart attack. She was wearing a skirt, too, so it provided easy access. He wondered if she still had a thing for lace thongs like she used to…and what color it was.

She looked up at him, her breath going shallow. He was so close, so damn close that all he had to do was lower his mouth to hers. Her good hand came up, and she placed it on his chest. He thought she was going to grab on to his shirt, pull him in closer... He'd been wrong.

"Don't even think about it." She pushed at him, halting his progress and giving herself more space.

"Think about what?"

"Kissing me. Your Neanderthal man moves don't work on me anymore, Nathanial. I'm immune."

There were only a handful of people who called him by his first name, and whenever they said it, it meant business. He took a step back, listening to the words she'd said, but he didn't believe her. Not because he was a cocky asshole—though he was one—but because he could see it right there in her eyes. She did want him.

But the truth was covered up a second later, like shutters slamming closed across a window.

She was lying to him.

Again.

What. The. Fuck.

* * *

It had taken everything in Hannah to push Shep away. Taken everything in her to lie to him, because if he'd pressed his mouth to hers she would've been done for. She absolutely refused to get hurt by this man again. She wouldn't survive it a second time around.

She didn't understand it. Didn't understand how in the less than ten minutes she'd spent with him, her resolve was disappearing. She was fighting with everything she had, because when he looked at her, she felt like that seventeen-year-old girl again. The one who had melted at his slightest touch.

He was right. She did have a problem with tripping all over herself when he was around. Proof in point, she'd landed on her ass again in no time at all. Well, it was better than him getting her flat on her back.

But how the hell was she supposed to react? He'd gone and said he'd been putty in her hands. She'd have to object to that statement, because whenever he'd been in her hands, he'd been anything but soft.

And she really couldn't think clearly when he was standing so close, when the scent of him was invading her lungs. That man had always smelled *soooo* damn good. He'd never used cologne. It was just his body wash and shampoo mixed with…well, him.

There'd been a few times over the years that she'd catch the scent from other guys—it was a fairly common soap after all—but it wasn't the same. It was close, but not close enough for Hannah. And now that she was breathing it deep? Well, it had been so much better than she'd remembered. She just wanted to inhale him for hours.

The fumes had gone to her head and it had taken her a second to come back to reality.

Hadn't he been doing the exact same thing last night? Pressing some other woman up against the wall and leaning down to kiss her?

Nu-uh, she wasn't doing this again.

He moved on from you, Hannah. Moved on and didn't look back. Didn't give you a second thought. And now he just wants to see if he can get into your pants again. For old times' sake…or, or something like that.

She wasn't the only one coming to her senses, either. The heat in his eyes from a second ago disappeared, and he took another step back from her, letting go of her hips. She was somehow both relieved and upset about his hands leaving her body.

"All right." He held up his hands in surrender. "I'll leave you alone."

But his words made her warring emotions pick a clear and definite side. That wasn't relief that she felt, and it made her lungs constrict.

What the hell was wrong with her?

"Just as soon as I take you to the hospital."

Oh, look at that; she could breathe again. She was a sick, twisted, sadistic freak.

There was a swish and a thud, and Shep pulled his gaze away from her, looking down to the ground. The cat food tin was lying beside his boot. Apparently, Henry had taken another valiant swipe at it, and his newest target was Shep.

He turned and dropped down to a squat in front of her, beckoning the kitten over. Henry came immediately, almost tripping over himself to get to Shep.

Hannah had long ago decided that Henry wasn't a normal cat. He loved affection. Craved it all the time. Ever since he'd become a presence in her life, she'd had to learn how to juggle both him and her computer on her lap at all times, because if she was sitting, he was lying on her.

And now he was soaking up every ounce of attention that Shep was offering, preening and purring as he ran his body under Shep's massive hand.

"Traitor," she whispered.

Though she wasn't sure why she was all that surprised. Shep had always known his way around a pussy.

"Why was the little guy staging a revolt in the kitchen?" he asked, interrupting her thoughts.

"He isn't the biggest fan of dry food. And I couldn't open the can this morning." She indicated her injured hand. "He wasn't very happy about that fact."

"Well, it looks like it's your lucky day, pal," Shep said as he grabbed the can and the half-empty bowl from the floor. He dumped the unwanted dry food in the trash before he put the bowl on the counter. It was such a simple thing, the actions he was making opening the can of food, but it made the muscles in his arms move. Her eyes focused on his tattoos, and man, were there a lot of them.

This was the first chance she'd had to see them up close and personal. The sleeves of his T-shirt came down to just above his elbows. So all she could see were his forearms. There was an intersecting shepherd's rod and staff on the inside of the left and what looked like a wolf on the back.

His right arm had a compass with the North Star in the center. There was a banner weaving back and forth with the words *I'll Always Find Home* across it. Different colored flowers surrounded it. They floated in blue and green water that filled the remaining space.

She assumed there was a meaning behind them—there was definitely meaning behind the only tattoo she had—so she wondered what his represented.

There had always been something about tattoos that she'd found terribly fascinating. Maybe because they reminded her of Shep. This was probably why she'd avoided men who had them.

She remembered the one on his right biceps distinctly. How could she not when she'd spent many nights tracing it with her fingertips? He'd always loved Superman, the comics, the movie, the TV show, all of it. It was the *S* with the blue and red shield, and she wondered what surrounded the emblem now. She also wondered about all of the other designs etched on his body.

Oh God, his body. She'd appreciated everything it had to offer before, but now? Now it was perfection.

It wasn't fair. Seriously.

And things were about to get a whole lot less fair. It was at that moment that Shep moved away from the counter and crouched down to give Henry the food. His jeans pulled tight, and she was lucky she didn't moan out loud as she took in the glory that was his ass.

Stop it, Hannah. Stop it. Stop it. That is not *yours.*

She hadn't quite been able to pull herself together and move her gaze from said ass before Shep turned and stood up.

Busted. The evident gleam in his eyes proved she'd been caught. But she wasn't backing down from his gaze. Not blinking or flinching. She'd checked him out. So what? There was a lot to check out.

"So," he said as he leaned back against the counter across from her. "When does your new mattress get here?"

She turned toward the clock on the wall, not paying attention as she set her injured hand on the counter and accidentally applied pressure. She hissed through her teeth, pulling her hand up to her chest as she breathed through the twinge of pain.

Shep immediately pushed off the counter and crossed the small space to her. "Why isn't your hand wrapped?" he asked, reaching for it. She didn't fight him as he ran his fingers across her skin. The gentle touch shot a shiver down her spine.

God, she'd missed his hands. Missed them when they were gentle like this. Missed them when they were rough, too. He'd always known just how far to go, how to make her weak with pleasure. He'd been the only man she'd ever been with—not that there had been that many men—who knew that perfect balance.

"Because I..." *Words. Find words, Hannah.* "I was taking a shower and didn't want to get the bandage wet. It's already complicated enough using one hand."

"All right, well, let's get you at least bandaged up until we go to the hospital." He dropped his hands and looked down at her, concern evident in his gaze. She wasn't going to fight him on his one. Her wrist was killing her.

She sidestepped him, walking out of the kitchen and down the hallway to the left. There were two bedrooms on this end of the house, and the one she was staying in had a Jacuzzi tub in the bathroom. The house might need some updates, but it still had a few perks.

What she'd told Shep had been true; Henry had picked this room. But really there had been no chance in hell she was going to sleep in the room she'd stayed in thirteen years ago. There were too many memories in there. Too many nights spent with Shep's hands and mouth all over her body. She'd gone in there only once since she'd been back. And chances were she wouldn't go in there again unless she had to.

She headed for the bathroom, which was still just a little bit steamy from her shower. The scent of her shampoo and lavender body wash lingered in the hot, wet air. She reached for the Ace bandage on the counter, catching Shep's gaze in the mirror.

His eyes were on her ass.

So, she wasn't the only one staring.

She cleared her throat, and his eyes came up, meeting hers in the mirror. He shrugged his shoulders unapologetically. "You started it."

Well, there was no denying that.

She handed him the Ace bandage, not even bothering to argue with him that she could do it herself. Besides, she really couldn't. The job she'd been able to do last night hadn't been all that impressive.

He put the bandage back on the counter before he reached into his pocket and pulled out a small tube of what she recognized to be horse liniment. The cure-all wonder for aches and sprains for equine and human alike.

Hannah had grown up riding horses. It was something Gigi had always loved to do. But she hadn't gone in years.

She missed it like crazy.

Both Shep and Finn had horses out at their aunt and uncle's farm. Springsteen, named after another of Shep's obsessions, was an Appaloosa. He had a white base coat and dark brown spots all over his body. Finn had Nigel, a bay horse that was solid brown with a shiny black mane and tail. She'd spent so much time out at that farm, and both of those horses had captured her heart by the end of it.

"How are Springsteen and Nigel?" she asked as she held out her wrist.

His mouth quirked to the side, his pride and affection for those two geldings evident. She knew how much he loved both of them, but Springsteen was his baby.

"They're good," he said as he unscrewed the cap. "I'm just glad that Finn is back permanently." He put the liniment on her wrist and worked the cool gel into her skin. She tried not to flinch at the pressure. Even though he was being exceedingly careful, it still hurt like a bitch. She attempted to distract herself, focusing on his voice and the spearmint scent filling her nose. "It wasn't like Nigel was depressed or anything. He just missed his owner. And it was difficult to split my time between the two."

"Where was Finn?"

He looked at her, even more pride in his eyes. "Veterinary school. The first Shepherd to go to college and he comes back a doctor."

"Wow. Finn's a vet. It's hard for me to replace the gangly little thirteen-year-old with glasses to him as an adult."

"Tell me about it." He grinned. "But no matter how smart and successful he is, it hasn't changed the fact that he's still a massive pain in the ass."

She smiled, trying to ignore the twinge of jealousy that ran through her. She envied Shep and Finn's relationship. They were close. Always had been. She didn't have that with either of her siblings.

She had absolutely nothing in common with her little sister, Sheri, who was a spoiled socialite just like their mother. She'd gotten married to Kelvin Sanford, the son of a Pennsylvania senator, two years ago. She thought she was a freaking Kennedy or something.

Philip was the baby of the family, and he'd always been treated as such. He was so incredibly entitled and immature that it was ridiculous. He was in his sixth year at Yale, and Hannah had a feeling that the only reason he was still enrolled was because of their parents' bankroll.

"What about you, Hannah?"

His words brought her back to reality. She shook her head and looked at him as he continued to massage her wrist. "What about me?"

"Did you go on to become your own big success, too? What happened after Columbia?"

"Columbia Law."

"Ahhh, so you're a hotshot lawyer now? What do you do?"

"I'm a partner at McAvoy and Sutter, a commercial law firm, and I specialize in contracts."

"Meaning?"

"I write them."

"Do you enjoy it?" He looked up at her for a second before he reached over and grabbed the bandage from the counter. Then he focused on her hand again as he slowly started to wrap her wrist.

Do I enjoy it? Well, it wasn't like it was exactly fun.

"I'm good at it."

"That's not the same thing." He shook his head. "What happened to teaching literature?"

Hannah had often had her nose buried in a book when she was growing up. Gigi had a library in her house; it was one of Hannah's absolute favorite places. That was another thing that Hannah had been left in the will, more than three thousand books.

But she'd learned that it didn't do well to dwell in fiction and fantasy, so she'd pursued facts. Reality. The law.

It was a different path than she'd planned when she was seventeen.

She'd had a lot of conversations with Shep about the future during that summer. What she wanted to do. What she wanted to be. Sometimes they'd talk about everything, and other times about absolutely nothing. That was usually when they had their tongues down each other's throats...or their hands down each other's pants...or when they were naked.

Though, come to think of it, they'd had a lot of good chats when Shep had been inside her, but those had mostly consisted of him talking dirty and her begging for more.

Stop it, stop it, stop it. Bad direction, Hannah. Baaaad. Reality. Stick to reality.

"It wasn't the right path for me."

His head came up, and he studied her for a second. He opened his mouth to say something, but shut it almost immediately before he nodded and looked back down.

She'd never known Shep to hold his tongue—not that she knew him all that much anymore—and she really wanted to know what was rolling around in that head of his. She bit down hard on the inside of her lip, trying her damnedest to not ask what he'd just stopped himself from saying.

She lasted all the way until he secured the clips into place and dropped her hand. Because when he looked up at her and focused those blue eyes on her face, she couldn't stop herself from opening her mouth.

"What? What were you about to say?"

"Nothing."

"Come on."

"I believe I was told I needed to stop acting like I know you. So I don't think I'm allowed to offer an opinion."

Well, she couldn't argue with that.

"But I do have a question. What are you doing back here?"

His change of direction threw her off, and it took her a second to regroup. "Gigi died. Four months ago."

Shep's face fell, his eyes going soft with sympathy. *Oh no. No, no, no. Don't do that. Don't look at me like that.*

"I'm sorry, Hannah." He reached out and ran his hand down her shoulder to her arm. His longer fingers wrapped around just above her elbow. His thumb moved back and forth, leaving goose bumps across her skin. "I know—I know exactly how you feel. My grandfather died three years ago."

Shep's relationship with Owen was similar to the one Hannah had with Gigi. But where he was close to his entire family, Hannah was only really close to her grandmother. Even with that difference he understood; he understood more than anyone.

Her heart couldn't handle this. Couldn't handle his hands on her, or his empathy, or his kindness, or any of it. She couldn't handle him.

She took a step back, his hand falling away and across the space she needed to put between them.

"Thanks."

"No problem." He folded his arms across his chest as he leaned back against the counter. "Why did Gigi's passing bring you here?"

"She left me the inn."

"And you're here for...what? A vacation?"

"No. I haven't exactly...dealt with it. She bought this place about a year ago and left it to me in her will. It's...I don't know..."

"Your last connection to her?"

"Yeah."

He continued to look at her in that way that only he could, like he was seeing into her. "How long are you here for?"

"Three months."

"Three months." He nodded. "Well, I hope you figure it out, Hannah."

"Figure what out?"

"Whatever it is that you need."

The thing was, she had no idea what she needed.

Chapter 3

The Power of a Well-Fixed Cup of Coffee

Hannah's mattress arrived not that long after their little chat, and while it was being unloaded and set up, Shep went about making a pot of coffee. He tried to process all of the information he'd just found out, filing it away to come back to as he learned more about what had happened since the last time he'd seen her.

One, Hannah was back in Mirabelle for three months. Two, she was a lawyer, something that thirteen years ago had been nowhere in the realm of her dreams. Three, she wasn't happy. She hadn't said this, but he'd seen it in her face. There were few laugh lines around her eyes, and he had a feeling that her smiles had been few and far between. It was a damn shame that the world had been missing out on Hannah Sterling when she was smiling.

Apparently, three months was long enough to make the need for a fancy new mattress a necessity. She'd bought one of those foam numbers that molded to a person's body. They were upward of a couple grand. He knew because he owned one, and they weren't something you bought for a temporary stay. They were an investment.

Just another thing to add to the clusterfuck that was his brain.

He shook his head, trying to clear it, and searched for coffee mugs among the cabinets. He hesitated when he found them, unsure if he should fix Hannah a cup. He didn't know if she still took her coffee the way she used to. He grabbed two mugs anyway and doctored hers up with lots of creamer the way he remembered.

She walked into the kitchen after letting the delivery guys out, and he handed her the mug. "Oh, thank you. I hadn't gotten around to making any yet."

"No problem." He nodded.

She leaned back against the counter and took a sip. Her eyes closed in satisfaction for just a second before they snapped back open. She stared down into her cup, chewing on her bottom lip. She took another tentative sip, and her eyebrows bunched together.

"Something wrong?"

Her head came up and she stared at him for a second, her mouth falling open and nothing coming out. She shook her head, closing her mouth before she finally answered. "It's perfect. Thank you again."

Well, he apparently still knew one thing about her: how she liked her coffee. Not the massive win he was looking for. But hell, he'd take it.

He had three months to figure this out. To figure her out. And he knew it was going to be more than a bit of a challenge.

She was resistant. She didn't want anything to do with him, or so she thought. He wasn't surprised by her hesitation. Things hadn't ended all that well. When she'd left Mirabelle, it had been a very painful parting. Full of tears but no promises. He hadn't made any that he knew he wouldn't be able to fulfill.

And then there was that phone call. It *still* haunted him. He remembered every ounce of pain in her voice, heard it clear as day whenever he thought about it.

Sometimes life liked to really kick a guy in the balls, and it appeared that this was exactly the case when it came to Hannah.

He'd been a miserable mess after she'd left. A real piece of work that absolutely nobody wanted to be around, and that had never been his MO. But that had just been phase one.

Phase two had been getting drunk. His family owned a bar, so he'd never had a problem getting his hands on alcohol. He'd been as responsible as somebody could be drinking underage... until those months right after Hannah left. He'd pushed the limits and his father and grandfather had noticed. They'd sat him down and set him straight.

Phase three had been moving on, with as many women as he could find. The part that was an unfortunate bit of fate? Hannah called him the very morning after phase three started. He'd taken it as a sign. There was no going back. No fixing it.

For ten years Shep did whatever the hell he wanted and whomever the hell he wanted. He took women to bed, the thought of a commitment nowhere in his brain. He just did what felt good.

He'd always played it fast and loose, much more so than his best friends Brendan and Jax.

Brendan had always been more of the middleman, having his fun but not pushing the boundaries too much. Then he'd met Paige and pursued her with a vengeance she'd never known was coming at her.

Jax was at the opposite end as Shep. He'd played it pretty safe, not getting too close to anyone really. That was until he finally got his shit together and made things work with Grace.

Since Owen's death, Shep had tried to start figuring out his life, and his sex life had slowed in the process. While he fumbled around in the dark, he'd watched as his friends began to settle down. They'd gotten married and had kids, while he did... what exactly? He had no idea.

And then, because fate was a fucking bitch, the very night he'd decided to make a move on a pretty girl at his bar, Hannah comes strolling back into his life.

So yeah, he had piss-poor luck.

After Hannah's little speech at the bar the night before, Shep had found Andrea again. She'd said something about having an early morning the next day and had promptly peaced out. He wasn't all that sorry, and he felt like more than little bit of an asshole for it. But the facts were the facts. There was only going to be one woman occupying his brain, and she had red hair and freckles.

Shep looked at Hannah as she sipped her coffee. He didn't care that she didn't want to be around him. That was just tough, wasn't it? Because he was going after her. No more regrets. No more *what-ifs*. This was his second chance, and he was going to take it.

* * *

Shep grabbed the keys from Hannah's hand as they walked out the front door of the inn.

"Hey." She rounded on him and watched as he made quick work with the door. "I'm capable of locking up, you know."

"I'm sure you are. But I'm doing it anyway." He reached out for her good hand, his fingers wrapping around her wrist and flipping it until it was palm up. He dropped the keys and pushed her fingers closed around them. "Get used to it, babe."

"Stop telling me what to do. And stop calling me that," she said as she put her keys in her purse.

"No. Now, come on." His hand went to the small of her back, and he led her down the steps. She would've shaken it off, but that wasn't the best idea as she was walking down a flight of stairs.

Plus there was a very stupid part of her that liked it there. Yeah, she'd lost every ounce of her sense.

She spotted Shep's black '67 Mustang parked next to her SUV, and the flood of memories that hit her were slightly overwhelming. Shep pushing her up against the door as he kissed the breath out of her. Him driving her around town, the windows down and the music up, her hair whipping all over the place as they both sang along. She'd loved Shep's voice, deep and rich. When he sang, she'd feel it all the way down to her toes.

They'd parked out in the middle of nowhere more times than she could count, making out for hours, the windows going all foggy. As they'd progressed in their physical relationship, they'd figured out exactly what they could do in those cramped quarters. A lot could be done when she crawled up onto his lap and straddled him, and dresses made for very easy access.

Hannah had gone many days that summer forgoing pants.

But the car in front of her had transformed into something new. Before the black paint had been missing in a few spots with rust showing through, but now it was solid and shiny. The windshield was intact, the crack that had split the center missing. As he opened the passenger door for her, she was greeted with soft red leather that covered the seats entirely and black carpet that was free of holes.

She slid into the seat, and when she turned to reach for the seat belt, Shep was already there. He pulled it out and across her shoulder, leaning over her as he buckled it into place.

She caught the scent of him again, and it made her stomach flip. It distracted her so thoroughly that she forgot to be annoyed with him.

He turned to look at her, his face so close to hers that his breath washed over her lips.

"You're welcome."

Hmmm, maybe not.

She didn't say anything as he pulled back and shut the door. He rounded the front of the car, and she couldn't help but notice that his cocky swagger had only gotten more pronounced.

Arrogant jerk.

He got into the driver's side and started the car. The steady purr of the engine was also something new. He reached out, adjusting the vents, sending a stream of cool air in her direction.

"I see you now have a working air conditioner," she said.

"Yeah, and the fuel gauge actually works, too. So no more keeping track of every single mile that I drive." He grinned over at her before he put the car in reverse and backed out of the small lot in front of the inn.

He grabbed the aviators from where they hung on the front of his shirt and slid them over his eyes. He looked so damn good it wasn't even funny.

She pulled her gaze from his sexy sexiness and turned toward the windshield, looking out at the road. The sun was blazing, and it made her eyes hurt. She reached for her purse, pulling out her prescription sunglasses and switching them out with the regular frames she was wearing.

She hadn't even attempted to put in contacts that morning. She couldn't have as she needed her right hand to put them in, and at the moment it was fairly useless. She probably would've lost an eye if she'd tried.

She wasn't sure why she even messed with them anymore. She'd never really liked wearing them. She needed help to see far away and not for reading, so when she spent hours looking over papers right in front of her, contacts would give her massive headaches.

Her mother had always been quick to tell her how unflattering glasses were, while her ex, Jeffrey, had made comments about how they were unnecessary in this day and age. He'd told her she should get LASIK more times than she could count.

But the idea had always freaked her out. A laser in her eyes? No, thank you.

"I always liked you in glasses," Shep said, somehow pulling her thoughts out of her mind and out into the open.

How in the world did he do that? She'd been bound and determined to think he didn't know her anymore.

That was what had confused her so much this morning with the coffee. How the hell had he remembered how she took it? Hannah was detail oriented, and how someone took their coffee was something she might remember, but she remembered weird stuff. Like the fact that she'd been wearing purple Converses the first time she'd met Shep, and he'd been wearing a blue Yankees T-shirt that she might or might not have stolen...and that she also might or might not still have.

She'd worn it so many times she was surprised the material was still intact.

There was a sarcastic quip about how happy it made her that he approved of her glasses just waiting on the tip of her tongue. But the truth was, it was another thing that she liked. Another thing that she was just going to have to ignore.

"Thanks." She pulled her bottom lip into her mouth again and started chewing. If she kept this up, she was going to gnaw the damn thing off. "So how long did it take you to fix it up?" she asked, changing the subject. Maybe if he wasn't focused on her, she could get through this day.

And she was genuinely curious, so it wasn't that much of a hardship. He'd been working on it when she'd been there that summer, looking for pieces to replace and fixing what he could when he could.

"Entirely? About three years. But the bulk of the work was done in a year. Brendan and Jax helped me with it. It's really convenient that Brendan is a full-time mechanic. Free labor."

"He works at his grandfather's shop?" Hannah asked.

"He owns half of King's Auto now. Bought himself into it a while ago."

"Well, you guys did a really good job. It looks amazing. If I didn't know any better, I'd think it wasn't the same car." But differences or not, it was still *all* Shep.

"*It?*" he asked, feigning offense. "Why do you keep calling her *it?* It's okay, Lois." He patted the dashboard with his hand as he talked to the car. "She didn't know any better."

"Lois Lane." Hannah snorted through a laugh. "I should've known. When did you name *her?*"

"After the paint job. I'd debated changing colors, and I couldn't be sure of the name until I knew the color."

Hannah shook her head at him. "That's ridiculous."

"Really? Says the girl who names her bookcases?"

"Hey, I used to read a lot of books. Don't scoff at my system."

"*Used* to?"

"I couldn't even tell you the last book I read for pleasure." She really couldn't tell him the last time she did anything for pleasure. But then his words clicked and she turned to look at him. "And I can't believe you remember that."

"I remember a lot of things."

"That so? Like what else?" The question was out of her mouth before she could stop it. Hadn't she wanted to steer clear of this? Apparently, she was a masochist.

"Your love for Cherry Coke, your hatred for peas—"

"They have a weird texture," she said.

"Your fear of lizards."

"I don't *fear* them. I just find them disgusting." She shivered involuntarily. "They're snakes with legs."

He continued. "Your fear of snakes."

"I just gave you that one."

"How about the reason you're scared of snakes? You were fifteen and went out riding when a snake crossed your horse's path. The horse freaked out and threw you off. You had to get thirteen stitches in your knee, and you still have the scar."

Hannah sat there stunned. *How the hell did he remember that?*

The air vents were pointed right at her, but they were no match for the suffocating pressure that settled on her, making her sweat. Her lungs weren't pulling in enough air, either. She wanted out of his car. Wanted to get away from him. He was too much for her.

This was way too damn confusing. One second he was infuriating the hell out of her and then the next… well, the next she had no idea what was happening. And she didn't want to find out, because in the end it would just be more pain.

* * *

The second half of the car ride to the hospital consisted of a silence that Shep just couldn't penetrate. Hannah had been willing to talk to him at first, but then she'd clammed up, and he had no idea as to why. He'd had a few ways of making her talk before, but he had a feeling that they wouldn't work now.

He was going to need to figure out another way to get under her defenses, because when her guard was down, he got to see glimpses of *his* Hannah. Got to see the girl he once knew and not the woman who was running from him like her pants were on fire.

The Hannah he got in the emergency room was the runner. The only time she really talked to him was when he was filling out her paperwork. She was right-handed, and as that was the hand that was hurt, he'd needed to do it for her. When he'd filled in her full name (Hannah Eileen Sterling) and date of birth (September 20), she'd started chewing on her bottom lip again, only letting it go between answers.

That was a habit of hers he wasn't used to. Like she was doing everything in her power to hold something back. But he'd never seen it before, so either it was a new habit or she just hadn't held anything back from him during that summer.

Even with his frustration at her lip biting, there was more than a small amount of satisfaction in him when he checked off the single box under marital status. But that satisfaction was short-lived when she was taken into a room for an X-ray and he was forced to sit in the waiting room.

He wasn't sure how long he stared blankly at the TV screen in front of him when someone kicked the side of his boot. He looked up at the owner of the green ballet flat to find Grace Anderson. The glow on her cherubic face was evident, not all that surprising, as her husband had knocked her up.

Shep's eyes darted to the man behind her, the knocker upper. Jaxson Anderson was not glowing. He didn't look all that put together in his deputy sheriff uniform, either. In fact, he looked so freaked out that he was about to throw up on himself. Maybe he'd gotten some of Grace's morning sickness.

"What are you doing here?" Grace asked. There was concern in her eyes as she looked down at him. He wasn't all that surprised. Enough of her friends and family had been in and out of the hospital in the last two years to cause concern.

"I'm fine," he said, getting to his feet. "And I don't think you should be worried about me when your husband looks like he's barely holding breakfast down. What's wrong with you?"

Grace turned to glance at Jax and laughed when she saw his expression.

"It isn't funny." He frowned, looking down at her.

Shep was more than used to his best friend's taciturn ways. Jax hadn't grown up in the friendliest of environments, and it had taken a toll on his demeanor. The guy's smiles were few and far between, except when it came to Grace. Ever since they'd gotten together, he'd been Mr. Freaking Sunshine, so the scowl currently plastered across his face was a little surprising.

Grace turned back to Shep and smiled. "He's worked himself into a state."

"Why?" Shep couldn't help but share her humor, and his own grin spread across his face.

"Because we just found out we're having a girl, and he doesn't know what to do with himself." Grace's hands came up to rest on her little bump. She was more than four months' pregnant and starting to show.

"Congratulations."

"She's never leaving the house," Jax said seriously. *"Never."*

"Good luck with that. It's going to take a much bigger force than her daddy to keep her locked up."

Jax paled, making his freckles more noticeable.

Shep had no idea how he'd feel about his own daughters—if and when he ever had any—but he could still understand Jax's fear. They were guys, so they therefore knew how men thought... what they wanted... and how often.

"Yeah, I'm with Jax on this one. I'll help out with whatever monitoring scheme you come up with. I'm sure Brendan will, too."

Grace rolled her eyes. "And how long is this security detail going to go on?"

The two men looked at each other for a second before Jax answered. "Until she's thirty."

"I think that's a good age," Shep agreed.

"Seriously?"

"Look, Gracie, your husband and I are fully aware of how men think when it comes to girls. And your daughter isn't going to be around that."

"You both are such hypocrites." She shook her head at them again, her lips pursed in disapproval. But a second later that look was gone. She did a double take at the area behind Shep, and her mouth dropped open. "Holy crap," she whispered.

Shep followed her gaze, and his eyes landed on Hannah. She was talking to one of the nurses, her wrist now covered with a black brace.

A small Grace-like hand wrapped around his biceps, fingers pressing into his skin forcefully. He turned to look at his friend.

"Did you know?" she whispered.

"Yeah. I brought her here. She fell last night at the bar and hurt her wrist."

"Why is she back?" Jax's reddish-brown eyebrows were so far up his forehead they might as well have been hidden in his equally matched hair.

"Her grandmother bought the Seaside Escape Inn and left it to Hannah when she passed away."

"Seriously?" Grace asked.

But Shep never got a chance to respond, as Hannah was heading in their direction.

"Hannah Sterling. Holy cow." Grace didn't even give Hannah a chance to respond before she pulled her into a gentle hug, careful of Hannah's hurt hand.

Hannah's back tensed, and she stayed that way until they pulled apart. It was more than a bit of a contradiction to the smile on her face.

"I'd ask how you're doing, but Shep said you got hurt last night. Are you okay?"

"I've dealt with worse. It's just a sprain. I should be back to normal in a few weeks. I just need to try to use it as little as possible and rest it." Hannah made a face like she wasn't sure that was going to be possible. "I don't even know when the last time was that I rested."

"Maybe that will be good for you," Jax said.

Hannah's eyes moved to him, and she grinned even bigger. "Jaxson Anderson, a man of the law. Will wonders never cease."

"What's that supposed to mean?" he asked as he took a step forward, giving her a gentle hug of his own. Hannah tensed in his arms, too.

Shep didn't think it was because she was uncomfortable. If the smile on her face was any indication, she was really happy to see them. It seemed that she just wasn't used to the physical contact.

Regardless, he was a little jealous that both Jax and Grace had gotten hugs out of her when he hadn't.

"Oh, you know," she said as they separated. "Just that you, Brendan, and Shep were always getting into trouble."

"I have no idea what you're talking about." He shook his head, a smile tugging at the corners of his mouth. He was apparently calming down a little from the recent baby news.

"So I hear congratulations are in order. I knew you two were going to end up together."

A loud laugh burst forth from Grace. "At least somebody did."

"Hey. I wasn't that bad."

Grace looked up at her husband with raised eyebrows. "Seriously?"

"Okay. I was. But I'm not going anywhere now."

"Well, that's good, considering I'm carrying your daughter."

The color disappeared from Jax's face again, and for just a moment Shep thought he saw Hannah's face pale as well. This was saying something, as she had very fair skin under her freckles. But she recovered fast enough that it wasn't too noticeable. Just to him.

"You guys are expecting? That's fantastic. When are you due?"

"September. Hopefully, he'll calm down in the next few months," Grace said as she put her hand on her husband's arm.

"Good luck with that." Shep didn't think Jax was ever going to calm down when it came to his family. Grace had been in three life-threatening situations in the last two years alone. If anything, she was lucky he let her out of his sight.

"Enjoy it while you can, Shep, 'cause the day you finally settle down and start having kids, I'm going to be standing there saying *I told you so* while you become the most overbearing ass in the world."

"Become overbearing?" Hannah snorted. All eyes went to her and she flushed. "He's just a little overbearing already."

"Really?" Jax asked, looking at Shep.

He shrugged. What the hell was he supposed to say? He

normally wasn't overbearing at all, but with Hannah he couldn't help himself.

"Hmmm, well, that's interesting." Grace pursed her lips together as she looked at Shep; then she turned to look at Hannah. "If you're going to be in town for a little while, you need to get together with the girls and me."

"That would be nice." There was genuine delight in Hannah's eyes at the prospect.

"I'll set something up. What's your phone number?" Grace asked as she dug her phone out of her purse. And as Hannah rattled off the numbers, Shep committed them to memory.

Chapter 4

Strawberry Jam and a Bearded Man

Despite the brand-new mattress, Hannah spent most of the night staring at the ceiling. It wasn't that the bed was uncomfortable; quite the contrary—it was like lying on a cloud. Not to mention the effect of the prescription pain pills that Shep had driven her to pick up after the hospital. They'd dulled the pain in her hand and wrist to something tolerable.

No, the reason she couldn't sleep was because of her Shep-soaked brain.

After the pharmacy excursion, they'd gone to the Piggly Wiggly, the only grocery store in Mirabelle. She'd needed to get Henry approved cat food that she could actually open, and she also needed to get some food for herself that she could prepare one-handed.

Hannah wasn't that great of a cook, except when it came to grilled cheese or BLTs. She'd learned to grill her creations years ago, and her peanut butter and banana was good enough to become a sandwich legend, if she did say so herself. And she did.

Shep had followed behind her, pushing the cart as she threw what she needed into it. The whole process felt too domesticated for her. Like they were a couple out shopping for groceries for the week.

And it had completely messed with her head.

If this was what a few hours with the guy did to her, she didn't even want to know what would happen with more.

Spending time with him was a huge mistake. She had no desire to get her heart stomped on again, and if she let him in, she knew exactly what was going to happen. She saw it playing out clearly, like a horror movie on repeat that wouldn't stop.

She wasn't sure how long it took for sleep to finally claim her, but when she woke up the next morning, it was to find Henry sitting on her chest.

He was staring down at her with big, pleading gray-blue eyes. It had been a shock the first couple of times he'd done it, but now it was a morning ritual.

"Meow."

"I know you're hungry. But can't I sleep for twenty more minutes?"

"Meeow."

"Ten?"

"Meeeeow."

"Fine. You win," she said, sitting up. He moved to the spot next to her and rolled over onto his back, exposing his belly and hoping for a little tummy scratch. Hannah complied like she always did.

Henry's loud, vibrating purr started up, and he wrapped his front paws around her hand, attempting to hold it in place.

"I thought you wanted food?" She raised her eyebrows at the cat.

He let go of her hand and rolled over, standing up and walking to the edge of the bed before jumping down. He circled, then sat on his back legs, looking up at her and meowing loudly.

"You're a royal pain. You know that?"

Another loud meow filled the room.

"I'm going to take that as a yes."

She got out of bed, relishing the fact that the only part of her body that hurt was her hand. Her back was delightfully pain free, the first morning she could say that since she'd been here. And her hand wasn't throbbing as badly this morning. She'd slept fairly stationary, with it resting on her chest. It was the most she could do for elevation.

She grabbed her robe from the chair next to the bed and put it on as she crossed the room. She couldn't exactly tie the sash, but it would somewhat shield her braless state from any eyes on the beach. Plus her shorts were rather short, and she wasn't one to flash a lot of leg to strangers.

She opened the French doors and stepped out onto the deck. The sky was a crystal-clear blue, and the waves crashed against the shore. She took a deep breath of the salty air and closed her eyes in pleasure.

God, she loved this place. Loved how peaceful and beautiful it was.

It was moments like this that reassured her she'd made the right choice coming down here. She was just going to have to figure out a way to deal with Shep. She could do that...couldn't she? She could make him keep his distance.

She snorted at the thought. She was pretty sure she couldn't make him do anything.

It probably didn't help her distance plan that she was going to hang out with Grace and her friends. But the prospect of a girls' night was something she just couldn't pass up. She hadn't done something like that in way too long.

She wanted to go, so she wasn't going to worry about any of the Shep stuff…well, at least not before she had some caffeine.

When she walked into the kitchen, she stared at the coffee-maker for a second. She was debating on whether or not it was even worth it to attempt to set the thing, or if it was a better option to just walk down to Café Lula to get a cup.

But that involved taking a shower.

And putting on a bra.

And putting on pants.

And brushing her hair.

All things she didn't want to do before a cup of coffee.

She let out an aggrieved sigh as she headed for the machine, but stopped when she heard a knock on the door.

"Oh no. No, no, no. He is *not* here." She headed toward her front door, looking through the peephole before she opened it. And there stood Shep, holding two cups of coffee and a bag full of what she could only imagine was sugary, carby goodness from Café Lula.

She rested her head against the wood and closed her eyes. Why in the world did he insist upon bombarding her in the mornings, when her defenses were low?

"I hear you on the other side. So why don't you just open up and let me in?"

"Or what? You'll huff and you'll puff?"

"You scared I'm gonna blow your house down?"

You already did.

"Look, I've got two steaming coffees *and* some of Grace's corn-bread muffins, fresh from the oven. Now, I know you've yet to try Grace's baking, which can't be beat in my opinion, but you *have* had my mother's strawberry jam. And, Hannah, when those two forces combine, you have no idea how incredible it's going to be."

Her stomach growled. Faye Shepherd's strawberry jam was what legends were made of. Hannah had more than indulged on the sticky sweetness the summer she'd been here. She was pretty sure Shep had cleaned out his mother's stock, because he'd kept giving her jar after jar. She licked her lips just thinking about having some again.

"How about you leave your loot on the mat and then step away nice and slow?" Hannah asked.

"Not gonna happen, babe. If I go, so do the goodies."

She didn't say anything as she reached for the lock and flipped the dead bolt. And when she opened the door, she realized how glad she was that Shep hadn't left and taken his *goodies* with him. The thing was, the food and coffee in his hands wasn't even the most delectable part.

Nope. It was him in a red T-shirt, those sexy aviators, and scruff. So much scruff that she just wanted to rub against it. Not to mention she was sure the jam would taste better on him than whatever pastries he had in the bag.

Hannah was so overwhelmed with the man in front of her that it took her a second to realize he was staring at her through his sunglasses. And even though she couldn't see his eyes, she knew he was giving her a scorching look. She glanced down to see that her open robe covered nothing. Her naked breasts pushed against the thin material of her teal cotton tank top, her nipples clearly visible, and her shorts were made of so little material they could be classified as panties in some parts of the world.

She made a quick grab for her robe, pulling the sides together, but the damage was already done.

"Nothing I haven't seen before," he said, giving her a slow grin.

"And something you won't be seeing again." She nudged the door open with her hip to let him inside.

"Hmmm," he hummed as he walked past her into the house. And she could have sworn he finished it with a *we'll just see about that*. But she wasn't going to ask for him to repeat himself.

She had to drop her grip on her robe to shut the door, but she gathered the material again as she followed him into the kitchen. Henry was already dancing around Shep's legs, seeking attention like only he could.

"At least someone in this house likes me." He bent down and ran a hand across Henry's back.

"Don't flatter yourself. He's just hungry."

"Still having technical difficulties with his food?"

"I can manage the pouches, thank you very much. I stayed up late last night and I just woke up, so I haven't had a chance to feed him yet."

Shep made an exaggerated move of looking at his watch. "It's after nine o'clock. What kept you up so late?"

You.

"I was reading." This wasn't a lie either. She'd downloaded a rather steamy romance novel on her iPad and had spent most of the evening devouring it. She hadn't realized how much she'd missed getting lost in someone else's words.

The problem? All of that fictional sex—and there was *a lot* of it—was making her think about actual sex…sex with Shep. This was why it had taken her hours to fall asleep, because there were just some thoughts a girl couldn't turn off.

"Well, good for you." He nodded as he continued to stroke Henry. "A little relaxing is good for you."

"How do you know I don't relax?"

"Just a guess. Anyway, since I'm here, I can help you out with one those cans of Henry's. Where are they?"

"The pantry," she said, pointing to the door in the corner. He stood up, and she found herself watching his movements closely. His sure and easy gate, the way his tattooed arms moved, how his hair was long enough to just brush the back of his shirt.

She pulled her eyes away from him before she was caught and focused on the coffee cups on the counter. They were turquoise with Café Lula printed in a deep purple pattern. Both of them had names written on the sleeves in big black letters. *Shep* on one and *Babe* on the other.

She rolled her eyes but reached for her cup anyway. He apparently wasn't listening to anything she'd told him not to do.

Shocking.

Just like yesterday, her coffee was perfect, and she sipped on it in delight... until she realized her bathrobe was open again. She put down her cup and pulled open the drawer next to her, looking for something to secure it closed with. A chip clip would do just fine. Once she MacGyvered it closed, she reached for the bag of pastries and pulled it open.

The scent that came out was mouthwatering and had her stomach growling. She wasn't used to eating too many carbs, or a lot of sweets, for that matter. She tried her hardest to keep her apartment free of them. Nor were they easily found at work. Which was a good thing, as she had more than bit of a sweet tooth, especially when she was stressed.

Her go-to drug of choice? Twix. Two for her, none for anybody else.

She attributed the ten pounds she'd gained in the last year to too much chocolate and caramel. But who cared? It wasn't like she was trying to impress anyone. So really she could eat two muffins.

The mason jar filled with jam was sitting on the counter, and she reached for it before she realized she wasn't going to get anywhere with the metal lid. She turned so that she could hand it to Shep to open just as he was reaching over her to grab it. Her face pressed into his chest, and much like the day before, she breathed him in deep.

She took a step back, her butt hitting the counter. "Here," she said, handing him the jar.

He didn't say anything as he took it, twisting the metal top, which made an audible pop. "Good thing I stayed; otherwise you wouldn't be getting any jam." He stretched his arm out to her, giving her the jar, but when she went to grab it, he pulled back. "You know, a please or a thank-you would be nice."

Was this worth it? Was it?

She eyed the jam in his hand and knew immediately that it was.

"Thank you," she managed to get out.

"See, that wasn't so hard—was it?" he asked as he placed the open jar in her hand and set the lid on the counter.

"Are you having fun with this?"

"Not as much as you'd think."

"Really?" She turned and opened the silverware drawer, grabbing two knives. "Could've fooled me."

His hand wrapped around her wrist, and he reached across her, pulling the knives away and placing them on the counter. He turned her around, looking down into her face as he held on to her shoulders, stopping her from moving anywhere. All traces of his sexy smugness were gone, replaced with a serious scowl that she wasn't used to seeing on his lips.

"Contrary to my time spent with you lately, I actually prefer it when people like to be in my presence. And you used to be one of them."

"What do you want from me, Shep? For things to be like before? They can't be. Too much has changed."

"I'm fully aware of the fact that we aren't teenagers anymore. I know that for the most part we're different people; we'd have to be, as it's been more than a decade since we last saw each other. But even though a lot of things have changed, not everything has. It doesn't matter how much time or distance there has been between us. I still care about you, Hannah. We went through too much together that summer for me to just brush it aside."

The problem was he had no idea how much they'd actually been through and how much she'd been through alone.

"So what do you want?" she repeated.

"For us to be friends."

She raised her eyebrows at him. "I don't think that's possible."

"Well, neither is us ignoring each other while you're in town. You should've realized that was a pipe dream the moment I saw you."

She had, and she'd been deluding herself with the possibility. "Okay, so what do we do?"

"Well, eating breakfast would be a good start. Then I thought I could take you out to the farm to see Springsteen and Nigel. You obviously can't ride, but we could take a walk. And then do lunch."

She chewed on her bottom lip, trying to decide.

"Come on, Hannah." He smiled at her as he reached up and gently pulled her lip from her teeth. It made her go tingly in her girly bits. "It won't be as painful as you think. You might actually have a good time."

"Two conditions," she said as she put her good hand on his chest and pushed. He didn't budge. "You keep your hands to yourself and you keep your distance."

"I will if you will. But first things first, because you look ridiculous." He reached down and removed the chip clip from her robe, not taking his eyes off her as the material fell apart. She gasped as his hands went to her hips, lightly skimming them before he grabbed the belt. He pulled the material together and cinched the belt, then took a step back.

The feel of his touch lingered on her body, and she wanted to reach forward and grab his hands, wanted to put them back on her. Yeah, it was going to be a testament to her self-control to keep those conditions, too. But keep them she would.

Or she'd just combust from all of the lust.

She was pretty sure the latter was a higher possibility.

* * *

Shep's aunt and uncle, Marigold and Jacob Meadows, lived about ten miles outside of the main part of Mirabelle. They'd turned their love for horses into a very successful business. Whiskey Creek Farm was on about forty acres. All of which were put to good use by the horses in residence, whose numbers ranged from twenty to thirty at any given time.

Jacob trained horses, so the numbers fluctuated depending on how many jobs he had going. Marigold gave riding lessons, and her schedule was always filled. People put their names on a long list, waiting for slots to open up. The farm also offered trail rides, and though Jacob and Marigold would lead them every once in a while, they had a couple of part-time employees who ran those and helped with the daily farm chores.

There were two barns on the property, one closer to the main house, where the family horses were stabled, and the other that was a little farther away, where people boarded their horses.

Shep parked in front of the family barn, and he and Hannah headed through the open doors together. She walked a little in front of him, her jean shorts allowing for those legs of hers to be seen in all their glory.

She came in at only about five foot six, so they weren't long. But they were shapely and freckled and he remembered quite clearly what they felt like wrapped around his waist. He wondered if the skin on her inner thighs was still just as soft. Wondered if she was just as sensitive there as she used to be.

His eyes wandered up to her little round bottom. It filled out her shorts in what could only be described as perfection.

He'd gotten a glimpse—an unfortunately very quick glimpse— of her body earlier that morning when she'd still been in her pajamas. First there'd been her shorts, which were nonexistent. Then there'd been her shirt, which perfectly showcased her breasts. He was pretty sure it had been made of the thinnest material known to man. Seriously, it might as well have been tissue paper, it had been so sheer.

Seeing her erect little nipples had done many things to him. And none of those reactions had been put to good use.

But really he couldn't complain about anything, because not only had he gotten Hannah to have breakfast with him, but he was also spending the morning and afternoon with her. And none of that was chump change.

Normally there were only five horses stabled in the family barn. At the moment all of the stalls were empty except for the last two, and Hannah was making a beeline in that direction. Both geldings stuck their heads over their gates as she stopped between them.

"Hey, big boys. Do you remember me?" she whispered as she ran her fingers up Springsteen's muzzle and then down his neck. "Man, did I ever miss you." Nigel took a step forward and nuzzled into Hannah's shoulder, wanting some attention of his own. "You too." She turned to the other horse and gave him a good pat down as well.

It would've been nice if she could say the same things to Shep...not that he was bitter or anything.

She looked over her shoulder at him with the biggest grin he'd seen on her face since she'd been back. There was some actual light in her eyes, and knowing that he'd been the cause of it— or the cause by association to his horses—made him feel pretty damn good.

Her hair had fallen in her eyes, not all that surprising, as she'd worn it down. It took everything in him to not cross the small space to her and brush it out of her face. But if he did, then he'd be violating both of her conditions. And since he wanted more of these mornings with her, he wasn't going to push his luck.

So instead he reached out and started scratching Springsteen's neck, which left Hannah free to give Nigel her undivided attention.

"How often do you get out here?" she asked, returning her gaze to the horse.

"I try to come out a couple times a week for a ride, but sometimes that just doesn't happen. Not that they don't get out almost every day anyway. Aunt Marigold's riding lessons are high in demand, not to mention the trail rides. My mom and dad like to come up here and go riding, too, so they both get a good workout. Plus Finn's back, and he's out here pretty often, as he's now the farm's official vet."

"God, I can't even imagine getting to go ride that often. It sounds amazing." There was more than a touch of longing in her voice.

"When was the last time you went?"

Hannah turned and looked at him, some of the sadness back in her eyes. "It's been about five years."

"I don't know if I could go that long."

"I've missed it so much. I wish I could go whenever I wanted. Just wake up and hop in the car and drive down here. You're really lucky."

An image flashed through his mind of the two of them coming out here to go riding together in the mornings, like it was part of *their* routine. He saw the whole thing clear as day, waking up together, wrapped around each other in the same bed, sheets tangled around their bodies.

He cleared his throat and tried to push the fantasy to the back of his brain.

"What's kept you from it?" he asked.

"Life. I've been juggling so many things that I've barely had time to sit down and breathe."

"When was the last time you had any fun?"

Hannah snorted humorously. "*Fun?* I don't even know what fun is anymore." Her shoulders slumped and her face fell. She turned away from him again, hiding. Another new thing that he really didn't like.

He wanted to ask why. Wanted to press her for information. But he was glad he didn't, because a moment later she took a deep breath and let it out on a sigh before she started talking.

"Gigi had a stroke right before I finished up with undergrad. She was completely there mentally, but physically? Not so much. It was really difficult for her to use her left side, and she needed a lot of help. My family wanted to put her in a home with assisted living. But I wouldn't let them, so I took care of her. I moved in with her and lived with her while I was in law school. She hired someone to come stay with her during the day, to help her out and everything. And it worked for five years, which in the scheme of things isn't a short amount of time. She had her second stroke three years ago. And after that she had to go somewhere with constant care."

"That must've been a lot. I'm sorry you both had to go through that."

She turned to look at him, a sad smile on her lips. "I wouldn't change it. Living with her. Taking care of her. It wasn't a lot. I would've done more. She was my best friend, and she did everything for me. I would've done absolutely anything for her, no questions asked. I miss her so damn much it…" She closed her eyes, and the tears ran over, streaming down her cheeks. And when she opened them again, more fell. "It hurts."

"Hannah." He whispered her name as he reached out for her.

She didn't hesitate, stepping into his arms and letting him pull her in to his chest. He tried to be careful of her injured arm between them, which was a battle, as he wanted to hold her to him as tightly as he could.

Her face was pressed into his shoulder, her tears soaking into his shirt as he rubbed her back. Up and down.

He didn't tell her it was okay. Because it wasn't. She'd lost somebody she loved, and that was something that would absolutely never be okay. The pain might become more tolerable to deal with, but it would never go away. Not completely. At least, not in his experience.

Hannah's good hand was on his side, balling his shirt up tight in her fist. She was holding on to him so fiercely that it made him ache.

He wondered if she'd truly mourned her grandmother yet. It had been only four months. Four months after Owen's death, Shep had barely been processing it…and there were some days he thought he still wasn't processing it. That he'd never process it.

But Shep had his people. His friends and family. A job that he loved. Two days with Hannah, and he'd come to the conclusion that she didn't have much of any of those things. Or at least not like she should.

Yet here she was, in his arms, seeking solace. Something he was pretty sure she hadn't had in a while. And he'd be damned if he didn't give it to her.

She deserved it.

She deserved *everything*.

So he did the only thing he knew to do. He held her until the sobs subsided and her body stopped shaking.

He knew the exact moment reality hit her because her entire body tensed and she pulled away from him.

He immediately felt the loss of her.

"I—I'm sorry." She ran her fingers under her eyes, wiping away the last of the tears as she took another step away from him. "I didn't mean for that to happen."

"Please don't apologize. Not about that. Not to me. Not ever."

She nodded, chewing on her bottom lip again. It fell from her teeth, and she licked her lips. "I just…I don't…I don't think it's really hit me yet. You know? That she's gone."

"I do know."

"Thank you for that." She gestured between the two of them.

"You don't have to thank me."

She just looked at him. *Really* looked at him for a moment. "I don't know what to do with you."

"Very few people do."

A smile turned up her lips as she laughed. She took a deep breath and let it out slowly, shaking her head. He had the feeling she was just about to say something when Springsteen leaned his head forward, pressing his nose into her neck and letting out a huff of air. She jumped back, startled, her hand over her heart.

"I guess he wanted to comfort you, too."

"I guess so." She reached over and scratched Springsteen's jaw.

"You know I'm here to talk? Whenever you need it."

Her hand stilled, and she didn't look over at Shep when she spoke next. "I'll let you know."

"I hope you do." Understatement of the day. He wanted her confidence again. Wanted her trust. Wanted her.

Chapter 5

Sugar Rushes, Head Rushes, and Shep Rushes

Crying still wasn't something that Hannah was all that accustomed to, and she definitely wasn't used to doing it around other people. She avoided being vulnerable at all costs, but it looked like there was no avoiding it now.

She hadn't quite recovered from her little emotional outburst. She felt more than slightly raw, which wasn't all that helpful when she was with Shep. He was the last person she should be exposing herself to.

Another thing she wasn't used to was being touched. Sure, it was easy to get jostled while walking down the streets of Manhattan, and there was plenty of handshaking when she met clients, but that wasn't the same thing.

She couldn't deny it had felt damn good being wrapped up in his arms. Having him hold her, his hands rubbing up and down her back. And then there was the fact that he knew when to be silent and when to talk. And when he did talk? He said all the right things.

She'd never really learned how to grieve, not when her world came crashing down thirteen years ago and not when there was a repeat performance four months ago. The only person who she'd had as a true confidant was gone. Now Shep wanted to fill that role, and she wasn't sure that she could let him.

In fact, she was almost positive she couldn't. Letting him in like that again would be…She didn't even know. She couldn't wrap her mind around it.

So she chose to try to not worry about it and just enjoy the rest of the day. Which wasn't that much of a hardship, considering what they were doing. Shep kept her busy enough that she didn't really need to think.

They spent a couple of hours out at the farm, brushing Springsteen and Nigel down before feeding them and letting them out into the pasture. Hannah had a few technical difficulties, as brushing them with her left hand was a little awkward. If there was one thing she knew for sure, it was that she was going to build up strength in that hand by the end of it.

For lunch, he took her to the Floppy Flounder, where they feasted on fried grouper, hush puppies, and sweet tea. In between stuffing their faces, they talked. She tried to be careful about what she said, treading lightly on the more sensitive issues. She told him about undergrad and law school. The long hours of what felt like endless studying and how even after she'd graduated those long hours had just gotten longer.

And then it was Shep's turn to talk. He told her about working at the bar. About Owen's legacy and how much he hoped he was living up to it. How much he loved it there. *Loved* working there.

It made her think about how he'd asked if she loved her job earlier and how she hadn't been able to say yes.

He dropped her off at the inn around three before he headed for the bar. He told her she should stop by, and though she smiled and said maybe, she most likely wouldn't go. She'd spent too much time with him already. He was breaking down her defenses, and she needed time to recoup and build up her walls again.

But that just wasn't going to be a reality.

Around seven o'clock that night, there was a knock at the front door. As Shep had been the only one coming around, she figured it was him, though he was supposed to be working tonight. But the man often did whatever the hell he wanted.

Imagine her surprise when she looked through the peephole to find a tiny little blonde on the other side.

"Grace." She opened the door as a smile turned up her lips.

"Hey." Grace grinned back. "I just wanted to stop by. See how you were doing. And I brought treats." She held up a hot-pink box. "Chocolate and salted-caramel cupcakes with cream-cheese frosting. But if you're busy, I can just drop these off and go."

"Not busy at all." Hannah opened the door wider and took a step back, allowing Grace to come in. Her little baby bump preceded her, the material of her dress clinging to her stomach.

A pang of longing that Hannah hadn't felt in years hit her, but she pushed it away. Far, far away and focused.

"I haven't been in here in ages." Grace looked around at the place, spinning in the living room and getting the entire three-sixty view.

"I don't think a lot of people have. It really hasn't been kept up. I spent the first two days cleaning the main rooms downstairs and one of the bedrooms. I haven't gotten to anything else, what with this and all," she said, holding up her injured hand.

"It has so much potential though...well, after this peach paint is covered."

"Oh, don't even get me started. The bathrooms have wallpaper that was more appropriate for the eighties. It's floral and gaudy as all hell."

"I bet." Grace nodded before heading into the kitchen. She set the box and her purse on the counter. "Milk?" she asked, pulling a bottle out.

"Yes, please. But I can get it." Hannah made a move for the cupboard, but Grace held up her hands and shook her head.

"I don't think so. You probably couldn't even screw off the cap. Sit down. I'll get it." She gestured to the bar stools at the island.

"Thank you." Hannah complied. It was true, she most likely wouldn't be able to get the little plastic bottle open without spilling something, but it was still weird being served in her own house...well, at least where she was currently living. The inn wasn't home.

"I would've brought wine, but as I can't drink in my current condition, I didn't have any." She grabbed two clean cups from the drainer in the sink and poured.

"No worries. Besides, milk goes better with cupcakes."

"True story. So, this place is yours now, right?" Grace asked as she started unboxing the cupcakes.

The light brown frosting was done up in a fancy twist, and caramel sauce was drizzled over the top. Hannah's mouth watered. She was going to need to go for a run soon; otherwise she was going to gain another ten pounds.

She pulled her eyes away from the confections and focused on Grace again. "Yes. Gigi left it to me when she passed away."

Grace looked up, her eyes somber. "Shep mentioned that. I'm sorry for your loss. Gigi was a fantastic woman."

"Thank you," Hannah said softly.

Grace nodded as she slid the cupcakes and glasses of milk across the counter. Then she rounded the island to sit on a bar stool. "Do you know what you're going to do with the place?"

"Not a clue."

"It's not a permanent move, though?"

"No." Hannah shook her head. "I have my job to go back to, and I'm actually still working while I'm here. Though it is a very different environment." She laughed. "It's the first time in a long time that I haven't had every minute planned out. Haven't had my schedule timed just so. We bill by the hour, so every minute is accounted for. If we aren't making money, we're losing it."

"How do you have time to just breathe?"

Hannah laughed. "I don't. Though I have been able to do that a little here."

"Well, here's to breathing again." Grace held up her cupcake, and Hannah grabbed hers, bumping them together. The frosting kissed in the middle, messing up some of the intricate swirl. But what did that really matter when Hannah was about to devour the thing?

They both fiddled with the paper, pulling it back, and it was then that Grace's earlier words sank into Hannah's mind. "What else did Shep say about me?" she asked before she could stop herself.

Grace's eyes sparkled with delight, and she grinned. "That you've been giving him a hard time. Which is good, because he needs it. You're the only girl who's ever gotten him all up in a twist."

"That can't be right."

"Facts are facts."

Hannah was under no illusions where Grace's loyalties lay.

She'd known Shep her entire life, whereas Hannah had been just a tiny blip on the Mirabelle radar, on *his* radar. But Grace hadn't been the first person to say something.

Hadn't Preston said something at the bar about Hannah being the only one to ever break Shep's heart? Yet he'd said that was just a theory of Grace's. And as Hannah knew full well, there were always different ways to interpret the fine print. A well-placed comma could change everything. Or a well-placed girl at a bar.

Facts were facts, and Hannah couldn't get the image from a couple of days ago out of her head. Of him and his not-girlfriend in the hallway, him leaning down to kiss her. And with that came the image she'd created thirteen years ago, of him in bed with another woman. Her voice saying "Sheppy" repeating on a loop.

* * *

Grace stayed over for about an hour. They'd had two cupcakes each, and the remaining two were sitting in the refrigerator, waiting to be devoured. Which wasn't going to take all that long, as they were the best damn cupcakes Hannah had ever eaten. Chocolate and caramel were her favorite combination, thus her love of Twix.

It had been nice sitting around with Grace and just chatting. Grace had filled Hannah in on all of the happenings around Mirabelle. She learned that Brendan, Grace's older brother, was married with a child. The little boy, Trevor, was almost a year old, and it took Hannah only a second to put two and two together.

The woman she'd seen Shep with at the Seafood Festival must've been Brendan's wife, Paige, and not another wide-eyed admirer of the tattooed man. The relief at that knowledge was another that Hannah pushed to the back of her mind and chose to ignore. Though she was very interested in meeting the long-legged brunette now.

Paige sounded like more than a handful. Brendan had always been such a good-natured guy, and she was eager to get to know the woman who had stolen his heart. Especially after Grace told Hannah all about how their little romance started. Another thing she was interested in was seeing Paige's artwork. Apparently, she was a fantastic artist and photographer. Her work was on display and for sale at many locations around Mirabelle, the café being one of them.

She also learned that Grace's best friend, Melanie O'Bryan, was planning her wedding to her fiancé, Bennett Hart. Hannah had never met Bennett, but she'd met the sweet-natured Mel and was eager to catch up with her, too.

When Grace left, she assured Hannah that she was going to put together a girls' night for the following weekend. She promised Mexican food, margaritas, and plenty of inappropriate conversation.

Hannah couldn't wait.

She went to bed that night with a stomach full of another cupcake and milk. She wasn't sure if it was the sugar or her time spent with Shep, but she had a few unexpected dreams that had her waking up breathing hard and sweating. Though it was a much better way to wake up than what she was used to.

She'd had more than enough nights of interrupted sleep. Nights where she'd wake up fretting about something job related. Nights where she'd go to sleep next to a man she'd never really been able to be herself around. She'd never slept soundly next to Jeffrey. Never been comfortable in his apartment. But as he'd flat-out refused to ever stay at hers, she'd had to go over there.

But none of that was the problem now. Nope, the problem was her very vivid Shep sex dreams. Dreams where he'd kiss her as he pushed inside of her. Dreams where he'd whisper her name as he moved between her thighs.

Okay, maybe those weren't so much the problem as the feeling of being thoroughly unsatisfied. She missed having a man-made orgasm. And though her past lovers hadn't necessarily been bad, they'd been selfish. She'd had more than a few nights of feeling just as unsatisfied with them as she did at that moment.

Even at eighteen years old, Shep had known full well what he'd been doing with her. Before him, all she'd ever done was kiss a guy. He'd been the first to ever slip his hand between her thighs, to ever touch her like *that*. He was the first man to ever be inside of her in any way, and he'd managed to always make her feel like she was on fire.

It was crazy how well he'd known her body. He would touch her in just the right way. Whether it was trailing his lips across her collarbone, pulling her hair back from her shoulder, or running his thumb across her cheek, he'd always managed to make her come alive with the simplest touch.

She remembered the night she'd given him her virginity quite clearly. They'd driven out to a field in the middle of nowhere to go stargazing. But the stars had been difficult to see with the clouds that had rolled in, so they'd moved on to other extracurricular activities. He'd laid her out on a blanket and slipped his hand beneath her dress.

Her body had still been pulsing as a result of his oh-so-talented fingers when she'd pulled back and looked at him, trying to catch her breath. His face had hovered inches above hers. She'd just been able to make out his features in the dim light from the semi-cloud-covered moon. His shaggy hair had hung down around his face and she'd reached up and put her hand in it.

It had started raining at some point, just a light sprinkle. She hadn't even noticed until she'd felt his damp hair.

"What's wrong?" He was breathing a little hard himself.

"Nothing," she said, shaking her head. "I want more, Shep." Her hand slid down to his cheek.

He stopped breathing in that moment as he looked at her. "How much more?"

"All of it. All of you." She'd fallen in love with him, and she wanted everything he was willing to give her.

It hadn't been a perfect experience that first time, but by the end of the summer they sure had perfected it.

And that was the dream that woke her at six in the morning. She stared up at the ceiling for about a half hour, wondering what it would be like now.

She'd promised herself she wasn't going to do this again, that she wasn't going to fall down the rabbit hole that was Nathanial Shepherd. Yet two days with him and she knew she was a liar. She was too late, in too far. But really, she'd always been in too far with him. Too far to ever go back.

And as that thought consumed her brain, she realized she wasn't going to be falling back asleep.

* * *

Going to bed at three in the morning and waking up at eight wasn't something that Shep was used to. He'd normally sleep to at least ten, sometimes eleven. But not the last three days. The second he opened his eyes in the morning, his first thoughts were of Hannah. Exhausted or not, once she was in his head, there was no hope of going back to sleep.

She was apparently a little easier to butter up with good food and caffeine, so after his shower, he took a quick stop by his refrigerator. As he'd gone to get groceries only the day before, Finn hadn't cleaned him out yet. He filled a bag with everything he needed and loaded up Lois. As he headed over to the inn, he found himself praying that Hannah wouldn't be as resistant today.

And it looked like God was listening, because the second she opened the door, she grabbed his wrist and pulled him inside. He was more than aware of how her fingers felt on his skin.

"Come here," she said as she dragged him through the house.

"Hold up." As they passed the kitchen, he slowed her down, putting his bag of groceries on the counter.

She picked up the pace as soon as his arms were free and led him in the direction of her bedroom. He had a fleeting moment of hope, but when she bypassed her still-unmade bed—with rumpled green sheets that had his mind racing—and kept going to the bathroom, his fantasies disappeared.

When he stepped inside the room, he looked around to see little scraps of paper littering the floor. Some places on the wall were bare, while others had torn as she'd tried to peel them away. It looked like floral flames licking up the walls.

"Do you know anything about wallpaper?" she asked, letting go of his hand and turning to him.

He immediately missed the feel of her, but he tried to focus on what she'd just asked.

"Wallpaper? Not exactly."

"I Googled it. And there are apparently three different kinds: strippable, peelable, and traditional. Strippable should come off in one piece, which this isn't. But as this is coming off in sections and the backing is staying on, I'm guessing it's peelable. Which is good, because traditional wallpaper is the biggest pain in the ass and you have to something with scoring...or sanding...or something. And then you have to use some sort of solution to soak into it to get it off." She didn't stop once. No breaths or anything.

"Wow. That was a lot of information."

"I've been up since six and already drank almost an entire pot of coffee."

"Up since six. Doing what?"

"This." She gestured around the room with her good hand. "I was brushing my teeth and saw the paper peeling in the corner, so I started to pull it off until my hand got tired, and then I decided to look it up on the Internet to see what the best methods were. I went into a couple of the other rooms to test those. Eleven of the bathrooms and five of the bedrooms are wallpapered in varying shades of horrible floral or seashells or seagulls. I'm hoping it's all peelable, but I'll just have to see. I have none of the tools, though, so I need to go to the hardware store. They don't open until nine, which it is now, so I could head over."

Shep took another look around the room, taking in her progress. If she was doing this all one-handed, it was going to take her some time, especially since there were sixteen wallpapered rooms.

"So what do you think?" she asked him.

"I think you need to switch to decaf."

She frowned at him and shook her head. "Come on, seriously?"

"I think I'm going to make you breakfast, and I'm going to call my friend Bennett to come over and get his professional opinion, as he deals with this stuff all of the time. Plus, he should have the tools."

"Bennett Hart? Mel's fiancé?"

"How do you know that?"

"Grace came over last night and brought me cupcakes. We talked. It was nice."

His mouth split into a grin. God, he loved that girl. Count on Grace to do something incredibly sweet like that. "What kind of cupcakes?"

"Chocolate and salted caramel. She brought over six, and I had the last one for breakfast."

"So it's caffeine and sugar that you're running high off of."

"Probably." She nodded.

"Well, let's get you some protein. Come on, I'm making you an omelet." He held out his hand for her, and to his complete and utter surprise, she grabbed it.

He led her into the kitchen and over to the bar stools. She placed one of her feet on the wooden rung at the bottom and stepped up. He reached for her on instinct, helping to guide her up and then down onto the seat. His hand slid along her back, her T-shirt pulling up a little and his fingers brushing her bare skin.

He took a step away from her, waiting for her to say something about not needing his help, but then he got another shock at the words that came out of her mouth.

"Thank you."

"No problem." He forced himself to pull away from her, something that took every ounce of strength that he had in him. He just wanted to keep his hands on her. Good thing he had something to occupy himself. "So I have onions, yellow and green bell peppers, mushrooms, tomatoes, chorizo, and sharp cheddar cheese. All of those things sound good?"

"Yes."

"Okay. Perfect." He started unloading the contents of his bag, putting the eggs and half-and-half in the fridge. "Want a glass of orange juice?" he asked, holding it up. "It might have sugar, but at least it's caffeine free."

"Shut up. I wasn't that bad."

He raised his eyebrows.

"I'm still adjusting to having some free time. Any at all is pretty new and different for me. So I might've gotten a little excited."

"You're right. There's nothing wrong with that. And we'll get you set up, figure out the best way to go about this."

He poured her a glass of orange juice and then fixed himself the remaining coffee in the pot. He called Bennett, putting his head to his shoulder to hold up the phone as he started to dice the onions. Bennett was just finishing up a job consultation and he'd be over within the hour.

"So," he said when he hung up the phone and set it on the counter. "You figuring out what you want to do with this place? What with your bug to fix it up and all?" He looked down, focusing on the knife that was slicing through the veggies.

"Not exactly. But if I'm going to sell it, I'm going to need to fix it."

His knife stilled, and he looked up. The amount of disappointment coursing through him was unreal. "Sell?"

"I mean, I don't know yet. But really, what in the world am I going to do with an eighteen-bedroom beach house?"

"Vacation home?"

"Shep, the last time I went on a vacation was thirteen years ago. And the next time I go on one will probably be in another thirteen years."

"Well, that's a damn shame."

"It's reality."

Well, it was a reality he didn't like one bit, and if he had any say, he'd be changing it.

As soon as possible.

* * *

Shep was right—again. Hannah had needed the protein. The sugar and caffeine running through her system had run their course and she crashed. Luckily for her, half of the very fancy and perfectly filled omelet was on a plate and in front of her moments after she started to fall.

It hadn't been a bad thing watching Shep move around her kitchen, cooking for her. Not a bad thing at all. Shep knew his way around a skillet, and as she bit into his creation, she couldn't stop the little moan that came out of her mouth.

Shep's fork had been on the way to his mouth, and he'd paused for just a second before it continued its journey up. After she swallowed, she grabbed her napkin, wiping away the string of cheese that had landed there.

"Holy cow, that's delicious." She looked over at him just as he was swallowing his bite. His throat worked, his Adam's apple bobbing. Never in her life had she found something so simple, so freaking sexy. "Thank you for making me breakfast," she said, trying to repress the other moan that was bubbling in her throat.

"Anytime."

She turned back to her omelet, focusing on the one thing she was allowed to devour.

When everything was nicely polished off, Shep grabbed her plate before she even had a chance and took it to the sink.

"You don't have to clean up, too."

"How about this? When your hand is good and healed, you

make me something." He turned on the water in the sink and started scrubbing the pan.

"I think you're drastically overestimating my cooking skills."

He looked up at her, shaking his head. "Hannah, when it comes to you, I don't drastically overestimate anything."

She snorted again, unable to stop herself.

"I bet you could make a five-course meal with lobster cooked to perfection."

"That…that's never going to happen." She shook her head. "You'd probably get food poisoning."

"Wanna take the bet?"

"No." A fresh dose of laughter hit her just as the doorbell rang. She slid off the stool and made her way down the hall, chuckling the whole way.

She managed to calm herself before she opened the door, offering a big smile to the man on the other side.

She recognized Bennett immediately. He was the guy who'd walked up behind Shep at the Seafood Festival, allowing her to escape. His gray-blue eyes were kind and seemed to promise a sort of honesty. It was something she liked a lot. He was tall and built, with toned arms stretching out the sleeves of his shirt. His dark blond hair was cut close to his skull in a military fashion and was only slightly longer than the five-o'clock shadow on his jaw.

What was it with these guys and the sexy scruff? Melanie O'Bryan was one lucky lady.

"Hannah?"

"That's me. And you're Bennett?"

"Contractor/handyman at your service." He stuck out his hand to shake hers.

"Sorry." She held up her right hand, which was currently in the black brace. Then she offered him her left.

"No problem," he said, taking it. "It's nice to finally meet you."

Finally? Shep had known she was in town for only a few days. She really didn't think that was enough time to warrant impatience...unless he'd heard about her before.

More information to be examined later.

Hannah took a step back, letting Bennett come into the house. "I've actually heard about you, too. I met your fiancée the summer I visited years ago. Mel was beyond sweet."

Bennett beamed. "She still is. In every single way."

"The wedding is in July?" she asked as they made their way down the hallway toward the kitchen.

"Fifty-six days and counting."

"He isn't eager or anything," Shep said as they walked back into the kitchen. "Pretty sure he's had the countdown going since they settled on the date."

"Damn straight. I'd have eloped if not for our mothers." He turned to Hannah. "They would've killed us both. The waiting is *killing* me, but what can you do?" He shrugged.

The more he talked about Mel, the more she liked him. He was beyond goners for his fiancée, and it was freaking cute. She was more than slightly jealous of Shep's group of friends. Grace, who would come over with cupcakes and conversation to make someone feel welcome. Bennett, who would drop what he was doing with relatively no notice to offer his expertise.

She wasn't used to people doing things selflessly. Nope. Most people in Hannah's life gave only to get. They always wanted to know what was in it for them. It was all about bottom lines and profits.

"So, let's take a look." Bennett rubbed his hands together, taking a quick scan of the kitchen.

This room wasn't all that better than the rest of the house. The counters and floors were the only things about the kitchen that Hannah loved. They were covered in a rustic stone that reminded her of an Italian villa—not that she'd ever been to Italy, but still they were beautiful.

There were two problems. One was they went with nothing. Like the rest of the house, there was no consistency. And two, the tiling job hadn't been finished. Only about seventy percent of the counters were done and about half of the floors.

None of the appliances matched. The dishwasher was a dingy yellow, the stove black, and the refrigerator stainless steel. The dark brown cabinets were in need of some repairs; they were more than outdated, not to mention banged up, dented, and hanging crookedly on their hinges.

She wasn't sure what things caught his eye as a contractor, and she was more than curious to know what his thoughts were. But first things first; he'd come over for the wallpaper problem.

"Not that this room couldn't use some attention, but this wasn't what I was working on. It's the bathrooms."

"Lead the way and I'll follow."

So Hannah did just that, heading toward the bedroom she was residing in and through to the gaudy floral-paper-strewn bathroom.

There were a lot of things about this house that didn't make any sense to her, and the bathrooms were at the top of the list, even above the kitchen.

The linoleum flooring—that occupied all of the bathrooms—was a dingy cream and salmon. It had a hexagon pattern that made her slightly dizzy when she looked at it for too long. The antique vanities had been painted in varying shades of peach, rose, and seafoam green. The one in this bathroom was the peach, which was chipping in more than a few places.

But then there was the situation of the showers and bath-
tubs. Out of the fourteen bathrooms, only six of them had the
massive tubs. They were more than big enough for two people
to sit in comfortably...or to try some water aerobics if they felt
so adventurous. The stand-up shower was covered with neutral
black, brown, and gray mosaic tiles and were completed with a
glass door. It was beautiful, but made no sense with the wallpaper, floors, or anything else, for that matter.

All of the fixtures were a generic shiny gold that looked more
than cheap. She suspected they'd been bought in bulk and without much thought.

"I don't remember the showers looking like this." Shep was
over on the opposite end of the bathroom, messing with the glass
door.

"It's definitely new since I was here last. Some of the smaller
rooms upstairs still have standard white tubs, and the tile was
added in those, too, for the backsplash behind them."

"I just don't understand what the Fergusons were thinking
with this." Shep shook his head.

"I don't think they were." Bennett was now facing one of the
walls that Hannah had made a little progress on. He worked his
thumbnail underneath a strip of the paper and started to pull
it down. "Well, this room is definitely peelable. Your best bet is
going to be removing the top layer and then getting the backing
wet with a paint roller. A plastic putty knife will get it off real
quick." He turned to look at her, his eyes dropping to her hand.
"But as you can't do too much yet because of your injury, I'd say
get all of the vinyl top layer off. Then, when you have the use of
both hands, you can start phase two."

Hannah nodded, looking around at how much more she was
going to have to do in this room alone.

"So you're going to fix it up?" Bennett asked.

"I think so. I'd like to do whatever I can on my own while I'm here. The linoleum and those awful gold fixtures have *got* to go. And the vanities all need to be sanded down and repainted. I think I'm going to work on what I can, and do a little research about the other stuff that needs to be fixed."

"Well, this place needs some work, no doubt about that, but it has a lot of potential."

"I think so, too," she agreed.

"You'll be able to do a lot of the work yourself. Taking things down is usually a lot easier than putting them up. The smaller things you need aren't that expensive and are the type of supplies that you'd just toss when you finish up with the job, so I don't have any of that to give you. But when it comes to the bigger tools that you're going to need, I have them, so you can just use mine."

"I wouldn't ask you to do that."

"Seriously, Hannah, it isn't that big of a deal. Depending on the job that I'm doing, there's a good chance I wouldn't need it. Besides, I don't do that much in demolition or remodeling like this anymore. I do custom woodworking jobs and furniture restoring."

"Is that so?" she asked, her interest more than piqued. There was a lot of antique furniture in the place, and it was in desperate need of some serious TLC.

"I think you might have another job in your future," Shep said.

"I think I might. Keep me posted, though. I'm very interested to see what you've got in store for this place."

"I'm very interested in figuring that out, too," she said as she walked with both men to the front door.

It was in those moments, those few steps through the house to let Bennett out, that the undertaking of fixing up the inn hit her.

What the hell am I doing?

Because it wasn't just the bathrooms or a couple of the bedrooms with wallpaper that needed fixing. No, it was every room in that house. There wasn't a wall that wasn't going to require a fresh coat of paint. None of the furniture was in an acceptable condition, and though some of the more solid pieces could be fixed by Bennett, there were more than a few wicker pieces that just needed to be trashed.

She said goodbye to Bennett, trying her hardest not to fall into a full-blown panic attack. What the hell was she thinking? What the hell had Gigi been thinking? What had been her plan in buying a half-remodeled inn? And a poorly planned remodel at that? And, why, oh why, had she left it to Hannah?

She was a lawyer and didn't have the first idea on how to fix up a place. Yeah, sure, she had ideas on how she wanted it to look. Ascetics were no problem. But doing it herself?

"Hey, what's going on? What just happened?" Shep was suddenly standing in front of her, and she was resolutely staring at his chest, desperate to not see his eyes because she knew the moment she did she was going to be even more lost than she'd been before.

If there was one thing that was confusing her more than the fate of this house, it was the fate of her heart when it came to this man. She'd been able to distract herself all morning, or maybe that had just been the high from all of the caffeine and sugar. She knew the moment she looked into those blue eyes that she was going to have to face another reality that was leaps and bounds more terrifying than wallpaper and paint.

She didn't think she could do it. Couldn't deal with this at the moment. But Shep wasn't letting her escape. Nope, his hand was at her chin, pushing her face up.

She couldn't handle this. Couldn't handle him. He was so close to her, almost no space between them. And then there was the concern in his eyes and the way his big hand gripped her waist, attempting to hold her steady. But she wasn't steady; she was reeling, spinning in circles and only moments away from falling on her ass, or her face. Either was a very distinct possibility.

"What am I doing?" she whispered.

"What do you mean?"

"I don't know that I was thinking coming down here. I can't do this." And though she was partly talking about the house, she was mainly talking about him.

His eyebrows lowered and his mouth turned down. "Did you seriously just say you couldn't do something?"

"I don't know what I'm doing."

"Where's the woman from this morning? The one who was ready to conquer everything?"

"Reality hit her in the face." Logic. Her go to. Where the hell had it been all morning?

"Well, I think she needs to kick reality right back in the balls."

A somewhat hysterical laugh burst forth from her lips. "Is that right?"

"Yeah." He nodded. "You have to take it one day at a time."

"But I don't operate like this. I always know the plan. Know the endgame. Where I'm going. But not with any of this. This is just so...so impulsive. I don't do that." *Not since you. Not since everything came crashing down.*

"Coming down here was a bit impulsive, wasn't it?"

"Yeah, but that had more to do with Gigi's plans than mine. I don't know what I was thinking, doing this. Coming here."

"Maybe it had to do with both of you, and maybe you should

stop overthinking for a little bit." He tapped her temple gently before he ran his fingers slowly down the side of her face, tracing her jaw. "Go with your gut." And then his hand was on her belly. His thumb circled over the fabric of her shirt, pulling it up just slightly as his fingers dipped, touching her skin.

And that was when the sheep turned into the wolf. The predatory gleam in his eyes wasn't a flare. It was a freaking inferno.

Her breath caught, her heart pounding in her throat. "Are we still talking about the inn?"

He shook his head, taking a step forward and completely invading her space. "I was never talking about the inn."

Chapter 6

The Problem with Being Impulsive

Shep's hand was on Hannah's belly and it moved, slipping around her side and to her back, gliding across her skin the entire journey. She shivered, and his grip on her side tightened, pulling her closer to him. She was completely flush against his body, and it was in this moment that she realized her good hand was at his side, too, twisting in the fabric of his shirt.

"Then... then what were you talking about?"

He leaned down, just barely skimming his mouth over hers, and damn if her knees didn't buckle just a little bit. Luckily for her, he took a step forward, pressing her back against the wall.

"I've missed you," he whispered, his lips moving against hers. "So damn much."

She wasn't sure what words she would've liked to use as a response, because the ability to speak was positively lost to her when he ran his tongue across her bottom lip. He didn't have to do much coaxing at all to get her to open up.

None. He had to do absolutely zero coaxing.

Her mouth parted on instinct, needing to taste him more than she needed to breathe. And he complied.

Holy hell did he comply. His tongue found hers, stroking and twisting. It was better than she remembered.

So.

Much.

Better.

His firm lips, the abrasive rasp of his scruff on her cheeks and chin, his hands on her body, his rough fingers working into her skin and holding her so close.

It was then that she noticed her hand was in his hair.

How in the world did that get there?

Oh, who the hell cared? It was exactly where she wanted it. Though she couldn't help but be frustrated that both hands weren't in it. Damn her injured hand. Damn it in all of its uselessness. But she'd just have to make do with what she had, and it wasn't too shabby.

Her fingers slid through the long strands. How a guy could have hair like silk she didn't know, but Nathanial Shepherd did. Oh God, did he.

He nipped at her mouth, biting down lightly on her lower lip and eliciting a moan in both of them. He shifted his body, and his erection pressed into her belly. Her stomach did that weird fluttery thing, an occurrence that she hadn't felt in forever, and not this strong. *Never* this strong.

He pulled back from her and looked down. There was more than just want in his eyes. There was *need*. Need for her.

"I keep thinking this isn't real." His breath was ragged as he leaned in and put his mouth to her neck. "That you're a dream. A complete figment of my imagination." He looked down her body as his hands went up, hiking up her shirt and exposing her stomach. "But when I'm touching you, when I…" He trailed off, his eyes fixing on a spot on her abdomen, just left of her belly button.

She knew exactly what had caught his attention, and as he reached out and traced the tattoo inked across her skin, she found it even harder to breathe.

Just moments ago his touch had turned her to fire. But now? Now it was like she'd just been doused in ice-cold water.

Okay, so maybe there were moments in her life when she'd done impulsive things. Getting the tattoo had most definitely been one of those moments. It was of a broken wing. Just the one separated from its partner. The feathers stretched down below the waistband of her shorts and out to her hip, the very tip tickling her side.

"When did you get this?" he whispered almost reverently.

She had to swallow past the painful lump that was lodged in her throat. "When I was twenty-one."

"What does it mean?"

What did it mean? Lots of things: hurt, sorrow, loss, things that would never be. What the hell was she doing letting him kiss her?

Stupid, stupid, stupid.

But that momentary lapse of judgment was over and done with.

"Nothing," she said.

His head came up, and he looked at her, his eyebrows bunching together. "What?"

"It means nothing." She started chewing on her bottom lip as she moved his hand away and pulled down her shirt.

"Hannah, what just happened? Why are you lying to me?"

"I'm not lying," she said as she put her hand on his chest and pushed him away from her. "And I told you to stop acting like you know me. Because you don't. You never really did. Now let go of me."

He did so immediately, his hand at her hip falling away, and took a step back.

"And you're seriously going to call *me* a liar? After what you did? I think you need to take a good long look in the mirror, Shep."

His eyebrows lowered, and any look of need or desire from a moment ago was gone. "When did I ever lie to you?"

"That entire summer was a lie." She stepped away from the wall, needing space.

"Are you kidding me with this?"

"How long did it take? How long did it take before you moved on? Before you forgot about me?"

Pain and hurt flashed through his eyes, but it was gone a second later, replaced with a fresh wave of anger. She'd never seen him mad before, at least not like this. He took a step toward her, and just like that she was back against the wall, entirely caged in again. He placed his hands on either side of her head as he braced himself and leaned in.

"First of all, Hannah, I didn't forget about you. Not even close. But *you* were the one who left. *You* were the one who talked about bigger and better things for the entire three months you were here. *You* were the one who suggested a clean break. Because it was *logical*. Because it would be *easier*. But what was easier about it, I have no clue. So you tell me what the hell I was supposed to do. Fight for you? Fight for us? I thought we were done. And the first I hear from you is a phone call two months later."

It took everything in her not to flinch at his words. "And you were already with somebody else. How long did that take you? How long after I left before you had another woman in your bed?"

"I don't owe you an explanation, or an apology, or anything for that matter. *You. Left.* I tried to move on."

"Clearly. And you just keep moving on, from girl to girl. Not three days ago you had somebody else in exactly this position."

He pushed off the wall and took a step back from her, closing his eyes as he reached up to pinch the bridge of his nose.

"Worst fucking luck in the world," he mumbled to himself. He took another step back before his eyes opened and focused on her. "You're absolutely right, Hannah. Before I knew you were back, I made a move on a woman. One consenting adult trying to kiss another consenting adult. *Unprecedented.* I'm sure that's something you've *never* done before. But the thing is, and I don't know if you've noticed this or not, since I found out you've been back, I've concentrated all of my efforts on spending time with you. I want to be around *you.*"

"For now. Until you find something new and shiny."

He breathed deep again as he took a few more steps away from her.

"You want to blame me for something that happened thirteen years ago? Something that ended because of a decision that we made *together*? You go right ahead. You want to blame me for something that happened before I even knew you were back? You can do that, too. But I'm not going to be around for it. You keep saying I don't know you anymore, but I'm beginning to think you don't know me, either, Hannah. Because if you can honestly say there's nothing here anymore, especially after that kiss, you really aren't the person I thought you were."

And with that, he turned around and walked out the front door, leaving Hannah so confused that she couldn't see straight.

* * *

Thursday morning started early, with a particularly needy Henry pawing and meowing at Hannah. The sun hadn't even risen yet, but there was no use fighting her demanding cat. She'd lose that battle anyway.

While he was munching away on his breakfast, she headed back to her room and changed. She'd started walking along the beach in the mornings. Vacationers were beginning to flood the area, so she'd take a good little stroll before the crowds started to show up and stake claim to all of the free space along the water. There were only a handful of people out at the moment, running along the beach or swimming laps, but other than that it was pretty much deserted.

She should go for a jog and really stretch her legs, but she wasn't sure how much her hand would hold up under all of that jostling. Maybe in another few days she'd be good to go.

It had been a little more than a week since she'd hurt her wrist, and though she wasn't going to be shooting basketball hoops—not that she'd ever shot one in her life—it was starting to be somewhat useful again. She could at least put on her clothes without having to become a pretzel.

Small miracles.

She walked out onto the sand, looking right and spotting the pier in the distance. She couldn't stop the image that filled her mind, of her and Shep walking down it hand in hand all those years ago. It felt like another life sometimes.

It had been five days since his little speech, and she hadn't seen hide nor hair of him since he'd walked out the door.

She'd wanted him to leave her alone.

Now he had.

She'd been wrong. Really, really wrong.

How was it that she missed him? Well, the answer was actually quite simple: It was because she'd missed him for the last thirteen years. And wasn't that just beyond complicated? She was beginning to think she had a personality disorder or something.

She kept replaying that freaking kiss. His lips and hands on her. His body pressed into hers, caging her against the wall. The silky strands of his hair between her fingers...

But that couldn't happen again. Missing him or not, that little bit of history just couldn't be repeated. There were only so many nuclear bombs a person could survive.

She needed a distraction. Doing stuff for work lasted a few hours, but once that was done, she was grasping at straws.

There was only so much brainpower used in pulling wallpaper off the walls. And there was only so long she could do it before her left arm was screaming in pain. She'd have gotten a lot further if she could use both.

So research it was. This was something she was more than used to doing for hours on end, but her focus during her nonwork hours was spent reading Do It Yourself Home Remodel blogs. After that, she'd done some other reading, plowing through a nice little series of books.

But all of these things provided only a tiny, insignificant dent in distracting her from one Nathanial Shepherd...or his scruff of glory.

Yeah, she needed to find another extracurricular activity. Pronto.

At least tomorrow night promised to be somewhat interesting, as she was going out with Grace and her friends.

Besides the phone call from Grace and the few calls from

work, Henry had pretty much been her only source of conversation for the last couple of days. Though he would look at her when she talked to him, his head tilted to the side, she was fairly certain he didn't understand. Nor was he capable of responding with anything besides a *meow*.

She needed a real, adult conversation, one that preferably didn't have anything to do with work and was absent of an argument in the beginning, middle, or end.

She'd actually been more than somewhat shocked when Grace had called her. After the incident with Shep, she'd been pretty sure that she was going to be getting the cold shoulder from more than just him. But Grace did call, and plans had been made.

There'd been a split second when the unidentified number flashed across Hannah's phone that she couldn't stop the little thrill as she thought it might be Shep. But as she hadn't given him her number, the odds were not in her favor. Plus, she didn't need to be talking to him anyway. See, she *did* have a personality disorder.

Whatever. She wasn't going to think about this anymore. Think about *him* anymore.

Fat. Freaking. Chance.

Hannah shook her head, turned left away from the pier, and headed northeast up the beach. She had about twenty minutes before the sun would peek above the horizon, but the distant glow was slowly starting up. It was so quiet out there, just the water crashing against the shore. No honking horns, or sirens, or cars rushing by on an endless loop.

She went on for a good two miles, the sun slowly working its way up in the sky. She was just about to turn around and head back when she saw a tiny figure shuffling in the distance. The person moved slowly, turning around in circles and stopping for a moment before they'd start again.

As Hannah got closer, she realized it was an older lady, her thin nightgown and robe blowing around her frail legs. She was wearing house slippers, dirty and damp from the wet sand. She was wringing her hands together as she looked around again, and a slight whimper escaped her throat.

"Are you okay?" Hannah asked.

The woman looked over, her long gray hair flying in her face from the breeze. "I can't find him. I can't find Owen." Her voice cracked, and tears started to fall from her eyes, eyes so blue they looked like sapphires.

Shep's eyes. His grandmother. Ella Shepherd was wandering around the beach looking for her dead husband.

Hannah's heart broke in two.

* * *

Shep pulled up in front of his parents' house at just after nine in the morning, yawning and needing a good, strong cup of coffee. He'd had another late night closing the bar, and though Thursdays were his day off and he should've been able to take things somewhat easy, that wasn't the case. His mother had called that morning and had *things* for him to do. What she'd promised would take only one hour was probably going to turn into five.

No rest for the weary.

Besides, it wasn't like he was sleeping all that well anyway. It had been pointed out to him by more than a few people that he was less than sociable the last couple of days. Not all that surprising given the circumstances.

But what the hell was he supposed to do?

Hannah didn't want to be around him? Fine.

She wanted to blame him? Fine.

Wasn't like it mattered anyway. She was down here for only a few months. Once she figured out what she was doing with the inn, the odds were she'd be out of Mirabelle, this time for good.

Well, if that wasn't a painful thought, he didn't know what was.

He pushed it to the back of his mind as he walked up his parents' front steps. Like the majority of the houses on this area of the Gulf Coast, they were built a good ten feet in the air on thick and sturdy pylons.

He was just about to open the front door when a light, fluttery laugh floated on the air. It was coming from the back of the wraparound porch.

Grandma El? Well, that's new. Her laughs were few and far between these days, her bad days far outnumbering the good. He couldn't even remember the last time he'd heard that sound.

He pulled back, letting the screen door slam shut, and made his way around. Another laugh went through the air, this one deep and rich. His mother. Now, that was a sound he was more than used to. Faye Shepherd was quick to laugh, always had been. And he loved it when there was a smile across that beautiful face of hers. So he was beyond curious to find out what was making two of his favorite women in the world happy.

But before he could round the corner, a third laugh hit his ears and he stopped dead. He'd know that soft, warm chuckle anywhere.

Hannah.

Well, this was bound to be interesting... and frustrating as all hell.

What is she doing here?

He took a deep breath before he turned the corner and took in the sight before him. All three women were sitting around the low wooden table. Hannah's back was to Shep, but her little red head was peeking out from the back of the Adirondack chair. There was an orange mug of coffee on the table in front of her, and she was tracing the handle with her forefinger in a thoughtless motion.

Top to bottom.

Lift and up.

Top to bottom.

Lift and up.

"Ohhh, Nathanial, you're here," his mother said when she spotted him. Of course he was, as she'd called for him to come more than thirty minutes ago. And now he understood exactly why.

Hannah's hand stopped moving and her shoulders tensed. She made a slow turn to look at him, and it was when her eyes caught his that he realized he was holding his breath, too. The trepidation in her expression was evident, from her eyes to the set of her mouth.

She wasn't happy to see him. *Shocking.*

"Look who's here. Why didn't you tell me Hannah was back in town?" Faye asked.

Shep pulled his eyes from Hannah and all of her uneasiness and focused on his mother, who was beaming brighter than the sun. There was no small amount of suggestion in her voice as her eyes darted between him and Hannah. She was practically bouncing in her seat.

To say that Faye Shepherd was anxious for her sons to settle down and start giving her grandkids would be an understatement. He would've thought she'd given up on him at this point, with his track record. But if Faye Shepherd was anything, it was determined.

He wasn't even remotely surprised that his mother was ignoring Hannah's body language and how she clearly wanted an escape route to appear.

"Must've slipped my mind. I guess I didn't think it mattered, as she's not staying long." He bent down and pressed a kiss to his mother's cheek before he went to do the same thing to his grandmother.

But Ella stopped him, grabbing his face with her soft little hand. "Nathanial Owen Shepherd. Where is your Southern hospitality? Of course it matters." The reprimand coming from her was sharp and stern, something Shep had been used to growing up, but something that had definitely dwindled lately. He'd always known that when she middle-named him, she meant business. And no one messed with Ella when she meant business.

Ella Franklin was born the second of two kids eighty-seven years ago. Her parents started out early, having her brother, Nathanial—Shep's namesake—when they were seventeen and sixteen years old. When Ella came along two years later, they still had no idea what they were doing.

Their father died shortly after Ella had been born, and their mother ran off with a man about four months after that. He was ten years older than her and provided the perfect escape from the burden of two children that she'd never wanted.

They were left with their grandmother, and though she wasn't abusive, her three sons definitely were.

Desperate to get out of that miserable house, Nathanial had joined the air force two years before WWII started. He trained and then fought alongside Owen Shepherd. The men became friends almost instantly, and before long they considered themselves to be brothers.

Nathanial died during the Battle of the Bulge, saving Owen's life. Before his death, Nathanial talked about one person more than anyone else, his little sister, Ella. He'd worried about her constantly, and all he'd wanted was to get her out of that awful house where their nightmares had followed them into the waking hours.

Owen was and always had been a man of honor, and he'd known exactly what he'd needed to do when the war ended. Every time Owen told the story of the first time he met Ella, he grinned like a fool. And he'd be the first to tell you that when it came to her, he was and always would be a fool.

Ella wasn't some sweet, shy little thing. She'd had to grow a thick skin and fend for herself over the years. Losing her brother had almost destroyed her. He'd been her only family, the only person she'd ever loved. So when Owen had come along, she'd wanted very little to do with him. He'd had to fight the good fight for a while before she finally let him in.

Ella had a tough exterior, but once anybody got past that initial barrier, they were in for life. She loved fiercely and without end, and that was why her heartache was debilitating. Her mind had started to go only after Owen died, maybe because it was too difficult to process life without him...or because she wanted to go back to a time when he still existed.

She still looked for him everywhere, and the pain in her eyes when she couldn't find him was awful.

But there was no loss or sadness in her eyes at the moment. In fact, she had a little bit of a spark that he hadn't seen in longer than he could remember.

"Sorry, Grandma El. Won't happen again."

"Good boy." She patted his cheek and smiled, which was her way of saying that he was now allowed to give her a kiss on the cheek.

He did so, and when he pulled back, she held up her coffee cup. "You should go get yourself some, and while you're at it, refill mine."

"Me too," his mother said before she mouthed *decaf* and nodded at Ella.

"Yes, ma'am," he said as he grabbed both of their cups. "Hannah? Need anything?" *Besides a getaway car?*

"Actually, I should probably be going."

Well, that had been predictable. He wasn't quite fast enough to bite back the scoff that bubbled in his throat.

Her eyes snapped to him and she frowned. "I have a meeting at the inn, and I need to get back and get dressed."

A meeting? With whom?

Didn't matter. It wasn't his business. Because she wasn't his business.

Faye waved off Hannah's words. "Have another cup of coffee and Nathanial can drive you back. You don't need to make that walk again."

"You walked here?" His eyebrows lowered as he studied her. Why the hell would she walk? It was about three miles between here and the inn.

His mother cleared her throat and shook her head slightly, casting an uneasy glance over at Ella for just a second.

Ahh, something to do with his grandmother. He could only guess what had happened. He'd have to get the full story later. Ella's moments of lucidity came and went with the breeze. She'd be without an episode for days, and then just like that she'd be gone, lost in the past, and there was no telling when she'd return, or if she'd return.

His grandmother was disappearing before his eyes, and it was just another thing he couldn't control. But she was here now, and he could have a cup of coffee with her.

"Is that okay with you?" Shep asked, looking at Hannah.

The shock on her face from his question was evident. She apparently wasn't prepared for him to be accommodating. But as she obviously didn't deal well when he was demanding, he'd have to be nice, even if she was driving him out of his mind.

It took her a second, but she nodded slowly, her uncertainty clear. He really hated that look coming from her. He turned around and headed into the house, his frustration growing with every step because he had no clue as to how to change it.

Chapter 7

Past and Present

The drive home was…odd. Shep got the story from Hannah about how she'd found Ella wandering around on the beach. His grandmother had been lost both physically and mentally, searching for Owen. It made his chest tighten painfully, and suddenly he was back to that fateful day three years ago.

He remembered the morning of Owen's death like it was yesterday. Finn had just gotten back in town for his summer break, and they were both having breakfast with their grandfather, something they did on the first Sunday of every month.

Shep had worked late at the bar the night before and had stayed up even later with a girl he'd brought home with him. When he got to the diner, only Owen had been sitting in the booth. He looked up from his newspaper and just shook his head.

"What?" Shep asked as he slid in across from his grandfather.

The thick, dark brown hair that dominated the Shepherd family had been inherited from Owen. It had to have come from him, as both Shep's grandmother Ella and his mother were blondes. Owen's hair had turned a dark salt-and-pepper gray in his old age, but it was still as thick as ever.

"When are you going to stop messing around with your life and settle down? You're twenty-eight years old. Start acting like it."

"Maybe I haven't found the right girl to settle down with yet. And I'm not going to settle for someone who isn't the right girl."

"Hmmm." Owen frowned. "I don't think you're looking."

Truer words couldn't have been spoken. He hadn't been looking. It wasn't that he thought the woman of his dreams was going to just magically pop up out of the ground or anything. It was more that he'd know her when he saw her.

And he wasn't seeing her.

"Not all of us can be as lucky as you and Grandma El. Maybe I'm destined to forever be a bachelor."

"Hmmm." Owen hummed again as he studied Shep. "I just don't think that's the case."

"And what is the case?"

"You're scared to fall in love again after Hannah. But if you keep up with what you're doing, you're going to end up alone. I just don't want you to miss out. Your grandmother is the best thing that ever happened to me. She made me the man I am. I didn't change because she wanted me to, but because for her I always wanted to be better. And I'd hate for you to not get your best thing.

"Nathanial, settling down in life isn't about settling. It's about being with the one person that makes waking up every day a gift. And you're wasting it. Every day that you keep up with these ridiculous shenanigans, you're wasting it. And, son, it should go without saying that I don't approve. Not one bit. There are consequences for your actions. And one day you're going to see them and not be too happy about your past decisions."

Disappointment had been all over Owen's face, and it had been a hard pill to swallow. In fact, it had never gone down.

Shep had definitely reevaluated his life after his grandfather's death. He might not have settled down with a wife and family, but he was settled in every other way. He owned a house and was part owner in the family business. He paid his bills on time, stayed out of trouble with the law...well, except for that one time a couple years ago when he and Brendan had landed in jail. But that had been Brendan's fault...mostly.

But none of that mattered, because reputations died hard and a person couldn't change their past. Well, at least that was the law, according to the woman next to him.

The woman in question was wearing a T-shirt and a pair of those cheerleader shorts. Light blue cotton top, black cotton bottoms. Nothing that screamed sexy. But even at her unsexiest—not that this was even a thing, as the woman was always sexy—she outsexied everyone. It didn't matter what she was wearing. He also knew any comparison would get even further apart if she wasn't wearing anything at all. She just did it for him, no matter the circumstances.

But Owen had been wrong, which was more than somewhat shocking. The man had almost always been right. He had a wisdom that was beyond anything Shep had ever known, and many others were drawn to it. A lot of people came to the Sleepy Sheep to talk to Owen. He probably listened to more confessions than the local priest. He was respected and admired, and his words were worth more than a lot of other people's words.

But he was wrong about why Shep hadn't moved on. It wasn't that he was scared of falling in love again. It was that he couldn't fall in love with anyone besides Hannah.

* * *

Shep was quiet as he walked Hannah up to her door, doing this whole moody broody thing that she wasn't used to with him. She didn't know what to do with it.

"Who's your meeting with?" he asked, pulling the keys from her hand.

"Would you stop doing that?"

"Nope." He opened the door and walked inside, not waiting for an invitation. She blew out a breath of exasperation before she followed him in the house. He held the door open as she walked through it. She turned around, hoping he was going to walk his very fine ass right back out of said door, closing it behind him and leaving her be with her very confused thoughts.

She was wrong.

He shut the door and then turned, walking past her as he made his way into the kitchen. She had no choice but to follow like some pathetic little puppy.

He deposited her keys on the counter before he turned to look at her, folding his arms across his chest as he leaned back against the counter.

"Who's your meeting with?" he repeated.

She debated not telling him. It wasn't like it was his business anyway, but with the way the rumor mill worked around this town, it would be only a matter of time before he found out.

"A Realtor."

The only visible reaction he had was a tic in his shadowed jaw. "So you're selling?"

"I'm not sure yet. I want to know all my options."

"Who's coming to look at it?"

"Topher Berk."

Another tic in his jaw and his frown seemed to deepen, something she hadn't thought possible. "What time?"

She glanced to the clock on the stove. "Twenty minutes."

"Well, you better go get ready."

"Would you stop telling me what to do? And maybe I could go get ready if you'd be on your way."

"Nope." He shook his head. "I'm sticking around."

"Oh, you are, are you?"

"Topher Berk is an opportunistic jackass, and I'm not leaving you alone with him."

Her eyes narrowed and her mouth bunched together as she took a deep breath through her nose. "I am thirty years old, Nathanial, and I've taken care of myself just fine without you. I don't need you to *stick around.*"

He shrugged his shoulders. "I don't care. I'm not going anywhere, and the longer you spend arguing with me, the less time you're going to have to get ready." He glanced at the clock before he turned back to her. "You have nineteen minutes now."

She stared at him, her anger increasing every second that ticked by. "It's real rich of you calling someone else a jackass."

"It is what it is, babe." He shrugged again.

She didn't say anything as she stormed out of the kitchen and headed toward her room. She didn't need this. His overbearing, Neanderthal, one-man show.

She would've slammed the door, but she didn't want to put more of her reaction to him on display.

Maybe a nice cool shower would calm her temper just a little bit. But as she stepped into the tepid stream of water, she realized that there was nothing in this world to accomplish that job when he was around.

He made her want to scream, both in anger and...well, all

the good ways, too. He'd had a knack for always making her let loose. Which had been a real problem when he'd snuck into the inn in the middle of the night. He'd needed to cover her mouth with his to muffle the sounds she'd made.

Besides him, no one had ever been able to make her scream in bed. It was possible that her agitation had more to do with her amped-up libido than anything else, and being around him after that kiss—*God, that kiss*—was killer. Because she wanted more.

So. Much. More.

But she couldn't have it. She'd already started down that slippery slope. One more misstep and she'd be falling on her ass, sliding all the way down.

She had to keep it together. No more letting her temper get the best of her. No more letting him affect her. She needed to push all of that to the back of her mind. Needed to focus on the task at hand. Which was figuring out what the hell she was going to do with this inn.

* * *

Hannah could be as pissed off as she wanted, because there was no way in hell that Shep was about to leave her alone with Topher Berk. The guy was much more than a jackass. He was a smarmy, pretentious prick who liked to screw anything that stood still long enough, both in business and in his personal life.

He'd been a few years behind Shep in high school, but his reputation had preceded him even then. He'd been known as Gopher Topher because the guy was a rodent if Shep had ever seen one.

People must've considered him charming or some shit, because he was beyond successful in the real-estate business, something that continued to baffle Shep.

So yeah, he'd stayed.

Water came rushing through the pipes in the wall behind Shep's back, and he took a deep, steadying breath, trying to calm himself.

Hannah was in there...naked...and wet.

And he was out here...alone...and frustrated.

A soft "meow" echoed through the kitchen, and Shep looked over as Henry padded in. He didn't even hesitate when he saw Shep. The little kitten walked right on over and sat down in front of his boots, looking up at him expectantly and meowing again.

"How can I help you?" Shep asked.

Henry stood and proceeded to climb up Shep's leg, stretching up with his front paws.

"You are a very odd cat." He shook his head and bent down, picking up the gray fur ball. He scratched the little guy's head, and the cat closed his eyes and started purring loudly in delight.

Shep had very little experience with cats. He was more of a dog person, but Henry wasn't half bad. He was actually pretty cool, especially when he was giving his owner a hard time. Apparently, Shep had something in common with the pint-sized creature.

Henry was more than content in Shep's arms, getting a good scratching everywhere. He shifted, moving his body so Shep could access new areas. Both man and cat were good and occupied for a few minutes, but nothing could distract the man when a certain redhead walked back into the kitchen, wearing skintight jeans and a loose yellow shirt that hung off one of her shoulders.

No bra strap, which meant she was wearing one of those strapless contraptions that seemed to defy gravity.

She came up short when her eyes landed on him, her focus darting between Shep's face and Henry. At this point the cat was lying belly-up, lounging in Shep's cradled arm, kind of like a baby.

Her eyes narrowed, and he distinctly heard her mumble "traitor" under her breath.

She headed for the fridge, opening the door and pulling out a bottle of water. She hesitated for a second before she cleared her throat. "Do you want one?" She didn't even turn to look at him.

Pissed or not, she hadn't forgotten her manners.

"Please."

Henry got one final scratch around the ears before he was placed back on the floor. He stretched, sticking his little butt in the air and the front pads of his paws separating.

"Here." She held out the chilled bottle, her mouth still in a severe frown. Shep was surprised she didn't throw the bottle at his head.

"Thanks," he said, reaching for it. He grazed her fingers with his and she jerked back like she'd been shocked, dropping the bottle on the floor.

Instinctively, they both went down to pick it and bumped into each other, Hannah going unsteady on her feet. Shep reached out and grabbed her shoulders, bringing her back to balance. If touching her hand a second ago was shocking, it was nothing to touching her now. His hand was on her bare shoulder. His thumb began to move, tracing the freckles on her skin.

She didn't pull away from him this time. In fact, she leaned in to his touch. Her eyes no longer held that look of agitation. Instead they were filled with need.

Was this all it took—his hands on her body—to make her agreeable? No, that couldn't be right. He'd had his hands on her before, and it was a flip of the coin as to how she'd react.

Apparently, the odds were in his favor at this exact moment.

There was another clatter as the other water bottle fell from her grip and hit the floor. This time neither of them made a move to pick it up, but they did move closer together, Shep leaning down and Hannah bracing her hands on his hips as she stretched up.

And much like last time, there was no hesitation at all as they kissed. Her lips were parted, her mouth already open and waiting for his. He skimmed his hands down her back, pulling her closer as he leaned back against the counter, bringing her with him. Her body pushed up against his, her breasts smashed to his chest.

Damn all these layers of clothes. Damn every last article. He wanted her naked. Wanted her underneath him, her legs wrapped around his waist. On top, riding him good and hard. Beside him, wound together so tight that nothing would separate them. In front of him, on her hands and knees with her fine little ass in the air. He just wanted inside of her, wanted to stay there for hours, and it didn't matter where they were while they went at it.

He wanted her on the counter, the floor, the wall, the shower, in a bed. God, in a bed, wrapped in sheets and surrounded by mounds of pillows. He could spend all damn day with her there and never get enough.

And they were in a building full of beds, the closest one brand-new and begging to be broken in.

He was just about to bend down and pick her up, just about to carry her across the kitchen and into that room of hers, just about to strip her down and bury himself inside of her when the damn doorbell rang.

"You've got to be fucking kidding me." He groaned against her mouth.

Hannah started to pull back from him, attempting to disentangle herself from his body, but he didn't let go of her. Awareness and uncertainty were back in her eyes…and more than a little bit of regret.

"That shouldn't have happened." She shook her head. "It was a mistake."

Her words pissed him off. Nope, he wasn't having any of that. Not for a single second.

"We're going to have a conversation, you and I. Just as soon as the jackass is done doing whatever the hell it is he's going to do. Understand?"

And now her anger was coming back to the surface. "Stop telling me what to do or what's going to happen like I'm some little girl." She pushed hard on his chest with her good hand and took a step back as she straightened herself out, but as much as she tugged on her shirt, it was going to do nothing for the state of her flushed cheeks and swollen mouth. "And feel free to leave."

"That isn't happening." He folded his arms across his chest and kept his position holding up the counter.

"You're infuriating." She turned around and marched toward the front door.

"Right back atcha, babe," he called after her. He needed a second to get certain aspects of his anatomy in check. But when the door opened and Topher Berk's voice drifted through the house, he found himself pushing off the counter and heading in that direction.

* * *

Okay, so Shep had been right. This guy *was* a jackass, and it took Hannah no time at all to figure it out. His charm was oozy and sticky and made her want to take another shower. His light brown hair was slicked back with gel, and his grin was wide enough to show off his overly white teeth. She suspected some bleach had been involved, because no one had teeth that unnaturally bright.

He looked like a wannabe Justin Timberlake—who besides Shep was the only man she'd pined after for years and years—but he came off more like Justin Bieber.

Topher's unctuous demeanor faltered every now and then, and Hannah caught him giving Shep a look that said, *What the hell are you doing here?*

As much as she didn't want to admit it to herself, and most definitely not out loud, she was glad Shep had stayed. Not because she couldn't take care of herself, because she most assuredly could, but because she wasn't used to someone having her back these days. And as he followed them around, his eyes on Topher and standing not much farther than a foot away from her, she knew he had hers.

But the close proximity was messing with her brain in more ways than one. She had their most recent kiss playing on repeat in the back of her mind, along with the look on his face when she said it shouldn't have happened. How he was able to pull off protective and pissed off and manage to turn her on, she had no idea.

Halfway into the walk through, Shep's phone rang. "I need to take this," he said, turning to her. She nodded, and he looked more than a little reluctant as he stepped out into the hallway.

It was almost instantaneous that Topher took a step closer to her. "This is a massive place. You've got quite a few things to get fixed up before it would be ready to sell for the best possible price."

"Yes," she said, retreating a step away from him.

"Well, I hope you know how very dedicated I am to my job and how important it is to me to get you a good deal. I make it a point to go above and beyond for my clients, so I can help you out on some of these minor restorations. I'm willing and able to add a little bit of my own elbow grease." He smiled widely.

How was it that the more he talked about selling her inn, the more she wanted him out of it? People actually fell for this crap?

"Also," he said, taking another step toward her, "I know this inspector who will let a couple things slide in your benefit, like the quality of the roof or the condition of the deck. I could tell you all about him over dinner sometime."

"Aren't you honest to a fault?" Shep asked as he came back into the room. He walked up beside Hannah, sliding his hand across her lower back and to her side, bringing her body in to his.

Well, damn. She didn't have a single problem with his hand on her body, or the way his thumb pushed up under her shirt and started tracing her bare hip.

"That won't be necessary. And I think this about sums up everything you need to see," Hannah said, looking at Topher. It was then that she realized she was leaning in to Shep. It was an automatic response that she hadn't even thought about.

Something flickered in Topher's eyes. Hannah was pretty sure he was repressing a sneer on that pointed face of his as he watched Shep's blatant display of ownership. This was another thing that Hannah didn't have a problem with. She'd rather give

Topher the wrong impression than let on she was available. As far as Topher was concerned, she was definitely off the market.

He wasn't getting his hands on her or her inn.

"Isn't there an entire other floor?" Topher frowned.

"It's pretty much identical to this one."

"So no need," Shep finished for her.

Hannah tried to repress her grin as they walked downstairs and Shep ushered Topher out quickly. She went back into the kitchen and busied herself unloading the dishwasher as Shep showed their guest out the door.

Their guest? Crap. What in the world was she doing? She had to stop right this instant. That kiss had messed with her head. His hands on her body hadn't helped either; nor had his alpha-man testosterone display.

Apparently, him being a caveman *to* her and *for* her had very different effects *on* her. The more time she spent around him, the more she knew she was becoming certifiably crazy. Men didn't have this kind of effect on her... well, men besides him.

His boots thudded across the wooden floor, and she knew he was standing in the doorway behind her.

He wanted to talk to her about the kiss and God only knew what else. But she didn't want to talk. She had no idea how she felt about any of it. About the kiss, about his hands on her, about him. She was all over the freaking board and she didn't know what she wanted. The further in she got with him, the more confused she became. When she'd come back here, she'd been bound and determined to keep him at arm's length.

Well, that obviously wasn't happening.

So instead of turning around and addressing his presence, she chose to focus on the silverware drawer.

His eyes drilled into her, making the back of her neck itch

as she continued to work. She couldn't show that he was affecting her.

Must.

Not.

Show.

Weakness.

Stay strong, Hannah. You can do this. You can handle Nathanial Shepherd and his face full of sexy scruff.

But as she finished with the top drawer and loaded the few dirty dishes on the counter into the dishwasher, she knew she was kidding herself. And she was proven correct when she turned around and found him leaning against the entryway, his shoulder pressed in to the wood and one boot crossed over the other.

His expression was neither angry nor happy, but more one of determination. And the direction of said determination was clear.

Her.

Chapter 8

The Second Coming
of Hannah

So, what did you think of Topher? Seem like the type of person you'd trust?" Shep asked with no small amount of smugness.

Jerk.

He was fully aware she hadn't liked the guy. It was obvious in the way she couldn't get him out of her inn faster. But she knew Shep, and he wanted her to say it.

Well, might as well get it over with. She sighed as she leaned back against the counter.

"You were right. And I was wrong," she said just a tad bit bitterly. Those words didn't taste so good coming out of her mouth. Not because she thought she was always right, but more because Shep continually proved to be so, and the arrogant ass was reveling in it.

"There it is." He pushed off the frame and crossed the room to her. "That's one thing down."

"And what's the next?"

He didn't say anything as he put his hands on either side of her and leaned in, bracing himself against the counter. "Kissing me was a mistake?" he asked, raising an eyebrow.

"Shep, what do you want from me?" She threw her arms up in the air. He let go of the counter and caught them, pulling them in to his chest as he took another step into her space.

"I want for you to tell me the truth. Tell me what you're really thinking and stop hiding from me."

She looked up at him, her heart in her throat. She couldn't give him what he wanted. Couldn't tell him the truth. She wasn't ready. Telling him the truth, all of the truth, would rip her wide open, and she couldn't handle that pain yet.

She wasn't sure if she'd ever be able to handle that pain.

"Fine. I'll go first." He somehow moved closer to her. "Me kissing you is *never* a mistake. There are a lot of things in my life that I'd take back, but my lips on yours? That's not one of them. I know that fact without a doubt."

He reached up and pulled her glasses from her face, setting them on the counter behind her before he lowered his mouth to hers. He nipped at her bottom lip, pulling it gently before his tongue darted out. He didn't even get it past her bottom lip before her mouth was covering his, her tongue sliding along his.

He let go of her hands, letting them drop to her sides before he wrapped his arms around her and pulled her entirely against his body.

He had her backed up against the kitchen counter again, their hot and hungry mouths eating at the others.

Every notion about fighting this thing with him flew out of her head, and she let herself go over to it. To all of it. All of him.

"Does this *feel* like a mistake, Hannah?" He pulled back, resting his forehead against hers as he looked down into her eyes. "Right now, in this moment. Does it?"

Her voice didn't want to work, and it took her a second to form a response. "No." She shook her head. "No, it doesn't."

"What about this? My hands on you?" he asked, his eyes not leaving hers as he moved his palms under her shirt, running them up and down her bare back before he moved them to her sides.

"No." She couldn't stop the shiver that ran through her body, and his mouth turned up in that predatory grin of his.

"Or this?" This time his eyes did leave hers as he dropped his head and put his mouth on her neck, his tongue flicking against her skin.

Her answer was a long, low moan that went all the way down to her toes.

"Do you want me to stop?" he asked right before he ran his tongue along her collarbone.

"No." Her eyes closed of their own accord as her head fell back. "Please."

"Please what?" Kisses across her shoulder.

"Please don't stop."

"Well, aren't those lovely words?" His lips were working back up her neck, and then he found her mouth again. He was consuming her with his kisses, inhaling her. And his hands. Holy hell they were still running wildly over her hips and back. And then he brought one between them, his fingers tracing around her belly button before it moved low on her belly.

He flicked the button on her jeans open and then went on to her zipper, pulling it down slowly. Maybe he was giving her another chance to protest.

There wasn't a chance in hell she was going to stop it this time.

His fingers ran along the top of her panties, just dipping beneath the lace. He worked down ever so slowly, making her desperate. And if the hard length of him pressing into her hip was any indication, he was pretty desperate for her, too.

Lower. Move your hand lower.

"All in good time."

She'd spoken that out loud? Whatever, she wasn't even remotely embarrassed.

But it appeared that Shep's practiced patience was lost on him a moment later. "God, Hannah," he groaned when he skimmed bare flesh. "This is new."

"I like the way it feels," she said between his kisses.

"So do I." He ran his finger between her folds, just barely skimming. Up and down, up and down. And then finally, *finally*, up and in, making her knees buckle. "You're so wet."

"Shep." His name on her lips was a plea; there was nothing else to it.

"Right here, babe."

It all felt so damn good, his mouth, his hands, everything. She never wanted him to stop. His hands were magic and they'd been made to be on her body.

He teased her for a good long while, alternating between stroking his fingers inside of her and applying the perfect amount of pressure to her throbbing clit. He would take her right to the edge and then back off before she came, returning to that delicious, yet torturous, stroking.

He brought his mouth to her ear, his voice a rough, low whisper. "Tell me how much you want this."

"So much." Her eyes rolled to the back of her head as he nipped at her earlobe and then ran his tongue down.

"Ask me to make you come, Hannah." His mouth was against her neck, and his scruff felt so damn good against her skin.

"Please."

"Please what?"

"Please make me come, Shep."

"Look at me."

Her eyes opened automatically at his command. Those sapphire-blue eyes of his held hers, the intensity so hot she was pretty sure she was going to burst into flames. She wouldn't have been able to look away even if she'd wanted to, and in no way did she want to.

This time he kept his fingers inside of her and moved his thumb to her clit. She was clutching his shirt, holding on for dear life as he devastated her with his fingers.

"Let go, babe. Show me how good it feels."

And let go she did, letting loose with an almighty scream that probably shook the rafters. She was pretty sure she'd never been this loud during sex. But it had never felt so good.

Apparently, Shep was like a fine wine, so much better with age.

Thirteen years did him damn good, and she was reaping the benefits. She couldn't even imagine what it would be like with him pushing her down onto a mattress, moving between her thighs while he thrust inside of her.

The image took root in her head and had her coming harder, tightening around Shep's still-moving fingers. He put his mouth to hers again, kissing her softly as he brought her down with slow strokes of his tongue.

When he pulled back, he looked like the cat that got the cream. No sooner was that thought in her head than he moved his hand from her body and brought his fingers up, putting them in his mouth.

Well, shit. She hadn't thought it was possible to get any hotter, but she was going to spontaneously combust any moment now.

"Even better than I remember."

She swallowed hard. How did somebody even respond to that? With a *thank you?*

But the playfulness left his eyes a moment later, a seriousness overtaking every feature of his face. He leaned in to her, getting so close that she couldn't look anywhere but at him.

"You said you wanted to know what your options were. Well, I'm one of them, Hannah. This. Us. *We're* an option. I know it's been more than a decade, but there's something between us, something that will *never* go away. It's too damn good to waste. I know you're scared. I know you were hurt during our last go-round. So was I. But we have a second chance, and I want to do something with it. You're here for many reasons, and I want to figure all of them out with you."

He put his hand over hers, the one that was still clutching his shirt, and pulled it away from his side. He brought it up to his mouth, placing a kiss in the center of her palm. Then he leaned in and pressed a kiss to her forehead before he took a step back from her. She immediately felt the loss of him.

"You know where to find me." And with that he turned around and walked out of her kitchen.

All she could do was stand there, with the top of her pants still unzipped, trying to remember how to use her legs again.

Slippery slope indeed. Yeah, the notion of escaping him was well and truly gone. She'd just fallen down a mountain in the middle of a freaking mudslide.

She might not have any earthly idea what she thought about this, but damn had it felt good.

* * *

The skirt of Hannah's green maxi dress flowed out behind her as she followed Grace through Caliente's and out onto the back porch. This side of the little restaurant looked out at the Gulf of

Mexico, and the ocean breeze whipped around her, blowing her hair every which way.

The place was packed, not all that surprising for a Friday night. Grace waved enthusiastically to a group of three girls at a table in the corner.

Hannah recognized Paige immediately, with her freckled nose and wavy brown hair pulled back into a stylishly messy bun on top of her head. And this time she was able to look at the woman without a spark of jealousy. Paige was Brendan's wife... and Shep was single and giving Hannah mind-blowing orgasms in the middle of her kitchen.

Her stomach fluttered just thinking about what had happened the day before and the way Shep had looked at her while he'd touched her. Not that she'd been thinking about that nonstop for the last twenty-four-plus hours or anything.

She still had no idea what the hell she was going to do with anything that had happened or with what he'd said. He kept doing this to her, leaving her completely and totally confused with his words... and his mouth... and now his fingers.

She needed to stop thinking about that and focus on what was going on around her.

No more Shep thoughts.

Yeah. Freaking. Right.

She made a valiant attempt as she looked at the next girl at the table. Mel's short blonde curls got caught up on the breeze and floated in the air for a second before they dropped back down, only to be picked up again a moment later.

Hannah guessed that the last girl at the table was Harper. Her long black hair was in a braid and hanging over her shoulder. She had a more than exotic look with her tanned skin and almond-shaped eyes that were so blue they looked violet. Grace had mentioned Harper the other day, saying she'd moved to Mirabelle after the summer Hannah had spent there. She was now a massage therapist at two of the spas in town.

All three women stood as Hannah and Grace approached the table, smiling warmly.

"Heya, ladies. Hannah, you remember Mel? And this is Paige and Harper."

They didn't even give her a chance to say anything before she was snatched up into three different hugs, all of the women embracing her like they were long-lost friends.

"We got margaritas for everyone, and a virgin one for preggers over there," Mel said as they all took their seats.

"Ohhh, perfect, thank you." Hannah reached for the salted lime drink that was gloriously already in front of her.

"Don't get to thanking them yet." Grace grinned. "They're probably going to try to get you full of tequila so they can get all of the dirt easier."

"Shhh." Paige shook her head. "Stop telling all of our interrogation tactics."

"What dirt?"

"We want the Shep secrets. And those have to be dirty." Harper waggled her eyebrows.

Hannah choked on her drink, inhaling a particularly strong sip of tequila. Her eyes watered as she coughed, trying to breathe. "Uhhh..." Shep secrets weren't exactly polite dinner conversation, especially the newer developments. She hoped the red blooming across her face could be misinterpreted as belonging to the coughing fit she was having and not the aftereffects of the orgasm she was still glowing from.

"It's okay. We're just kidding." Mel reached over and gave Hannah's hand a reassuring pat.

"Speak for yourself," Harper said as she munched on a chip. "I'm dying to know what happened that has Shep in a state."

"What do you mean?" Hannah couldn't stop herself from asking.

"Apparently, he's been rather pissy the last couple of days, and as this is coming from my husband, who used to always be the moody and broody one, I think that's saying something. Not that it's any of our business," Grace added before she took a sip of her drink.

"It also wouldn't be any of our business to tell you that he's been hung up on you for the last thirteen years," Paige said.

Hung up? That couldn't be right. Sure he'd said there was something between them that would never go away, but that didn't mean he'd pined for her that entire time.

He said he'd been hurt, too, but how hurt could he have been when he'd moved on so fast? She wasn't a fool. She knew he had to have been with countless women since her. It was Shep. He was a bartender, and she was sure there were very few women who wouldn't drop their panties when he smiled at them...or looked at them...or generally just breathed in their direction.

Yes, focus on these facts, Hannah. Because it's the only way you're going to keep your head straight and your legs closed.

"So the last thing that isn't any of our business." This time it was Harper speaking, and she eyed Hannah over the rim of her margarita glass, taking a slow, deliberate sip and swallowing before she put the glass back down on the table. "Would be to tell you that since you've been back in town—"

"And angry or not," Mel interrupted.

"Yes, angry or not, he's had this..." Harper trailed off, waving her hand in the air, looking for the words.

"*Change*," Paige said.

"This *spark*," Grace added.

"Like the thing he's been waiting for—but didn't know he was waiting for—is back," Harper finished.

"Not that it's any of our business." Mel shook her head.

"Nope. Not our business at all." Paige's eyebrows rose as she pursed her lips and gave Hannah what could be classified only as a significant look. "So, lets order. What are you all getting?"

As if on cue, all of the women looked down at their menus, leaving Hannah staring off in shock. What in the world was she supposed to say to any of that?

* * *

In the beginning Hannah fought the good fight and was able to hold her liquor and her tongue. The other girls had dropped the subject of Shep and his secrets and his being hung up on her…or being hung like a horse.

Which was a fact. The man's erection had been pressing into her belly long, hard, and huge. She was sure he'd been desperate for a release of his own, but he'd walked out of that kitchen and not turned around.

Why, though? She would've let him lay her down on just about anything, or really he could've just taken her right there up against that counter.

Hannah had never really been the type of girl to sit around pondering the mysteries of men. She hadn't had girlfriends to confide in before. But this group of girls, no matter how wonderful they were, had loyalties to Shep. That was obvious.

But it didn't matter that they weren't talking about him, because Hannah couldn't stop thinking about him. The more her brain got soaked with tequila, the more her thoughts got soaked with Shep and all of his Shep-like powers.

He was and always had been her Superman...made her fall for him faster than a speeding bullet...was more powerful than a locomotive...and able to give her mind-bending orgasms in a single bound.

But as it turned out, he was her kryptonite, too.

Go fucking figure.

It hadn't taken very long for Hannah to get nice and comfortable with the girls. Though that could be attributed a little bit to the third round of margaritas, it was also because the group of ladies was just flat-out fantastic.

First, there was Paige, who was fiery as all hell and just as much of a handful as Hannah had expected. She heard all about Paige's series of unfortunate events that had brought her down to Mirabelle and how it had all led to her meeting Brendan, the man of her dreams.

Then there was Harper, who was in no short supply of sarcastic quips. She seemed to have a bit of a hard edge to her, something that would soften whenever she talked about her boyfriend, Brad Nelson.

Mel was exactly as Hannah remembered, sweet and usually more held back, but just as capable of delivering a snappy one-liner as anyone else. She was a high school math teacher, and Hannah had a feeling that her students loved her. The curly haired beauty beamed as she talked about her future husband. She was just as eager as he was to get down that aisle.

Hannah had already had the opportunity to see Grace and her overprotective husband in action. Five minutes around the two of them and it was obvious that his wife was his world and he'd do absolutely anything for her and that little baby in her belly.

Not that she was jealous of them or anything...no, not at all. Not jealous that they were happy and settled and loved...loved unconditionally.

Who wanted any of that?

Not her...nope.

She was just fine without a man...without friends...without any real family to speak of. What she did have was her cat and enough delusions to fill the Gulf of Mexico.

It also wouldn't be any of our business to tell you that he's been hung up on you for the last thirteen years.

Those words replayed in her head for the umpteenth time and she tried to shake them out.

No such luck.

They were there, permanently imprinted on her brain along with Shep's gravelly Southern voice in her ear and his lips moving across her mouth.

Ask me to make you come, Hannah.

She shivered just thinking about his words. She'd been begging for it, and she felt no shame.

She reached for her margarita and sucked down the last of it, and like magic another one appeared in front of her. Ice floated in the lime-green liquid, and the salt rocks around the rim begged to be licked. So she complied, starting in on her fourth margarita of the night.

"How do you know Shep's been hung up on me?" How did those words come out of her mouth? And with so few slurs?

The conversation around the table came to an abrupt halt, and four sets of eyes focused on Hannah.

It was Paige who spoke first, her mouth split in a grin. "Well, in the three years that I've been here, I haven't really seen Shep with any women." Her eyes squinted like she was looking back through the years. It must have cost her some effort to peer through the haze of tequila because she'd been partaking in just as many drinks as Hannah had. "Nor has he talked about any. But I *had* heard about you, more than once *and* not only from Shep. Brendan can get chatty when I want him to be." Paige's grin widened, and Hannah had a feeling they were no longer talking about her and Shep.

"Ewwww, that's my brother. Keep your sex talk to yourself." Grace frowned, shaking her head.

"You're a fine one to talk." Mel leaned forward, whispering, though it wasn't all that necessary for her to drop her voice. The back deck had cleared for the most part, and there was absolutely no one by their table. "That lovely glow coming from Grace has nothing to do with her pregnancy. Never in my life have I seen someone's complexion this affected by regular orgasms."

"Shut up." Grace laughed, throwing a chip at Mel.

"They're just making up for lost time." Harper winked.

"Not enough hours in the day for that, but Jax sure does try," Grace said more than somewhat smugly.

"All right, let's focus here, ladies." Paige rubbed her hands together as she zeroed in on Hannah from across the table. "That's not the topic at hand. What we're supposed to be talking about is our favorite tattooed bartender and our new friend here."

"Mel and I have been witness to BH, DH, and AH," Grace said. Hannah just looked at them, dumbfounded.

"Before Hannah, During Hannah, and After Hannah," Mel clarified.

"Whereas Paige and I have only seen After Hannah," Harper explained.

"Though we are all now privy to TSCoH," Paige said, and everyone nodded.

"And what is that?" Hannah's confusion was multiplying the more they talked around her.

"The Second Coming of Hannah," Grace answered.

"You can't be serious."

"Oh, I can assure you, we are." Mel reached over and patted Hannah's hand. "And we aren't the only ones who've seen the proof. If you'd like to call more witnesses to the stand, I'm sure Bennett, Brendan, Jax, and Finn would be more than happy to testify."

"None of us know what's been going on between the two of you lately." Harper was talking now. "He's kept that to himself, and we aren't asking for you to tell us."

"'Cause it isn't any of our business," Paige said.

"Nope, but what we are telling you is that he's been all over the place." Grace this time.

"That boy has no idea what to do with himself," Mel said.

"Well, I have no idea what to do with him, either." Hannah shook her head, which probably wasn't a good idea as it was now spinning, and that had very little to do with the alcohol.

"Hmmm," Paige hummed. "Well, maybe you should figure that out, sweetie." She grabbed her margarita and toasted it to Hannah before she brought it to her mouth and took a good, long, healthy swig of it.

Maybe Hannah *should* figure it out. The thing was, that would involve a conversation with Shep, and she had a feeling the next one was going to end with her naked.

* * *

Hannah Sterling was good and thoroughly drunk, something she hadn't been in years.

Yeeeeaaaarrrrsssss

She had a lovely little buzz going, and she was going to ride it all the way nice and easylike. This was probably why she didn't protest at all when Harper suggested that they go get another drink at the Sleepy Sheep.

Besides, confused or not, she wanted to see Shep. Wanted to ask him about all of the things she'd found out. That was if she'd be able to string any of those sentences together, or if she'd be able to stop herself from climbing all over him.

The only person who had driven to the restaurant was Grace. Paige, Harper, and Mel had all been dropped off. Apparently, it had been the plan for everyone to have a grand old time. As Grace wasn't going to be partaking in the next stop on the agenda—one, because she was exhausted, and two, because she thought it would be weird to go to a bar pregnant—she said she'd drive them all over before heading home.

The guys had been having a night out of their own, so they were heading over to the Sleepy Sheep at some point that evening as well.

"I miss your Bug," Mel said from the backseat of Grace's little SUV. She was sitting in the middle between Hannah and Paige, her head resting on the back of the bench and looking up at the ceiling. "But I do so love this new car smell."

"And not having to climb behind the front seat to get to the back." Harper was in the passenger seat, looking through the iPod that was connected to the stereo.

"Oh my gosh. Could you imagine all five of us in that? It would look like we were trying to cram ourselves into a clown car," Paige said.

"Though, considering how drunk we are, it would be pretty entertaining," Mel added.

"Well, the Bug is not gone, just shelved for now."

"Hmmm, good luck getting the keys from your husband." Paige

looked over Mel at Hannah. "Jax is a little overprotective." She held her thumb and forefinger in the air before she made a move, pulling both hands a good distance apart and mouthing *massively*.

"I noticed." Hannah nodded.

"Puh-lease. Like Brendan, Bennett, and Brad aren't overprotective?"

"Brendan, Bennett, and Brad...try saying that five times fast." Mel snorted, and everyone promptly fell into the giggles.

"Anyway," Paige said when she was able to control herself. "He said that Grace wasn't going to be driving the death trap anymore. He wanted a safe car for his woman and child."

"Isn't he sweeeeeeet?" Harper asked, laying on an accent that was much thicker than normal.

"He's something, all right," Grace said. Hannah couldn't see her face, but the grin in her voice was evident.

"Ohhh, I found one." Harper bounced in her seat before she reached over and turned up the volume.

Hannah new the opening beats immediately. She wasn't even remotely ashamed to admit that she'd been obsessed with *NSYNC in their heyday. Hello, she was still massively crushing on Justin Timberlake now.

Nope. No shame.

"Hey, heeeey," Harper started.

"Bye, bye, bye...bye, bye," everyone else sang in unison.

The best part? Everyone in the car knew all the words...and the hand motions.

* * *

Shep stared at the front door of his bar as four fairly intoxicated women stumbled through it, laughing.

He'd known that Hannah was going out with the girls for dinner—his girls, though not *his* in a sexual way. In a brotherly way, that is, because he'd always seen them more like sisters.

That was how he viewed all of them...except for the one who came in last.

He believed that Hannah was, for all intents and purposes, *the* girl for him.

He'd thrown down the gauntlet in her kitchen the day before. Told her she knew where to find him if she wanted to see where things could go with him.

And she was here.

So what did that mean?

The second she was over the threshold, her gaze met his. She faltered for just a second, her eyes going warm as she looked him over. She licked that bottom lip of hers, her cheeks blooming with color.

His dick was hard in an instant.

Well, this was going to be inconvenient. He'd walked away after making her come, not getting his own satisfaction. There was only so much self-stimulation he could do, and it wasn't doing much.

Though that wasn't exactly true. He'd been pretty damn satisfied. Hannah had come apart in his hands, proving that he still knew her body. Holy hell had she screamed when she came. The fact that it had been his name bursting forth from her lips still had him grinning like a freaking moron.

She looked at him for a good couple of seconds before she turned away and followed the others girls to a table in the corner. Her long green dress trailed behind her as she walked, making her look like some goddess, or siren, or temptress sent here to taunt him.

Or torture him.

He still had her breathy little pants and moans echoing in his ears, the feel of her body tightening around his fingers, the taste of her on his tongue.

She'd been an overload to his senses when she hadn't been around, but having her in the same room when he couldn't touch her? Couldn't feel her against him?

Too fucking much.

"Well, that was interesting."

Shep looked over at his father, who was standing next to him. Nathanial Shepherd Sr., or Nate as everyone called him, wasn't as tall as his two sons. He just barely cleared six feet.

Shep and Finn's sapphire-blue eyes hadn't been passed down from their father, either. No, Nate had Owen's stormy gray eyes, and they were currently focused on the group of girls settling into their seats.

"So what's going on there?"

"I don't know yet."

"She the reason you've been in a mood the last couple of days?"

"I haven't been in a mood." Shep frowned.

Nate just raised his eyebrows at his son.

"She's proving a little bit more difficult than before." Understatement of his life. She was proving to be the *most* difficult damn woman he'd ever encountered.

Nate chuckled. "So really the problem is she isn't a blind teenage girl anymore and now sees through your charm."

Shep's frown deepened. *What the hell is that supposed to mean?*

"No one is perfect, son. Everyone has their own set of issues, their individual flaws, their own special brand of crazy. And being with someone for the long haul is about accepting all of that. When the rose-colored glasses come off is when it starts to get real, and it's so much better."

The long haul echoed in Shep's mind. The longest relationship he'd ever been in had been with Hannah. Three months, thirteen years ago.

This wasn't all that shocking, either. When it came to other girls, as soon as he realized they weren't the one, he moved on. There was no point in prolonging the inevitable. He'd just had a little fun before he moved on.

"Maybe you should head on over there and get their drink orders. First round is on the house as your redheaded troublemaker helped my mother yesterday."

"All right," Shep said, fortifying himself. Paige, Mel, and Harper wouldn't hesitate for a second to bust his balls, and normally he could handle it. But not today. Not when he had no idea what was going on in that mind of Hannah's and he couldn't pull her away to find out.

He'd have to get her alone for that conversation. But what with the way he was feeling at the moment—combined with the way she was dressed—there would be very little talking. He'd most likely have his hand up that dress of hers in seconds.

"No need to act like you're going into battle. It's a table full of pretty ladies."

"Dad, that is a battle. And the redhead in the middle is the bomb that's blowing up my life." And with that he ventured out into no man's land, determined to get his head and his dick under control.

The odds were not in his favor.

Chapter 9

The Men of Mirabelle

What the hell had Hannah been thinking?

Oh, right. She hadn't.

The alcohol had added to her lust-filled brain and had taken control of her body and marched her ass right on in to Nathanial Shepherd's domain.

She was the sheep in the lion's den.

And as the man in question crossed the space to their table, he had eyes only for her. Eyes that said he wanted to eat her alive.

"Damn," Harper whispered under her breath. "Did your panties just catch on fire?"

"Yes, but my girly bits put it out." Hannah's hand flew up to her mouth, horrified. She couldn't believe she'd said that.

Paige, Mel, and Harper burst into laughter just as Shep made it to the table.

"Something funny?" he asked, looking around at all of them.

"Yup. Someone has a sense of humor," Mel told Shep as she glanced over at Hannah.

Or no filter.

His gaze followed Mel's and landed on Hannah as well.

"That so?" He raised one of his sexy eyebrows. How were eyebrows sexy? She wasn't quite sure, but his were.

And then the doubt in his words processed in her brain.

"Hey, I'm funny when you aren't pissing me off," she protested.

"Babe, you're funny even *when* you're pissed off."

Her eyes narrowed on him and her mouth pursed together. "Stop calling me *babe.*"

"Never." The cocky grin that spread across his face was massive and solely for her.

How he was able to annoy the hell out of her and turn her on simultaneously, she'd never know. The man was going to send her to the loony bin.

Okay, she was going to have to play dirty. She leaned back in her seat, folding her arms across her chest. Her dress was a V-neck, so she knew the move plumped up her breasts. "Okay, Nathanial." She smiled wickedly at him and had no small amount of satisfaction when his eyes flared.

"What can I get you ladies to drink?" he asked, pulling his gaze from her. "First round is on the house, courtesy of Hannah there and her sense of humor."

"As we've been drinking margaritas, let's stick with something that has tequila." Paige looked around the table, and everyone agreed.

"Tequila? I think I can handle that." He nodded. But he didn't walk away. Instead he moved to Hannah's side and placed both of his big hands on the table as he leaned down. He brought his mouth right up next to her ear so only she could hear the next words that came out of his mouth.

"It doesn't bother me when you call me *Nathanial,* 'cause that's what you scream when I make you come."

Weellll, Hannah's moment of triumph had certainly been

short-lived. She couldn't even formulate a response as he pulled back and walked away from their table.

"Your mouth is hanging open, dear." Mel reached over and touched Hannah's chin. She snapped it up in a second, and all of the women at the table burst out into laughter.

"What in the world did he just say to you?" Paige asked, leaning across the table.

"Uhhh…He…umm…" Yeah, she wasn't repeating that.

"Sweetie, you are so totally done for." Harper grinned.

Hannah couldn't even find the words to disagree with that statement, mainly because it would have been a lie. And she was sick and tired of lying to herself, especially when it came to that man and her feelings for him.

She was all sorts of confused, but was given a reprieve a moment later when six very attractive men approached the table. All of the women stood as the men circled around them.

She recognized Bennett Hart and Preston Matthews immediately. Brendan took her a second longer to place because he wasn't the same eighteen-year-old boy she'd known, plus the alcohol was making her a little slow. He was way more muscular and scruffy, but those light blue eyes of his hadn't changed.

The last three men she'd never seen before. One had blond hair, dark brown eyes, and a big smile that was directed at Harper. She guessed this was Harper's boyfriend, Brad Nelson, and was proved correct in her assumption when he pressed a kiss to his girlfriend's cheek, whispering something in her ear that had her grinning.

The next guy had sandy blond hair, hazel eyes, and a lopsided grin. Like Brad and Preston, he was clean shaven. But scruff or not, he was pretty damn good-looking.

And the last guy was another one of those tall, dark, and

handsome types. He had thick brown hair and matching chocolate-brown eyes that would've probably made her a little melty had she not been entirely focused on someone else. He was sporting the scruff like Brendan and Bennett, though none of them had the length of Shep's beard.

Brendan placed an affectionate kiss on his wife's mouth before he turned his focus on Hannah. "I can't believe you're back," he said, pulling her in for a hug.

Holy hell, he was a huge man with all of those muscles. She was pretty sure his biceps alone could crush her head. But he was gentle with her. She wasn't used to all of this affection from people. It was beyond different for her, but so freaking nice.

"You've wreaked havoc on Shep's mental state." He grinned as he grabbed her shoulders and pulled her back. "Keep it up."

"Oh, I think he's doing a pretty good job of wreaking his own havoc," Mel said. She was currently snuggled into her fiancé's side.

"No doubt about that." Brendan agreed. "Well, before we leave you ladies be, let me introduce Hannah. This is Tripp Black," he said, indicating the scruffy guy with the warm brown eyes. "He's Atticus County's resident fire chief."

Brendan went around the circle, moving on to Brad next. And last was the hazel-eyed guy, Baxter McCoy. He was another deputy sheriff for Atticus County, spending most of his time in Mirabelle like Jax.

"All right, we're going to shoot some pool and enjoy a few beers until you ladies are ready to go," Brendan said before he pressed another kiss to Paige's mouth.

The guys said goodbye and headed off to the bar.

"Holy hell." Hannah shook her head as they all took their seats again. "They should make a calendar or something. The Men of Mirabelle. They'd make millions."

"Right?" Paige agreed while all of the other girls just nodded. "But only one of them is single, so that might be a little disappointing to the ladies."

"Who?" Hannah asked, looking over at the men.

"Fire Chief Tripp Black."

"What about Preston and Baxter? Where are their significant others?" Hannah returned her gaze to the table.

"Preston and Baxter are each other's significant others," Mel answered.

Hannah's gaze immediately returned to the men just as Baxter reached out and ran is hand across Preston's back in an affectionate gesture. Preston looked over at him with an expression that was so sweet it made her teeth hurt.

"If they kiss, I think my ovaries will explode," Harper said, her voice wistful.

And just as the words had been spoken, Preston moved in toward Baxter. There was a collective intake of breath around the table, but a second later they all let it out. Preston had only whispered something into Baxter's ear. Though whatever it was must have been good, because it had a light blush coming to Baxter's cheeks.

"Damn," Harper whispered, disappointed. All of the women looked away from the men and back to the table. "So back to this Men of Mirabelle calendar. Who would be what month?"

"Brendan would be a good August, I think," Paige said immediately. "Him working underneath the hood of a truck covered in grease...sweaty and shirtless. Yeah, that would be perfect."

"Bennett in July...sounds like Christmas in July." Mel's face was overtaken by a dreamy smile. "He could be building something...shirtless."

The girls proceeded to go around the table, figuring out the months and themes for Brad, Jax, Tripp, Preston, Baxter, and Finn.

"So what about Shep?" Harper asked Hannah, raising her eyebrows suggestively. "Set the scene."

Hannah's eyes darted to the man behind the bar, where he was putting some concoction together. He poured in a generous amount of tequila before he put the top on the shaker. His biceps flexed, making his tattoos move.

Her gaze returned to the girls at the table and she shook her head. "Oh, no. I'm not playing this game."

"Come on. Spill. I know you have delicious thoughts in that pretty red head of yours," Paige said.

"How do you know?"

"Because you licked your lips when you just looked at him," Mel answered. "And I'm pretty sure it had nothing to do with the drink he's making."

"How do I know you won't tell him?"

"Cross my heart," Harper said, making the sign over her ample chest.

"What's said at this table stays at this table," Paige agreed.

"Yup." Mel nodded.

Hannah looked over to Shep again where he was pouring the drinks. As he filled the last glass, his eyes came up and automatically landed on her. She squirmed in her seat but didn't break contact, and he gave her another look that made her go sweaty all the way down to her toes.

"He'd have to be behind the bar." She found herself talking before she realized it, her gaze not wavering from his as she continued. "I'm thinking March because of St. Patrick's Day. He'd wear a kilt and … and nothing else."

What the hell is even happening?

She wasn't a sharer about this sort of thing, most definitely not her fantasies, and the image she'd just conjured up was most definitely climbing to the top of her list.

There could be a body shot...or ten. She'd never done body shots and could just imagine licking tequila off his chest, him sucking it up from her belly button. Heat spread through her body, settling low in her belly.

It took everything in her to pull her gaze from Shep's. If she didn't stop looking at him, she was likely to do something embarrassing. She was never drinking again. She had absolutely no control over her mouth or her body. It was getting ridiculous.

She glanced around the table at the other women, who were looking at her with shock and wonder.

"*Damn*, girl," Paige whispered.

"I've never seen him look at anyone that way." Harper shook her head.

"I have," Mel piped up, and everyone's gaze moved to hers questioningly.

Hannah couldn't stop the sinking feeling in her stomach at those words. Her reaction must have registered on her face, because Mel reached across the table and grabbed Hannah's hand.

"I'm talking about you." She squeezed reassuringly. "He looked at you like that thirteen years ago, sweetie. Though it's way more intense now."

"Intense doesn't quite seem adequate," Paige said.

Well, wasn't that an understatement. She was going to be lucky if she survived this night, let alone anything else that included that man.

* * *

Frustrated or not with the current unknown that was Hannah and their status, there was something about seeing her sitting in his bar, laughing with his friends, that made Shep so unbelievably happy.

She was having a good time, her cheeks flushed from the alcohol and probably the conversation. He knew those girls with Hannah very well, and they held nothing back. He also knew he had a little something to do with the stain that colored her skin. She looked over at him fairly often, and that need and desire in her eyes was only for him.

He was giving it right back to her, too. What the hell else was he supposed to do?

"That eye fucking the two of you are giving each other is getting a little ridiculous."

Shep pulled his gaze from Hannah to find Brendan on the other side of the bar. The guys had showed up not that long after the girls, and they'd stationed themselves at a pool table in the back.

"Isn't that a bit of the pot calling the kettle black? You and Paige going to go home and play Parcheesi or something?"

"Is there such a thing as naked Parcheesi?" Brendan asked, grinning.

Shep shook his head at his best friend and went to get two more pitchers of beer to send the smug ass on his way. On a less busy night he would've been able to pull himself away from the bar to join the guys for a round or two of pool, but not tonight. It was winding down now, as it was after one and they closed at two, but the Sheep had been packed for most of the evening.

Being a bartender and part owner of the only bar in Mirabelle,

Shep had dealt with some inebriated people in his day. People made mistakes, which was understandable, so there was a two-strike policy.

Once was forgiven; twice was never again.

The locals knew the rules, but visitors didn't. So sometimes visitors weren't given a second chance.

School had just let out for the summer, and the college students were down and invading the beaches. These kids had a tendency to test his patience.

Especially when they were drunk.

There was a group of guys in the corner who were getting rowdy and pushing the limits of what Shep would allow in his bar. He'd been trying to keep an eye on them for the last hour, which was made more than somewhat difficult because of his need to watch Hannah.

The ringleader of the bunch had spiky light brown hair and an air of arrogance that made Shep want to hit him. Every time the guy would come to the bar for a drink, he'd slap the wood a couple of times with his palm before he'd start snapping his fingers in the air.

Now the little shit was holding court, standing up and talking loudly about some girl he "banged." The guys around him pounded their fists on the table as they laughed, and the leader started up with another story.

"Those kids need to calm it down," Nate said as a loud *whoop* filled the air. "I'm about to lose my patience."

As Nate Shepherd was a pretty patient man, this was saying something.

Shep looked over just in time to see the moron dry humping the air.

"Yeah, he's about reached the limit," Shep agreed. But his

attention was pulled elsewhere as he went to serve a few patrons at the other end of the bar.

When he finished up, he looked in Hannah's direction again, as he'd been prone to do all night, and his blood went cold.

The little shithead and two other members of his posse were talking to her and the other girls. The guy's hand reached out and he caressed her shoulder. She flinched away from him, clearly uncomfortable with the little slime.

"Son of a bitch." Shep was heading in that direction immediately, tempted to vault over the bar as opposed to walking the few extra feet to use the door on the side.

He couldn't get over there fast enough.

* * *

"That dress looks good on you. It'd look better on my bedroom floor."

The laughter died in Hannah's throat, and she looked up and into the face of a twelve-year-old boy.

Okay, so maybe he was more like twenty-one, but he was a puppy, and not a cute, adorable one. He was the sort that would eat the drywall and would be impossible to house train. Plus he had droopy drunk eyes and spiky hair that probably could take someone's eye out. Not to mention his too-tight shirt that was an eye-popping highlighter yellow.

"Excuse me?"

"You heard me, sugar. I've got a thing for cougars, and you've been making eyes at me all night." He managed to slur only a few of those words.

Okay, she was pretty sure she'd just been insulted. *Cougar?* She was thirty. Didn't a woman need to be about ten years older to be classified as that? Not that sleeping with him was even remotely a possibility. With any chance of Shep on the horizon, she had no need to explore anything with him, or anybody else for that matter.

"Eyes at you? I don't think so." Hannah shook her head.

"Yeah, you need to step away from our table, little boy," Harper said.

"Little boy? I think I could give you a run for your money, sweet cheeks." Droopy's eyes darted to Harper, and he gave her a smarmy grin.

"Yeah, you've got a banging body," one of Droopy's friends said. This guy was wearing a muscle T-shirt and he had a pierced eyebrow. "I'd like to bang it, too."

"And, sweetheart, your legs are something I'd like to feel wrapped around my waist." This from the last friend, who had a blond ponytail and wore a hat backward. His comments were directed at Paige. "I think we could all have some fun. And we have some more friends over there," he said, pointing at the other end of the bar, where four other guys were sitting.

"You too, Curly Sue. I think we could make your hair go straight," Droopy said to Mel. "There are enough of us to go around for all of you lovely ladies." He reached out and ran his fingers down Hannah's bare shoulder. His skin was hot and clammy, and she automatically flinched away from his touch. "Awe, come on. Don't be like that," he said as he reached forward again.

"Don't." When she moved this time, she braced her hands on the table as she leaned away. She'd put too much weight on her sore wrist and flinched again, this time in the opposite direction she'd intended and right into the guy's hand.

"You need to stop touching her. *Now.*"

Hannah looked to find Shep standing next to Droopy.

He was seething.

Droopy looked over at Shep with a shocking amount of disdain coming out of his drunken eyes. "Listen, Farmer Fred, why don't you head back over to whatever hovel you crawled out of." He let go of Hannah and made a shooing gesture with his hand. "This doesn't concern you. Your presence isn't needed here." Droopy turned away from Shep, but he was more than a little unsteady on his feet, and his other arm came up in the air as he tried to find his balance.

Problem was his free hand had a mug full of chilled beer in it. Ice-cold beer that proceeded to slosh out of the side and all over Hannah.

It covered the front of her dress, going all the way from her chest down to her lap, where it went through the fabric, right to her panties. She gasped, shocked, and stood up, bumping into Droopy and getting the rest of the beer dumped on her.

Hannah looked down. The front of her dress was soaked, and her lace bra wasn't holding up against the freezing-cold liquid. Her very erect nipples were poking through for the world to see...or at least everyone in the bar was getting a pretty good gander.

"Shit. I'm sorry." Droopy made a move to wipe at the front of her dress, but his hand was snatched out of the air and wrenched back.

"Touch her again and I will break your hand," Shep said as he pulled Droopy away from her.

"Dude. Get your fucking hands off me." Droopy struggled against Shep's hold, but he wasn't successful as Shep pulled him a good couple of feet away and turned him in the direction of the pool tables.

That was when Hannah noticed all of the guys, standing there with their arms folded across their chests, looking like a big wall of pissed-off men.

"See that guy in the front?" Shep asked, indicating Brendan. "That's his wife right there." He nodded at Paige. "I'm pretty sure he could snap you like a twig. And the one behind him? He's former military and wouldn't hesitate to protect his fiancée, who's at this table. Then there's that guy in the back whose girlfriend is also sitting here, and I'm pretty sure he'd be more than willing to show you what a boot up your ass would feel like. And, finally, we get to the lady you just spilled beer all over. You see, dipshit, she's someone I would do absolutely anything for. And as she's made it clear she doesn't want you near her, and you won't listen, I'm going to make that happen."

Droopy wrenched his arm away from Shep's grasp. "What the hell are you going to do?"

"You have ten seconds to walk your drunk ass out of here," he said, pointing toward the door. "Before I throw you out."

"Who the hell gave you that authority?"

Shep's grin was a mean one. "It's my bar. Get the fuck out and take your friends with you. And don't come back."

Once Droopy and all of his friends cleared out, Shep turned his focus back to Hannah. "You okay?" he asked, looking down at her.

"Yeah, I..." She couldn't think anymore.

Hannah had never really had those moments where everyone else disappeared, where a crowded room seemed empty besides her and some man.

Except Shep wasn't just some man. He was *the* man.

We have a second chance, and I want to do something with it.

She still wasn't sure she could do it. She could take the leap or run away. With either of those options there was the possibility of losing everything.

But with the leap there was the chance of gaining everything.

He'd just very publicly defended her honor and it had been… so damn hot. Her next move was most likely fueled by the alcohol and that look of intensity that was just for her. Her hand moved up his chest to his neck and she tugged him down. He came willingly and without a moment of hesitation.

She kissed him this time, her mouth working over his, her tongue dipping in and tasting him.

And, God, he tasted good.

His arms banded around her, and he brought her in to his body. He didn't even flinch when the cold, wet fabric of her dress soaked into his shirt. But really it wasn't that cold anymore; his heat radiated out, warming her instantly.

Now her nipples were erect for an entirely different reason.

And it was then that Hannah was brought back to reality, when the room around them burst out into a round of applause.

Chapter 10

How to Remove a Wet Flannel Shirt

Shep pulled back, more than reluctantly, and looked down at the stunning woman in his arms. "We have an audience."

"I don't care." She kissed his jaw.

"How drunk are you right now?"

"Pretty drunk. Take me home."

He laughed at her insistence, feeling decidedly better than he had a minute ago, when he was dealing with dipshit and all of his friends. "Anything you want, babe." It was at that moment that the very wet dress of hers registered in his brain. "I really don't think you could look any more indecent if you tried. And as much as I like this look on you, I'm not letting anyone else see this."

He moved back just enough to give himself room to pull off his flannel shirt, but not enough to let the rest of the room see how the green fabric of her dress clung to every single one of her delectable curves. He would've stood in that bar bare chested to shield her from the view of the guys who were around them.

Luckily, he was wearing a T-shirt underneath, so he was spared that problem.

"Let's get you covered up." He pulled the sleeves over her arms and then buttoned the shirt up just enough to conceal her breasts... and those nipples.

God, those nipples of hers were going to kill him.

"That's better," he said as he reached down and grabbed her hand, lacing his fingers with hers. Then he turned to face his friends, who were all looking at him with shit-eating grins.

"You guys good?" he asked.

"We sure are." Brendan pulled Paige in close to his side. The rest of the guys just nodded.

Shep looked up at his father behind the bar, who made a shooing motion toward the door with his hand. "I got it."

"Come on." And with that he led her out of the bar and into the night.

The woman by his side was intoxicated and wearing heels that were high enough to take a pretty good topple of off, so he carefully steered her toward Lois.

"God, this car is so sexy," she said, running her fingers across the hood. "It fits you perfectly."

"You think I'm sexy?" He raised an eyebrow at her.

She grabbed on to the front of his shirt as she leaned back against the door. She looked up at him and gave him one of those smiles that almost made his heart stop. "Don't play dumb with me, Nathanial."

"Wouldn't dream of it."

"Good." Her hand loosened from his shirt, and she trailed her fingers up his chest.

"You know, you're pretty damn sexy yourself."

Hannah looked down at herself, and when her head came up,

skepticism was clear on her face. "I look ridiculous and smell like a brewery."

"It works for you."

Her head fell back, and she laughed long and loud. He fucking loved that sound. It was his favorite... well, maybe second favorite. Her moaning was number one.

But *that* wouldn't be happening tonight. Hannah was pretty toasted, and there was no way in hell they were doing anything that she might possibly regret the next day. When they had sex again, he wanted there to be absolutely no doubts in her mind before, during, or after said glorious event.

Because it would be glorious. That he could damn well guarantee.

"I'm serious." He reached up and brushed his fingers across her temple and down the side of her face. "Everything you do works for me."

"Is that so?" She let go of his shirt and moved her hands up his chest, tracing the emblem on his shirt. "Will you do something for me?"

"What's that?"

"Kiss me again."

"Never have to ask that." His hand moved to the back of her head, his fingers spearing through her hair as he brought her mouth to his. He kissed her. A soft and slow tangling of tongues that wasn't anything less than perfect.

When he pulled back to look at her, she reached up and pushed some of his hair off his forehead, her fingers trailing down before she gently rasped his beard. "Thank you."

"For the kiss?"

"No." She shook her head, smiling at him. "Well, yes for that, too. But I was referring to what you did in there."

"Anything for you, babe. Let's get you home and into something dry."

"Hmm." She sighed dreamily. "I think it would be better if you got me into nothing at all."

"That's not happening tonight," he said as he ran his thumb across her jaw.

Her lips formed into a pout. "Why not?"

"I'm not taking any chances on you regretting something with me. It's been thirteen years. I can wait a little longer."

"What if I don't want to wait?" She raised her eyebrows as her fingers skimmed down his body. She was messing with his belt, tracing the metal buckle. Her hand started to dip further and he snatched it up, shaking his head.

"You're going to be trouble tonight, aren't you?"

"Absolutely." She stretched up onto her tiptoes and kissed his jaw, working down his neck and driving him damn near insane.

"It's still not going to happen," he whispered in her ear.

She pulled back, frowning at him. "When did patience become your virtue?"

"Believe me, Hannah, it's not." He shook his head as he opened the door and helped her into the car, wondering how the hell he was going to survive the night.

But as it turned out, he had absolutely no reason to be concerned about Hannah and her intentions. Because by the time they pulled up in front of the inn, she was asleep.

A total of three minutes and she was out like a light.

His car triggered the censor of the flood lamp at the bottom of the steps, and it came on, illuminating her face. Her head was leaning back against the seat, her eyes closed behind the square black frames of those glasses of hers, and her mouth partially opened as she breathed.

She was so damn beautiful. He'd thought so from the very first time he'd seen her.

He remembered that moment like it was yesterday. It was exactly a week after he'd graduated high school, and he'd still been flying high on his newfound freedom. No more classes for him. The family business was in his blood, and he couldn't wait for the day he was working behind the bar at the Sleepy Sheep.

But until that day, he was going to enjoy the time his life was relatively responsibility free. And what better way than with girls?

But there'd been no way in hell he'd ever have been able to prepare himself for Hannah, for everything that had happened that summer, for how fast and far he'd fallen for her. It had been an at-first-sight thing for him. Something he'd never experienced before that moment and something he'd never experienced again...until she'd shown up again.

He'd been parked across the street from the Seaside Escape Inn, leaning against what had then been his very beat-up Mustang. Hannah had been unloading the back of an SUV, an SUV that had been parked exactly where they were parked in the present moment.

She'd grabbed the straps of a couple of bags and hung them from her shoulders. Her long strawberry-blonde hair—a few shades lighter than it was now—stretched down her back. She was wearing cutoff jean shorts that showed off her freckled legs, a plain white T-shirt, and purple Converse sneakers. He hadn't seen her face yet, but he'd known without a shadow of a doubt that she was beautiful. And a second later he was proven right.

She closed the hatch and turned. Her eyes caught his and

she froze, one of the bags sliding down her arm and catching at her elbow. They'd just stared at each other for that one magical moment, neither of them moving, and then her mouth had quirked up into a big grin.

That was it. That was all it took. That one smile. He'd been done for when it came to her.

He still was.

Shep pulled himself back to the present and the drunken woman who was fast asleep in his car. He turned and eyed the steps in front of him.

"Well, this is going to be interesting."

And interesting it was. He fished her keys out of her purse before he pulled her from the car and carried her up the stairs. She snuggled into him, her face pressed into the crook of his neck and her breath washing out across his skin.

It was the sweetest torture.

He somehow managed to get her into the house with little jostling, or maybe she was just too drunk to notice. A very distinct possibility.

She'd left a light on in the living room, so he was able to navigate to her bedroom without running into anything. Henry had been asleep on the back of the sofa. He jumped down when they walked in, meowing to let his presence be known as he followed.

Shep laid her out on the bed, and she rolled over, hugging the pillow. He really didn't want to wake her up, but her clothes were wet and covered in beer. Her dress was a halter, so he figured if he just untied the top he'd be able to slip it down her body.

He started with removing her glasses first, placing them on the nightstand for her to find easily in the morning. Her shoes were next. He unbuckled the straps at her ankles and freed her feet. Then he put his knee on the bed, bracing his weight as he brushed her hair away and worked at the knot at the back of her neck. He managed to get the dress off of her with a couple of minutes of maneuvering and only a slight glimpse of the turquoise material of her panties.

He looked over at Henry, who'd stationed himself on a chair in the corner, watching with what Shep could only imagine were judging eyes.

"Hey, this isn't all that easy."

Easy wasn't even remotely the word he would use. This wasn't the way he'd imagined getting Hannah in bed and undressing her.

Not even close.

The flannel shirt was only slightly damp, and he was pretty sure he wouldn't survive trying to get her out of it. So it looked like she was going to be sleeping in it.

He got her underneath the covers and leaned over to place a kiss on her cheek. Her eyes fluttered open, and it took her a second to focus on him.

"I missed the fun part where you undressed me."

"I promise to do it again. Very soon."

"Good," she said with a sleepy grin on her face.

He leaned down and pressed his lips to her forehead, but when he went to pull back, she grabbed his shirt, her fingers fisting in the fabric. "Stay with me."

"Anything you want." It wasn't like he didn't want to stay. He'd take sleeping next to Hannah anytime.

Every time.

"Just going to go lock up and turn off the lights."

"Okay." She closed her eyes.

"Okay."

Shep pulled off his boots before he stood up and made his way through the house. He stopped by the kitchen to grab a bottle of water and fished out two Advil from the bottle next to the sink. He placed them on the nightstand next to a sleeping Hannah before he started to strip down.

He kept his boxer briefs on but hesitated before removing his shirt. It would probably be in his best interest to keep as many layers of clothing between them as possible.

He reached behind him, grabbing the back of his shirt and pulling it over his head.

But when have I ever played things safe?

He crawled into bed next to her, slipping his arm around her waist and pulling her back against his body. She rolled over in his arms, her head resting on his chest. Her shirt—well, really his shirt—had moved up her body when she moved, and her bare stomach pressed against his.

He wanted all of her bare, wanted both of them to be naked, wanted every inch of her skin on his. No space. No separations. Just the two of them wrapped up in each other.

His body ached for her like nothing he'd ever known, which was probably why he couldn't stop himself from groaning when her bare thigh moved up his leg. It felt so good, causing him no small amount of discomfort. He knew this was exactly as far as it was going tonight, but his dick hadn't gotten the message.

But even with that, he was more satisfied in that moment with her in his arms *not* having sex than with any woman he'd ever slept with before. Hell, more satisfied than he'd ever been with all the other women he'd ever slept with combined.

Hannah Sterling was back in his life. And he was going to do everything is his power to keep her there.

* * *

The reality of the situation was slow to process in Hannah's sleep-hazed brain. She opened her eyes to sunlight streaming through the French doors and had to close them quickly.

Her head hurt. Not as bad as it could have, considering the circumstances. Hannah was no fool when it came to alcohol. Hydration was key, and she normally kept up with a steady stream of water when she was drinking. Last night had been no exception.

But she'd had a lot of tequila. Thus her slow processing skills. Really slow.

It was then that she registered the fact that she wasn't alone. She slowly opened one of her eyes, peeking at the man who was asleep next to her. Or really underneath her, as she was currently sprawled across him.

He stayed.

Even in her thoroughly fuzzy brain she could appreciate how truly breathtaking Nathanial Shepherd was in sleep. Not that he wasn't just as beautiful when he was awake, but this was different.

He had a slight widow's peak that was mostly disguised by his long hair and the way it fell over his forehead. It was currently falling in his face, and she itched to reach up and brush it aside. She stopped herself, though, because she didn't want to wake him up.

His long, thick eyelashes fluttered against their resting place, dancing across his skin. There were laugh lines by his eyes, not all that shocking either. The Shep she remembered had always been smiling, and she was glad to know that this was something that hadn't changed. There was a tiny scar on his forehead. It was thin and just sliced through his left eyebrow. She wondered how he'd gotten it, wanted to hear the story.

Wanted to hear every story.

What the hell am I talking about?

She couldn't think that way. The past needed to stay in the past. She wasn't quite sure what the future would bring with Shep... or if there would be any future at all. She needed to focus on the present. Which included a very full bladder and a headache.

She disentangled herself from Shep nice and slow, pulling herself from his warm embrace and sitting on the edge of the bed. She reached for her glasses, noticing the two Advil and the bottle of water.

Shep. Always taking care of her.

She popped both pills and drank a good portion of the liquid, which was a nice little relief to her desiccated mouth.

She stood up, shaky on her feet at first, and made her way into the bathroom. She was a little slow at her normal tasks, but she managed to wash her face and brush her teeth, feeling distinctly more human after this was accomplished.

She stared at her reflection in the mirror, taking in Shep's shirt covering her body. The soft blue and green flannel fell past her thighs. She grabbed the collar and turned her face into it, breathing in the scent of Shep and beer.

Yeah, she was going to need to shower soon. That lovely beer aroma was coming from more than just the shirt.

But first, coffee. That would definitely help her fuzzy brain get into fighting shape. Then she could figure out what to do with the semi-naked man in her bed. But when she stepped back into the bedroom, she stopped dead in her tracks. Shep was still asleep, the sheet high up on his chest and not allowing her to see any of the spectacularness underneath.

She should've explored his chest when she'd been sprawled across it. She was too late now. Too late to see more of that eagle tattoo that was just peeking out from under that stupid freaking sheet. If only she could just pull it down...

No, Hannah. Stop it. Stop it, stop it, stop it.

God, she was screwed. She closed her eyes and rubbed her sore temples. This wasn't supposed to happen. She wasn't supposed to want him like this. This wasn't practical; nothing with him was.

When he walked into a room, all logic went out of her head and she started thinking with her girly bits. Something that only he'd ever been able to do to her. Something that she needed to get under control immediately. She was a loose cannon around him, and it terrified her.

She turned away from the glorious sight of him in her bed and walked toward the kitchen. Maybe if he wasn't in the room with her, he wouldn't overwhelm her senses.

She pushed her face into the fabric of his shirt again and inhaled deeply.

Or maybe not.

She made a grab for the coffee grounds but was stalled when a loud meow echoed behind her. Henry ambled into the room, looking a little rumpled himself.

"Where did you sleep last night?" she asked him.

He just meowed again, stretching his little body.

"Okay, you get food first." Her wrist was getting decidedly better, so she was able to open the cans with the pull tabs. She dumped the food into his dish and put it on the floor for him. He walked over immediately, making quick work of his breakfast.

Hannah returned to her mission of coffee, throwing out yesterday's filter and grabbing a clean one. She filled it with grounds and then grabbed the pot, heading over to the sink to fill it.

When she turned the knob, a thudding noise filled the kitchen. The pipes behind the sink vibrated louder and louder, and then there was the unmistakable sound of them bursting. She turned the knob off before she dropped to her knees, but the damage was done. She opened the cabinet doors and was immediately sprayed with a steady stream of water.

Well, this wasn't exactly the shower she'd been planning on having.

* * *

Shep woke to an empty bed, not too pleased at all. This was not how he'd imagined starting his morning. He frowned as he looked around the room, but Hannah was nowhere to be seen. If she'd planned on pulling a runner, or was going to push him away after that kiss she'd planted on him last night, she had another thing coming.

He got out of bed and headed for the bathroom, grabbing his clothes on the way. He had no idea if he was going to have to track her down, and being dressed was probably in his best interest.

He was just pulling his shirt over his head when the wall behind him started to vibrate and a shout filled the air. He bolted in the direction of the kitchen, crossing paths with a wet Henry, who was sprinting in the opposite direction, toward the bedroom.

Shep wasn't exactly prepared for the sight that greeted him. Hannah was on her knees on the floor, her head underneath the sink and her ass in the air.

He'd gotten a glimpse of her panties last night, but he'd only gotten the color: turquoise. He hadn't gotten make or model. He wasn't too sure on the make. There was too much fabric to be a thong, but they did ride high, exposing a good portion of those lovely cheeks of hers. And then there was the model, which was a hybrid of some sort. They were mostly cotton, but the outer edges were lace.

So it was a little understandable that it took him a second to realize that water was spraying out everywhere.

"Shit!" she shrieked.

He crossed the room just as her head came out from under the sink. She reached up on the counter for a towel, but he grabbed her hand, stopping her. She jumped in surprise and looked up at him.

"I got it." He was gentle pulling her out of the way, but he was also quick about it.

He got down onto the ground and was immediately assaulted with a steady stream of water. It hit his face and then soaked into his shirt. He found the valves through the assault and wasn't surprised why Hannah couldn't get them closed. They were good and stuck, and he had to put a lot of effort into loosening them.

When both were shut off, he pulled back, wiping his face as he stood up. He turned to find Hannah behind him, and for the second time that morning he almost swallowed his tongue.

Hannah was drenched. Every single inch of her.

Water beads covered her glasses and her hair was dripping wet. The flannel shirt was completely molded to her body like a second skin. And her breasts…well, they were very prominently displayed, those damn nipples of hers making another appearance and causing his mouth to water.

His eyes skimmed to her legs in all of their bared glory. He might've slept with them tangled up with his last night, but it was a nice little view he was getting of them this morning. His gaze slowly traveled back up her body, taking it all in again. She was every single one of his wet dreams come to life…literally.

And Shep wasn't the only one doing the checking out. Hannah pulled off her glasses and set them on the counter next to her. He was sure they weren't helping her see all that much as they were spotted with water. He knew that she had problems seeing far away, but he guessed that she was close enough to see him just fine, because her eyes were tracking all over his body, too. His shirt was plastered to him and so were his jeans, which were showcasing the ever-growing bulge in his pants.

Her breathing was erratic, but when her eyes landed on his, she stopped.

"Yes or no, Hannah?"

Chapter 11

Four-Letter Words

Yes or no, Hannah?"

She knew exactly what he was asking her; there was no doubt about his intentions.

To bang or not to bang, that was the question.

Logic was Hannah's go-to tool. It was how she'd made herself a success. What she thrived on. What she survived on.

But how could she possibly use logic when the man in front of her was short-circuiting her brain. She ceased to breathe, her lungs unable to pull in any air. Her body was on fire, and she was pretty sure steam was about to start pouring out of her ears.

There was no logic as she looked at Shep, only lust.

Lust that made her want to climb up his body like a cat, wrap herself around him, and not let go for hours. Lust that demanded him inside of her, thrusting into her as he pushed her up the wall, across the floor, or anywhere really.

She wasn't picky.

She wanted moaning and panting and sweating. Biting and licking and kissing. Wanted to map out his tattoos with her fingers. Wanted to taste every inch of his body with her tongue.

She wanted all of it. All of him.

So bang it was.

"Yes."

He was on her in an instant, his arms coming around her body and his mouth crashing down hard on hers. She didn't hold back for even a second, opening up and letting his tongue in. He licked at her mouth, sucked and sipped on her lips.

He had her up against the island in the middle of the kitchen, the hard granite digging into her back. Though it wasn't anywhere near as impressive as his hard erection pressing into her front.

His hands were at her sides and sliding down. The second he touched the bare skin of her thighs, he groaned into her mouth.

"So soft. So. Damn. Soft." He pulled back, licking his lips.

Her knees buckled just a little as she imagined that mouth of his licking something else.

"Maybe later," he said, correctly guessing her thoughts.

How? How does he do that?

One of his hands went to the apex of her thighs. He ran his fingers down the front, tracing the material and pressing just slightly when he got to her entrance. He moved up to her clit and pushed just a little bit harder, rubbing the spot.

This time she was the one moaning. She grabbed on to his arms for balance, needing to hold on to something so she didn't slide to the floor.

"*Definitely* later." His mouth was on her neck, and he sucked on her skin, licking his way up to her ear.

She whimpered, desperate for him to remove the obstruction that was preventing him from sliding inside her. He pulled back just a little to watch what he was doing with his hand, moving his fingers up and down.

And then he was pulling back the material, and his fingers dipped inside of her. She was panting, freaking *panting.* That whole breathing thing was becoming a bit of an issue.

"Soft, warm, and wet. The trifecta." His eyes were still focused down, not moving from where he slowly fucked her with his fingers. "Hannah, this is exactly where we were the other day."

"I know, and you were the one who stopped."

"An action I won't be repeating today." He put his mouth to hers again, inhaling her in one fell swoop. He removed his fingers from her body, and both of his hands were at her waist, lifting her up onto the counter.

Her hands skimmed up his chest, the wet fabric somehow hot beneath her hands. But this wasn't what she wanted. She wanted his skin bared. Wanted his tattoos on display. Wanted him naked.

She fisted her hands in his shirt and tugged it up, an action that was made difficult by the fact that it was stuck to him. The right wrist was still sore, and she'd twisted it when she'd been trying to work at those unbudging knobs underneath the sink.

Working at Shep's shirt wasn't making it any better, but she really didn't care in the slightest.

As soon as he realized her mission, he assisted in her endeavors, reaching behind him and grabbing a fistful of the fabric. He pulled it over his head and threw it to the side. But he didn't give her even a second to admire him in all of his glory. She only just caught a glimpse of the ink across his chest before he was on her again, his mouth covering hers.

She might not be able to study him with her eyes, but she didn't hesitate with a hands-on exploration. She started at his neck and down his shoulders. When she got to his pectoral muscles, she placed her palms flat. Her thumbs rasped his nipples, and he groaned into her mouth.

"Now it's your turn." He was working at the buttons on the bottom of her shirt, and when the last one was undone, he pulled it open, taking a step back and looking at her.

She'd slept in her bra the night before. It was strapless and matched her panties, the cups made of the same turquoise lace. Shep licked his lips as he reached out and traced the top of the cup with his finger. A second later he pulled it down, her breast popping out of the top of it. He repeated the same action with the other cup, putting both of her breasts on display.

His eyes and hands traveled down, taking all of her in. Then his focus landed on the tattoo at her hip. He reached out, tracing the wings that spread up and out across her skin and down to where it dipped past the top of her panties.

And this was when reality started to penetrate her lust-filled brain.

No. No, she didn't want that. That wasn't what this was about. She wanted hard and fast. Nothing gentle. Nothing sweet. She didn't want to think about anything, and especially not about that.

But Shep didn't linger. Instead his fingers hooked into the panties on either side of her hips, and he pulled them down her legs. And just like *that* the urgency was back. He reached behind her, unsnapping her bra with a single move and leaving her entirely exposed to his gaze.

"Damn, woman." He shook his head in wonder as he reached between her legs, pushing her knees apart before running his finger along the seam of her folds. "This bare thing you've got going on definitely works for me."

"Glad you approve."

His eyes came up to hers, and they were so damn hungry. "I do, and at a later time I'm going to spend a good amount of time enjoying it with my mouth."

"Later?"

"Yes. I need to get inside you now." He started working at this belt, pulling it open in one swift move.

Need was a powerful word, one she thought described her pretty accurately in that moment as well.

Hannah put her hands at his hips and grabbed ahold. She shoved his jeans and boxer briefs down his thighs. His erection sprang free, and she was distracted with the task at hand, putting something else in her hand entirely.

She wrapped her fingers around his glorious cock and stroked him. His mouth went down to her neck as she worked him over, lightly nipping at her skin before soothing the area with his tongue.

"God, that feels good." The vibration of his voice went through her body, settling in her bones.

"What about this?" She brought her other hand down and cupped his balls, squeezing just so.

"Shit." He groaned, bucking in her grip. His reaction had more than a small amount of satisfaction running through her.

He was off of her again, breathing hard as he pulled his wallet out of his back pocket. He dug out a condom before he threw his wallet over his shoulder. He had that sucker on before he even pushed his pants the rest of the way down his legs and stepped out of them.

He was climbing on top of the counter within seconds, pushing her back and knocking everything off to make room for their bodies. The wire rack holding the fruit crashed first, quickly followed by the dish she kept her keys in.

He was a man on a mission.

She would've wished him Godspeed, but as her mouth was currently occupied with his tongue, conversation wasn't exactly on the table.

Nope. Sex was on the table...or the counter, as the case may be.

The tile was cold on her back, but it felt good with his hot body over hers. She planted her feet flat, adjusting and making room for him. He slid up and over her, moving his hips against hers. He pushed against her entrance, gliding through her folds and making her squirm.

She wasn't above begging at this point, but he didn't let it go that far. Apparently, his patience was wearing thin, too, because a second later he was inching his way inside of her.

"You're still so damn tight. I'm going to come before I'm even all the way in."

"You better not." She arched her hips, taking him all the way to the hilt in one swift move.

"*Fuuuuck!*" he ground out between his teeth.

Her sentiments exactly.

He kissed her again, claiming her mouth and her body at the same time.

Damn, she'd missed this. The hot, uncontrollable need to have someone...to have him. Because really, it had only ever been like this with him. That can't stop, can't let go, clawing desperation.

And there was clawing involved. Hannah raked her nails down his back all the way to his ass. His glorious ass.

But she might've been a little too overeager in this endeavor, because when she grabbed it, pain shot through her hand.

She gasped, and Shep pulled back.

"You okay?" he asked.

"My hand."

"Don't hold on so tight." He buried his face in her neck, his labored breaths washing out over her skin.

"Have to." If she didn't hold on, she'd float away.

The grin against her throat was unmistakable, and he moved faster inside of her.

Harder.

He was demanding.

Relentless.

It was perfection.

She arched up again and again, meeting him thrust for thrust. She was coming apart at the seams. Her body...no, her entire being was overwhelmed by him.

"Oh God, oh, oh, ohhhh, *Nathanial.*" She went over the edge, the next string of sounds coming out of her mouth indecipherable. It wasn't part of the English language. That much she knew, and she really didn't care.

Shep didn't stop. He moved throughout her orgasm, keeping it going nice and long. Just when she thought she couldn't take it anymore, he followed her over the edge, his body shaking as he pumped into her.

She ran her hands up his sweaty back, his muscles trembling under her touch. He pulled his face from her neck. She expected there to be a cocky grin plastered across his face, in true Shep form.

But there wasn't.

He looked...staggered.

His mouth lowered to hers, and he placed the sweetest kiss across her lips. She was sucked in before she knew it. Kissing him back and reveling in the gentle way he touched her body. It was all such a contrast to how he'd been just moments before, and she couldn't take it.

"God, I could make love to you for hours on end."

And that's when reality came back in full force. No tiptoeing around anything. She just slammed right back into it. Like a slap to the face...followed by a car crash.

"No." She pulled away, shaking her head. "Not that."

"Not what?"

"Make..." She couldn't even say it. "The *L* word."

"What do you think we just did?" he asked, incredulous.

"Fuck."

The look that flashed through his eyes was none too pleased... In fact, he was pissed. Those blue eyes of his turned icy, making her freezing cold in the process. "That's what you think just happened?" he practically growled at her.

"Yes. That's what this has to be, because it's not going to be anything more."

"You're right about that." He pulled out of her, the cold intensifying at the loss of him, and got off the counter.

Hannah sat up. She watched as he grabbed his pants from the ground and walked out of the room, anger radiating off him the whole way.

What did I just do? What the hell *did I just do?*

She got down, too, feeling exposed beyond words. She crossed her arms over her chest and rubbed at her shoulders, but it did nothing to ward off the chill. She needed clothes.

His shirts were in a puddle on the floor, along with her bra and panties. She wasn't pulling any of that back on. One, because it was all sopping wet. And two, and more important, because *he* had just stripped her out of them and she...well, she just couldn't.

She had no choice but to follow in the direction that Shep had just gone. She needed to get to her clothes. Otherwise she was going to be stark-ass naked when he walked back out.

And there was no need for that.

The bathroom door was shut when she walked into the bedroom. She was grabbing a pair of shorts when the toilet flushed. She snatched up a shirt from her dresser, jamming it over her head before the door opened.

Her eyes just cleared the fabric when Shep walked out. He stopped dead at the sight of her. His wet jeans were on and buckled, but he was still shirtless.

When her eyes found his face, she immediately wanted to look away. It was full of an emotion that she didn't even want to contemplate. That she couldn't deal with. But somehow she held his gaze.

He shook his head and walked out of the room.

And she followed him. Why? She didn't know. She should just let him leave. Let him walk out the door. Out of her life.

That was how it was supposed to be, wasn't it?

If it was, why did she feel so damn hollow all of a sudden?

She didn't say anything as he snatched his shirt up off the floor. Didn't open her mouth as he wrung it out over the sink. Couldn't get her throat to work as he pulled it over his head. She couldn't make a single sound until he got to the front door, his hand closing over the handle.

"Shep."

He stilled for just a second, but he didn't turn around. "I hope I was the fuck you wanted, Hannah."

And with that he walked out the door.

* * *

If Shep was pissed after that first kiss with Hannah and her calling him a liar, it was nothing to how he was feeling after their "fuck" session on the counter.

He hated that damn word. He was no saint when it came to his past sexual endeavors. He'd been with plenty of women, no thoughts of anything besides getting them into bed and having a little fun for as long as it lasted. Then he was out the door.

He was fluent in meaningless sex. He'd done it well and he'd done it often. But that wasn't how it had been with Hannah. Yeah, it had been hot. *Really* hot. He was surprised they hadn't set the kitchen on fire. But it hadn't been an *itch* he was scratching. It hadn't been meaningless.

That word and Hannah didn't equate. At least not for him.

Apparently, that wasn't the case for her.

The irony of the whole situation? The reason he hadn't been able to commit on any level had been because of her. He wasn't blaming her in any way. It was just that nobody else compared. And now she was doing to him what he'd been doing to other women for years.

It sucked beyond words.

He slammed the door behind him when he got home, making the house shake.

"What the hell's wrong with you?"

Shep walked into the kitchen to find his little brother staring intently at the coffee machine like it held all of life's answers. Judging by the fact that Finn's hair was sticking up every which way and that all he was wearing were a pair of boxers and his glasses, it appeared that he'd only just rolled out of bed.

Finn hadn't gone the same route as Shep with the multiple tattoos. He had only the one on his left pecs and going up to his shoulder. It was identical to the one that Shep had in the exact same place. They were of Owen's dog tags from WWII, the chain stretching up to his left shoulder, where it was grasped in the talons of an eagle.

"So what's your damage?" Finn asked, turning around and looking at Shep. He reached up and ran his hand through his hair, somehow making it stand up even more. "I'd ask if something finally happened with Hannah, but as you look like you're about ready to get into a fight with a wall, I'd guess not."

"Something happen? *Something* happen? Everything happened, Finn. I don't understand that woman to save my life. She infuriates me to a level that I can't even begin to put into words."

"Want to talk about it?"

"No." Shep pulled out a chair so he could sit at the table.

A grin spread across Finn's mouth. He grabbed two mugs from the cupboard and filled them both with coffee. He grabbed the creamer from the fridge, then set everything down at the table and pulled out a chair for himself. He doctored his coffee first before he passed the creamer across to Shep.

Shep stared at the bottle for far too long before he reached out and grabbed it. He poured just enough into his cup to turn it a lighter shade of brown. He watched the creamer swirl with the coffee, mixing only slightly.

"It would appear that we don't want the same things."

"What do you want?"

"Her."

A dark shadow overtook Finn's face. "Sometimes we don't get what we want," he said more than somewhat bitterly as he brought his coffee cup to his mouth and took a drink.

"What happened with you?"

"Becky is engaged."

Becky Wright and Finn had dated all through high school and a good portion of college. They'd gone to different schools and were separated by a few states. The plan had been for them to both come back to Mirabelle after they'd graduated. But when

Finn figured out that he wanted to be a veterinarian, and a few more years were added on to his schooling, Becky had decided that waiting wasn't in her nature.

Finn had put on a pretty good show of moving on since he'd been back. But apparently that show was about to end.

"To who?" Shep asked.

"Brett Milton."

"Shit." Shep let the word out in a commiserating whisper, shaking his head before he took a sip of his own coffee.

To say that Brett Milton and Finn hadn't gotten along would be an understatement. They'd always tried to one-up each other, in sports, in academics, in their personal lives. Brett had gone and become a dentist, coming back to Mirabelle and opening his own practice. And now it appeared that he'd gone and won over Finn's ex.

"Here's to moving on," Finn said, holding his coffee mug in the air before he took another sip.

Shep held his in the air, too, before he took a drink of his own. But all he could think about was the fact that he'd never once mentioned anything about moving on.

He was pretty sure that was impossible.

* * *

It had been four days since Shep had seen Hannah. Four days since he'd been inside of her. He wasn't doing any better with the whole *moving on* thing than he had been right after it had happened.

Out of sight definitely wasn't out of mind. She was never out of mind. Hadn't been for thirteen years, and that was when she hadn't even been in the same state, let alone the same town.

This was torture.

Cruel and unusual punishment.

Was this his penance for all of the shit he'd done before? Was he finally getting his comeuppance?

There are consequences to your actions, son. And one day you're going to see them and not be too happy about some of your past decisions.

Yet another thing that Owen had been right about, and Shep was experiencing it in full force.

And it didn't take long for even more consequences to hit him in the face. He'd been doing his damnedest to try to distract himself from any and all things Hannah related, but life had other plans.

Shep didn't think it was possible to feel any worse about everything.

He'd been wrong.

A few days after the *counter incident*, he found himself the target of Mirabelle's notorious Bethelda Grimshaw. The article in question had been written a few days previous, but as Shep avoided all things that had to do with the woman, it took some time for the newest bit of gossip to trickle into his bar.

Years ago Bethelda had worked for the local newspaper, writing human-interest pieces. But somewhere along the way, her articles stopped being about the news and started becoming more about gossip. Yeah, a lot of it was true in some way or another, but the good people of Mirabelle didn't want to read about the scandalous goings-on in their little town while enjoying their Sunday brunch. Especially when the gossip was about them.

No one was safe from Bethelda's vitriol. It wasn't long before people had had enough of it and fought back.

When Bethelda was fired from the newspaper, she'd found another way to spread her poison by going to the Interwebs. She might use her own inventive code names, but she gave more than enough context clues for it to be beyond obvious as to whom she was talking about.

Considering the fact that most of the town hated her, it was shocking how many hits her website got a day. Once Bethelda got ahold of a story, it spread like wildfire across the town and out into Atticus County, too.

Shep had been caught in her crosshairs before. It was something he was quite familiar with. Not to mention that his friends and family had been part of her headlines as well. Bethelda had had a vendetta against Paige and Brendan a couple years back. Then she'd gone after Grace and Jax with gusto. Even Bennett and Mel hadn't been able to escape it when their relationship had been on the up-and-up.

It shouldn't have been all that shocking when Shep hit her radar again, especially after the drunk guys at the bar…or the chain of events that followed.

THE GRIM TRUTH

BAA, BAA, BLACK SHEEP, HAVE YOU ANY WHORES? YES, SIR, YES, SIR, ONE BAG FULL

Wild Ram, Mirabelle's resident womanizer, is up to no good. *Again.* I'm sure this comes as a shock to absolutely no one. He might've laid low for the past couple of years, but a tiger can't change its stripes after all. Sooner or later past behaviors come to the surface.

If I've said it once, I've said it a thousand times: Ram is nothing but a wolf in sheep's clothing, and he's sharpening his teeth on a rather unfortunate bit of scrap. Mirabelle seems to attract the Yankees for some reason that I just can't understand.

The newest unwelcome invader? Red Riding Hood.

And she needs to march her little freckled nose back up to the city where it belongs. We don't need her and her big-city ideas coming down here and disrupting our little town. It appears that a beloved (albeit slightly neglected of late) landmark has fallen into her care.

Mirabelle is a small beachside town, and we pride our-selves in keeping to our roots. We've had enough of devel-opers with certain ungodly monstrosities popping up and tarnishing our beaches. All we need is for this city girl to come in and destroy what makes us *us*.

And it isn't just in real estate that she's making a scene. Riding Hood has joined the likes of Brazen Interloper, Little CoQuette, and their band of merry ladies. The group was seen getting publicly intoxicated before making a show over at Wild Ram's disreputable establishment, the Den of Iniquity.

This isn't Riding Hood's first trip to Mirabelle. She came down here years ago. She and Ram have a bit of a history together, one that I'm told did not end well. And now their drama is resurfacing.

Riding Hood appeared to be making eyes at a rather young group of boys (which is just disgusting, if you ask me). Never one to appreciate being upstaged, Wild Ram felt the need to put a stop to it. Words were said. Threats were made. And people were thrown out.

Apparently, Riding Hood has a need for attention. A flair for the dramatics if you will. And Ram is giving her all of the attention she wants, and in more places than one. The two quickly gallivanted off into the night, and Ram's car was parked outside of that inn well after the sun came up.

If Riding Hood thinks that Ram is her knight in shining armor, she has another thing coming. The man will tire of her like he has with the rest. He's just scratching an itch, as dogs tend to do.

"Man, you just have to ignore it," Bennett said before he took a sip of his beer. He was keeping Shep company and enjoying a drink while Mel worked on wedding stuff with her mother and Grace.

It was a fairly tame Wednesday evening at the Sheep, and both Finn and Shep were working behind the counter, though Finn was keeping himself occupied on the other end of the bar with a group of girls spending a week at the beach.

Finn was taking up the whole moving-on mission with gusto.

"I wasn't scratching an itch."

"You don't need to explain that to me." Bennett shook his head. "Believe me. It's all garbage and not worth worrying about. She likes to stir things up and mess with people's heads. So don't let her mess with yours."

"That's easier said than done. You ignore her when she was messing with your head?"

"Not at first. And it screwed me over in the long run. Not talking to Mel was my downfall. But sometimes you have to hit rock bottom before you can figure your shit out."

"Well, that was a wise little nugget."

"Sometimes I have a good line or two. It's rare, but it happens." Bennett grinned.

"You wouldn't change the hitting rock bottom?"

"I *can't* change it, so why waste time thinking about it?" He shrugged. "All you can do is move on."

"You sound like Finn."

Bennett's eyes moved to the other end of the bar, where Finn was leaning against the counter, grinning at the blonde in the middle just a little bit more than her friends on either side.

Bennett turned back to Shep and shook his head. "Nah, Finn's definition of moving on is different from the one I'm talking about for you. I mean you need to figure out what your next move is, stop worrying about the past."

"I don't know that there is a next move."

"You giving up?"

"I don't know what I'm doing." Shep went to grab a few empty mugs on the bar.

"Well, if it's any consolation, I don't think Hannah knows what she's doing, either."

"That so?" he asked immediately, turning back to Bennett.

A smile tugged at the corner of his friend's mouth. As Bennett had been at the inn the last couple of days, he had firsthand information as to exactly how Hannah was doing. He'd gone over and fixed the pipes under the sink, and while he was there, she'd hired him to finish up the tile in the kitchen.

Bennett had done the job in the evenings, bringing along Hamilton O'Bryan and Dale Rigels, Mel's little brother and his best friend, to help with the job. Bennett had taken the two teenage boys under his wing, and he'd been teaching them a few skills along the way. Since school was out for the summer, they were going to be working with him on a couple side jobs to earn some extra money.

"She's pretty excited about that inn, more excited than she planned. She's taken a liking to Hamilton and Dale, too. I think when she finally got that bathroom painted, she realized she needed more help with those rooms than she'd originally thought. She hired them to come and work for her."

"Really?"

"Yup. They start on Monday. From what I've seen during the little I've been there, she's getting pretty invested in the place."

"She talked about selling it when I was there last week. Topher Berk was there."

Bennett scoffed. "That guy is a total prick. And I don't see her selling." He shook his head. "Not at all."

"I don't see her staying here."

"Hmmm, I don't know about that."

"She didn't last time."

"What did I tell you about worrying about the past?" Bennett asked, raising his eyebrows. "It's a complete waste of time, and you don't have that much of it, my friend."

"How the hell am I supposed to forget about it?"

"I didn't say forget about it. I said stop worrying about it. And you better figure out the difference," Bennett said simply. Except it wasn't simple at all.

* * *

On Thursday afternoon Shep was making a run to the Piggly Wiggly for the second time that week. It appeared that his brother really was hell-bent on eating him out of house and home.

Not that he was bitter or anything, but really, he hadn't signed up for this shit.

He was loading a bag up with tomatoes when out of the corner of his eye he saw strawberry-blonde hair. He looked up, getting a full blast of the last person he wanted to see...and somehow at the same time, she was the only person he wanted to see.

How was it that when she walked into a room he immediately saw her? Like a fucking sixth sense. Yeah, whoever gave him that ability could just take it back. He didn't want it.

But it wasn't like he was going to have to deal with it when she wasn't here anymore...Damn, he didn't like that thought at all. Not one little bit.

He'd kept going over Bennett's words, about not worrying about the past and focusing on the future. But he wasn't sure that separation was possible, because the past almost always influenced the future.

Hannah looked around the produce department as she pushed her cart, and when her eyes landed on Shep, she came up short. There wasn't exactly delight in her eyes as she looked at him, either.

Shocking.

She took a quick breath, her shoulders going up and down before she sucked that bottom lip into her mouth.

"Hey." Well, wasn't he Mr. Eloquent. But what the hell was he supposed to say? *How's it been since I screwed you?* Yeah, that probably wouldn't be the most appropriate thing.

She shook her head, letting her lip drop. "How's this going to work, Shep?" Well, she wasn't going to mince words.

"How's what going to work?"

"This." She gestured between the two of them. She used her right hand—the swelling was completely gone.

He wanted to ask her how it was healing. If it was completely better. Wanted to ask her how she was doing. What was going on with the inn. What plans she had for Hamilton and Dale. Wanted to ask her five thousand different questions. But he couldn't, because there was no point.

"That's the thing, Hannah. There is no this." He repeated the gesture she'd just made, waving his hand forward and then back at himself. "I'll see you around." And with that he put his tomatoes in his cart and walked away.

Apparently, he wasn't going to listen to Bennett and his words of wisdom.

* * *

Hannah couldn't move for a second as she watched Shep walk away from her. He was getting good at it. She felt like after every encounter they had lately, he was the one walking away. Leaving her feeling...what exactly?

She didn't know. She didn't like it. She tried to push it down and into that place where she wouldn't need to examine it.

It was something she'd gotten good at over the years, but she'd been failing spectacularly since she got here.

She couldn't stop thinking about the events of the other day. Getting lost in the good. Shep's hands, his mouth, his body. Him moving over her, against her, inside her.

And then agonizing over the bad. The hurt in his eyes, his bitter words, him leaving. Him walking away...like he'd just done...again.

She was going to have to get this under control as soon as possible

There would be no mixing of the head and the heart. She had to keep them separate. That was just how it was going to have to be. That was the only way for her. Had been the only way for almost her entire life. The only blip had been Shep thirteen years ago. And, well, Gigi. But there had been no escaping her grandmother.

They were the only two people to ever break her heart.

Well, there'd actually been three…but…but the third…She couldn't talk about the baby.

And she wasn't doing any of that again.

Couldn't do that again.

Focus, she told herself as she made her way around the store. It was her mantra as she loaded her cart with groceries. And it worked up until she got to the checkout line.

It appeared that everyone and their brother was out grocery shopping on this Thursday afternoon. There were only a few registers open, and the lines were about seven people deep.

An older man with a slight belly stretching his black polo came up to Hannah. "Miss? If you make your way over to register thirteen, it's open." He pointed at the register where a young girl with a curled blonde bob was staring off into space and popping her gum.

Hannah pulled her cart over just as another customer was directed to the same register.

Shep.

Perfect.

They both got there at the same time. He stopped, holding his arm wide, and smiled, but it wasn't a smile she was used to. It wasn't warm, didn't reach up to his eyes. "By all means. Ladies first."

"Thank you." She didn't even bother arguing. It was pointless.

She pushed her cart over and started unloading it, Shep standing behind her, his arms folded across his chest. She didn't want to look at him. Didn't want to see how he was looking at her like she was somebody else.

She was beginning to doubt what she'd thought she'd wanted in every way.

She pulled her thoughts from the man, offering the cashier

a smile. But the cashier wasn't looking at her. She was making eyes at Shep, her pale skin turning pink as the blush crept up her cheeks and chest.

"Hi, Shep," she simpered, no longer looking bored in the slightest.

Oh. Please. The girl couldn't be a day over eighteen. Like that was going to happen, Shep had higher standards than that.

At least she hoped he did.

Really, why did she care?

"Hey, Kat. How's it going?" He gave her that same practiced smile, which came as more of a relief to her than it should have.

Focus! Unload your cart, woman.

So she did just that. She was just reaching in for the gallon of milk when long fingers wrapped around the handle and pulled it out. Hannah looked up at Shep, his face unreadable as he placed it on the conveyer belt.

"You don't have to—"

"Would you just let me do something?" he asked as he started pulling more of the contents out of the cart and loading them onto the conveyer belt.

This was another one of those moments that felt like it could become part of the routine of her life. Shopping with Shep for groceries. Planning their food for the week and the dinners that he would obviously be making, as she was relatively inept in the kitchen. Sitting at the table together as they ate.

Really? That was the vision she got from him pulling milk out of her cart?

She had to stop her imagination from running wild. Dreaming about what wouldn't, or couldn't be, was impractical. It was pointless. But so was arguing with him, so she took a deep breath and pushed such thoughts away.

The two of them finished unloading everything, the silence between them so loud she thought her ears were going to burst. When she went to swipe her credit card through the machine, Kat asked to see her driver's license.

Hannah was surprised the girl was able to take her eyes off Shep long enough to verify it.

Kat's mouth dropped open as her eyes darted between Hannah and Shep. "Oh. My. Gosh. You're Red Riding Hood."

"Excuse me?" Hannah asked.

"Red Riding Hood. The Yankee troublemaker. The one Shep's scratching his itch with."

"Excuse me?" she repeated. Who the hell did this little girl think she was?

Kat's hand flew to her mouth as her eyes went wide. "Sorry." The word was more than somewhat muffled. "I shouldn't have said that."

No shit.

"What are you talking about?"

Kat just shook her head, horrified with herself.

Hannah turned to Shep. His jaw was ticking under all that scruff, the only thing readable in an otherwise unreadable expression.

"Listen, Kat, I would discount all of what you read. Okay? No itches are being scratched, and Hannah isn't a troublemaker. Bethelda is just stirring everything up, and you don't want to get involved in that, do you?"

"No."

"That's what I thought."

"Who's Bethelda?" Hannah asked, starting to get agitated. What the hell was going on?

"Bethelda Grimshaw," Kat answered.

"Who—" But Shep cut her off with a shake of his head, reaching over for the receipt and pulling it from the printer.

"Kat, I'll be right back." He moved his cart to the side so that the person behind him could be rung up. "I'm just going to help Hannah here out with her groceries."

He grabbed the bags with ease, holding them with one hand before he reached out with his free hand, linking his fingers with Hannah's. She was so baffled by the last minute that had passed that she didn't even protest as he led her out of the store and in the direction of her car.

It wasn't until they were halfway across the parking lot that she realized her hand was still in his. She pulled it out and started digging around in her purse, using the pretense of finding her keys as the reason for the move.

She just couldn't have him touching her. She tended to do stupid things when his hands were on her, which would in no way be helpful, as she needed to keep her focus and figure out what had just happened.

He didn't even give her a chance to press the button on the remote before he was pulling the keys from her hand.

"Why do you insist on doing that?" she asked, rounding on him.

"Because I know how much you love it when I take charge." He popped the latch and unloaded the bags into the back.

"You going to tell me what that was back there?"

"We've been targeted by Mirabelle's resident gossip. I wouldn't worry about it. It's just a stupid blog."

"Wouldn't worry about it? How did that girl back there know we had sex?" Hannah certainly hadn't told anyone, and despite all of her issues with him, she knew Shep wouldn't be opening his mouth about it.

"That we *fucked*," he corrected her.

Hannah couldn't help but flinch at the bitterness in his voice.

"Your guess is as good as mine. But it's all speculation. The post just said that we left the bar together and that my Mustang was parked outside of the inn all night."

"You knew about this?" Her voice went up higher than she'd intended, and an older lady walking through the parking lot looked over at them, alarmed.

"I found out the other day."

"And why *exactly* didn't you tell me?"

He closed the back of the SUV and turned to her. "Because sometimes it's better not knowing."

She was pretty sure he wasn't talking about the damn article at all.

"The blog is called the Grim Truth. Bethelda Grimshaw is nothing but a miserable old hag who likes to cause people misery because she's alone and hates life. Read it. Don't read it. Do whatever you want. You obviously know what's best." He reached out, wrapping his fingers around her wrist and gently pulling it up. "I'll see you around, Hannah." He dropped the keys into her palm before he turned and walked back to the store.

Chapter 12

Wild Abandon

The wineglass refused to stay full, and the bottle was now empty. Every last drop had been poured. It was a shame, but no matter how much Hannah shook it over the glass, nothing else was coming out. It was almost all gone.

Gone.

Gone.

Gone.

She'd been planning to go to the liquor store after the Piggly Wiggly, but she'd been more than a little distracted from the task. Seeing Shep...hearing him...finding out about that damn article...wanting to read the damn article...then reading the damn article.

She hadn't listened to him. She'd never been good at that. But this time she wished she had, because none of it had been good.

Understatement.

She tossed the empty bottle into the trash can, staring at it for far too long before she let the lid slam shut.

Sometimes it's better not knowing.

Did he really think that? Truly?

For the last thirteen years she doubted her decision in never telling him about the baby. Told herself she should have called him again. Just picked up her damn phone.

But then one month went by. Then two. Then three. Then it was four years. How did somebody just call out of the blue at that point? How could a person from the past pop up and drop a bomb like that?

She convinced herself that he'd moved on. Replayed that phone call in her head over and over again until everything was numb. He'd been in bed with another woman not that long after she'd left. Not that long after they'd ended their ridiculous summer of love.

Love? Pshhh.

"It's a hoax, Henry. It's *all* a hoax. Love doesn't exist." She held her barely filled glass up in the air to her cat. He tilted his head to the side as he looked at her from his perch on the back of the couch.

If Riding Hood thinks that Ram is her knight in shining armor, she has another thing coming. The man will tire of her like he has with the rest. He's just scratching an itch, as dogs tend to do.

She'd started drinking to stop thinking about that damn post…Now, a bottle in, all she could think about was that damn post.

She wasn't wanted here? Well, that was nothing new. She grew up in a household that should have never had one kid, let alone three. She didn't even know what she'd be like if it weren't for Gigi.

Indifferent and self-involved like her parents?

A spoiled socialite like her sister?

An entitled little jerk like her brother?

The possibilities were endless.

She wasn't sure if she had any of those qualities…or maybe she had a little bit of each of them all rolled up into one big ball of messed up.

That sounded about right.

She knocked the rest of the wine back in one gulp and then regretted it immediately.

"There has to be someone around here who delivers wine. Right?"

No sooner were the words out of her mouth than there was a knock on the front door.

She looked over at it, like if she stared long enough she could figure out who was on the other side. Well, it sure as hell wasn't Shep. She was pretty sure he wouldn't be walking through that door ever again.

Crap, she needed more wine.

She took a deep breath and walked over to the door. She stretched up on her tiptoes, and the sight that greeted her on the other side had a genuine smile spreading across her face. The first one she'd had all damn day.

Grace, Paige, Mel, Harper, and a woman with auburn hair who Hannah had never met were standing on the other side with what appeared to be multiple bottles of wine, two boxes of pizza, and an entire box of cupcakes.

* * *

There had been more than a little hurt in Hannah's eyes when Shep had walked away from her in the parking lot, and he couldn't get her expression out of his head.

He was still pissed about everything, and apparently acting like an asshole was the only thing he knew how to do.

And that's why the subsequent guilt had set in.

Shep's evening was going to be spent helping Jax and Brendan paint the soon-to-be Rose Mae Anderson's new bedroom, so he'd decided to enlist the help of Paige in something that he needed done.

As Trevor's first birthday party was on Saturday, Paige's best friend, Abby Fields, was in town for the weekend. Grace was hanging out with them to avoid all of the fumes, so he got her to help out, too. He'd told them about the article, given them a few bottles of wine, and they'd promptly been on their way to the inn.

He had a pretty good feeling that their evening was going to be a hell of a lot more fun than his.

At least there was beer on his end. Though this had been provided by Shep was well. He'd just gotten his most recent batch of home brews bottled, so that was what the guys were imbibing on for the evening.

"Wow, this one might be your best yet." Jax held the bottle in the air. "Cheers to you, man."

"When are you going to open up this brewery you keep talking about?" Brendan asked. "You need to start selling this stuff at the Sheep."

"You'd sell out faster than you could make it."

"Maybe one day." Shep nodded, taking a swig of the beer.

Starting his own little brewery next to the Sheep had been a dream of his for a couple of years now, ever since he'd tried his hand at it and realized he wasn't half bad.

Actually, he was pretty damn good at it.

He'd had this idea of building onto his grandfather's legacy with something of his own, and the idea had never really gone away. It had just been a matter of timing, and what with business booming and all of the extra bartenders they had on hand, the timing was good now.

But then, as his mind filled with Hannah, he wasn't so sure it was the right time anymore… not until he figured out what was going to happen with her.

If anything even was going to happen with her.

"I feel like we just painted this room," Brendan said, bringing Shep back to the moment.

"Yeah," Shep agreed as he looked around at the green walls. "It hasn't even been a year."

He turned to watch as Jax started to open the can of paint that was sitting on the middle of the tarp. The lid was popped off a moment later, revealing a soft pink that was such a contradiction to the man who hovered over it.

Sometimes Shep didn't even recognize Jax anymore. He was a changed man since he'd settled down. Not that any of those changes were bad—quite the contrary in fact. The things Jax had gone through in his life were no picnic. He'd been raised by a drunk father who hated him and an indifferent mother. He'd had this thought in his head that he hadn't deserved happiness, that he hadn't deserved Grace.

It had been a long road for those two to get together, and Grace had had the patience of a saint, waiting for Jax to pull his head out of his ass. But he figured it out in the long run.

The same had happened for Brendan; he'd met Paige and he'd been done.

Shep knew what that was like, except in his case the woman in question didn't feel the same way about him.

"So you going to talk about it, or are you just going to continue brooding?"

"What?" Shep asked, looking up.

"You've been standing there staring at this pink paint for about two minutes like you expect it to start giving you the answers to life," Jax said as he handed Shep a roller.

"You going to start talking about all of this shit with Hannah or not?" Brendan asked.

"There's nothing to talk about." He dipped the roller into the paint tray and started in on the first wall.

"So that's a no," Jax said from behind him. "Brendan, you know anything?"

"Just what Bennett told me. There was that post from the hag Bethelda. He and Hannah slept together that night she kissed him at the bar. He wasn't scratching an itch. And—"

"Would the two of you stop talking about me like I'm not in the room?" Shep glared at the wall as he covered it with the pink. It was such a happy and sweet color, two emotions that he wasn't even close to feeling.

"Nah, we figure the more we needle you, the higher the chance you're going to crack and start talking."

There wasn't anything to talk about. Hannah was leaving. She didn't want a relationship with him. She just wanted meaning-less sex.

Who would've thought that Shep of all people was going to turn down meaningless sex? But that wasn't what it was with her.

Never had been. Never would be.

And it wasn't just about the damn sex. It was about sleeping in a bed next to her, having her curled up in his arms for hours, that ridiculous cat curled up on his other side. It was about going grocery shopping with her, cooking for her, drinking coffee with her in the mornings. It was about how when she smiled he forgot how to breathe, or about how he wanted to listen to her laugh every day for the rest of his life.

And about how none of that was possible. She didn't want him the same way he wanted her. Apparently, she didn't want any of the things he wanted.

"I don't even know what to do anymore." Shep turned around to look at his friends.

"There it is."

"Finally."

Both men turned around with huge grins on their faces, but the grins disappeared immediately when they looked at Shep.

"All right, let's have it. All seriousness," Brendan said as he dropped the edger onto the tarp in the middle of the room. "What exactly do you want this to be with her? She's just here temporarily."

"You think I don't know that?" Shep's voice was a little louder than was probably necessary.

"Hey." Brendan held up his hands in surrender. "We're just trying to get a feel for the situation, Shep. Trying to help you figure this out."

"Are you falling in love with her again?" Jax asked.

Shep looked at his best friends for a moment before he could get the next words out of his mouth. He hadn't said it out loud yet, thought that it wouldn't be as painful in the long run if he didn't.

Yeah, he was only kidding himself.

"I never stopped loving her."

He got a "shit" from Jax and a "you're screwed" from Brendan.

"You guys are so helpful it's ridiculous."

"So what are you going to do?" Jax asked.

"I have no idea."

"You have no idea? *You* have no idea? What the hell, Shep?" Brendan shook his head. "Aren't you the guy who told me that

I had to go to Paige when everything was going down with us? That I needed to stand outside of wherever she was and make her talk to me?"

"Yeah," Jax said. "And aren't you the guy who told me that you didn't get how I could have the woman I love in front of me and not do anything about it. You're doing the exact same thing. She's here now."

"What the hell am I supposed to do?"

"You fight," Brendan answered, like it was the easiest damn answer. "You fight until you have nothing left. Until you know that you've exhausted everything you have."

"And when I'm still left alone?"

"You know that you tried. You've got nothing to lose," Jax said.

"Except my pride."

"Nah," Brendan disagreed. "You'll find that when you fight for something like this, fight for the person you love, you'll only respect yourself more. But if you don't try? You're gonna hate yourself. You will always ask yourself *what if?* What could've happened? You have a finite amount of time. You have to use it wisely, man. Every second of it."

"She's already proven to not listen to what I have to say." She didn't listen to anything really.

"Words are useless." Jax waved his hand in the air as if to wipe *words* off the table. "Actions are what matter. You have to prove it. You know, it doesn't get any easier on this side of it, either. It's a constant fight. Every damn day. But it's worth it. I'd give Grace whatever the hell she wanted, whenever the hell she wanted it."

"You're a fucking sap." Brendan grinned.

"You think you're any better? I'm pretty sure you're tripping all over yourself when it comes to your wife and child," Shep said as he dipped the roller back in the paint tray.

"Hey, I never said I wasn't a sap. Just glad to see that it's happened to him. And it's happening to you, too."

"Happening? Already happened. Thirteen years ago, and it's finally catching up to me." Shep turned back to the wall and focused on a task that he knew he could accomplish and tried to figure out what to do next with the mystery that was Hannah Sterling.

* * *

It was shocking what a good dose of girls, greasy pizza, ganache, and German wine could do for Hannah's mood.

They were all sitting around the coffee table, Grace and Paige on the lumpy couch, Harper curled up in the God-awful floral chair, petting a purring Henry, who was sleeping in her lap, while Mel and Hannah sat on pillows on the floor, cheering before they started to inhale their third cupcakes of the evening.

Abby Fields, the previously unidentified redhead who had been at Hannah's doorstep, was Paige's best friend. It was a title she'd had since the two of them were five years old and they'd met on their first day of kindergarten. She was a publicist in Washington DC, and Hannah had no doubts that she was good at her job. She had just as much sass as the rest of the Mirabelle ladies, and maybe just a tad bit more fire. Hannah liked her immediately.

Abby's red hair was much darker than Hannah's strawberry blonde, and her pale complexion was freckle free. She was currently stretched out on the love seat, her feet resting on the arm while she sipped her wine.

They'd gone through more bottles of wine than Hannah could keep track of. She hadn't been the one pouring it, and the alcohol combined with the sugar and laughs had her feeling like she was on cloud nine.

Which was so nice she could barely see straight…and she knew that feeling had nothing to do with the alcohol.

"You have to ignore that woman." Grace shook her head, her blonde hair brushing her shoulders. She was the only one who was sober. Obviously.

"She's corrosive. Like battery acid." Paige tapped her wineglass before she took a sip.

"Full of bitterness and rust," Harper said.

"And absolutely no pixie dust." Mel took another bite of her cupcake.

Abby finished up. "Covered in crust."

The laughter that went around the room was working like helium, buoying Hannah up in an instant.

"How do you guys manage to avoid it all?"

"Have to." Paige spoke first. "Brendan…he doesn't exactly deal with Bethelda all that well. Or at all. He has a bit of a temper when it comes to me."

"Jax isn't any better."

"Nor is Bennett."

"Have you been in any of her articles before?" Hannah asked Harper.

"Other stuff yes, but not anything with Brad."

"Just you wait," Paige said.

"Yup. It's only a matter of time." Mel licked the chocolate from her fingers.

"She can write whatever she wants to write. I'm not going to read it." Harper shrugged.

"Now, that's the best philosophy," Abby said, holding her glass in the air and cheering Harper before she took a sip.

Hannah looked around at the girls, something clicking in her brain. "So none of you read it?"

"Nope."

"Then how did you find out about it?"

Silence as they all stared at Hannah. Then Paige cleared her throat. "Shep told Abby, Grace, and me about it."

"Oh…he…he did?"

"Yeah, I…um…he didn't want you to be alone," Paige finally got out.

"He…" Hannah paused as the word came out a little croaky. Damn emotions were getting to her, or maybe it was the wine. She cleared her throat and started again. "He said that?"

"Well, the very fact that he mentioned you and the article was enough to know that was the case. Plus, he's the one who gave us all this wine." She gestured wide with her arm. "So you see, there were a couple of context clues that I picked up on."

"Smart girl." Abby nodded.

"You better believe it." Paige grinned. "I also picked up on the fact that something else might have happened. Which is why he isn't here himself."

"Uhhh…" Words failed her. Her guard was dropping when she was around these women…probably because being around them had involved drinking.

All the drinking.

She looked down at her empty wineglass. "More wine?" she asked, getting to her feet and heading into the kitchen. "Who needs a refill?"

"Oh my gosh. You two totally had the sex," Harper called out.

"Harper!" Mel scolded. "It isn't any of our business."

"Her silence says it all." Abby laughed.

"No need to answer," Paige finished.

"Ignore them, Hannah. They're meddling meddlers," Mel said.

"That's what we do to those we adore. And that includes you now, Hannah darling."

Hannah stilled at Grace's words as she reached for the refrigerator door, her heart in her throat for so many reasons. This wasn't a permanent thing. She wasn't staying here. These girls weren't going to become her best friends. They weren't going to keep in touch after she left.

Hannah would just be another blip on their radar...kind of like Shep.

Shep.

Shit.

He hadn't wanted her to be alone. He'd known she'd be upset. He cared.

He freaking cared. So did all of those women in her living room. Well, not *her* living room, the inn's living room. She didn't need to start thinking of this place as hers.

She opened the fridge and grabbed the bottle of wine, turning to place it on the island in the middle, but she had to stop herself. She'd been avoiding said island for the last week, because all she could think about when she touched it, or saw it, or really just walked into the kitchen, was Shep.

Shep.

Shep.

Shep.

Shiiit.

She needed to stop it.

You're leaving. You. Are. Leeeaving.

She needed to remember that. *Had* to remember that. But no one was making it easy.

Not one little bit.

* * *

The girls stayed at the inn until well into the night, laughing and drinking some more. Hannah had been concerned as it was only a Thursday, and she was pretty sure that they were going to have headaches the next day when facing the workday.

"Not a problem." Harper waved off Hannah's concerns. "Mel is out of school, Paige doesn't work on Fridays, Abby is on vacation, Grace isn't drinking and she's going into work late, and my first massage client isn't until noon. Absolutely nothing for you to worry about."

So Hannah didn't worry. She just enjoyed their company until about midnight, when they decided to call it an evening. But as they were leaving, Paige turned to Hannah at the door while the other girls headed toward the car.

"I'll be seeing you on Saturday at Trevor's birthday party." It wasn't a question coming from Paige's mouth, more a statement of fact.

"I don't know. I should probably lie low. But I do have a gift. Let me go grab it." As Paige had invited Hannah to the party last week, during the evening of all of the tequila, she'd already ordered a present for Trevor.

"Nu-uh." Paige reached out and grabbed Hannah's hand, stopping her from walking away. "Bring it on Saturday."

"Paige, I really don't think I should go."

"Well, I do. And the only way Trevor will get that present is if you show up. Party starts at noon. If you aren't there by fifteen after, I'll send Abby over here to get you."

There was no doubt that Abby would accomplish the mission, too. It had taken Hannah about five seconds to realize that the woman was no-nonsense. But none of that changed the fact that this probably wasn't a good idea.

"Paige—"

"Noon," she said, leaning in and kissing Hannah on the cheek.

Hannah was so taken aback by the affection that she didn't even know how to respond. Paige smiled and squeezed her hand gently before turning and following the other girls down the steps.

She stood there in the open doorway for a few seconds at a loss, realizing Shep wasn't the only one she was going to miss when she left Mirabelle.

* * *

Saturday morning dawned gray and wet. The skies weren't promising at all and even without the weather report, Hannah knew that it was just a precursor for something way worse on the horizon.

When she pulled up in front of Paige and Brendan's house, there were a handful of cars parked in the driveway, Shep's Mustang, Lois, among them. The house was on the water but not on the beach. A dock stretched out behind it, a boat bobbing in the waves at the end of it.

She grabbed the present that she'd wrapped in paper covered in cartoon safari animals, pulled her purse over her shoulder, and got out of her car. She took deep calming breaths as she made her way up the stairs, trying to relax.

She could still turn around.

Still go back to the inn.

Something stronger than her had her knocking on that front door. But that strength was gone, gone, gone when the door opened.

Never in her life had she wanted to run more.

Shep was on the other side, holding a giggling Trevor in his arms. It wasn't like she hadn't been witness to him doing this exact thing before, because she had the first time she'd seen him after her return to Mirabelle, when she'd spotted them at the Seafood Festival.

But there was something about being so close to the scene, not being able to turn around and get away unnoticed, that had her head spinning and her breathing coming up short.

She'd imagined what their child would've looked like more times than she could count. A boy with his dark hair and her green eyes. A little girl with her pale, freckled complexion and his sapphire-blue eyes.

This was the life that could've been, right here in front of her, literally so close she could touch it. But it still wasn't hers.

And it hurt so damn much.

Speak. Open your mouth and say words. Say words, dammit!

"Hi." Shep's eyebrows climbed up his forehead.

"Paige told me I had to come. She pretty much demanded it."

"Why am I not shocked?"

"I told her I shouldn't. I'm sorry. Here, I'll go." She held out the gift for him to take so she could leave.

Shep looked between her and the present for a second before he shook his head. "I don't think so, Hannah. Come on." He reached out and grasped her other hand, pulling her into the house and shutting the door behind them.

"Really, I can go. I don't want to...to..."

"To what?"

"Make you uncomfortable."

"I'm anything but uncomfortable. This isn't my house; nor is it my party. It's this guy's party." He looked at the child in his arms. "Do you want Hannah to stay?"

Trevor just giggled, clapping his chubby hands in the air before he leaned forward, reaching for Hannah. She didn't even have a second to think before Shep was handing the little boy off to her and grabbing the present from her so she had two free hands.

She held Trevor out and away from her body, gripping him underneath his arms. He laughed, trying to reach out for her face. She'd never held a child before. Never really been around them. She looked at Shep, desperate for him to take the little boy back.

"He isn't a bomb about to detonate, you know." Shep was no help at all. He was grinning at her, fighting a laugh.

And as if on cue, Trevor let out a high-pitched squeal and promptly burst out into another round of giggles.

"Here, hold him close to your body." Shep took a step close to her, guiding Trevor to her side, where she balanced him on her hip.

She looked up at him, catching his gaze. Something that she could describe only as longing flickered through his eyes, all traces of humor gone. His hand moved down her side for just a second before he pulled away from her like he'd been burned.

"Shep, I don't know what I'm doing."

"You'll be fine." And with that he turned around and pretty much fled down the hallway.

* * *

Okay, so Shep had purposely left Hannah with the baby. What else was he supposed to do? She'd looked like she was on the verge of turning right back around and running out the front door. But since he'd passed off Trevor, he knew she'd have to come and find someone to give him to. The thing was, as soon as she was spotted, there was no chance that any of the other girls would let her leave.

He headed toward the present table to add Hannah's to the pile. He had to be careful where he put it. Paige's best friend, Abby, had organized it just so, and she'd given Shep more than the evil eye when he'd put a gift on the table earlier and messed up her system.

"Big packages on the bottom and then you stack up," she'd said somewhat snappily as she'd rearranged it to her specifications.

Shep had always been intimidated by the auburn-haired beauty. She might be just over five feet tall, but she was a little general if he'd ever met one. Besides, she wasn't the redhead for him.

That specification was for Hannah.

"What is she doing here?"

Shep turned around to find Finn, who handed him a Coke. He nodded in the direction of Hannah, who was currently being swarmed by Mel and Harper.

"Paige invited her," he answered before he took a swig of the cold soda.

"Why?"

"Because she wanted to."

"You okay with that?"

Was he okay with that? Well, judging by the fact that he'd

been happy to see her on the other side of the door when he'd opened it, he'd guess that he was in fact okay with Hannah being here.

She was still holding Trevor somewhat awkwardly. Her shoulders were tense, and her back was ramrod straight. Trevor kept reaching for her glasses, making grabbing motions while she attempted to dodge him. When she turned to the side, he touched her cheek and something came over her face. A warmth in her eyes that was different from anything Shep had ever seen there before.

But he understood it; that little boy had the ability to win anyone over.

"Another one bites the dust."

"I know. Everyone loves that kid," Shep said as he looked over at Finn again.

"Not talking about the kid." He shook his head pityingly. "I'm talking about you. You better be careful, Shep. She's trouble for you, and I don't see this ending well."

"I got it under control."

"Yeah, I don't think you do though."

The odds that Finn was right were pretty high...but it changed absolutely nothing.

* * *

It didn't take Hannah very long to realize that a child's first birthday party was more of a party for the adults than the child. Trevor was more interested in crawling around in the tissue paper, bags, and boxes than anything else.

That was until the cake was pulled out.

She had to admit that watching him dig in and cover himself

in icing while he brought fistfuls of the cake to his face was pretty entertaining.

"You think it would be more fun if we could eat cake that way?"

Hannah turned to find Shep behind her. He was grinning as he watched Trevor.

"I think everything in life would be more fun if we could do it that way, with wild abandon," she said, turning back just in time to see Trevor run his icing-covered hand across the top of his head.

"Not caring what others think at all."

"Yeah." She nodded.

"And not letting logic get in the way," he whispered close to her ear. His breath washed over her skin, making her shiver in that way that only he could. "I'm glad you're here, Hannah."

She turned to look at him. This time those blue eyes were focused on her.

"I told you, Paige didn't give me any other choice."

"No." He shook his head. "I mean I'm glad you're in Mirabelle. Glad you came back."

She wasn't exactly sure how she felt about being back here. Too many mixed emotions. And being around Shep was confusing as all hell.

But one thing she was sure about was that she wanted to lean in and kiss him so damn much it was ridiculous. The only thing that stopped her was the fact that people surrounded them. Last time they'd been in this situation she hadn't exactly restrained herself. She'd just kissed him in the middle of that bar, people be damned. There'd also been the added influence of tequila, something she was lacking today.

And she wasn't the only one who wanted some kissing. His eyes dipped to her mouth for just a second before he licked his lips.

A bright flash went off and had both of them turning and looking over in the corner. Paige's camera had veered from her son for just a second. She was grinning as she glanced down at the screen. She looked back up and winked at Shep and Hannah before she returned her attention to her son, who was doing an awesome job of thoroughly destroying his cake.

Wild abandon indeed.

* * *

The birthday party ended around three, the skies opening up with what Hannah guessed was just the first act for the storm that was on the horizon. Shep had insisted on walking her out to her car, finding an umbrella and holding it over their heads as he did so.

The rain prevented him from lingering by her car longer than the amount of time it took her to get in it, but she got the feeling he wanted to say something to her. Most likely about the moment they'd shared at the party.

Well, she wasn't exactly ready for that, so she thanked the Lord for the storm. Though she was regretting that thanks about seven hours later when said storm was in full swing.

Lightning lit up the window outside her bedroom about a second before the thunder boomed, making the entire inn shake. The lights flickered before they came back on to full power. The lightning was doing a little dance out on the Gulf of Mexico and the thunder was rocking out with it.

Henry was more than a little skittish and wasn't dealing with the storm very well at all. He was currently buried in the clean pile of clothes in the middle of the bed, the top of his head barely sticking out.

He wasn't used to loud noises. It had taken him some time to recover from the burst pipe and his little bath a week ago. But Hannah understood that...She hadn't recovered from the events of that day, either. Or things that had happened not all that many hours ago.

I'm glad you're here, Hannah.

But she wasn't staying, so he shouldn't get used to her being there.

Nor should she get used to it. To him, or his friends, or the inn with its creaking floors, or waking up to the ocean pounding against the shore right outside her window. She would soon be returning to honking horns, crowded sidewalks, no weekends, no fun, none of that.

But she didn't need fun.

Fun led to bad things like heartache and disaster.

All the things she didn't want.

Another clap of thunder shook the house and brought her back to the moment and the lovely chore before her.

Laundry.

Henry burrowed himself deeper into the warm clothes.

"It's okay, buddy." She tried to sound reassuring, but she was pretty sure she failed miserably.

She pulled a towel out of the pile, still warm from the dryer. She was working on the outside, trying to leave Henry's nest intact. He was probably shedding all over everything, but that's what lint rollers were for.

She worked steadily through it, and when Henry's cave was no more, he gave her a rather pathetic look before he got up from the bed and went to hide in her closet. She froze when she got to the last article of clothing: Shep's flannel shirt. It no longer smelled like him, the laundry detergent having washed him away.

She ran her fingers down the fabric, tracing the buttons, remembering exactly what it had felt like when Shep had been stripping her out of it.

"Stop it," she whispered to herself.

She folded the shirt and walked over to the dresser, pulling it open and putting it in with the rest of her clothes, right on top of a Yankees T-shirt that was about thirteen years old and three sizes too big.

She was beginning to start a little collection of Shep's shirts. She closed the drawer, placing both of her hands against the wood and bracing herself as she looked at her reflection in the mirror.

"It's going to be okay." No wonder Henry hadn't believed her. Those words were beyond hollow. "What the hell did I get myself into?"

No sooner were the words out of her mouth than lightning struck again. This time when the thunder hit so did the darkness.

* * *

The bar closed early because of the storm, which was saying something considering it was a Saturday. But bad weather and drinking didn't exactly mix well. It was around ten when Shep headed to Lois, getting more than soaked during the short walk. He'd just shut the door behind him when the sky was split by a massive lightning bolt.

The buildings around him were plunged into immediate darkness.

"Lovely." He started up the engine, pointing his car toward home. The only light was coming from his headlights and the few other stragglers out on the road. The darkness over the next three miles proved that the entire area was out of power. Which meant that the inn was no doubt affected. Hannah was there alone. Well, except for Henry, but what was the cat going to do to protect her?

He rolled to a stop at a stop sign. Right would lead him toward his house. Straight would take him to Hannah.

He sat there for only a moment before he lifted his foot from the brakes, keeping his hands steady on the wheel. Actions were what mattered. Well, he was about to go full-on Operation Sterling.

He pulled up next to her car, putting Lois in park and shutting her off. He reached around to the backseat and grabbed the Maglite from the floor. Next was his cell phone, which he dug out of his pocket, scrolling through the numbers until he found hers. He hadn't used it yet, and there was no time like the present. He figured it was better to inform her of his presence than to bang on her door like a madman in the middle of a typhoon.

That was likely to scare her.

"Now or never," he said before he hit Dial.

She answered on the third ring. "Hello?" There was only a slight inflection to her voice, but he could tell immediately that she was scared.

"Hey, are you okay?"

"Shep?" The relief in her voice settled in his bones.

"Yeah. I'm outside. Open the door for me?"

"Yes. I'll be right—*Shit!*" A thud and the line went dead.

He clicked on the flashlight, opened the door, and sprinted out into the rain. There was no other thought besides getting to her. That damn building had more stairs than he could count, and all he could see was her falling down them in the dark.

He took the steps two at a time, his heart hammering in his throat, prepared to shove the Maglite through the glass to get the damn door open if he had to.

But his plan of attack wasn't necessary; the front door was opening before he even cleared the last step. And there stood Hannah, using the light from her cell phone to shine out into the darkness.

He walked straight in and she shut the door behind him, flipping the bolt before she turned around to look at him.

"You okay?" he asked, taking a step toward her. She didn't back away as he reached out and cupped her chin in his hand.

"Yeah." She closed her eyes and leaned into his touch. "Just tripped. I'd been using my phone as a flashlight and couldn't when I was talking to you." She opened her eyes and turned the light on her phone off, the Maglite making the need for it useless.

"Your hand okay? You didn't fall on it again?"

"No, I caught myself." There was enough light for him to see her face. She gave him a soft smile, but it didn't cover the confusion in her eyes. "How did you have my phone number?"

"You gave it to Grace when you ran into her at the hospital. I saved it in my phone."

"That's not weird or stalkerish at all." She shook her head, a smile dancing on her mouth.

"I didn't think so. Good thing, too. Otherwise you'd be alone. Terrified in the dark."

"I wasn't scared."

He raised an eyebrow.

"Okay, maybe a little... or a lot." She reached up, her fingers tracing the water on his beard. "Why do you keep doing this?"

"Doing what?"

"Worrying about me. Sending other people to spend time with

me when I'm upset. Running to my rescue even though most of our encounters end with you mad at me. Caring about me."

"It would take a lot more than me being mad at you to stop caring, and I'm not mad at you." His hand moved along her jaw and back, his fingers delving into her hair as he palmed the back of her head. He tilted her head back and looked down into those gorgeous green eyes that no one anywhere would ever come close to.

"Then what are you?" she whispered.

"Frustrated. Stop fighting me, Hannah."

"I don't think I can anymore."

"Thank God."

Her lips quirked to the side, and he couldn't stop himself from pressing his mouth to the corner of hers. She melted into him, her body going pliant against his. Her arms wrapped around his neck, holding on to him as he continued to move his lips over her mouth. When he got to the center, she let him in immediately. Their tongues tangled wildly, and he had her backed up against the wall.

He was just about to open his mouth and start begging to spend the night with her. He wasn't above it in the slightest. He'd get on his knees right now... Well, he'd get on his knees in front of her for many reasons actually.

But Hannah spoke first. "Take me to bed. *Please*, Shep."

Chapter 13

Here and Now

Shep didn't need to be told twice. He pulled back and grabbed Hannah's hand, pointing the flashlight in the direction of her bedroom and leading her through the house. When they got to the room, he found candles flickering on her dresser, bathing the space in a dim glow.

He let go of her hand as he walked across the room, turning off the Maglite and setting it on the nightstand. He turned around and the sight he found had his heart hammering in his throat and his dick growing hard behind the fly of his jeans.

He just had to stop for a second to look at her. To commit this moment to memory. Hannah was wearing those minuscule shorts and that paper-thin shirt again. The material was damp from when he'd pushed his body against hers. It was almost transparent as it clung to her chest and belly. She wasn't wearing a bra, and her nipples were on full display.

Her hair was down and around her shoulders, the strands wild from his fingers. She bit her lip and shuffled on her bare feet, fiddling with the phone that was still in her hands.

"You're nervous?"

"Yes." She nodded.

He crossed over to her, pulling the phone from her grasp and putting it down on the dresser behind her. He removed her glasses next, setting them next to the phone, before he reached out, running his hands up her arms. She shivered beneath his touch.

"You always do that when I touch you."

"I like your hands on me."

"I like my hands on you, too." He stepped in closer, his hands going up to her neck. He touched her chin, tilting her head back so he could look into her eyes. "Why are you nervous, babe?"

A smile tipped her lips.

"What?"

"You called me *babe* again. You hadn't been when you were mad at me."

"Frustrated, not mad, and I thought you hated it."

"I don't hate it." Her breathing was becoming erratic. Her hands were at his sides, holding on to him tight.

"Good." He leaned down, his lips hovering right above hers. "Why are you nervous?"

"I can't think straight. Can't focus. All sense and logic are gone."

"You don't need any of that."

"But that's all I have. All I know."

"No, it isn't." He shook his head, bringing his hands down, his fingertips tracing her collarbone. "You know *this*. You know *us*." He let his fingers trail down to her breasts, circling her nipples. She moaned, her head tilting to the side. Shep's mouth went to her throat, kissing her, licking her skin. "Wild abandon, remember?"

"And what happens after?"

"Stop thinking about the next step. Just be here. Now. With me."

Her hands were moving now. She still had her death grip on the fabric of his shirt and she was pulling it up.

Up.

Up.

Up.

He let go of her, lifting his arms and letting her strip him of his shirt. When he was free and clear of it, she dropped it to the floor. Her hands were on his bare chest in seconds, her fingers spreading wide as she moved her palms over his skin.

"Here and now." She leaned forward, kissing the center of his chest, her lips moving over before she opened her mouth wide, her tongue going flat across his nipple.

"God, Hannah." His hands went up, his fingers spearing in her hair.

And then her hands were at his waist, unbuckling his belt and pulling down his zipper. Before he could even take his next breath, she was making her way beneath the waistband of his boxer briefs, her fingers curling around his shaft.

He pulled her mouth back up to his, kissing her as she worked him up nice and good. Just before he was about to lose his damn mind, he covered her hand with his, stilling her movements.

"Can't take anymore. Not if you want this to go any further."

She pulled her hand away and took a step back. "Yes to further."

The words stuck in his head, taking shape and sprouting wings. *How much further? How much more?* He wanted those answers, but they wouldn't come tonight.

Time. He had to give her time. Had to prove that he was the man she wanted. The man she *needed*.

Her hands dropped to the hem of her shirt, and she pulled it up and over her head, baring her breasts to him. She hooked her fingers in her shorts a second later, shimmying them down her legs.

She stood before him completely naked, her skin glowing in the light from the candles.

"Do you have any idea how beautiful you are?" His eyes traveled up and down her body. He wanted inside of her.

Here and now.

He got rid of the rest of his clothing, kicking off his boots before he pulled his jeans and boxers down his legs. The second he was free, he held out his hand.

"Come here."

Her palm slid over his, and he closed his fingers around it, pulling her to him and crushing her against his chest. His mouth found hers, another beacon in the darkness.

They moved slowly through the room, and he held her tight as he walked her backward. When they got to the bed, he laid her down, covering her body as he continued to work her mouth with his.

He had all night.

All damn night, and he was going to take his time. Savor every inch of her body.

His mouth moved from hers, down her neck, and to her chest. He flicked his tongue across her right nipple first before he moved to the left and sucked it into his mouth.

Her body bucked, her hands going to his hair as her moan filled the room.

He wanted her screaming.

He continued his southward descent, dipping his tongue in her belly button before he lightly nipped down her belly. Then he was pushing her legs apart, settling between her thighs.

He slid his palms underneath her bottom, bringing her to his mouth. Her hands tightened in his hair when he ran his tongue across her core. He lapped at her, and she melted on his tongue.

She tasted fucking perfect. Warm and sweet...and...and something that was uniquely Hannah. Something that was impossible to find anywhere else. Something that he didn't know how he'd gone without.

His goal was to ruin her for other men. The reality? She'd ruined him. Ruined him thirteen years ago.

He worked her up, nice and slow. He was intent on making her desperate, and when she let go of his head and started clawing at the sheets, he knew he'd succeeded.

"Please, please, pleeeease."

So he did just that, focusing on that little bundle of nerves until she was coming hard. He stayed with her through the end, not stopping until she was boneless, her body relaxing into the mattress. He sat back on his heels and looked down at her, his eyes skimming every inch of her body.

Holy. Hell.

Her chest was rising and falling erratically, her skin glistened with sweat, and her hair was a mess scattered over the pillows. The cherry on top? She looked up at him and grinned, her satisfaction evident. He'd done that. He'd made her look blissed out beyond words.

He needed to do it again.

He started to get off the bed, and that smile of hers faltered. "Where are you going?"

"Condom." And then reality hit him; he only had one. That wasn't going to be enough.

Not even close. He grabbed his jeans and dug his wallet out of the back pocket. When he pulled out the little package, he held it up. "We're going to have to make this count."

"I, uh...I have some."

His eyebrows rose up his forehead. He wasn't sure how he felt about this. She had condoms? Intended to be used with whom exactly?

"I bought them after you made me come against the counter." She looked at him, her gaze unflinching. "Just in case."

Okay, he took it back. He knew exactly how he felt about it. He 100 percent, wholeheartedly approved. He didn't hesitate to rip the package open, and then he was rolling it down his length.

When he looked up he caught her gaze as she unabashedly checked him out, her eyes lingering on his erection before she licked her lips. The thought of her mouth wrapped around him was enough to have him almost losing it now, but he had plans. Many, many plans.

He got back on the bed, settling over her body and between her thighs. He seriously thought it just might be his favorite place in the world to be.

But when he pushed inside her, he realized *that* was his favorite place to be.

He kissed her, needing his mouth working over hers as he thrust his hips over and over again. They moved together for God only knew how long. Her legs coming up and wrapping around his waist, letting him go deeper.

But he wanted more.

He wanted everything.

He wanted it all.

She came about a second before him, his mouth still over hers, taking her screams of pleasure and feeling them all the way to his bones.

This was what he'd been looking for. *This* was what he hadn't been able to find anywhere else. *This* was what he wanted. Needed. And he'd only ever find it with Hannah.

Because she was the love of his life.

The only woman there had ever been, the only woman there would ever be.

She survived on logic, but there was no logic in love. And he was going to do his damnedest to prove it to her. *This* was the real thing, and she needed to realize it, too.

He pulled back to catch his breath, but lost it just as quickly when her eyes opened slowly and focused on him. Her hands came up to his face, her fingers trailing down either side of his jaw.

She was wide open to him. He knew this wasn't meaningless. Knew there were more emotions running behind those eyes than even she knew how to deal with. But she wasn't running this time.

No, she was tracing his lips with her fingertips.

"Kiss me." It was a plea, and he understood it completely. A need so strong that it was painful.

He leaned down, barely brushing his lips with hers.

"Don't break my heart again, Nathanial Shepherd," she whispered against his mouth.

"Same goes for you, Hannah Sterling."

* * *

Shep slid inside of Hannah, and her back arched off the bed as she cried out.

She was lost in him. In his kisses and his hands. Lost in how he moved over her. In her. Through her.

They'd been at it for hours.

Hours.

She wasn't sure how long they dozed before they reached for each other again. The storm raged around them, lightning tearing up the sky, as their sweat-soaked bodies moved together. It was perfect.

So.

Damn.

Perfect.

This man knew her body better than anyone ever had. Knew where to touch, where to linger, where to kiss, and nip, and bite. Knew how to make her moan, how to make her scream.

She was going to lose her voice by morning.

There'd been no doubt in her mind when she'd asked him to stay that this time around would be different. No more running or hiding. No more ignoring it, acting like things weren't happening, praying that her feelings didn't exist.

Because they did exist, like a giant neon arrow pointing toward the one man who'd gotten to her. He was the only man who'd ever gotten her body and her soul. And tonight she was giving in to him.

Again.

And again.

And again.

* * *

It wasn't the bright lights from overhead that woke Shep up the next morning. No, it was the shivering woman burrowing into his side. The power had come back on, kicking on the air conditioner and setting the fan above them into motion.

He had no idea how long they'd been asleep, but when they'd passed out they hadn't bothered with any covers. No need as they'd been hot and sweaty.

Which wasn't the case now. Hannah was cold and seeking out heat from him. He looked at the foot of the bed, searching for a cover of some sort, but everything had been kicked off in their endeavors.

He couldn't even stop the grin that spread across his face. Hannah had had no problems keeping up with him throughout the night. She'd wanted him just as much as he'd wanted her.

He reluctantly pulled himself away from her, but he didn't get very far.

"No," she mumbled into his chest. "Cold. Don't leave me."

He stilled for a second at her words. If he had his way, he wasn't going anywhere that she wasn't. "Not leaving." He kissed the top of her head before he pulled out from underneath her.

She made a sound of protest as she curled up into a ball in the middle of the bed. The blankets were in a pile on the floor, and when he went to grab them, a little gray head stuck out from the top.

"Meow." Henry stretched before he crawled out of the blankets. He sat back on his heels, staring at Shep for a second before he let out another long, loud *meooooow.*

"Ughhh, noooo." Hannah groaned from the bed. "Sleep. Need sleep."

Shep pulled the blanket from the floor and threw it over Hannah. "I got it," he said as he kissed her head again. His words were unnecessary; she'd already fallen back asleep.

He grabbed his boxer briefs from his pile of clothes on the floor and pulled them on.

"Come on, cat. Let's get you fed."

Henry trotted out in front, his little gray tail in the air. Shep blinked his eyes a few times, trying to get used to the bright light streaming in through the windows. The storm had definitely passed, and the sun was out in full force. He couldn't be sure of the exact time, as both the clock on the stove and microwave were blinking, but if he had to guess, it was somewhere around nine.

He had no idea how much sleep he'd gotten. There'd been no concept of time when he'd been in that bed with Hannah. Nor did he care. He could sleep when he was dead. He had years to make up for.

Years.

He pulled a can of food out of the pantry and popped the top, pouring the contents in a clean dish he found on the counter. The cat pounced on the food the second it was on the floor.

"I swear you'd think I never feed him." Hannah's voice filled the kitchen, more than a little bit raspy.

Shep looked up as she made her way over to him. She was wearing his T-shirt from last night. It hit her midthigh, and was more than slightly rumpled from being on the floor. Her hair was a glorious mess of soft red tangles, and they framed her sleepy face. She was wearing her glasses, but her eyes were barely open. She was apparently struggling with the light as well.

"I thought you wanted more sleep."

Her arms wrapped around his waist, and she leaned her head against his bare chest. "Wanted you more."

And that was the second time in five minutes that her words had him coming up short.

"I like the sound of that." He ran his hands up and down her back, and she snuggled into him. He buried his nose in her hair and inhaled deeply.

"I wanted coffee, too."

* * *

The laugh that burst out of Shep blew through Hannah's hair, making her shiver. She hadn't quite gotten over the chill she'd had that morning. This was why she'd vacated that bed after he left; she wanted the warmth from his body. Something she was currently getting.

Mission accomplished.

"Need to check the state of your refrigerator first. Power was out for a little so you might have to toss some stuff."

"I better not. I just bought all of that." She groaned. "And I hate grocery shopping."

"Well, aren't you delightful in the mornings?"

She pulled back and looked up at him, frowning. "Normally I am, but somebody kept me up most of the night." A smile fought the corner of her mouth.

"I didn't hear you complaining, and if I remember correctly, you were instigating just as much as I was." He leaned back against the counter for support, his hands at her hips, holding on to her.

Her smile won over, a grin breaking through. "This is true," she said as she ran her hand down his chest. It had been about a fifty-fifty split.

She took a moment to look at him. *Really* look at him, and oh boy was there a lot to look at. She hadn't exactly gotten to admire much of his body last night. Well, not with sight at least, because there'd been plenty of admiring that body in other ways.

But now she could fully appreciate it in the light of day, and she was going to do just that. She grasped his forearms as she leaned back, her eyes moving down the length of him. He was wearing a pair of black boxer briefs that left absolutely nothing to the imagination. The bulge pressing against the thin cotton fabric was…impressive. That was the only word for it.

And that wasn't the only thing that was drawing her attention.

He had huge thighs, strong and muscular, powerful. Damn were they ever powerful. The feel of him moving between her legs was branded into her brain. Hell, he'd done it for most of the night.

"Like what you see?" he asked.

Her eyes went back up to his and she shrugged her shoulders unabashedly. "Yes."

"I like what I see, too." He pulled the T-shirt up slowly, baring more of her thighs to his gaze. When he was able to see the light purple fabric of her panties, he grinned. "I like that even more."

"Stop it." She lightly swatted his hands, and the fabric fell back down around her thighs. "I'm going to need more recovery time than that before the next round."

His eyes came back up to hers, and his grin widened. "Now, those are future plans I approve of."

"That so?"

"That *is* so. Come here." He pulled her in to his chest again, and she rested her head over his heart.

She looked down at her hand running up and down his left forearm. She watched as her fingers traced over the intersecting shepherd's rod and staff that had been tattooed into his skin.

Shepherd's tools for a Shepherd.

She'd seen these before, along with the wolf in the forest at the back of this arm. But the portion between his elbow and shoulder was a blank canvas waiting to be covered.

She pulled back slightly from his body to continue her exploration. He kept his hands firmly on her hips, preventing her from moving out of the space between his legs.

She reached out and touched his chest. His left pectoral muscle jumped when her fingers glided over it. She traced the pair of dog tags and the chain that stretched up to his left shoulder, going all the way to the soaring eagle and out to the tips of his wide wings.

"Owen?" she whispered, looking up into his face.

"Yeah." He nodded, sadness flickering in his eyes. "Finn has the same one."

"When did you get it?"

"The first anniversary of his death."

She shifted over to his right arm. The Superman emblem she remembered had been incorporated into the sails of a pirate ship that was sailing through stormy seas. Blue and green waves crashed up and around the base, and an anchor took up the majority of the back of his arm.

"That one took a couple of months, the longest one to finish." Not all that shocking, as it covered the entirety of his upper arm.

"The meaning?" Her eyes flickered back up to his.

He let go of her hip with one of his hands and reached up, brushing her hair back from her shoulder. He went up to her neck, his fingers running across her skin.

"The battle between man and nature. Sailing stormy seas. Surviving the infinite abyss."

"So they make it out alive?"

"I like to think so," he said seriously, his fingers tracing her ear and making her shiver.

"So there's some hope in there?" she asked, trying to get

control of herself. If he kept touching her like this, she had a feeling that recuperating was going to be taken off the table.

"Babe, there's hope everywhere."

Something about the pure honesty in his eyes and voice made her look away. She couldn't handle it at the moment. It was like staring into the sun, so she returned her gaze to his arm.

The blue and green waves continued down past his elbow until they got to the flowers. The different colored blossoms looked like they were floating in the waters on the side and back of his arm. The majority of his forearm was taken up by a compass. The North Star was at its center, and a banner with the words *I'll Always Find Home* weaved back and forth above and below it.

"When did you get this one?"

"I was twenty. It was the first one that was plainly visible, and my mom freaked out. She was only slightly placated when I told her this flower was for her," he said as he pointed to the bloom at the top. "Yellow because of her blonde hair."

"So the colors are significant. Do they all represent somebody different?" she asked as she studied them.

"Yes, important women in my life."

Women? She shouldn't do it. Shouldn't keep asking about this tattoo. Should move on.

"Who's this one?" she asked, pointing to the blue that was directly in the center of the back of his arm.

Curiosity killed the cat.

"Grandma Ella."

"Blue because of her eyes." Her head came up and she looked into his face. "*Your* eyes."

"Yes." He nodded. "The orange is my aunt Marigold, because of her name." He apparently figured out that she wanted them all explained. She looked to the flowers again, jumping from bloom to bloom and tracing the petals with her fingers at his words. "Green is my cousin Meredith because she was born in May, so an emerald birthstone, plus it's her favorite color. The pink is Grace because she was and always will be a princess. Periwinkle is Lula Mae, as that's her favorite color. The dark purple is Claire, Brendan and Grace's mother."

He'd explained all of them except for one. Heart hammering hard in her throat, she went to the red one that was over his right wrist. She'd only glanced at it before, but as she studied it now, she noticed the green detailing in the petals.

"That's you," he said softly.

She had no idea where it came from, but tears burned her throat. She couldn't swallow. Couldn't breathe. She just stood there staring at the flower. But when she blinked, it went blurry and a tear splashed down onto his arm, quickly followed by another. And another.

"Hannah." He touched her chin, gently pushing up, but she fought it, turning her head to the side.

For thirteen years she'd told herself he hadn't ever really cared about her. Never really loved her. She'd been wrong.

He'd inked it on his skin. It was there. *She* was there, permanently.

She wanted to run. To disentangle herself from his grasp and get the hell out of there. Somehow she didn't do either, but she wasn't quite sure how she managed it. Maybe it was the steady weight of his hand at her side, his fingers wrapped in the fabric of the T-shirt.

She was in his hands again, his mouth at her ear, his breath on her skin as he spoke the words, "I *never* got over you."

She couldn't...she just couldn't deal with this. It was more than just the numbing sadness; it was the mind-bending anger.

Those were two emotions that were hard enough to deal with on their own; combined was a force beyond her.

She put her palms on his chest and pushed away, trying to step back, needing space before she suffocated

"Hannah, look at me." He caught her hands and held her in place.

"I can't. Please don't." She pulled at her hands uselessly, and though he wasn't holding on tight enough to hurt her, he was succeeding in not letting her run.

He spun, pushing her up against the counter, caging her in, trapping her with his body. He bent his knees, putting his face right in front of hers. His eyes locked on to hers and didn't let go. "I told you to stop fighting me last night, and you said you couldn't anymore."

"I know, but you said here and now. Not *then*. I can't...I can't deal with that yet."

"The past? Why?"

Why? *Why?* Because it hurt so much it was crippling.

The fear that came over his face was immediate. "What are you not telling me?"

Here it was, the opportunity to tell him everything. To tell him about their baby that had never been. To tell him about the loss and the pain. Oh God, the pain. Hours of feeling like something was being ripped out of her. And even when the physical pain was gone, the emotional had lingered. Most of her heart had gone along with that baby.

And then there'd been that damn phone call. That had been it, the final nail in the coffin. She'd needed him more than she'd ever needed anyone in her life, and he'd been with somebody else.

Yet he'd just told her he'd never moved on. How was that even possible? It didn't make any sense and it infuriated her.

"I…I…" What? She what?

"Talk to me."

"Who was she?" The question was out of her mouth before she even realized it. Not all that shocking, as it had plagued her for years.

"Who was who?"

"The girl who was with you when I called?"

His grip on her faltered, and he took a step back from her, reaching up and running his hands through his hair. "I don't even know." He shook his head, the shame radiating off of him evident.

It pissed her off even more.

"You don't know? How can you not know?" Her voice went up of its own volition. She had no control of it whatsoever.

"I was fucked up when you left, Hannah. Really fucked up. I distracted myself with alcohol and girls."

"So you drowned your sorrows and then screwed yourself into oblivion?"

"I'm not proud of it."

"It doesn't change it. Dammit, Shep! I still hear that girl's voice in my head, and you don't even know who she was. Do you have any idea how much that messes with my head? I'm sorry that you were fucked up, but so was I. And I had nothing, *nothing,* to distract myself. And I've had to deal with it. For thirteen years I've had to deal with the idea that I meant nothing to you."

Anger flashed in his eyes. "Stop saying that. It was *never* the case."

"But I didn't know it!"

"What was I supposed to do? You left. You walked out of this town, away from me, and didn't look back. How the hell was I supposed to know? How was I supposed to know there was still a possibility of anything? I thought it was done. I thought *we* were done. So tell me, Hannah, what do you want?"

"I don't know!" Her chest was heaving, her eyes still burning, and her heart wouldn't stop thundering in her ears.

She couldn't process all of the things he'd just said. Or how she was feeling. So it should've come as no surprise that she really didn't understand what she did next. There was no logic anywhere; there never was with him.

She took a step forward and grabbed his face, kissing him hard.

The fact of the matter was she *was* starting to figure out exactly what she wanted. She'd spent far too many years without it. Without him. She wanted Shep, and she was going to take him for all he was worth.

He bent down, grabbing her thighs and pulling up. Her legs wrapped around his waist and he carried her through the house, straight to the bedroom.

He had both of them stripped down, her on her back, him between her thighs and inside her in moments.

Nothing about how he moved was slow. There was a desperate need coming from both of them. They apparently hadn't gotten everything out the night before.

She didn't think they ever really would. What had Grace said? That there wasn't enough time in a day to make up for lost time?

She understood that entirely.

"I want this," she gasped as she looked up into his eyes. "I want *us*." She didn't add on the *for as long as it lasts* that was at the tip of her tongue, though.

Here and now. Stay in the here and now.

Chapter 14

An Itty-Bitty Mint-Green Bikini

The need for something beyond caffeine forced Shep and Hannah to leave the inn. Sure she had some food, but neither of them were all that interested in cooking at the moment. He would've preferred to keep her in a constant state of undress, but sustenance was a necessity. And they should get out of the house, otherwise they were going to screw themselves into an early grave.

What a way to die.

They took a shower together before they headed out, and Shep quickly discovered one of his new favorite pastimes.

Her hands glided over his soapy chest and up to the back of his head. She kept getting distracted as she lathered up the shampoo in his hair.

He had absolutely no complaints.

The hot water rained down around them, steam filling the bathroom. Her nails raked his scalp, and he was pretty sure his eyes rolled into the back of his head. Who knew washing his hair could be complete and total ecstasy?

It also didn't hurt that her very warm and wet body pressed up against his accompanied the experience.

This was how he needed to start every day for the rest of his life.

Hannah might not be allowed to think about the future, but it didn't mean that he couldn't. And really, he didn't care what happened as long as they were together. She just needed to realize that, too. They'd figure it out.

They had to.

When all of the suds had been washed from his hair, he bent his head down to hers, needing her mouth. He reached around, palming her ass in his hands and holding her firmly against him.

"If you do that, we're never going to get out of here," she said against his lips.

"And that's a problem?"

"Not at all."

"Good," he said as he took full advantage of the situation at hand.

It was about thirty minutes before they were heading out the door. As they were going to be among the living, even for a little while that day, he needed to get a clean change of clothes. This was something he had mixed feelings about. As Hannah had worn his shirt for most of the morning, it smelled like her. Words couldn't express how much he loved that.

They headed over to his house, the sun so damn bright it was ridiculous. Apparently, even Mother Nature was smiling just as widely as he was.

Finn's big blue truck was absent from the front of the house when Shep pulled in. As the two of them had opposite schedules, it wasn't all that shocking that Finn wasn't there. But as it was a

Sunday, Shep had expected him to be lounging around the house in boxers and eating everything in sight, as was the norm.

It wasn't that Shep didn't love the guy. He did, dearly. But Shep had been living on his own for ten years, and having a roommate was not something he'd signed on for. But how was he supposed to kick his little brother out?

Another reason Shep was glad Finn wasn't there was because Finn hadn't exactly been positive about Hannah being back in town. He'd made it perfectly clear that he thought Shep messing around with her was a bad idea.

Finn was just going to need to learn that Shep wasn't *messing around*. It was better that they had that conversation when Hannah wasn't there anyway. But there was no need to worry about it at the moment. He'd deal with that later.

There were more important things to concentrate on, like the woman next to him. As he helped her out of Lois, he was tempted to push her up against the car and kiss her. But if he did that, they'd probably stay at it for a good long while, and the last thing he needed was to get distracted again.

"I forgot how beautiful this place was," Hannah said as they made their way up the front steps to the house.

The two-story A-frame stood on stilts, the Gulf of Mexico stretched out behind it. Dark gray shingles covered the roof, while the wood paneling in the front and back was a lighter gray. The doors and windows popped with their bright red paint. It had seen its fair share of repairs in the last fifty years. There'd also been a few remodels, the kitchen and bathrooms being the biggest changes.

But even with those differences, it still had Owen's touch running through it.

"When did you move in?" she asked as he opened the door for

her and she walked through, turning to look at him as he followed her inside.

"Three years ago. Ella couldn't handle living on her own after Owen died, and there was no question of selling. That just wasn't going to happen."

She nodded thoughtfully before she turned around and walked down the hallway, passed the small den on the left and the bathroom and storage to the right. As it went with most houses on the water, the view was at the back of the house. Owen had used it to its full advantage, splitting the downstairs in half. The kitchen was to the right, the living room to the left. The rooms flowed together perfectly, one big space filled with natural light.

Glass windows composed more than half of the back wall, showing the water in all of its glory. Even though the house wasn't on the sandy beaches, it still had a mighty fine view of the Gulf of Mexico. The tide came in and out, the sea grass forming a sort of marsh when it was high and a muddy trap when it was low.

Three bedrooms and two more bathrooms were upstairs, the master getting the benefit of the back of the house.

"Does it make it easier or harder, living here?" she asked, turning to him.

"Both. It's the same as the bar. It makes it easier in some ways because I'm in a place that he built with his own hands, and it's like a part of him is living on. But at the same time, he isn't here anymore. And that's still hard."

"Yeah," she said, looking away from him.

He crossed the room to her, standing in front of her. He reached out, running his palms up her arms. "Hannah?"

She looked up at him a wealth of sadness in her eyes.

"What's up, babe?"

Her mouth quirked to the side in a bittersweet fashion. "I feel like that at the inn sometimes. Like Gigi is a part of it. It's ridiculous really. It was only a couple months out of the thirty years that I spent with her, but she's still...there."

"It's not ridiculous at all." He shook his head. "It's the last thing she left you. The last thing you have of her."

It was on the tip of his tongue to ask if she'd figured out what she was going to do with the inn, but he kept the question to himself. It wasn't the time or place.

Hannah was thinking about her grandmother, letting the grief take hold for just a moment. He had a feeling this was something she didn't do all that often, that she avoided the grief.

It was very different for him. He'd never been able to run from his grief. He'd just had to feel it, as he was pretty sure he wouldn't have survived if he'd buried it deep. The pain would've turned into a bomb and destroyed him.

There was also something to be said about having a massive support system around him. He had friends and family. Hannah's family left something to be desired, and her friends didn't sound all that much better.

"You know I'm still here when you're ready to talk."

"I know."

She still wasn't there yet, apparently. She could give him her body now, no problem. But her heart and her mind? That was going to take more time.

That was fine. He had patience. He'd wait for the rest of his life if he had to. What other choice did he have?

But right now he knew she needed space, so he'd give it to her.

"Okay." He leaned in, pressing his lips to her forehead before he pulled back. "I'm going to run upstairs and change. You good here?"

"Yeah." She gave him a small smile, the sadness still lingering in her eyes. There was only so much that could be hidden when you pushed the pain down. "If I go up there when you're changing, we probably won't go anywhere for a while."

"This is true." He kissed her on the mouth before he took a step away from her and headed toward the steps.

"Shep?"

He turned to look at her, and that small smile on her lips was just a little bit bigger. "You should bring your toothbrush and a change of clothes...or a few."

"On it." He turned and practically sprinted up the stairs.

Well, at least there was some progress. And really it was a good thing she wanted him to stay at the inn, because he'd already been planning on it.

* * *

Hannah had about ten minutes to recover from the conversation she'd had with Shep. It was just enough time, and she appreciated him giving it to her.

She wasn't ready to talk about Gigi yet...She wasn't ready to talk about a lot of things yet. But she'd get there. Sooner or later.

Maybe.

She spent the time looking around his space and was distracted with a dark wooden cabinet in the corner of the kitchen. The doors were clear glass, so she was able to see inside. It was stocked with more than a hundred brown beer bottles. Each shelf was filled, different colors of bottle caps distinguishing the groups. There were about eight sets of caps.

Footsteps echoed down the stairs, and she turned to see Shep making his way into the room. His green T-shirt was rumple free, and his jeans were light blue and worn soft in all of the right places.

It took everything in Hannah to not lick her lips.

"Storing up for the winter?" She waved her hand at the cabinet.

"Not exactly. Those are my home brews."

"You brew beer?" she asked, fascinated. Throwing together a soup was beyond her skill set, so the concept of brewing beer was akin to rocket science in her brain.

"I've dabbled in it."

"This doesn't look like dabbling. It looks like an investment. Is it any good?"

"I sure as hell think so." He threw the bag next to the couch and crossed the room to her.

"Well, I want to try it. Can you bring some with us?"

"You know, you don't have to get me drunk to get lucky."

She raised her eyebrows at him and frowned. "Do you think about anything besides sex?"

He looked up at the ceiling, thinking, before he dropped his gaze back to her. "With you around? Very little else crosses my mind."

"Well, calm yourself, buddy."

"Did you just call me *buddy*?" he asked, coming to an abrupt halt.

"Yes, I did. And there's nothing you can do about it." She shook her head and smiled sweetly.

"Oh really? I wouldn't be too sure about that. If I remember correctly, you're very ticklish just under your ribs."

That sure wiped the smile off her face. She held up her hands and took a step back. "You wouldn't." She hated, *hated*, being tickled.

"Wouldn't I, though, Hannah?" He held up his hands in the air, wiggling his fingers at her.

She took another step back nice and slow before she turned and bolted. Where she was going she had no idea, but she didn't get farther than the living room. He caught her up around the waist and had her down on the sofa in a matter of seconds. Then she was pinned beneath him, his legs locking hers down and both of her hands held above her head in one of his. His other hand was at her side.

She laughed hysterically as she squirmed. "No, no, noooo! Stooooop!"

"Concede."

"Never!"

Words from what seemed like years ago echoed in her head. *I never concede. Not to you or anyone. Not again. Not ever.*

She'd said a lot of things that first night she'd seen him at the bar. One, that she didn't want him calling her *babe*. Well, that obviously hadn't been the truth. That little term of endearment made her feel all warm and tingly.

Two was that he needed to stop acting like he still knew her. That had been proven wrong. Spectacularly so. He did still know her, better than anyone else, in fact. She liked it just as much as it scared the crap out of her.

Third was she'd wanted him to stop bossing her around like she was his little woman. Okay, she'd be lying if she didn't admit to maybe, possibly, liking his he-man macho stuff...sometimes. Besides, she gave it right back to him most of the time with her own bossiness. So she could handle him taking away her keys and opening the door for her.

Last was the whole not conceding thing. But hadn't she already conceded to him in every other way?

It was remarkable that all of these thoughts flashed through her brain in an instant, especially in her current state of duress. It could never be said that Hannah Sterling wasn't more than capable of multitasking.

It just went to show how significant it was that Shep could obliterate this ability when he was moving inside of her. Because there was absolutely no multitasking when he was making her come. She wasn't even coherent in those moments.

Though she wasn't all that coherent now.

"I...I can't...I can't breathe," she gasped.

"Give up."

"No!" She squirmed harder, but it didn't matter. He was unrelenting.

"Well, isn't this special?" a voice said somewhere to their left.

Shep immediately stopped, letting go of Hannah as he sat up and pulling her vertical with him. She looked over to find Finn standing in the entryway of the living room, a big old frown on his face.

"Hello, Finn," she said more than somewhat awkwardly. Really, what else could it be? Shep was still straddling her, and she was breathing like she'd just run a marathon.

"Hey." The word might've been clipped, but it seemed to linger in the air.

Shep's body tensed. "What's wrong?"

Finn just shook his head before he turned and headed upstairs, his boots echoing dully every step of the way.

Shep tracked his brother's progress while Hannah watched Shep. The frown at his mouth was etched with a certain amount of agitation, but there was worry there, too.

He turned to look at her, his hands running up her sides. "I'll be right back. Pack some of those bottles up for us to take."

He kissed her on the nose before he got up and headed for the stairs.

* * *

It was obvious that something was going on with Finn, but that didn't excuse the cold shoulder he'd just given Hannah.

He pushed open the bedroom door just as Finn pulled his T-shirt over his head and threw it to the ground. The bedroom floor was littered with dirty clothes. His brother was a slob. Apparently, laundry wasn't his forte either, much like grocery shopping.

There wasn't a lack of dedication in the Shepherd family. All of them had their passions. But Finn's was of a different make and model. He'd get so focused on one thing that other stuff fell to the wayside. Like normal everyday tasks. His focus was one of the reasons he'd graduated at the top of his class and he was a damn good veterinarian.

Still.

That didn't make up for him being a shitty human being at the moment.

"You want to explain to me what the hell that was down there?"

"Knock much?" Finn asked as he kicked off his boots.

"It's my house, jackass."

"It's Owen and Ella's house. You were just the first to take over."

Shep was more than taken aback by the bitterness and anger that was radiating off of Finn. This wasn't like his little brother at all. He generally had the same good nature as the rest of the family. Not today.

"What crawled up your ass and died?"

"It's the first Sunday of the month."

"Shit." Shep closed his eyes and shook his head. They'd made a point to keep up with their brunch tradition with Owen when both of them were in town. "I'm sorry."

"Too busy getting laid this morning?"

Shep's eyes snapped open instantly. "Fuck you."

"What the hell are you doing with her anyway? There was an expiration date on anything before she even walked into town. She's just going to leave again without any regard for you, and you're going to be more messed up than you were last time. I really hoped you were beyond making stupid decisions with her. Apparently you can't think straight when you throw your dick into the mix."

"You need to stop now. You have no idea what's going on with us."

"*Us?*" Finn scoffed. "You need to open your eyes to the reality of the situation. There is no *us* when it comes to you and her. You're separate entities. The hotshot lawyer from New York and the tattooed roughneck who serves up alcohol for a living."

Shep stood there in stunned silence. He couldn't believe what his brother had just said. Nor, it seemed, could Finn. The hardness is his face faltered for just a second.

But Shep didn't give him a chance to say anything. "As previously stated, you can go fuck yourself. I'm done talking to you, Finn."

He turned and walked out of the room, needing to get the hell away from his little brother before he punched his fist through a wall. He headed back downstairs to find Hannah standing behind the couch, shifting from foot to foot as she watched him.

And this was another thing that pissed him off. Finn had made Hannah uncomfortable in Shep's house. *Shep's* house. And what the hell had that been about? *It's Owen and Ella's house.*

Whatever, Finn could be a jackass all he wanted. Shep didn't have to deal with it.

"Everything okay?"

"Nothing for you to worry about. Come on. Let's go." He grabbed the bags from the floor before he reached out and took her hand, leading her toward the front door.

* * *

Hannah didn't push Shep to talk, but she knew he was upset. She hadn't been able to hear the conversation between him and his brother, but certain things had carried down the stairs. Like when Shep had told Finn to "fuck off."

Shep was pretty good at masking his facial expressions, but the tension hadn't left his body. No, it had all just gone to his shoulders, where it stayed all through brunch and their trip to the Piggly Wiggly for more groceries.

He was hell bent on making her something fancy for dinner. Besides, if he was going to be staying with her, they were going to need more than sandwich fixings.

When they got back to the inn, they unloaded all of the groceries and cleared out some space in the fridge.

"I'm going to take this out," he said, tying up the trash bag and heading for the door.

She watched him walk away, a weird little flutter in her belly. The whole afternoon had been positively domestic. This feeling was becoming more commonplace when she was around him, and she still didn't know how she felt about it.

She reached back and gathered her hair into her hands, twisting it and pulling it up. The back of her neck was hot and sweaty and her hair was sticking to her skin. It was either from the humid weather or the freak-out she was trying to keep at bay.

Or both.

She headed toward the bathroom in search of a hair tie when she spotted her mint-green bikini hanging on the back of the door. Well, a dip in the ocean would be a nice little way to cool off, and Shep shirtless would be the perfect sort of distraction.

She changed quickly, dropping her shorts and panties to the floor before pulling on the bottoms. She'd just gotten the top on when Shep called her name.

"In here." She was adjusting the clasp at the back of the strapless top when he stepped into the room, stopping dead in his tracks.

His eyes slowly ran down her body, taking everything in before he made the return journey up, a smile splitting his mouth

"Want to go swimming?" she asked.

"Babe, I'm down for any and all activities that involve you in that bikini."

"That so?"

"Absolutely."

For the most part Hannah was pretty comfortable in her own skin. Maybe it was because the first man she'd ever given her body to had worshipped it. And Shep's actions since she'd been back proved that he was of the same mind-set despite the changes to it. So what if her ass had gotten bigger or if her breasts weren't as perky as they were when she was seventeen?

She lifted her hands above her head and spun around slowly in what she hoped came off as a seductive move. Based off the way Shep's eyes dilated when she looked at him, she figured she'd succeeded.

"I'm sorry. My brain short-circuited for a second there. Could you please do that again?"

"Well, since you asked so nicely." She lifted her arms and repeated the move. She knew each and every place that his gaze lingered.

She turned to face him again, and a new tension had overtaken his body. His fists were clenched at his sides and his breathing was uneven. He took a step back, his eyes still on her body, before he shook his head and left the bathroom.

"Where are you going?" she called out after him, grinning.

"Need a second."

"For what?"

"To learn some self-control. I'd really like to do something today that doesn't involve you flat on your back."

Well, didn't that open the door to all sorts of possibilities.

Hannah grabbed the sunblock from the counter before she headed into the bedroom. Shep was standing by the bed, pulling a pair of red swim trunks out of his bag. She walked past him, heading for the chair in the corner, where her cover-up was thrown over the arm. She didn't get very far before Shep snatched her up and pulled her onto the bed.

He kissed her, his tongue dipping in and tangling with hers, before he pulled back and looked down at her.

"I thought you said you didn't want me flat on my back."

"No." He shook his head, his hair falling in his eyes. "I always want you flat on your back. Or really in any position where I'm inside you, but just touching will have to do." He bent his head, kissing her lightly on the mouth again. "Might as well make the most of this situation."

He reached over and grabbed the lotion from her hand before he sat back, moving his legs so he was straddling her. He held up the bottle, waggling his eyebrows.

He grabbed the bottom of the swimsuit top, pulling it down around her ribs and exposing her chest. He cupped one of her breasts in his palm, running his finger across her nipple. "These seem bigger than I remember."

She laughed, reaching down and cupping him. "Interesting, I was thinking the same thing about you."

"Oh, the sweet things you say to me." He grinned.

She moved her fingers back and forth for a second before he pulled her hand away.

"Behave," he said as he placed her hand on the bed. Then he popped the top of the bottle and poured a generous amount of lotion into his hand. He tossed the bottle on the bed before he rubbed his palms together, warming the lotion before he reached down.

His hands started at her shoulders, working the lotion into her skin. He grabbed her right arm first, pulling it up and covering her upper arm before moving to her forearm. Then to her hand, where he worked her wrist and each of her fingers and then massaged it into her palm.

Her right hand was only slightly sore from when she hurt it, but his gentle ministrations felt like magic. He repeated the process with her left arm, all the way down to her hand, where his fingers moved between hers.

He put her hand down on the bed before he grabbed the bottle again, filling his palms with more lotion. He went to her collarbone, his fingers moving in soft, circular motions. It was taking everything in her not to close her eyes and just feel, but there was something amazing about watching Shep, the delight in his eyes as he explored her body. She just couldn't look away.

She knew what was next as he looked down at her chest, his

tongue darting out and licking his lips. He'd repeated the warming motion with the lotion, but it was still cool when he touched her breasts. When he ran his fingers around her nipples, she shivered, and it had very little to do with the temperature.

His hands opened wide and he palmed her breasts, massaging them. She couldn't stop her body from bucking.

He looked up at her, the heat in his eyes overwhelming. "This feel good?"

"Yes, but I don't think you need to put the lotion where the bathing suit goes."

"You complaining?"

"Never." She moved her arms up above her head, stretching out beneath him.

"Perfect." He reached for her top and started to pull it lower. "Though I don't think I thought this out very well."

"The clasp is at the back."

"Problem solved." He spun it around, undoing the clasp and pulling it from her body. He threw it somewhere on the bed above her head.

And then his hands were on her again, his fingers tracing her ribs. This time she did close her eyes, giving in to the pleasure of it. Shep worked the lotion into her skin with skilled movements that had her melting into the bed.

When he got to her belly, he ran his fingers around her belly button and out to her sides. Her eyes opened as he put lotion onto her tattoo. She tried not to tense up as he traced the feathers in gentle strokes.

"You know, I had to explain all of my tattoos, but you've still yet to explain this one. I don't believe that it means nothing."

Explain it? How the hell was she supposed to do that? How was she supposed to explain that it represented a baby they'd created? A baby that had been lost? A loss that he still didn't know about?

She *still* wasn't ready.

She sucked her bottom lip into her mouth, and some of the heat disappeared from Shep's eyes.

Okay. She had to say something. Something…

"It was after Gigi's first stroke." This was true. "And I was feeling…lost. Broken." Also true. Though the brokenness had to do with the miscarriage, too…and a little bit of Shep.

"So, a broken wing."

"Yeah."

"You can't fly with a broken wing." He looked down, watching as he continued to trace the feathers.

"I know."

His eyes came back up to hers. "Babe, you need to learn how to fly again."

Her breath caught as she looked at him. *How the hell am I supposed to do that?*

Shep leaned down, bracing his hands on either side of her head. His face hovered just inches above hers. "We'll figure it out," he said before he pressed his mouth to hers.

Yet again, he'd known exactly what she was thinking. It was a good thing he couldn't read all of her thoughts. Otherwise she'd be totally screwed.

Though part of her knew she already was.

* * *

They finally made it out onto the beach about an hour later. It had taken Shep a little while to get Hannah nice and covered in suntan lotion. He'd taken his sweet time and loved every second of it. He'd also loved when she'd taken the bottle away from him and proceeded to do the exact same thing to him.

She'd pulled his shirt off his head, massaging the lotion into his shoulders, her hands like magic on his muscles. It had felt incredible, and her fingers had melted away the knots that had formed after his conversation with Finn.

He pushed the whole thing with his brother out of his mind and focused on the red-haired siren in the wet green bikini in front of him. Now, this was the perfect way to spend his day off.

Hannah was smiling as she splashed Shep, taking a step back into the water. The waves lapped at her thighs, and the damp ends of her hair stuck to her shoulders.

"We've already established that you aren't faster than me."

"Have we?" she asked as she took another step back.

"Are you challenging me?"

"Yes."

"Good." He ran toward her, gaining on her quickly and throwing her over his shoulder. She laughed and squirmed as he walked deeper into the gulf.

The ocean was perfect, the cool waters beyond refreshing in the summer heat. When the water reached past his waist, he lightly smacked her butt.

"Hold your breath," he said before he took them beneath the waves.

She sputtered when they surfaced a second later and slid down his body, his hands at her waist guiding her. As she'd worn her contacts, her face was obstruction free, but the bright sun caused her to squint as she looked at him.

"You need to learn that I'm always going to catch you," he said.

Her hands went to his hair, her fingers spearing through the wet strands. "Good. I was counting on it."

She kissed him as he reached down, bringing her legs up and around his waist. He walked farther into the water, pulling them both below the surface, their mouths never separating.

Chapter 15

The City Girl and the Country Boy

Monday morning dawned bright and early, and Shep woke with a cat perched on his chest, swatting at his face.

"You should feel privileged," Hannah mumbled into Shep's shoulder. "He only does that to people he likes." Her leg was thrown over his, and she moved it, her knee riding up the inside of his thigh.

"Who else has he done this to?" he asked, reaching up and scratching Henry behind the ears. The cat's eyes closed, and he started purring in delight.

"Just me," she said as she ran her hand across Shep's lower belly, her nails lightly raking his skin. He was about to start purring like Henry.

"So just people who feed him?"

"Pretty much. What time is it anyway?"

Shep turned to look at the alarm clock on the nightstand next to him. "Eight twenty."

"You just couldn't wait ten more minutes, could you?" she asked the cat. "Come on, let's get up."

At her words, Henry got off of Shep, jumping down from the bed and heading out of the room toward the kitchen. Hannah made to follow, but Shep grabbed her hand, pulling her back down so she was now sprawled across his chest.

"Kiss first," he said against her mouth.

"You're so demanding."

"Only when it comes to you." He gave her a slow, sweet kiss; anything else and they'd be staying in bed for a while.

On second thought...

"Don't even," Hannah said, putting her hands on his chest and pushing away. She threw the covers back and got out of bed. "Dale and Hamilton are going to be here in forty minutes. So nothing inappropriate when they're around."

"They're two teenage boys. Most of what they know is inappropriate."

Actually, that could pretty much be said for men in general. But Shep realized he wasn't going to win the battle. Instead he settled in for the show in front of him, stacking his hands behind his head and watching as she walked her very naked body over to her dresser.

"Then maybe you should be a shining example around them." She opened the top drawer on her dresser, pulling out something that looked purple and would most likely be littering the floor in a few hours.

"What was that?"

She turned to look at him as she put on a bra, covering up those perfect breasts as she hooked it in the back. "Never mind." She rolled her eyes as she pulled up the straps and turned back around. She grabbed a shirt and shorts from the second drawer and started to pull those on. "Maybe you just shouldn't talk when you're in the same room as them."

"Nah. Dale and Hamilton have already been corrupted. They hang out with Bennett far too much."

"Bennett corrupt them? Really? I don't believe it."

"Hey, he's not as sweet and innocent as he looks."

"And neither are you." She grabbed a pair of his pants from the floor and threw them at him. "Get dressed." She shook her head at him, but she wasn't quick enough to cover up her smile before she turned around and walked into the bathroom.

* * *

It was very true that Bennett Hart was not a sweet and innocent guy, but he was definitely a good influence. Proof in point, Dale Rigels.

The kid wasn't even recognizable from how he'd been nine months ago. Last September Dale had been smoking pot, walking around with his pants around his ankles, and wearing a permanent sneer across his face.

But as Shep hadn't exactly dealt with his own grief in the best ways, he understood Dale. Four years ago, a roadside bomb in Afghanistan had taken Vince Rigels's life. He'd left behind his wife and his twelve-year-old son.

At the beginning of the last school year, Bennett had done a project with Mel's math classes. He'd made an impact on many of those kids, most specifically Dale. Now he was drug free, knew how to use a belt, and actually smiled every once in a while.

Another big influence on Dale was his best friend, Hamilton O'Bryan, Mel's little brother. Hamilton had always been a good kid, more interested in music than in getting into trouble. He'd gotten pretty close to his future brother-in-law, idolized him in a lot of ways.

Bennett cared a lot about both of those boys, too. That much was evident, as they would be standing up on that altar when Bennett married Mel. Actually, there would be quite a few people standing up on that altar, Shep included. The wedding party was eighteen, twenty counting the bride and groom.

Not that he wouldn't have a lot of groomsmen at his wedding, but...

Shep shook his head. *Holy shit.* He'd never had a thought like that before. His wedding?

Yeah, maybe he needed to calm himself down...think about something else. He thought about the endless possibilities as he ripped the linoleum from the floors.

As Hannah was more than in love with the tile that was in the kitchen and there was plenty of it left over after Bennett had finished it up, they were going to be using it in some of the bathrooms.

First up was the one attached to Hannah's room.

She'd already made significant progress over the last couple of weeks. The paper had been completely removed from the walls, and she'd painted it a light gray. The color was going to pull out a lot of the tones in the tile.

This was what a well-designed bathroom should look like. Not the hodgepodge that it had been before. Hannah had a good eye, a *very* good eye, and he had no doubt that it was going to look spectacular when it was all said and done.

Shep had laid tile before, when he'd been helping out with work on Jax's house, so he knew what he was doing, but so did Hamilton and Dale. The two kids were working machines, picking up the boxes of tile with ease.

"I see Bennett's weight training is paying off," Shep said as Dale put one of the boxes on the floor.

"Man, you have no idea." Dale wiped the sweat from his fore-head. "He's relentless."

"Oh, believe me, I know. I've worked out with him before."

"That why you don't work out with him anymore?" Hamilton asked, coming into the room with a box of his own and stacking it on top of the other one.

"Yup. Once was enough."

"He's a beast for a reason," Dale said.

"I have a feeling the two of you won't be that far behind if you keep up with what he's got you doing."

"Yeah. It's just a matter of keeping up." Hamilton reached for his water bottle and drained it. No sooner was it empty than Hannah appeared, four chilled bottles in her hands.

"Here you go," she said as she handed them to the boys.

"Thank you, ma'am," Hamilton and Dale said in unison before they started drinking from the fresh bottles.

"There's more in the refrigerator. Help yourselves whenever you need one." She turned to Shep, holding out his bottle. When he went to reach for it, he grabbed her hand instead, pulling her in close.

"Thanks...ma'am," he whispered in her ear.

"Stop it." She pushed at his chest, shaking her head. "Young, impressionable minds, remember."

Dale snorted.

"I wouldn't worry too much about our impressionable minds. We're subjected to my sister and Bennett all the time. Talk about public displays of affection. I swear you'd think those two don't know the meaning of *behind closed doors*."

Hannah couldn't help but laugh. "Do you two have girlfriends?"

"I did, but we broke up," Dale said. "We're better as friends." He shrugged.

"And what about you?" she asked Hamilton.

"Nope. Flying solo."

Dale snorted again.

"What?" Hamilton asked, rounding on his friend.

"Nora," Dale coughed into his hand.

"She's just a friend."

Dale turned to Hannah and Shep, shaking his head. "He's blind. The guy is in love with her."

"I'm sixteen. What the hell do I know about love?" Hamilton protested.

"Ahh, don't discount it based on age." Shep couldn't stop himself from glancing over at Hannah. He'd fallen in love with her when he was only two years older than Hamilton was now. There was no telling when the person you were supposed to be with was going to walk into your life.

The thing was, you just had to make sure that person didn't walk out of it.

If anybody knew that, it was Shep. And he wasn't letting Hannah walk out again. He'd been stupid once and he wouldn't be repeating it.

Not *ever* again.

* * *

Shep woke up with Hannah every single morning that week. They worked with Hamilton and Dale on whatever project she'd lined up for the day, and he'd keep going right up until he'd head in for work.

Hannah's bathroom was completely done within a few days. Bennett came over on Tuesday and sanded down the antique vanity. On Wednesday he stained it, Dale and Hamilton watching his every move and learning exactly how to do it.

Shep had no doubt that after they helped Bennett fix a few

more of those pieces, they'd be able to do it on their own. This was a very good thing, because there were many pieces of furniture in that house that needed some attention.

There were also quite a few that needed to be trashed.

Hannah had hired a company to come in and haul out all of the old mattresses and a good portion of the unfixable furniture. On Thursday, they'd headed up to Tallahassee and he'd helped her pick out a new living room set. On Saturday, the lumpy sofa and floral chair were gone.

On Sunday morning, exactly a week after the blackout, Shep woke up alone. He reached over and ran his hand across the empty sheets. They were still slightly warm, so Hannah hadn't been awake for too long.

Sounds from the kitchen traveled down the hallway and slipped through the cracked door: a pan being pulled from the cabinet and put down on the stove, the coffeemaker beeping a second before the refrigerator door opened.

He rolled out of bed and rubbed the sleep from his eyes. He looked around the room, searching for his boxers, and spotted them on the back of the chair in the corner where Hannah had tossed them not that many hours ago.

He grabbed them before he headed into the bathroom.

When he walked into the kitchen five minutes later, it was to find Hannah in front of the stove, her hair thrown up in a messy bun and wearing his T-shirt from the night before.

She had a habit of wearing his T-shirts, and they'd mysteriously disappear afterward. He'd had to go to his house to pack another bag, because he was apparently clothing both of them from his wardrobe.

"This is a sight I like to see," he said as he wrapped his arms around her waist and buried his face in her neck.

"Me cooking?"

"You cooking half-naked."

She turned her face toward him, and he kissed her, his lips lingering on hers until she broke the kiss, looking back to the stove.

Shep rested his chin on her shoulder and looked down at the pan, where a thin layer of batter cooked. It covered the entirety of the pan, all the way up the edges. "Crepes?" he asked as his hands moved to her thighs, running up and down her bare skin.

"Yup." She pulled the pan from the stove, grabbing the spatula and running it around the edge. The crepe loosened and rolled up as it went down the pan, flopping onto the plate.

"You can't boil pasta, but you can make thin French pancakes?"

"My cooking skills are confined to a frying pan. Grilled cheese or other sandwiches, scrambled eggs, and crepes."

"You never cease to amaze me." He kissed her neck before he pulled back, going to the coffeemaker and pouring a cup. He grabbed the caramel creamer that Hannah loved from the fridge, adding a dash to his before filling the rest of the space with half-and-half.

He leaned back against the counter, watching Hannah cook, and sipped his coffee. She lifted the pan from the stove, tilting it from side to side and spreading the batter out.

"I was thinking we could go riding today." He hadn't been out to the farm all week, and he was itching to get on a horse.

"I'd like that." She looked over at him and grinned. "Oh, I'd like that a lot."

"We can pack some lunch, eat out on the trail."

"A picnic?" She tilted her head to the side thoughtfully. "I'm pretty sure the last time I went for a picnic was with you."

"You and your city life." He shook his head.

"You and your country life," she said as she turned back to the stove.

If only it could be *their* country life.

* * *

Shep had high expectations that the afternoon was going to be awesome. How could it not be with the riding outfit Hannah was wearing? She was in tight jeans that she'd tucked into a pair of high boots. He'd been walking behind her pretty much as soon as she'd come out of the bedroom. He was going to trip and fall on his face if he didn't stop looking at her ass.

It didn't stop him from staring.

When they got to the barn, Shep's aunt Marigold was inside brushing down Betsy, her black-and-white pinto.

Marigold was so much like Ella it was crazy. There was no doubt that they were mother and daughter. Same blonde hair that had gone white with age, same button nose, same golden brown complexion, same sassy demeanor. The only difference was that Marigold had Owen's gray eyes.

Shep put his hand on Hannah's back as he led her over to his aunt. "Hannah, you remember Marigold, my favorite aunt." He let go of Hannah and moved to Marigold, wrapping his arms around her and kissing her on the cheek.

When he pulled back, Marigold was fighting a smile as she shook her head at him. "I'm your only aunt."

"Still my favorite."

The smile took over Marigold's face as she rolled her eyes. Then she turned and wrapped Hannah up in a hug. "It's so good to see you again, sweetheart."

"You too." Hannah's shoulders were tight and unsure at first, but she quickly melted into the hug.

It was something Shep had noticed the last couple of weeks. His friends and family were very quick to hug people, something that Hannah wasn't used to. She'd always be taken aback for just a second when people wrapped their arms around her, and then she'd eagerly accept it, like she was starved for it.

"You two going on a long ride?"

"Probably not too long. City Girl over here hasn't been in a while, so I don't know how much she can handle."

Hannah looked over at him, the challenge clear in her eyes. "I can handle whatever you throw at me, Country Boy."

Marigold laughed. "A girl after my own heart. Well, you two have fun. Stick to the north trail. The river came up high on the west side during that storm on Sunday, and it's still really muddy."

"Yes, ma'am," he said as he headed for the horses at the end of the barn.

It took them a good twenty minutes to get Springsteen and Nigel groomed, saddled, and ready to go. Shep grabbed two helmets and handed one to Hannah. She might not have been riding in a while, but she tightened the strap under her chin with quick efficiency. When she was done, she rounded in front of Springsteen again, scratching his neck and saying something into his ear.

"You whispering sweet nothings to my horse to try to get him to switch allegiances?"

Her eyes came up and landed on him, a smile across that mouth of hers. "Don't you know it. You're my cat's favorite these days, so I'm commandeering your horse." She grabbed Springsteen's reins and led him out of the barn.

This was true, but that was because Shep was usually the first one out of bed and therefore fed Henry more often.

"I don't think that's a fair trade," he called out after her, too focused on her walking away to follow.

"I don't really care."

"She's nothing but trouble," Shep turned and whispered to Nigel. "This is why I love her. But don't tell her."

Nigel moved his muzzle to Shep's ear and let out a huff of air, his way of saying *your secret is safe with me*. Then he shook his head, his black mane moving across his broad back, signaling that he was ready to get the show on the road. Shep scratched his muzzle before he grabbed the reins and followed Hannah and Springsteen outside.

* * *

Hannah exercised regularly; she kind of had to, as kettle-cooked potato chips were a staple sidekick to her sandwiches. Not to mention her sweet tooth attacks when she'd grab more than one pack of Twix. But after two hours on Springsteen, she knew without a doubt she was going to be paying for it the next day.

She'd stretched before they'd headed out, but the twinges were more than present and they were only going to get worse. How could they not when she hadn't gone riding in years?

Well, on a horse, that is. She'd ridden Shep nice and good more than a few times in the last week. The night before being one of them. But her sexcapades had only warmed her muscles a little bit, because, man, was she ever hurting.

She tried not to show weakness, especially in front of Shep, because he would no doubt be unrelenting. She attempted to hide her wince as she got off Springsteen. She was pretty sure she was unsuccessful in this endeavor, but Shep didn't say anything as they unsaddled the horses, brushed them down, and gave them water. Springsteen kept snuffling his nose into her hair through most of the process.

"He wants a treat," Shep said from behind her.

Hannah turned and he handed her a carrot before he headed off to give one to Nigel. She was a little annoyed at how easily he moved. The man obviously wasn't hurting after their little ride, not one little bit.

And he looked too damn sexy for his own good as he walked off. His jeans were a little tighter than the ones he normally wore, and holy hell were they giving her all the dirty thoughts.

All of them.

At least she had that as a distraction.

They led the horses out of the barn and walked them around for a little cooldown before putting them in the pasture.

Hannah leaned against the wooden gate, and Shep came up next to her, putting his boot up on the bottom post. They watched Nigel and Springsteen walk away, joining the other horses grazing on the many acres that stretched out around them.

"So how bad are you hurting?" he asked.

She didn't need to look over at him to know that there was a smug grin on his face, but she looked over at him anyway.

"I'm fine." She shrugged. Somehow even that hurt.

Shep just did his one-eyebrow-raise thing, and as he was wearing his aviators, it made the whole gesture exponentially more appealing.

"Okay." It was beyond obvious that he in no way believed her. "You ready to head back?"

"Sure am." She smiled widely before she turned and headed to the car, twinges be damned.

Well, she'd just show him, wouldn't she?

* * *

Okay, so six hours later Hannah's plan of "showing Shep" wasn't working out all that well.

Or at all.

She was struggling. *Really* struggling. Her abdominal muscles, inner thighs, and rear end felt like they'd been worked over six ways to Sunday. But none of that was as bad as her back.

Though Shep still hadn't said anything, his smug little smile whenever she winced was more than a little obnoxious. She knew he wasn't laughing at her pain but at the fact that she was too stubborn to say anything.

He was only slightly forgiven with his dinner of applewood-bacon-wrapped pork chops, cheddar-cheese mashed potatoes, and asparagus. And then a little bit more than slightly forgiven when he pulled out two slices of dulce de leche cheesecake from Café Lula.

His cooking was freaking phenomenal. She'd never eaten this many home-cooked meals in a row that didn't involve a slice of bread somewhere in the mix.

After dinner, Shep banished her to the living room, where she was able to sit on the new sofa, which had been delivered the day before, and look over a contract that needed immediate attention. It had to be sent back to the office by the following morning. It didn't matter that it was the weekend because those didn't exist.

He kissed her on the cheek, setting a filled glass of red wine on the table next to her, before he went back to the kitchen.

Okay, so maybe she wasn't all that annoyed with him after all.

Hannah turned her attention to the contract in front of her, distracting herself from the pain in her body. She might be very good at multitasking, but she was also very good at focusing.

She'd always had the ability to tune out the world around her when she needed to concentrate on a task at hand.

But it made her somewhat oblivious to her surroundings when she did it.

She'd been working for about an hour when she finished. She sent the document and closed her laptop, taking advantage of Shep's absence and stretching slowly as she stood. She grabbed her glass of wine—she'd been nursing it, so there was still a good amount left—and went to the kitchen, finding it empty, the counters cleaned, and the dishwasher running.

She headed toward the bedroom and heard the sound of running water coming from the bathroom. The door was open, and a shirtless Shep was leaning over the massive tub, which she swore was built for three or four people, not that she'd ever be in there with three or four people.

But being in there with Shep sounded glorious.

She leaned against the doorjamb and sipped her wine as she watched him test the water gushing from the spout. A second later he grabbed a box of salts and added them to the tub. His muscles flexed as he moved, and she noticed a light flickering across his skin.

Lit candles glowed from the counters and shelves on the walls. He'd also hooked up his phone to a set of speakers, and a soft beat filled the room along with the running water.

"Well, isn't this a sight to be seen."

He turned to look at her, and she about swallowed her tongue. His jeans were unbuckled and unzipped, hanging dangerously low on his hips. A nice little smattering of hair stuck out of the waistband of his boxers and stretched up his abs.

She took back her words from a second ago. *This* was a sight to be seen.

"I didn't know you were a bubble bath kind of guy."

"I'm not. There are no bubbles in there, babe. And this"—he gestured at the tub behind him—"is for you. Purely therapeutic for your poor muscles."

"I don't know what you're talking about." She shook her head. "I'm fine." She straightened and winced.

His eyebrows climbed up his forehead. "You still sticking to that?"

"Yup."

"I guess I'll just have to enjoy this bath on my own." His hands went to his hips, where he pushed down his jeans and boxers.

Nope. She'd been wrong again. This was the epitome of all the things: Shep completely naked, his dark brown hair hanging in his eyes, and that heated gaze of his directed at her.

Who would've thought that eyes that blue could be so hot?

And then there was the matter of the situation between his thighs. Even at rest his cock was impressive.

That arrogant grin of his only got bigger. He knew exactly where she'd been staring, not that she'd tried to hide it or anything.

Hello. The man was naked. Her eyes were obviously going to drift to her favorite places.

But he changed the object of her ogling when he turned his back to her, shutting off the tap. Yeah, she could stare at his ass for a long, long time. But even that view came to an end when he climbed into the tub and sat down. He leaned back in the water, his head resting on the ledge, and closed his eyes.

"Damn, this feels good."

Hannah watched him settle into the steaming water for about three more seconds before she gave in to her screaming muscles— and her never-ceasing libido.

Her entire body hurt, and all she wanted to do was jump him. Seriously?

She downed the rest of her wine before she put the glass on the counter, and then pulled her shirt over her head. The shorts she'd changed into earlier dropped to the floor a moment later, quickly followed by her bra and panties.

When she looked up again, she found Shep's eyes on her, no smirk to be seen as he gazed at her naked body.

"Come here." He held his hand out to her, and she moved to him automatically.

He kept her steady as she lifted her foot over the ledge. The instant her toes dipped in to the gloriously hot water, her entire body sighed in relief, and it only got better as she lowered herself inch by inch, past her ankles, her calves, her thighs, and around her belly as he guided her down.

She sat between his spread thighs, and his hands moved slowly up her back. She shivered as goose bumps sprang up across her skin. He gathered her hair and moved it over her shoulder, leaning in and pressing his lips to the top of her spine.

"Lean forward." His breath washed over her skin, and another shiver overtook her body.

She pulled her legs up, bending her knees and wrapping her arms around them as she leaned forward. He moved behind her, and a second later she heard the sound of a bottle being popped open.

He rubbed his hands together before they landed on her back. Lavender filled her nose as his oiled palms moved easily across her skin. He started at her shoulder blades, kneading into her muscles with just the right amount of pressure.

"Oh God," she moaned.

"You can just call me Shep."

Her moan turned into a laugh, more of the tension melting off of her as his hands continued to move down to her lower back. He had magic hands.

Magic.

She wasn't even sure how long he worked her over for, but her muscles were nice and loose when he finished. She rolled over in the water, lying down on his chest. Her legs tangled with his as she pressed her face into his neck, breathing in his spicy scent mixed with the lavender from the salts and oil.

It smelled so damn good.

He added more hot water to the tub, and it reached up to her shoulder blades now. His hands moved up and down along her spine in a slow, lazy pattern. She melted into him, her body sighing in blissful ecstasy.

"I don't ever want to move. Can we just stay here forever?"

His movements faltered for only a second before he continued. He turned his head, pressing a kiss to her temple. "Whatever you want, babe."

She trailed her fingers down his abs, tracing his skin. His muscles jumped under her touch. She opened her mouth on his throat, her tongue darting out and tasting his skin before she shifted, her body sliding up his. Her free hand moved up and into his hair, pulling his head down so she could press her lips to his.

He dipped his tongue inside her mouth, his hands moving to her butt and squeezing. His shaft hardened beneath her belly.

"Ignore that," he said against her mouth.

How on earth was she supposed to ignore that? Didn't matter. She wasn't going to listen.

"Stop telling me what to do." She shifted slightly to the side as the hand she had on his stomach moved down between his legs.

She wrapped her hand around his erection, running her thumb across the head. She couldn't stop the satisfied grin on her lips when he bucked and moaned into her mouth, water sloshing over the side of the tub.

"I think you need a massage, too," she said as she began to stroke him. "I'll relax this muscle for you."

"You aren't relaxing it." His head fell back onto the ledge of the tub, and his eyes closed as his chest heaved.

"Want me to stop?"

His head snapped back up, his eyes narrowing on her as he continued to breathe hard. "Hell, no."

She covered his mouth with hers again, her grip on his cock tightening as she moved her hand up and down. His hands gripped her bottom, his fingers sliding between the cheeks before one slipped low. He traced her folds, playing with them in the warm water before he found her entrance.

Her mouth fell away from his in a gasp as he entered her. The hand at the back of his head slid down to his neck. She used it as an anchor as she began to move, thrusting herself against his fingers. More water sloshed over the edge of the tub, splashing against the tile floor.

"We're making a mess," she whispered against his mouth.

"I don't care."

It was at this point that he found her clit, applying pressure and making her move harder against him. It was requiring a whole hell of a lot of effort for her to split her focus at the moment and continue to work him over.

But somehow she managed, her hand keeping up with the pressure and pace.

Shep's hand that wasn't working her over slid up her lower back, his fingers and palm spreading wide and guiding her movements.

"Shep, I'm going to come." She moved her face to his neck again, trying to catch her breath.

"Let go, babe. I've got you. I've always got you."

She started to move her hand to the tip of his cock, applying just the right amount of pressure before she slid her hand back down.

"Just like that. Just. Like. That," he said as his hips started to move faster. "*Hannah.*" The desperation in his voice had her looking up, and his mouth claimed hers in an instant.

They fell over the edge together, coming hard.

She collapsed against his chest, both of her hands going to his hair. Their mouths continued to move against each other, and that was how they stayed until the water turned cool.

Chapter 16

Unfinished Business

Bennett and Mel had decided to do a joint bachelor/bachelorette party the weekend before their wedding. There was a music festival up in Tallahassee on the Fourth of July. Five different acts were scheduled to perform throughout the day, and a fireworks show capped off the night.

Shep hadn't expected a crazy bachelor party with strippers. None of the guys had gone for that. Both Brendan and Jax had chosen to go fishing. It was something that Shep had mocked them for, but he understood it now. Why in the world would he want to see some other woman naked when he had Hannah?

There was no point.

And really, what better way was there to spend an evening? He got to listen to good music with a beer in one hand and Hannah in the other. And it only promised to get better when he took her to bed and stripped her out of the sexy-as hell white dress she was wearing.

The top was some sort of lacy material, and it plunged down deep on her back, exposing all of those freckles he loved so much.

Freckles that he planned on counting with his tongue just as soon as they got home.

Home.

Except the inn wasn't home. It was more like limbo. Where they were staying until they moved on from the here and now. It had been a little more than a month since the blackout, since Hannah had stopped running from him, since she'd started running toward him, and it had been perfect.

They'd developed a routine: up in the mornings, coffee and breakfast in the kitchen, and then working with Hamilton and Dale on whatever she had planned for the day.

Some of his nights at the bar were cut a little bit shorter. He'd go in around four like he normally did. But on nights that the bar was plenty covered with either his dad or one of the other bartenders who worked there, he'd head out around midnight. Besides, the day labor at the inn was exhausting.

Hannah was usually awake when he got back, sitting at the massive dining room table and sipping on a glass of wine or on one of his beers. She spent her evenings working on a contract of some sort or returning e-mails. But as soon as he walked in the door, she'd close her laptop. It was guaranteed that he'd pretty much be on top of her within a matter of seconds. Or, she'd be on top of him.

Both were pretty awesome.

The progress on the inn was steady. They'd been working only on the bottom floor, and as there were five bedrooms, five bathrooms, the living room, dining room, and kitchen, there'd been a lot to tackle.

After Hannah's bathroom had been finished, they'd moved on to her bedroom. She'd gone with a darker shade of gray than the bathroom for these walls, put up a new ceiling fan that actually had all of the lights working in it, hung gauzy white curtains above the windows on fancy rods, and replaced all of the blinds. Bennett had also completely refinished all of the antique furniture in the room.

After that, they'd moved on to the kitchen. All of the appliances were brand-new and black, and the fact that they all matched brought Hannah great joy. As the counters were finished and looking pretty good, it was more work than it was worth to replace the cabinets. The frames were sturdy and in pretty good condition, so Bennett came up with a better solution. They sanded and restained all of the bases a sandy brown and then replaced the drawers and doors. As he was a custom cabinetmaker, Shep was pretty sure the guy knew what he was doing.

They'd also put up a backsplash behind the counters with those tiles that Hannah loved so much and painted the walls light beige.

She was obsessed with paint colors and had brought back more swatches than should be legal. She wanted neutral colors in the main rooms, but couldn't figure out what to do in the rest. So a palette of colors had been taped to the walls. Reds in one room, blues in another, yellows, greens, et cetera.

She had a lot of ideas rolling around in that head of hers, and the more she talked about it, the more excited she got. But it was nothing to the excitement when something was finished.

In all of the conversations they'd had since she'd arrived in Mirabelle, she'd never talked about her job with as much enthusiasm as she talked about the inn. As he'd watched her work on it, he knew she was getting attached. And she wasn't the only one.

Shep had to continually tell himself he couldn't get used to any of it. He was under no delusions that Hannah was going to pick up her life and move here. Staying in Mirabelle just wasn't an option.

But neither was losing Hannah.

"I've seen that look before."

Shep pulled his gaze from Hannah, who was in line at a food truck with Mel and Harper, and looked over at Brendan, who'd just joined him in line for beer.

"And what look is that?"

"The *I'm going to do anything to keep her* look. I thought you'd recognize it, as it was pretty much a permanent feature on my face after I met Paige."

"Was?"

"Okay, you're right. It's not going anywhere. And I have a feeling yours isn't, either."

"No." Shep shook his head and scratched the back of his neck. "It's not."

Brendan studied Shep for just a second before he nodded, clapping him hard on the back. "Good for you, man. I'm glad you got her back."

"Me too," Shep said, automatically looking back to Hannah. At that exact moment she looked over her shoulder and smiled at him.

Yeah, he'd do anything to keep her.

* * *

The second they were through the door of the inn, Shep had Hannah pushed up against the wall. His hands were at her hips, working their way down until he got to her thighs.

He pushed his palms up under the white skirt of her dress,

his fingers gliding across her bare skin until he slid around to her lace-covered bottom. She gasped when his hands tightened on her ass, and he moved his hips against hers, pressing his erection into her belly.

"Bed," she whispered against his mouth.

He didn't need to be told twice. He bent down and grabbed her, throwing her over his shoulder in one quick movement. She let out another gasp, her legs flailing in the air as he headed for the bedroom.

"Shep! I'm more than capable of walking." She laughed.

God, he loved that sound.

"This is quicker. Besides, you need all of the energy you can save. I'm going to be keeping you occupied for the next couple of hours. I'm going to show you exactly what it is I can do to your body. That *only* I can do to your body."

She stopped struggling, and a content sigh escaped her as her hands trailed down his back. When she got to his ass, she squeezed, and he rewarded her by placing a light smack to her bottom.

"Hurry up." The desperate pleading edge to her voice had him grinning.

When he walked into the room, he lightly tossed her onto the bed, and her hair scattered out across the comforter. The contrast of her red hair against the green was stunning. She should only wear green, should live in the color.

Her lips curved up in that sexy little way of hers as she stretched her arms above her head. He kneeled down on the mattress and wrapped his hand around her ankle, pulling it up so he could undo the buckle. Her dress fell down and puddled around her waist, exposing light-blue lace.

Hmm, something could be said for that color on her body, too. Who was he kidding? She looked good in everything.

But on second thought, she looked even better in nothing.

If he wanted to get there, he was going to need to focus. He returned his attention to her sandal and worked the buckle with quick efficiency. When it was free, he tossed the shoe to the side and placed her ankle on his shoulder. He ran his hand up her calf, all the way to the apex of her thighs. His fingers brushed under the lace, stopping just short of where they both wanted him to go.

She let out a frustrated whimper when he pulled his hand away. He grinned as he turned his head, placing a kiss on her ankle before he put her bare foot down on the bed. Then he grabbed her other ankle and repeated the process, but this time when he got to her panties, he ran his fingers up her center.

He pushed into the wet lace and her body arched up off the bed.

"You want me." Not a question, but he wanted her to say it.

She nodded, moving her hips and pressing herself firmly into his hand, seeking more pressure.

"Uh-uh. I want the words, babe."

She took an unsteady breath before she got the words out. "I want you."

"Good girl." He pulled the lace to the side and slid two fingers inside her.

Her eyes closed as her hands clutched at a pillow.

"Look at me." The demand in his tone brooked no argument, and she obeyed immediately, those sea-glass-green eyes landing on him. "I want your eyes on me when you come. Understand?" He moved his thumb to her clit, pressing down and making her body writhe.

She just nodded again, words apparently failing her. Well, that just wouldn't do.

"Say it."

"I understand," she whispered.

"What was that?"

"I understand." This time she shouted it.

"Frustrated?"

"Yes. How about you stop talking about making me come and actually do it?"

"Yes, ma'am." He pulled his fingers from her body and wound them in the lace at her sides. "Lift."

She did as she was told, and he shimmied the fabric down her legs. He tossed the blue lace over his shoulder before he shifted back on the bed, settling himself between her legs and pushing her thighs apart with his shoulders.

He kissed the insides of her thighs before he slid his hands under her bottom and pulled her to him. The second his mouth was at her core, she bucked against him, her hands fisting in his hair like they always did. He slid his tongue along her folds, licking and sucking.

And then he was at her clit, flicking his tongue against it and making her writhe and moan his name. He looked up and found her eyes on him. She was so lost, so beyond herself, so damn gorgeous as she soaked up every ounce of pleasure.

If he didn't watch himself, she wouldn't be the only one coming.

He brought his hand down and slipped two fingers inside her again. The knowledge that she wasn't going to last much longer hit him about two seconds before her body started pulsing and she was screaming.

"Oh, ohh, ohhhhh!"

And that was it. She was gone.

"Don't move." He pulled himself from between her thighs and got up from the bed.

"Not even a possibility." She sighed like a content cat, snuggling further into the comforter. She looked like something else, all right, with the skirt of her dress bunched up around her waist.

God, he needed to be inside of her.

"Don't fall asleep, either." He reached behind him and grabbed a fistful of his T-shirt, pulling it off in one movement. His eyes were back on Hannah the second his shirt was over his head. She was up on her elbows now, licking her lips as she looked at him.

"That's also not a possibility."

"Didn't I tell you not to move?"

"Stop telling me what to do. Now, take off your pants."

"Take off your dress," he countered.

For someone who couldn't move a moment ago, she sure did pull herself up with ease. She moved to the edge of the bed and turned slightly, gathering her hair and pulling it to the side.

"Help me with the zipper?"

He kneeled on the bed behind her, his knees on either side of hers. His hands were at her waist in an instant and he leaned down, pressing his mouth to her now-bare neck.

"That's not my zipper."

"I'm getting there." His tongue flicked out against her skin, and her hand came up to the back of his head. Her fingers dived into his hair again, her nails gently raking his scalp. He trailed his lips up her neck and to her ear. His teeth grazed her earlobe, and he bit down gently before he let go.

He moved his hands from her waist, anchoring the base of the zipper while he pulled the metal tab down. Her hand fell from his head as he slid his hands into the back of her dress. He pushed the straps from her shoulders where they caught at her elbows.

He continued his journey forward, palming her breasts. His thumbs rasped over her erect nipples, the thin fabric of her bra doing nothing to hide his effect on her.

"Shep," she moaned as her head fell back on his shoulder. "I need you."

He pulled his mouth from her throat at her words, his heart somehow beating more erratically than it had been a moment before, and for an entirely different reason.

"What was that?"

She turned and looked at him over her shoulder, her eyes landing on his. "I need you."

There was so much meaning in those three words. She didn't mean just in this moment, and he knew it. They might not be the three words he'd been dying to hear for a month now, but they came in at a close second.

"I need you, too. Always have, always will," he said right before he pressed his lips to hers.

He dipped his tongue inside her mouth, tasting her, as he pushed her dress the rest of the way down her arms, where it fell to her waist. He unclasped her bra a second later, pulling it from her body.

His hands skimmed under the skirt of her dress, his fingers going to the apex of her thighs again, sliding inside her. She moved against him, her ass pressing into his erection, and he couldn't take it anymore.

He pulled his fingers from her body and grabbed a condom from the nightstand, which thankfully was close enough that he didn't have to move too far from her. He didn't even bother getting rid of his jeans. He couldn't wait that long.

He undid the buckle and zipper, pushing everything down just far enough to free himself. The condom was open a second later, and he was rolling it down his erection. And then Hannah did something that almost had him coming on the spot.

She moved to the center of the bed, getting into position on her hands and knees.

He moved quickly, the need for her clawing at him, and pushed her legs apart as he kneeled behind her. He balled the skirt of her dress in one hand, pulling it up and to the side. He took in the sight before him, Hannah half naked with her sweet little ass in the air. And she was his.

All.

Fucking.

His.

"You're so damn beautiful." He moved closer, lining up the tip of his cock with her entrance. He'd barely touched her when she pushed back, seeking more of him. "Easy, baby." He grabbed on to her hip with one hand as he slowly sank inside her.

"Ohhhhhh, Shep." She fell onto her elbows, before her arms stretched up toward the headboard.

Nothing, *nothing*, had ever felt this good. The different angle made her tighter around him. He had to stop and breathe, letting her body adjust before he could start moving.

"Feel good?" He pulled out of her before he slowly sank back in.

She nodded.

He brought his hand down sharp on her ass. She gasped in surprise, her body jerking back against him, taking him all the way to the hilt and making him groan.

"Words, Hannah. You have to talk to me."

"Yes. It feels incredible. Don't stop. Don't *ever* stop." She was desperate. Desperate for this. For *him*.

He pulled out and sank back in. "Not going anywhere." He

ran his free hand up her spine as he moved, grinding his hips into her ass. "God, do you have any idea how good you feel, Hannah? Any idea at all?"

"Tell me." It was a strangled request, one that she apparently had a hard time voicing. Probably because she was putting every effort into using the headboard to hold her in place; otherwise Shep's persistent thrusting would have moved her up the bed.

"Perfect. That's how you feel. So fucking perfect I can barely breathe. Looking at you, touching you, I'll never get enough."

He brought his hand down on her bottom again, and she bucked against him wildly.

"Good?" he asked, soothing the spot with his fingers.

"Yessss!"

He did it again on the other cheek, and she cried out, the sound muffled in the pillow by her head.

He grabbed on to her hip with one hand, his fingers digging into her flesh as he held on, his thighs hitting hers. His other hand ran up her back and along her spine. They moved together, their sweat-soaked bodies begging for each other. He tried his hardest to hold out, waiting for her to come first, wanting her body clenching around him to be the trigger to his own orgasm.

"Babe." His voice came out strangled, barely under control. "You close?"

Her answer was a muffled scream. Her arms trembled, and her legs shook, giving out. She fell flat on to the bed, forcing him to follow her down, hovering over her as she let go. And then she was pulsing around him as she went absolutely wild underneath him. He couldn't hold back, not for a second longer. He picked up the pace of his hips, pushing into her harder and faster. She pulled him under with her, wringing it all out of him. Every last drop.

Everything in him wanted to just collapse on to her, still buried deep inside. He never wanted to move from the warmth of her body again. But somehow he managed to stay upright. She moaned as he pulled out of her, making a blind grasping motion toward him, saying something that was muffled by the pillow at her mouth.

He grinned, leaning over her and pressing a kiss between her shoulder blades. "I'll be right back."

He went and cleaned up in the bathroom, and when he stepped back into the bedroom, it was to find Hannah in almost exactly the same position. The only difference was her head was resting on her arm and she was looking at him.

"You didn't even get your jeans off." She grinned.

"Wasn't enough time."

"I suppose not. Next time, though, I want your naked thighs slapping against mine."

"Keep talking like that and next time is going to be very soon."

"That's what I'm counting on." She rolled over onto her back, stretching. "Now, are you going to get over here and finish the job you started with this dress, or what?"

He was across the room in two seconds flat.

* * *

The sound of crashing waves filled Shep's ears about a second before he inhaled a warm salty breeze. He hadn't even opened his eyes when he registered that he was alone in bed.

The room was dark, the only light coming from the alarm clock next to him. It was just after six in the morning. The sun wouldn't be making an appearance on the horizon for at least another thirty minutes.

He sat up, the sheet falling to his waist as he rubbed his face and looked around. The French doors were cracked, the source of the sound and breeze. He pulled back the blankets and got out of bed, grabbing his boxers from the floor and slipping them on before he made his way across the room. The blinds clattered when he pulled the door open, and Hannah looked over at him.

She was sitting on one of the Adirondack chairs, her legs pulled up to her chest and her chin resting on her knees. She was wearing his T-shirt, like she always did, and she'd pulled it over her legs.

"Why are you up?" he asked, closing the door behind him before he walked over to her.

"Couldn't sleep."

"Everything okay?" He bent down, kissing her on the top of the head.

She looked up at him, chewing on her bottom lip, before she slowly shook her head.

He reached out, tracing her jaw, her eyes filled with an uncertainty that had his knees going just a little bit weak. "Babe, what's wrong?"

She pulled her legs out from under the shirt, putting her feet flat on the deck, and leaned forward. Her arms came out and she wrapped them around his waist as she rested her forehead against his stomach.

"Hannah, talk to me." He brought his hands to the back of her head, running his fingers gently through her hair.

"I was wrong," she whispered. Her lips brushed across his skin, her breath washing out in a warm wave. She pressed a kiss right next to his belly button before she looked up at him

"Wrong about what?" All traces of sleepiness vanished from his body. He was now wide-awake. *What is she saying?*

"Thinking I needed to get over you. Thinking I'd ever be able to walk away again. I—I can't."

"Okay..." He shook his head and tried to remember to breathe. "And you want to be able to walk away?"

"No, I don't. But what are we going to do? I know you said to stay in the here and now and not to worry about the future, but we've gotten past that point."

"I think so, too. Come here." He reached down, grabbing her by the elbows and bringing her to her feet. He turned, pulling her away from the chair so he could sit down. Then he held out his arms so she could crawl into his lap. She did so immediately, her legs hanging off the side of his, and her face pressed into his neck.

He grabbed her hand, lacing his fingers with hers and bringing it up to his mouth. He kissed each of her knuckles before he brought their hands to the center of his chest.

"My boss called yesterday," she whispered, her breath washing out across his skin. "They need me back by the fourth of August. So we have a month before I have to leave." Her hand tightened in his, holding on to him. "All I can think is that this is just thirteen years ago all over again."

"It's not."

"Then what do we do? Long distance?"

"No, not long distance." He moved, pulling her face from his neck so that he could see her eyes. "I want this every day. I want *you* every day."

She shifted in his arms so that it was easier to look at him. "I want you every day, too." Her free hand was in his hair, her fingers running through it and down to the ends. "It scares me."

"What?"

"How quickly I fell back in love with you."

Everything in him froze as he looked at her. He was lucky he was sitting; otherwise he would've fallen flat on his ass.

"I didn't think it was possible." Her mouth curved up at the sides. "I told myself over and over again before I came down here that it was all just history. The past. Something to be dealt with and finished up so I could move on."

He shook his head. "No moving on. You and I will always be unfinished business."

His hands moved to her face, holding her head as he looked into her eyes. The sky was still dark, a dim glow just coming up over the horizon. He couldn't see that sea-glass-green color he loved so much, but it didn't matter. Only one thing mattered in that moment.

"I love you, Hannah."

She closed her eyes and took in a slow breath like she was savoring his words before opening them and focusing on him.

"I didn't know that was possible, either. That you could love me again."

"There is no *again*, babe. I never stopped loving you. Not once. It's you. It's always been you, and it always will be you." He leaned in, pressing his mouth to hers. He pulled back again, running his thumb across her cheek. "That's why I'm going to move to New York."

"What?"

"Thirteen years, Hannah. That's how long I've had to be without you. I'm not doing it again."

"You're going to pick up your life and move across the country?"

"Yes, because I want my life to be with you. I'm all in." He kissed her again, long and slow. "All. In."

"I am, too."

* * *

Shep sat at the diner, spinning the saltshaker on the table as he waited for Finn to show up. He had absolutely no idea if that was going to happen or not. Finn had been less than eager to talk to Shep over the last month.

But he needed to talk to his brother.

Had to talk to his brother.

He'd left a sleeping Hannah in bed that morning. Something that had taken a force stronger than himself, because it had been hard. He was pretty sure he'd never get tired of waking up next to her, not for as long as he lived.

That was the plan, anyway.

"Can I get you a refill, honey?" Wanda Little asked, coming up to the table, one hand on her hip while she held the coffeepot up in the air.

"Please." He pushed his mug to the end of the table.

Wanda was backing away when he spotted Finn over her left shoulder. He was just standing there, his arms folded across his chest as he stared at Shep with a stern expression.

"This one, too," Shep said, flipping the cup in the saucer across from him and holding it at the end of the table.

Wanda tipped the carafe over the cup, filling it before she turned.

"Thanks, Wanda." Finn spared her a smile before she walked away, but when he looked at Shep again, there was no smile to be found. "Able to pull yourself away long enough to remember the other people in your life?" he asked as he sat down on the other side of the booth.

"Is that really how you want this to go?"

Finn didn't say anything. Instead he reached over for the sugar packets, grabbing three and ripping the tops off in one move. He dumped them in, grabbing a spoon and stirring before he added a little cream.

"You're here. So talk," he said before he brought the mug to his mouth.

Shep sat back in the seat and looked at his little brother. "What the hell do you want from me, Finn?"

"An apology would be nice."

He took a deep breath and let it out in a rush through his nose. "I need to apologize? For what, exactly?"

"Forgetting about your family and friends, for one. You've been so caught up with *her* you can't even see straight."

"Hannah. Her name is Hannah," Shep said through clenched teeth. Maybe he wasn't going to get through this conversation.

"What does it matter? She'll be gone soon."

"And so will I."

Finn paused in the middle of raising his cup to his mouth, and he set it back down on the table. "What?"

"If you'd stop being an ass long enough, I'd be able to tell you."

"Tell me what?" Finn's eyebrows bunched together on his forehead.

"I'm going with her."

"You're serious?"

"Yeah."

Finn shook his head. "What the hell are you doing? You're just going to walk away from everything? For her?"

"You don't get it, man."

"*I* don't get it?" Finn's voice rose as he put his hands flat on the table. "I think *you* don't get it. You're going to leave everything behind, *give* everything up, for her. Your family, your friends, Springsteen and Nigel, your house, *the bar.*"

"I know exactly what's at stake, Finn. I've thought about this, long and hard."

"*Long?* She's been here for two months, and you guys have been playing house for only one of those months. How is that *long?*"

"One day you'll get it. When you meet the person you're *supposed* to be with, you'll get it."

"You're living in a fantasyland." Finn shook his head. "And you're so fucking selfish."

"I'm selfish? *I'm* selfish? Are you kidding me with this shit? You left, too, Finn. You've been gone for eight years. And you walk back in here telling me what my life should be? What the hell gives you the right?"

"I left to make something of myself."

All of the air left Shep's lungs as he looked at his little brother. He took a deep breath, trying to calm himself. "You're on a roll."

Finn looked down, running his hands across his face. He looked back at Shep a second later, shaking his head. "I didn't mean that."

"Oh, but I think you did. That's the second time you've pretty much said I've amounted to nothing. And as enlightening as that is, I don't care." Shep slid out of the booth and stood. "The house is yours now," he said before he walked away.

Chapter 17

Red Lipstick, Green Dresses, and White Lies

It had become a bit of a tradition for the rehearsal dinners to be held at the Sleepy Sheep. First Paige and Brendan, then Grace and Jax, and now Mel and Bennett. They actually turned out to be more rehearsal parties than anything else. A live band would play music from the stage, drinks would be in no short supply, and food would be provided by Lula Mae and Grace.

Shep would split his time between working and celebrating, occupational hazard being as it was his bar.

His bar for just a little while longer.

The thought of leaving it all behind was…painful. But the thought of losing Hannah? Well, that was unbearable. Sacrifices had to be made, and he'd sacrifice it all for her. That was just how it was.

He hadn't told anyone besides Finn about his plans. He was waiting until after the wedding. The focus at the moment was Mel and Bennett, not the massive life change that Shep was about to embark on, picking up his life and leaving the only place

that he'd ever called home. He hoped that when the news came
out, everyone would be supportive, or at least more supportive
than his brother. Which wouldn't be all that hard, really.

As Bennett and Mel were getting married in her church and
the pastor was a bit old-fashioned, the groomsmen needed to do
the whole button-down shirt and tie thing for the rehearsal.

Shep leaned in toward the mirror, trying to remember how to
tie a Windsor knot. It wasn't all that shocking that formal attire
wasn't part of his normal attire, so he was having a little bit of
difficulty with this particular task.

And it didn't help his endeavors at all when Hannah walked
out of the bathroom wearing a bra and panties that covered
nothing.

Nothing.

It was pretty much just scraps of black lace placed strategically
over her body. Her breasts were only half covered, her nipples
seen plain as day through the thin material. Then there was the
excuse for panties that his fingers itched to rip from her body.

Her makeup was on, red lipstick painted across that mouth
of hers, and her eyes had that sexy, smoky thing going on. She'd
styled her hair, and it hung in curls around her face and shoulders, completing the whole picture in a way that even he couldn't
have come up with in his wildest dreams.

He stared at her reflection in the mirror, his hands freezing
and his mouth falling open. He turned, leaning back against the
dresser, and watched her walk across the room to the closet. It
was then that he got the back view.

It was a thong. The black lace disappeared between the cheeks
of her ass.

"Are you doing this on purpose?" His voice came out a little
more pained than he'd intended.

"Doing what?" She shrugged her shoulders as she pushed hangers around. "I don't know what to wear. Black just doesn't seem appropriate. Hmmm." She hummed, bringing her hand to her mouth and tapping her fingers to her lips. "Maybe I need to figure out shoes first." Then she bent over, reaching for a pair on the floor, and Shep about lost his damn mind.

She straightened before she placed her hand on the door-frame, bracing her weight as she bent just slightly at the waist and slipped one on. She repeated the motion with the other foot before she straightened and turned to look at him.

Her mouth moved and sound came out, but he had no idea what she said. The blood had rushed from his head in about a nanosecond, and it was all sitting painfully behind his now-throbbing dick.

He was going to have a heart attack. Right then and there. Nothing to save him. Absolutely nothing.

He swallowed, trying to remember how to speak.

"What...?" He reached up, pulling at his tie to loosen it before he choked. "What was that?" he managed to get out. He was pretty sure she'd asked how she looked in the shoes, but as he'd gone temporarily deaf, he wasn't sure.

"The shoes." She held her leg out. "What do you think?"

"I think I'm going to be walking around with a hard-on for the rest of the day, which is going to be a massive inconvenience." He reached down, holding on to the dresser so that he didn't move, because if his hands touched her, they would both be naked, which was going to result in a wrinkled suit, ripped lace, and lipstick all over his mouth.

"That so? Mmmm." She walked over, her hips swaying with every step.

She stopped in front of him and reached out, wrapping his tie around her hand and tugging lightly, bringing his face down to hers.

His hold on the dresser turned into a death grip as he tried to remember how to breathe. But then she stretched up and pressed her body against his, and all of the air left his lungs in one fell swoop. She dragged her lips across his neck, her hands running down the front of his shirt.

"What are you doing?" He turned his head, his nose skimming her hair.

"Taking care of the *massive* inconvenience." It was then that she traced his erection through the front of his gray slacks.

"Hannah, I—" But the words died in his throat as she lowered herself to her knees in front of him.

Now, this was every fantasy of his come true. Hannah in lace and heels, kneeling in front of him, licking her lips like she was going to devour him. She popped the button of his pants before she pulled down the zipper. And then her hands were at his hips, pulling just enough for his cock to spring free.

She gave him one long stroke before she moved her hand down, her fingertips gliding down his balls. His knees buckled, and he had to brace his weight against the dresser. A good thing, too, because he would've found himself on his ass a second later when she leaned in, her tongue swirling over the tip like it was an ice-cream cone.

Those red lips of hers wrapped around the head of his dick, and he thought he was going to die. She sucked him into that warm, wet mouth of hers, which was so damn perfect it was ridiculous.

He wasn't going to survive this.

Nope.

And he didn't care.

One of his hands came up to the back of her head, his fingers spearing through the strands as he guided her up and down. He closed his eyes as his head fell back on his shoulders, giving way to the sensations of her tongue and the slow pull of her mouth.

Whatever inarticulate sounds he managed to get out of his mouth were pure male satisfaction. Hannah hummed in approval, the vibrations traveling along the length of him and going all the way to his spine.

He brought his head back down so he could watch her pretty red head moving between his thighs, and he knew it was going to be over soon. He'd reached his limit.

"I—I can't hold on anymore, babe. I'm going to come."

She just hummed around him again as she brought one of her hands to his balls and lightly squeezed.

And that was it. He was gone, pumping into her mouth while she sucked him dry.

She dragged her mouth down his length one last time, her tongue wrapping around the head. She ended it the exact same way she'd started, licking the tip with a smile. Though those lips of hers weren't nearly as red as they had been.

It was then that he realized her lipstick was all over the base of his cock.

Well, shit. She freaking marked me.

It wasn't like she didn't already own his ass. She could do whatever the hell she wanted, really.

She reached for his boxers, tucking him into place, before pulling his slacks back up. He was still at a loss for words as he reached for her, pulling her to her heeled feet and wrapping his arms around her. He kissed her hard, needing his mouth on hers more than he'd ever needed anything.

"What was that?"

"Something for you to think about for the next few hours."

"Hannah, I'll be thinking about that for the rest of my life."

She smiled, pressing her mouth to his. "Good. Now let's get you straightened out," she said as she leaned back, grabbing his tie and undoing the messed-up knot he'd failed at tying correctly.

His hands rested at the base of her back, his thumbs moving back and forth over her skin. He watched the look of concentration in her eyes, the way she bit her bottom lip as she maneuvered the ends of the tie around.

Two months. She'd been back in his life for two months, and there was no way in hell he was going back to how it'd been without her.

He'd known thirteen years ago that she was the only one for him, and he'd let her walk out of his life. That wasn't happening this time. It wasn't happening ever again. He'd made the right choice; he knew it without a shadow of a doubt. Moving to Manhattan? That was nothing.

He'd follow her anywhere.

* * *

The only wedding Hannah had ever been around was her sister's, and that had been beyond stressful. The term bridezilla had been coined for Sharon Sterling-Sanford. It had been months of *me, me, me*. And Hannah's mother had let Sherri have whatever she wanted. After all, throwing money at the problem to shut up their kids was the Sterling way.

Mel, on the other hand, was the polar opposite. Not all that shocking, as she was pretty much the sweetest, most down-to-earth person Hannah had ever encountered. And as Hannah had pretty much been raised by a pack of wolves—excluding Gigi, that is—it was a breath of fresh air.

Mel had everything planned to a tee, and the few things that veered from the plan, as things did, didn't have her going off the rails. She was so calm, cool, and collected that Hannah couldn't help but be in awe of the woman.

"As long as we get down that aisle, I don't really care how it happens," Mel said as she took a sip of her wine. "I get to marry the love of my life tomorrow. That's all that matters." She looked across the bar at Bennett, who was standing with Brendan, Jax, and Shep, laughing.

Shep was behind the bar, serving up drinks. He'd lost that tie of his a while ago, and the sleeves of his buttoned-up shirt had been rolled up to the elbows. He was just as edible as ever.

And he was hers.

This was still hard for her to believe. The fact that he was giving everything up for her? Well, she just couldn't wrap her mind around it. What kind of person did that?

His eyes landed on hers, and a grin overtook his face. This was what it was all about, sharing a private smile in a crowded room with the man she loved.

Because damn did she love him.

Someone was calling to Shep on the other side of the bar, and he winked at her before he turned away.

Hannah finished her glass of wine and excused herself to go to the bathroom. When she stepped out a few minutes later, she was barely across the threshold to the hallway when hands came around her from behind. She jumped, startled, and was spun around, her back pressed against the wall and Shep pressed against her front.

Both were hard.

"What are you doing?"

"Do you have any idea how crazy you're driving me in this dress?" he asked as his hands ran up her thighs and to her waist.

She'd opted for an emerald-green number because of how much he liked her in the color. The back plunged low and the hem came up high. She'd also gone with the sparkly silver heels she'd worn while giving him that blow job.

"I want to take you to bed and strip you out of this dress," he whispered against her ear. "Want to make love to you for hours on end."

She shivered, clutching his sides. She wanted all of that, too, but as he was doing manly things with the guys after the rehearsal, that wasn't going to happen. Hannah was on her own tonight, and the thought made her more than a little unhappy.

"We might not have hours, but we have a few minutes now."

His eyes went wide as his hands tightened on her waist. "Are you serious?"

"I'm thinking fast and hard. That office still locks, right?" She nodded over his shoulder at the door behind him.

Shep didn't even hesitate, grabbing her hand and turning around. He fished his keys out of his pocket and had the door open in seconds. He flipped the light on as he pulled her inside, shutting the door behind them and locking it.

Hannah was pushed up against the wall again, Shep's mouth coming down hard on hers. He pulled her small clutch from her hands and dropped it somewhere to the side.

"Try to be quiet," he said as his hands pushed up the skirt of her dress.

"Me? You're just as loud." Her hands were at his belt, pulling at the buckle.

"Care to make this interesting?"

Her hands stilled, and she looked up at him. "How so?"

"The quietest person gets to tie up the loudest."

"Deal." Her hands continued on their earlier mission, and the second the zipper of his pants was down, her hand was diving into his boxers. She wrapped her hand around his erection, making him groan.

She grinned against his mouth in triumph.

But a second later her grin was wiped off her face. Shep wrapped his fingers in the thin strap of her panties at her side. He ripped it away in one quick motion, making her gasp.

"What the—" But her words were cut off when he slipped his fingers inside her. Her head fell back against the wall, and she had to bite her lip to keep herself from moaning.

His other hand was moving down her thigh to her knee, and he pulled her leg up and around his waist. He pressed his thumb to her clit, and her body bucked against him.

"Fast and hard, right?"

She just nodded, her bottom lip still clamped between her teeth so she didn't cry out as he moved his thumb in circles.

He pulled his hand from her body and grabbed her other leg, bringing it up and around his waist. He stepped back from the wall and walked to the desk, sitting her down on the edge. He grabbed his wallet from his back pocket, finding the condom that he'd told her he made sure was on him at all times these days.

Hannah snatched it from his hand and ripped it open. She took her time rolling the latex down his erection. His jaw tightened, and he took slow, steady breaths out of his nose as he watched her.

"You're doing this on purpose."

"No idea what you're talking about." She reached the base, her fingers running across the smudged lipstick that was still there, making her smile. "I think I need to freshen this up."

"I don't think so." His hands went under her thighs and he pulled, making her fall back on the desk.

"Why?" she asked as he hooked her knees at his elbows, spreading her wide.

"Because if you put your mouth on me, I'll lose."

"You don't play fair."

"Just trying to keep up with you," he said as he pushed inside her.

"Oh God!" She gasped. "Oh God, oh God, oh God." Her back arched off the desk, and she gripped the edge.

He dropped her legs, pulling them around his waist, and hovered over her. "That's not quiet."

"I don't care." She grabbed his shirt and pulled him down, needing his mouth on hers.

This worked out well for her for a couple of reasons. One, she was kissing Shep, which was never *ever* a bad thing. And two, when they both came a minute later, it muffled her screams.

But muffled or not, she still lost the bet.

"I win," he said, brushing his mouth across her jaw.

"Really? The way I see it, I crossed the finish line just before you did."

He pulled back and looked down at her, grinning. "Yeah, you did."

She brought her hands to his head, running her fingers through the soft strands of his hair. "I love you."

The words came out of their own accord. She hadn't been able to stop them—not that she'd wanted to.

"I'm never going to get tired of hearing you say that." He

pressed his mouth to hers, kissing her long and slow. "I love you, too."

He pulled from her body a moment later, and she sat up on the desk, her body deliciously sore in all the right places. She stretched, and her eyes landed on the bit of lace on the floor.

Her panties.

She turned to him as he buckled his belt. "What the hell am I supposed to do about those?" She pointed to the floor.

He looked up, his eyes following where she was pointing. His mouth turned up into a smug grin. "Don't bend over."

She rolled her eyes at him, rising from the desk. She pulled her dress down over her thighs and tried to straighten herself out.

"Yeah, that's useless." His voice rumbled through the room.

Her head snapped up, and she found him watching her. The way his eyes eagerly moved over her body, she'd think he hadn't just had her flat on her back.

"You look well and thoroughly fucked." He stood in front of her, his arms wrapping around her and folding her into his body. He kissed her again, one of his hands sliding down to her butt, where he squeezed not so gently.

"Stop it." She smacked his hand and pulled away from him. "Walk out in front of me so I can sneak into the bathroom."

He moved across the small room, grabbing her panties from the floor and sticking them in his pocket, before he opened the door and walked out in front of her. She grabbed her clutch from where he'd tossed it to the floor earlier and dashed across the hall to the bathroom.

She stood in front of the mirror and shook her head. The grin on her face couldn't be helped. He was right. She did look well and thoroughly fucked.

That was twice tonight that he'd done a spectacular job

messing up her hair. After the blow job earlier that evening, she'd had to pin it in a messy up-do, as her perfectly curled hair was no longer. But she couldn't really blame him for that. She'd wanted him to lose control, wanted to prove that he was hers and put her own little brand on him in the process.

It was a shame he hadn't let her touch up the lipstick... though nothing else that had taken place in that office had been a shame.

She pulled out a few of her bobby pins and tried to fix the new mess that was her hair. The door opened behind her, and Harper walked into the bathroom, her face splitting into a grin as she looked Hannah over. "So that's where you disappeared off to."

"Hmm? I've been in here," Hannah said, ducking her head and turning the faucet on. She let the cold water wash over her wrists, hoping it would help with the heat in her face.

"Oh, don't play coy with me. I just walked passed a very relaxed Shep with a certain pep in his step. And you look... well, that scruff burn across your neck is pretty telling. Not to mention your flushed skin and that glow on your face."

"I don't know what you're talking about."

"Mmm-hmm. All right, Hannah." Harper laughed as she opened her purse and rummaged around. "Here you go." She handed Hannah a compact. "Should help a little."

"Thanks." Hannah grinned.

"Anytime. And your secret is safe with me," Harper said before she ducked into one of the stalls.

Hannah pulled out the brush and dusted a little powder across her nose and forehead.

"Dammit." Harper's voice echoed against the tile. "I swear to all that is good and holy, my period has the worst timing on the face of the planet. Do you have a tampon?"

"Uhh, let me check." Hannah grabbed her clutch from the counter and opened it, her fingers searching through the contents. She normally had a few stashed in the side pocket, but she came up with nothing.

When was the last time she'd used this purse?

When was the last time she'd had her period?

She froze, staring at the lipstick at the bottom of the bag, her heart hammering in her ears as she tried to focus and think that far back.

It had been two days after the blackout...so the beginning of June...It was July now...eleven days into the month to be exact.

She was more than a week late.

They always used condoms. Shep made sure of it. But that was the only form of birth control they used. Hannah had been put on the pill after the miscarriage, but she'd had horrible side effects so she'd stopped taking it. And condoms had always worked in the past.

Well, except with Shep.

"Hannah?" Harper was out of the stall now, a look of concern on her face.

"I...I don't have a tampon." And that wasn't the only thing that was missing.

"No need to look horror-struck. A pad's fine. I'm not picky."

"It's not that. I'm sorry. I don't have anything."

"That's fine. Sweetie, are you okay?"

"Yeah." Hannah took a deep breath, and the smile that she forced across her face took a will that she didn't even know she possessed. "Just tired." She waved her hand in the air vaguely. "You know...things. I'll see you tomorrow." She took a step toward the door, Harper looking at her like she was possibly a little crazy.

Hannah turned and headed out of the bathroom, walking into the still-heavily-crowded bar.

Don't freak out.

Must not freak out.

You don't know anything yet.

She forced herself to take deep, calming breaths. She just needed to get out of there. Needed to be alone to think. Process the situation. Figure out what she was going to do next.

* * *

Shep and Finn had done a pretty decent job of avoiding each other since their *talk* at the diner. But that hadn't been an option the night of the rehearsal, as not only were both of them manning the bar, but they were also both in the wedding. Finn wasn't a groomsman like Shep was, but as he'd grown up with Mel and they were relatively close, he was acting as an usher for the service tomorrow.

He was also acting like a jackass for the evening.

The few words they'd managed to exchange with each other were clipped and pretty much consisted of one of them being in the other one's way. Not to mention Shep's little disappearance into the back office hadn't gone unnoticed.

"Unbelievable," Finn had muttered under his breath as he'd snatched a glass from the counter and moved to the other side of the bar.

And Finn and Shep's interactions weren't going unobserved by their parents or their friends.

"Why does it look like Finn has been sucking on a lemon all night?"

Shep turned around to find Grace standing on the other side

of the bar. Her eyebrows were raised, and that little mouth of hers was pinched in concern.

"You need a refill?" he asked, nodding at her empty glass on the bar.

"Another virgin mimosa." She pulled herself up onto the stool across from him, which was a bit of an endeavor now that she was almost seven months pregnant.

"How are you feeling?" He grabbed a clean champagne flute from the shelf behind him before he filled it with orange juice.

"Nothing I can't handle. Jax is hovering, though." She rolled her eyes. "He freaks out when I do anything more strenuous than brush my teeth."

"I can only imagine." Shep grinned as he added ginger ale and a splash of grenadine.

He wasn't even remotely surprised. Jax had always been over-protective when it came to Grace, and he'd gotten only more intense in the last couple of months, since Rosie had been on the horizon. Shep understood that, too. Grace was carrying Jax's child. They were the two people he cared about more than anyone else on the planet.

One day that was going to be him and Hannah, her round with his child. Him hovering like an overprotective moron. He couldn't freaking wait.

"Back to my earlier question—what's going on with you and Finn?" she asked.

That wiped the grin from his face. "Nothing for you to worry about."

"Nathanial Shepherd, don't you bullshit around with me. You've always made me be straight with you. I expect the same."

He added a slice of orange to the rim before he slid Grace's filled glass across the bar.

"Come on. Tell me what's going on." She leaned over, wrapping her mouth around the straw of her drink and taking a long pull.

He rested his hands on the ledge and leaned in. Sometimes blood really didn't define family, because Grace was his sister in every other way. He'd been there since the day she came home from the hospital. Watched her grow up. He was going to miss her a whole hell of a lot.

It hurt like hell that he wasn't going to be there when she and Jax had Rosie, wasn't going to be there to watch Jax be a crazy, overprotective father.

"When Hannah leaves, I'm going with her."

Grace's face fell as she looked across the bar at Shep. She dropped the straw from her mouth and sat up.

"You're leaving," she whispered. She took in an unsteady breath, and her eyes filled with tears.

"Grace, don't. Please don't cry." He reached across the bar and grabbed her hand.

"When?" She blinked, and tears ran down her cheeks.

"Hannah has to be back up there by the first week of August. I don't know how long it's going to take me to get things settled here, but as soon as they are, I'll be up there, too."

She nodded as she reached up and wiped at her eyes. "I'm happy for you, Shep. Hannah is fantastic, and she's good for you. But I'm going to miss you." Her bottom lip started to tremble.

He let go of her hand and rounded the bar, pulling her into his arms. She pressed her face to his chest, her tears soaking into his shirt. "Don't cry Grace. We'll visit. You'll still see me." He rubbed his hands up and down her back.

"Swear?" she asked, pulling back, running her fingers under her eyes.

"Cross my heart." He made the motion over his chest. His eyes moved over her shoulder for an instant, where he saw a frowning Jax crossing the room straight to them. "I haven't told anyone besides Finn yet. And your bulldog husband is heading over here. I'd like to be the one to tell Jax and Brendan."

"Don't worry. I cry all the time these days. I got this."

"What's wrong?" Jax asked, coming up next to her, running his hand across her lower back.

"Just tired." She turned, giving him a watery smile. "Wedding emotions are getting to me."

He leaned in, pressing his lips to her forehead. "When are you heading to Mel's?"

The night before Grace's wedding the girls had all stayed together, so they were apparently going to make a tradition of it. But as there were nine girls in the wedding party, plus Mel, Shep suspected that they were going to get very little sleep.

Though it wasn't like the guys' night was going to be all that restful, either. They'd started their own tradition before Brendan's wedding, and they were heading over to Jax's after this, where a night full of poker and scotch was in order.

"We're leaving soon. The stripper is showing up at ten, so we need to be ready for that."

"You're hilarious," Jax deadpanned.

"I know."

He just shook his head at her before he looked to Shep. "Thanks for taking care of her."

"Anytime." Except that wasn't going to be the case soon.

Jax pulled Grace away just as Hannah came walking in from the hallway. He grinned at her, but the weak smile that turned up her face was pained. She was pale, too. The flushed complexion she'd had when he left her five minutes ago was gone.

"I think I'm going to head home."

"What's wrong?" he asked, reaching up and touching her face.

"Nothing. I'm just tired." She stretched up and pressed her lips to his before she pulled away from him. "I'll see you tomorrow. Have fun with the boys."

"I will. You sure you're okay?"

She hesitated for just a second before she nodded. "Yeah. I love you."

"I love you, too." He kissed her lightly on the mouth before he let go.

She turned, and he watched her walk out the door, something stirring in the back of his mind. She'd said she was *just tired* exactly like Grace had said to Jax.

But he didn't have all that much time to worry about it. When he turned around, he was face-to-face with Finn, who had barely contained anger simmering in his eyes.

"You *love* each other? You guys barely even know each other. You're rushing into this blind. And when you can see again, you're going to regret it."

"You don't understand—"

"No, you don't understand."

Shep took a deep breath as he looked at his little brother, trying to rein in his impatience before he spoke. Losing his temper in front of everyone wasn't the best idea. He grabbed the bin of dirty glasses and headed through the door to the small kitchen in the back. He put the glasses in the sink, and when he turned, Finn was behind him again.

"Nothing I say is going to make you realize this is a mistake?"

"No, Finn, because it's not. Look, not everyone is Becky."

"Don't bring her into this." A whole different type of anger lit up his face.

"Why?" Shep asked, completely fed up. He didn't care that he was poking the bear anymore. Didn't care at all. "She's the reason you're so pissed off, right? You're jealous. I get my girl and you don't get yours—"

And that was as far as Shep got before Finn punched him in the jaw.

Shep fell back against the counter, rattling the glasses, before he pushed off of it. He pulled his arm back and punched Finn in the face.

He got in only the one hit before their father came into the room, pulling Shep off.

"What the hell is going on?" Nate shouted as he pushed his two sons apart. There'd been very few times in their lives that Nate had raised his voice, and it made both Shep and Finn stop.

"Tell him," Finn said, wiping the blood from his lip before he straightened his glasses. "Tell Dad your big news."

Nate looked at Shep, his eyebrows raised.

"You're an asshole; you know that?" he said to Finn before he turned to his father. "I was going to tell you, when everything settled down after the wedding. Not like this."

"Nathanial?"

"I'm going with Hannah. I'm moving to New York."

Nate nodded his head slowly, understanding in his face. "I figured that was going to happen."

"What?" Finn looked at their father in shock. "You're okay with this?"

"Finn, listen—"

"No." He cut him off, leaving the kitchen without a backward glance.

Shep and Nate stared at the swinging door for a moment before Nate turned to look at Shep again.

"Dad, I was—"

"I knew, Shep. So did your mother. You need to know that we support this decision." Nate smiled. "And we're happy for you that you have Hannah back. I don't think it's too fast, or that you don't know what you're doing. I think it's the Shepherd way, actually. Your grandfather knew immediately that he was going to marry your grandmother when he first met her. There was no doubt in his mind. It was the same with your mom and me. I won't even act like I was a saint before her, but after her, there was no one else that even came close."

"No one compares to Hannah, Dad. Not for me, at least. And they never will."

"I know. And you had it much harder. You met the one and then had to live without her for thirteen years, and I don't envy that at all. I think that would've damn near killed me if something like that had happened with your mom. Your brother doesn't get it, and he won't until it happens to him."

"Yeah, I know."

"I think that coming back wasn't exactly the reception he thought it would be. He hadn't really been here since your grandfather died. He hadn't seen your grandmother at her worst, and Becky moving on hit him hard. He's had school as his focus for the last couple of years, and it's not the same here as when he left. I don't think he was ready for that. And now you're leaving, and he as to deal with that." He reached out and grabbed Shep's shoulder, squeezing tight. "And he will. Just give him time."

"How much time?" As his jaw was currently throbbing, he wasn't inclined to give his jackass of a brother anything.

"However much time it takes. You should get back out there." He nodded toward the door.

Shep turned, and just before he walked out of the kitchen, his father called after him, making him turn around.

"For the record, Owen would be proud of this decision."

There was nothing else that his father could've said to make Shep feel better.

* * *

Hannah stared at the pregnancy test that sat on the bathroom counter. She'd run over to the Piggly Wiggly as soon as she'd left the bar. It had been five minutes from closing, and the cashier behind the register had glared at her from the moment she'd walked in the store until the moment she walked out.

The test was still in the package. Hannah just couldn't bring herself to open it. Couldn't bring herself to pop her thumb underneath the cardboard flap and pull it out.

It was Pandora's freaking box, and the only safe thing to do was to keep it shut.

She placed her hands on the edge of the counter, closing her eyes as she bowed her head.

It was thirteen years ago. She was back in the dorms at Columbia, huddled in a bathroom stall, staring at the positive test in her hands.

In all of the years she'd been in school, none had ever offered her a test harder than that one. And the fallout after? Well, she'd barely survived it.

First the pregnancy.

Then the miscarriage.

And, finally, Shep destroying what remained of her broken heart.

She knew the truth now—that Shep hadn't in fact moved on

from her—but it in no way made that past pain easier. In fact, it was harder. She'd been devastated by something that could've been fixed.

But would it have been?

What could've possibly happened?

He'd have come up there. That she didn't doubt. He would've dropped everything and gone to New York to be with her. But what would've happened after? He *wouldn't* have stayed. He *couldn't* have stayed. There'd been nothing for him there. Nothing for him except her.

How was that any different from now? He was giving up everything to move across the country for her.

Just her.

So would he have stayed thirteen years ago? If she'd asked?

She couldn't stop the questions that flooded her mind.

What if no one had been there when she'd called him? What if she'd called him before?

What if she hadn't lost the baby? Where would they be now? What would've happened? Would it have all worked out?

But that was all in the past. And there was absolutely nothing she could do to change it.

Here and now, Shep's voice echoed in her head. And the here and now involved that test on the counter.

What if she was pregnant now? What if she lost this baby, too? The fear was crippling, and the only way she was going to get past it was to find out.

Be brave. This time it was Gigi's voice.

She opened her eyes and straightened, grabbing the box from the counter.

She could do this. She *had* to do this.

Her hands shook as she opened the box, and they continued

to tremble as she took the test. It wasn't until the little negative sign popped up in the window that they stopped.

And as she fell to her knees, her head in her hands, she knew it wasn't relief coursing through her body that had brought her down.

Chapter 18

Nothing Ever Hurt Like You

Sleep would've been a welcome relief for Hannah's poor brain, but the thoughts running around in there were like a stampede that she just couldn't stop. Her mind was spinning just like the fan she was staring up at. The constant whirring provided no answers.

She rolled over, burying her face in Shep's pillow and breathing in deep. The scent of him was only a small comfort, as was his T-shirt, which she'd pulled on before crawling into bed.

Who would've thought she'd already be this dependent on his body next to hers at night? Sure, there'd been more than one evening when she'd fallen asleep before he'd gotten back, but she'd known she'd wake up with him next to her.

He'd always come home to her.

Home.

But *home* wasn't the inn. *Home* was in Manhattan. *Home* was her brownstone on the Upper East Side. *Home* was more than one thousand miles away from here.

She still had absolutely no idea what she was going to do with the inn. It needed way more work than could be done in another month. The thought of not being here to make decisions and be a part of it every step of the way didn't sit well. She'd loved working on it the last two months, and even more so over the last month with Shep, Hamilton, and Dale.

It was *her* project, *her* baby.

She clenched her eyes shut at that word. *Baby.*

How could she be sad about something that never was? Nothing had been lost because it had never been. Well, not this time.

What had she wanted, anyway? For that test to be positive?

She'd pretty much written off pregnancy after the miscarriage. Not to mention she'd never really been around children all that much in the last thirteen years or before. She had absolutely no idea what to do with them, and they scared her just a little bit.

She hadn't exactly had the best examples with her parents. Whenever Kendra Sterling had to touch her children, she did it with a grimace and held her hands in a way that reminded Hannah of the way women acted when their nails were wet.

As little contact as possible.

Maybe this was why Hannah was desperate for Shep's touch all the time. Or why she craved hugs from his friends and family. Or why she loved holding Trevor.

There was something so wonderful about that child that she couldn't even wrap her mind around. Like the way he would hold her face in those two chubby little hands of his, leaning close while he gave her a kiss. Or how he'd make that high-pitched squeal before he'd burst out into a round of giggles.

She hadn't dodged a bullet earlier with that negative pregnancy test. Because a positive was what she'd wanted. She wanted a baby. *Lots* of babies. With Shep.

A family.

She wanted all of that, and she wanted to raise them in the inn. Wanted to raise them in Mirabelle.

This was home. *This* was where she wanted to be. She just needed to tell the man whom she wanted to be here with, and she was going to have to tell him everything. If she had any hope of having a future with Nathanial Shepherd, he had to know about the past.

But it would have to wait until tomorrow evening, because she couldn't tell him at the wedding.

And what *was* she going to say? Well, she'd better figure it out, because she had less than twenty-four hours before all of the truth was going to be laid out in the open.

* * *

The guys headed over to Jax and Grace's house around midnight, and Bennett's best friend and best man, Danny Provo, pulled out a box of cigars. Everyone lit up out on the back porch as they sipped on the bottle of Johnnie Walker Blue that Shep had brought.

"So did you get into a fight with Finn?" Jax took a pull on his cigar and let the smoke out into the hot night air.

"You the reason he had a bloody lip when he left tonight?" Brendan asked.

"Yup."

Jax studied Shep for a second before he spoke. "Why?"

"Because he's leaving," Brendan answered before Shep could. "You're moving, aren't you?"

Shep just nodded.

A smile that could be described only as bittersweet turned up

Brendan's mouth. "I knew, man. I knew as soon as she was back that you would be going with her."

"I don't have any other choice. She's it for me."

"I get that," Brendan agreed. "What about that bar?"

"My dad knows that I'm leaving, but we haven't talked about that yet."

"And the inn?" Jax asked. "What's she going to do with it? Sell?"

"I don't know. I hope not. I hope she keeps it."

"A place for you guys to stay when you visit?" Brendan asked.

"Which better be every few months," Jax said before he took a sip of his scotch. "I can't believe you're leaving. I mean, I can because it's Hannah, but I can't believe you won't be here."

"I know. It's hard for me to wrap my mind around, too. Mirabelle has always been home."

"And it always will be." Brendan held his glass in the air

"And it always will be." Shep nodded as he and Jax clinked their glasses with Brendan's.

But as Shep took a drink of his scotch, he found that it got stuck in his throat, burning more than he was used to.

* * *

The wedding ceremony went off without a hitch, and if Shep didn't have to pose for pictures again in his life, it would be too soon.

It was lucky that Finn had gotten only one hit to his face and the bruise on his jaw was mostly concealed by his beard. The only damage done to Finn was his busted lip, so they hadn't messed up the pictures.

The two brothers had come to a mutual understanding to

just not talk to each other. There was no need to ruin the day. Besides, it was the last time in what would probably be a while that Shep was going to get to be around all of his family and friends like this.

So he chose to enjoy it. Which wasn't all that hard when Hannah was by his side. She was absolutely stunning.

Her dress was a light peach, one of the sleeves hanging off her shoulder, exposing a good portion of her freckled skin. And she was wearing heels, this pair gold and somehow sexier than the pair she'd worn yesterday. She'd curled her hair again, though this time it was hanging down around her shoulders, as he hadn't had the opportunity to mess it up.

A mission for later.

He'd had her out on the dance floor for most of the reception, his arms wrapped around her body, holding her close. After a few dances she'd been out of breath and flushed, so he'd gone off to get them both a drink.

But before he'd made his way to the bar, Finn was walking toward him, two beers in his hands. He looked more than slightly chagrined as he took a deep breath and stopped in front of Shep.

"Can we talk?" Finn asked, holding out a bottle.

"Yeah." Shep grabbed it, clinking the neck against Finn's.

They both took a drink, not saying a word for a few moments as they looked out at the room full of people.

Bennett was dancing with Mel, his arms wrapped around her as he smiled down into her face. He said something, raising his eyebrows, and she threw her head back, laughing before she grabbed his face and pulled him down for a kiss.

Finn cleared his throat. "Sorry I've been a dick."

Shep laughed, choking on his beer, before he looked over at his brother.

"I was wrong," he said seriously.

"What made you realize this?"

Finn held out his beer, pointing the neck of the bottle at Bennett and Mel. "Seeing the two of them get married today." Then he moved the bottle over to Grace and Jax, who were also out on the floor slow dancing. "Those two who are about to start a family." He finally moved the bottle over to a table on the edge of the dance floor, where Paige was sitting in Brendan's lap, laughing as they talked to Hannah. "And them."

Shep's stomach did a funny little flip. Hannah was holding Trevor, bouncing him in her arms and grinning down at him. It was such a change from the first time she'd held him, like he was a grenade about to explode.

"I've grown up with all of these people," Finn said. "I think I know them all pretty well. Seen a lot of ups and downs. Witnessed some of the relationships they've been in before. Watched those relationships end. But not *these* relationships. The difference is…unmistakable." He paused for a second before he spoke again. "You and Hannah have it, too."

Shep looked over at his brother at the same time Finn turned to him. "She's it for me, man. She always has been. I can't lose her again. I wouldn't survive it."

"Yeah, I know. I didn't get it before, how you could walk away from everything. But it isn't about what you're walking away from. It's about what you're walking toward."

"It is." Shep nodded. "Well put." He raised his beer, clinking the glass to Finn's again before he brought the bottle to his mouth.

"I hadn't really seen the two of you together before today. Maybe if I had, I wouldn't have missed out on the last month. And maybe I wouldn't have found out you might be a father from Bethelda fucking Grimshaw." He said the last part somewhat bitterly, but he recovered a second later.

Shep, on the other hand, did not recover. "What?" he sputtered on his beer.

His eyes automatically landed on Hannah. *Pregnant?* No. She would've said something...wouldn't she have? She'd been upset last night, but she was fine today. If she'd thought there'd been a chance for something like her being pregnant, wouldn't she have told him?

"But I get it, and I respect it." Finn continued on, oblivious to Shep and his spinning mind. "You guys are going to start a family, and you're both going to be great parents. It just sucks that you won't be living here. But that's what planes are for. And, anyway I figured you should know about the article, because the cat's out of the bag, and everybody is going to know that Hannah's pregnant."

"Finn, man, what the hell are you talking about? Hannah isn't pregnant."

"She's not?" Finn's eyes went wide.

"No. And what the hell did Bethelda Grimshaw say?"

"Umm." Finn reached up and scratched the back of his neck uncomfortably. "You know I don't read that shit. Brent Larson's here, and he thought he was being funny, showing me the article. You remember him? We were in the same year in school, total prick."

"Finn, focus."

Finn took a deep breath and shook his head. "Man, this wasn't what this conversation was supposed to be. Bethelda saw Hannah buying a pregnancy test last night. It's all over her blog."

Shep had never taken stock in the words of Bethelda Grimshaw. *Never.* The woman took the truth and twisted it into a garbled mess. The problem? She usually started with a seed of fact before she went off on one of her tangents, and he was going to get to the bottom of it.

* * *

Trevor let out that high-pitched squeal that Hannah loved so much as he clapped his hands together in the air. He was standing on her thighs now, bouncing up and down to the music while she kept him balanced at the waist.

His parents were sitting across from her, Paige in Brendan's lap as he ran his hands up and down her back. She had her hand on his neck, her fingers trailing through his short hair.

"So when do you have to be back in Manhattan?" Brendan asked.

Well, as Hannah had quit her job that morning, she didn't. But she wanted to tell Shep before she told anyone else.

She'd been surprised to learn that his plans to move to New York with her had been revealed by Finn, and not all that happy.

It hadn't made Shep all that happy either, as was proven by the bruise to his face and the cut on Finn's mouth. She didn't like that everyone was misinformed. Talking about this when she hadn't talked to Shep about everything was making her a little twitchy.

"The date they gave me was August fourth." Which wasn't a lie. That was when they had wanted her back. It just wasn't happening.

"Oh." Paige nodded, disappointment clear in her gray eyes. "I'm really happy for you and Shep, but as I am a selfish individual, I wish you two weren't leaving."

Paige would soon be getting her wish.

"We have a problem."

Hannah turned as Harper sat down next to her. She took the bouncing Trevor from Hannah's hands and settled him in her lap before she passed over her phone.

"You need to read this," she said seriously. "Now."

Hannah looked down, her stomach making an uncomfortable lurch as she stared at the words.

She was going to be sick.

THE GRIM TRUTH

MARY HAS A LITTLE LAMB, AND OTHER UNFORTUNATE NURSERY RHYMES

God help us all. He's gone and done it, ladies and gentlemen. Wild Ram is procreating.

Well, maybe…

With the way that man has gotten around, I wouldn't be too surprised if there were a couple of his offspring running around somewhere, either known or unknown to him. Let's face facts: The man probably has a flock.

There hasn't been a woman in Ram's life to make him change his rowdy ways. An argument could be made for the current woman keeping his bed warm, but I have my doubts. I thought that Red Riding Hood would be just another passing whim, but if she's carrying his child, we might be stuck with the redhead indefinitely.

How do I know that this might be a possibility? Well, it would appear that Red Riding Hood isn't the best about being discreet. She made a pit stop at our local Piggly Wiggly late last night. Yours truly observed her walk into the store shortly before closing and make a beeline to the pregnancy tests, a certain amount of fear radiating from her pores.

I mean, I would be scared, too, if I were linking myself to a good-for-nothing bartender. But what can you do? Well, maybe she could've kept her knees together, but that isn't the motto of this generation. It's *do now* and *think later.* Well, she's going to be thinking for a mighty long time if that little test of hers turned up a positive, something I can assure you would be a negative.

But only time will tell, and I have a sneaky suspicion that the whole thing is going to fall apart. Kind of like Humpty Dumpty falling from the wall. And nobody's going to be able to put that disaster back together again.

Hannah looked up, horrified.

No. No, no, no. This isn't happening.

Her ears were ringing, blocking out everything else around her. She handed the phone back over to Harper before she stood, more than a little unsteady on her feet. Her head was spinning and her lungs weren't working properly.

She looked around the room, searching for Shep, and it didn't take long for her to find him. He was making his way across to her. His expression was...unsettling, a mixture of anger and hurt.

The only time she'd ever seen him look like that was after they'd had sex for the first time—well, their first time since she returned to Mirabelle—and she'd said it had been *fucking* as opposed to *making love.*

He knew. He knew about that stupid article.

"Shep, I can explain."

"We need to talk somewhere private." He reached out and touched her elbow, leading her through the room.

He was barely touching her, just his thumb and forefinger. The absence of the full weight of his palm was more than a little bit painful.

The long hallway outside of the reception was relatively empty, just a few stragglers going back and forth between the bathrooms. Shep was heading down to the very end. She thought he was going to go through the side exit door and lead her outside. But he veered at the last minute, pushing open a door to his right that had been cracked open.

He let go of her as she walked into the darkness, flipping a switch and illuminating the room before he shut the door behind them.

She turned to look at him, her mouth trying to find words. Where the hell was she supposed to start with this? But it didn't matter, because Shep apparently knew exactly where to start.

"Did you buy a pregnancy test last night?"

"I...I was going to tell you."

"Are you pregnant?" For a second the longing in his face overtook the confusion and anger. And the hope that was in those words? There was too much there. It broke her.

She shook her head, unable to say anything.

His entire face fell, and he closed his eyes tight as he took a deep breath. When he opened them again, she wanted to look away from the pain. "I asked you straight out last night if you were okay, and you said you were just tired."

"I know. I—"

"You lied to me. Why? Why didn't you tell me?"

"Yesterday, at the bar...before the wedding...when everyone was so happy, it wasn't the time or the place to do it. This wasn't how it was supposed to happen. Not like this. *Dammit!* An hour. If this had waited an hour, it wouldn't have been like this."

"Why, Hannah?"

"I was scared."

He crossed the space to her, his hands coming up to her shoulders, holding her as he looked down into her face. "What were you scared of?" he asked. "Of me? What did you think I was going to do? Walk out on you and our child?"

"No. I didn't think that at all." She shook her head. "I don't think I was scared of the future, so much as the past. I had to tell you everything."

"What's everything?"

There was no more running away from the truth. No more waiting. It was here and now. "Shep...I...I'm not pregnant now, but thirteen years ago I was, with our child."

His hands fell away from her body. It was like somebody had just punched her in the stomach. And then he took a step back, moving away from her.

Another punch.

"You *were* pregnant?"

"I had a miscarriage."

He took another step back, shaking his head as he looked at her, like he couldn't see straight, or like he didn't know whom he was looking at. "How far along?" His question was barely audible.

"Almost three months."

"The night you called me?" he said slowly. "You were calling to tell me this?"

"Yes."

"And because you heard someone with me, you felt that I no longer deserved to know?"

"I thought you didn't care about me, and therefore wouldn't care about that."

"Are you fucking kidding me?"

"I was wrong. I was *so* wrong. I was eighteen and terrified. It destroyed me, and then you broke my heart on top of it. I didn't know what to do. I didn't know how to deal with it. I was so sad, Shep. For weeks after Gigi and I left Mirabelle, I just...I couldn't do anything. I could barely get out of bed. I missed you so damn much that it hurt to breathe. And then school started, and I hated it. I hated every damn minute of it." She couldn't stop the words as they poured from her mouth. The darker his face got, the more she tried to explain.

"I'd stare at the phone, desperate to call you, to hear your voice. But I couldn't do it. You'd said it. You'd said it was just a summer thing. That even though you loved me, it couldn't go further because I had to go to school. That it was over."

"You're blaming this on me?" he asked, incredulous.

"No! I'm not. That's what I'm trying to tell you. I didn't know what to do!" And there was the burning at the corners of her eyes. She blinked, and tears fell down her cheeks. "It was only a few weeks after I left Mirabelle when I realized I was late. But I ignored it. Told myself it wasn't happening. By the second month, I knew I couldn't ignore it anymore." Tears were streaming now, and she ran her fingers under her eyes to wipe them away.

"I took the test, and when I saw that positive, I knew I had to tell you. Knew you deserved to know. And I tried. So many times over the next few weeks I tried to pick up the phone. But the fear was paralyzing. Or at least I thought it was. I didn't know what real fear was until it got so much worse."

"You tried?" he asked slowly.

"Shep, I—"

"Did you try this time?"

"What?"

"Two months, Hannah. You've been back here for *two months*. I've gone after you since the moment I saw you. I've been willing to give up everything for you, have been trying to prove myself. And you still can't let me in? How could you not tell me now?"

"I didn't know how. I'm sorry. I—"

"Stop." He held up his hands, shaking his head. "You're sorry? You're *sorry*?"

"Shep, please." She reached for him, but he pulled away.

"I…I can't," he said as he backed farther away from her. "I just…I can't. I need to get out of here."

He turned and walked out of the room. Walked away from her.

It was worse than she'd thought it would be. The pain was crippling. So much so that her legs gave out from underneath her. She fell to her knees, her head falling into her hands and the tears coming like a dam had burst.

She'd lost Shep once before. And she couldn't do it again.

Chapter 19

Next to Me

Hannah wasn't sure how long she sat on the floor of that room, staring at the taupe wall. She vowed in that moment that absolutely no rooms in her inn would be painted that color.

She hated taupe.

Hannah got that life wasn't fair. She did. But an hour? Really? She couldn't have been given an hour? She'd been prepared to tell him *everything*. All of it. But it had been taken out of her hands.

That was why she was sitting there staring at a taupe wall that she hated about as much as she hated Bethelda—who hopefully would one day be eaten by her cats—Grimshaw.

A knock sounded at the door. She turned as the door jiggled and it was pushed open. Harper came into the room first, closely followed by Paige and Grace. She turned back and stared at the wall, unable to look at any of them straight on.

"Hannah?" Harper said her name gently as she kneeled down.

"What happened?" Grace asked.

"Sweetie, are you okay?" Paige shut the door before she came over and sat on Hannah's other side.

"No." She shook her head and promptly burst into tears.

Harper didn't say anything as she pulled Hannah into a hug, and as much as she felt undeserving of the comfort, she couldn't pull herself away.

"I don't know what to do." Hannah sobbed.

"We'll figure it out." Paige rubbed her hand up and down Hannah's back, more comfort that she didn't deserve.

"Start at the beginning," Harper said.

Hannah wasn't sure she was going to be able to talk, but somehow she opened her mouth and the words fell out.

She told them everything, like she was confessing all of her sins. But when she was done, all she felt was empty. Empty and alone.

Now all she wanted was to go home and crawl into bed. Go to sleep and wake up to realize this was just a really bad dream. That it hadn't happened.

"I know what it's like to mess up, to mess up so royally that you don't know if there's any going back," Paige said, handing Hannah another tissue. "I did, with Brendan. I blamed him for things that weren't his fault because I had no one else to blame. Sometimes grief leads us down a path that isn't the best. Shep... he...he'll figure it out."

"What if he doesn't figure it out?"

"He will," Grace said seriously. "You just can't give up. And you have to prove it to him. Prove that this is it. Prove that you want this and that you're going to fight for it no matter what. You can't walk away, Hannah."

"I know I can't."

"He's worth it, you know," Harper said.

"I know that, too." She nodded, a fresh wave of tears running down her face.

Paige leaned forward, running a tissue under Hannah's eyes. "So fight."

* * *

Mel and Bennett had already left the reception when Paige, Grace, and Harper had found Hannah. So when they emerged from the taupe room from hell, most of the guests had cleared out.

The guys obviously hadn't, though, as their ladies had been consoling Hannah. Brendan, Jax, Brad, and Finn were standing in a circle in the parking lot when the girls walked outside.

"It's going to work out," Harper said as she continued to rub Hannah's back. She leaned in and kissed Hannah's temple.

Hannah took a deep breath and continued on toward the guys, who were all looking worried. "Can I talk to you?" she asked Finn.

He looked surprised for a second before he moved off to the side with her.

"Do you know?" she asked.

"Not everything. Just what was in the article."

"It's worse than that," she whispered, closing her eyes for a second before she opened them again.

"Where is he?"

"I don't know. I know you don't like me very much, but—"

"Hannah, I don't dislike you. I don't know you. But I do know you love my brother."

"I do." She nodded, running her fingers under her streaming eyes again. Years of not crying and now she couldn't turn it off. "I love him so much. I need to fix this, Finn. I *have* to fix this. And I need your help."

* * *

Shep stared down at Owen's headstone, reading the words engraved into the granite over and over again.

Beloved Husband, Devoted Father, and *Trusted Friend.*

He closed his eyes at the wave of pain that ran through him. Never in his life had he needed Owen's guidance more. He took a mouthful of whiskey. It burned down his throat before it settled nice and warm in his stomach.

"Are these the consequences? Is this my punishment? Is this what I deserve for all the shit I did? 'Cause I can't deal with this. How does a person deal with this?"

A baby. There'd been a baby. A baby that he and Hannah had created together. A baby that had died.

It had happened thirteen years ago, but for him…for him it had just happened.

He would have been a father. Their child would've been twelve years old now. Another wave of pain ran through him, so he tipped the bottle back again, attempting to dull the ache.

It wasn't really working.

The graveyard around him was quiet and slightly eerie in the dark. The moon was large in the sky, more than half full, with the stars clear as anything around it.

He'd just found out that he'd lost a child and he'd run to the graveyard. He was surrounded by death. Surrounded by pain and loss.

Is this what it was to love? To hurt?

"You lied to me." Shep shook his head. "You *lied.* You said it was worth it. You said this was what life was all about, finding the person you love. But what happens when they do this? What happens when they withhold and they lie and they never let you in? What happens then?"

"You keep trying."

Shep turned around as Finn made his way over to the grave. "What are you doing here?"

"Didn't want you getting drunk alone." Finn grabbed the bottle from Shep's hand, taking a drink before he passed it back.

"You know?"

"Hannah told me everything."

Shep closed his eyes at her name and turned away.

"She's really upset, you know."

"She should be." Shep threw the bottle back and took another swig.

"So what are you going to do now?"

"What is there to do now?"

"You're fucking kidding me, right? You're giving up? After everything you've said? After all of your words of *she's the only one for me?*"

"Yup. That should make you happy." Shep turned to look at Finn again. "I'm not going anywhere now."

"You're an idiot. You know that?"

"Seriously? You're on her side?"

"No, you moron." Finn grabbed the bottle from Shep. "I'm on *your* side. I'm a selfish ass. That was why I didn't want you to go. I've been gone for eight years, and I get back and you're about to pack your bags, and it pissed me off. Yeah, I'm bitter because of Becky. I'm pissed because she moved on. But I let her move on. I never did anything to keep her in the first place. I thought I could go off and do my own thing and then come back and she'd be here waiting for me. And when that wasn't the case, all I could think about was how you get your second chance and I didn't get mine. But now? Now I'm pissed because you're throwing it away."

"I'm throwing it away?"

"What does it change, Shep? What does knowing it all change? She was pregnant, and, man, I can't even begin to imagine what it's like to lose a child. And yeah, I get that you didn't find out in the best way."

"You think?" Shep laughed bitterly.

"Does it change anything? Does it change how much you love her?"

"No. I'll always love her. But sometimes that's not enough." Shep held out his hand for the whiskey bottle, but Finn shook his head.

"I think you need to stop drinking."

"Why?"

"Because whiskey obviously makes you stupid. You're not mad at her."

"I'm not? You sure about that? 'Cause I think I'm pretty fucking infuriated with her."

"Okay, you're a little bit mad at her. But you're pissed at yourself."

"You might be a doctor, but I don't think you're qualified to psychoanalyze me." He turned back to stare at Owen's grave.

"I think I am. You're upset because you think that if you had known you could've done something to stop her from losing that baby. But you couldn't stop it, Shep. There wasn't anything that could've been done. And no matter how much you want to, you can't fix it, either."

"I had a kid. *We* had a kid. How can losing someone that you never knew hurt this much? I don't even know if it was a boy or a girl. Never got to hold my child in my arms. I could've had this entire other life. A life with Hannah where I didn't lose thirteen years, where we didn't lose our child." The words on the headstone blurred as Shep's eyes burned. The tears started to fall from his eyes, and he couldn't breathe.

Finn was right, he couldn't fix any of it.

* * *

For the second night in a row, Hannah stared up at the spinning fan, sleep nowhere on the horizon. It was two o'clock in
the morning, and she was wide-awake. One would think that the
constant crying would've made her sleepy.

Not so much.

Her brain was on overdrive as she tried to figure out what she
was going to do. She had no freaking clue. There was no logic
when it came to any of this. No logic when it came to the pain,
or the hurt, or how much she loved that man.

Finn had left the parking lot and gone out in search of Shep.
She'd wanted to go, too, but what the hell was she going to say
to him?

I'm sorry? That hadn't gone over very well the first time.
Chances were it wouldn't this time, either.

So what the hell was she supposed to do?

How could she repair this?

Paige had said she needed to fight. And she would. She'd
fight for Shep for however long it took. He'd been right. He *had*
proven himself, and now she needed to prove herself. She just
had to figure out how.

A loud bang at the front door pulled her from her thoughts.
Henry had been asleep next to her, and he streaked off the bed,
bolting into the closet.

Hannah's heart hammered in her throat as she got out of bed.
She flipped lights on as she stumbled through the house. There
was more banging the closer she got, and loud voices. Well, one
loud voice and the other making a shushing sound.

"Don't you shush me! You shush!"

"Dammit, Shep! Stop doing that."

"No. She's here. I *need* to see her." Shep's slurred words came through the door. "Hannah! Hannah!"

She flipped the dead bolt and opened the door, finding a very drunk Shep being supported by his brother.

"There she is," Shep said to Finn. "Isn't she beautiful? She breaks my heart, and all I can think is how fucking beautiful she is. How does that make sense?"

"Sorry," Finn apologized, looking at Hannah. "He told me to take him home, but when I took him back to his house, he wouldn't get out of the car."

Hannah immediately crossed the threshold, coming in on Shep's other side and putting his arm around her shoulder so she could help Finn guide him into the house.

"'Cause that's not home," Shep said as they walked through the living room. "Home is with Hannah the breaker of my heart. Isn't she beautiful?" he asked Finn again. "So fucking beautiful it hurts. And, man, does it hurt. Don't do it, Finn. Don't fall in love. 'Cause you can't go back from it. It's irreveribles. Irreversbiel. Irreversible."

"I don't know how much whiskey he drank before I got there, but it's hit him pretty hard in the last thirty minutes."

"'Cause they lie to you," Shep continued when they sat him down on the bed. "And it doesn't change how much you love them. It just makes it that much worse when you still love them after all that hurt. Because the love doesn't go away, man." He grabbed on to Finn's shirt. "It. Doesn't. Go. Away."

"You need to get some sleep," Finn said, pulling Shep's hand off his shirt. Shep fell back onto the bed, and Finn turned to look at Hannah. "You going to be okay? I can sleep on the sofa or something."

"I'll be fine." Hannah shook her head before she looked at

Shep, who was already passed out in the bed. "Can you just help me turn him?"

"Yeah." Finn reached down and pulled Shep's legs onto the bed, settling his head on the pillow before he moved away.

Hannah was used to seeing Shep asleep, and his forehead would always be relaxed. Tonight it was bunched together in confusion, still trying to work things out even though he was unconscious. She turned away and walked with Finn to the front door.

"He's really drunk, Hannah. I wouldn't put too much stock in his words. He didn't know what he was saying."

"It doesn't mean it isn't true."

Finn stopped and turned to look at her when he got to the door. "Maybe not, but I'd focus on the good over the bad."

She couldn't stop the pained laugh that came out of her mouth. "What good?"

"How about the fact that even after everything, the only person he wants is you? I don't think that's going to change. No matter what. Focus on that. And figure out what to do in the morning."

He opened the door and stepped outside but turned before he walked down the steps. "I owe you an apology. Even with all of this…" He waved his hand in the air. "I—I can't even imagine that kind of loss…a baby." He shook his head. "He doesn't know how to deal with it. But he will. My brother is one of the smartest people I know. He just can't think straight when it comes to you."

Hannah was so taken aback by Finn's words that all she could manage to get out was a "thank you."

"I'll see you later, Hannah. And this will get worked out. I have no doubts about that." He waved before he turned around and headed off toward his truck, leaving a very shocked Hannah in his wake.

She turned all of the lights off as she made her way back to the bedroom. She stood in the doorway for a minute, watching Shep sleep before she moved to the bed, pulling off his shoes and socks.

She moved to his pants next, unbuckling his belt before she slowly shimmied them down his legs. She started on his shirt next, undoing his buttons. When she got to the last one, Shep's hand came up, grabbing on to hers.

She looked up into his face, his unfocused eyes watching her.

"I love you."

"I know. I love you, too."

"So why? Why do you keep hurting me?"

"Shep." She reached up to touch his face, but he turned away from her, gently grabbing her hand and pulling it away.

"What did I do?" he asked, sitting up. "What did I do wrong?"

"Nothing." She shook her head, running her hands up his shoulders and pulling his shirt from his arms.

He let her slip it off, and when his hands were free, he reached up, touching her face. "Then why can't I have you?"

"You can. Shep, I—"

"Don't leave me." He leaned in, burying his face in her neck as his arms wrapped around her. "Please, Hannah. Don't leave me." His voice cracked, and tears hit her skin.

"I'm not going to." She wrapped her arms around him, running her hands up and down his back.

"I'm sorry. I'm so sorry."

"Shep..." She couldn't say anything. Her own tears clogged her throat, making it painful to talk.

He pulled her down onto the bed, and they stayed that way for God only knew how long until he finally fell asleep.

But sleep never came to Hannah, and she held him until well after the sun came up.

* * *

Shep cracked one eye open, and he was pretty sure his head was about to split in two. The bright light streaming through the windows was surely going to kill him. He slammed his eyes shut and groaned, rolling over onto his back.

He did an assessment, a very slow assessment considering the jackhammer that was in his skull. He was in a bed. No shirt. No pants. Boxers...yes.

So whose bed was he in?

Not his. The sheets were too soft and they smelled like lavender.

Hannah.

He was at the inn? How the hell had he gotten to the inn?

Images of the night before flashed in his brain. The wedding. The article. Hannah's face as she told him what had happened thirteen years ago. The graveyard. Whiskey. Finn showing up. More whiskey. Him losing it. Even more whiskey. Banging on the front door of the inn. Hannah. Hannah in her pajamas with red-rimmed eyes. Her hands in his hair as he cried into his shoulder. Him begging her not to leave.

He was pretty sure he'd made a total ass out of himself ten times over. It all made his head hurt more. He needed to talk to her; that much he knew. Where it would go after, he had no clue.

Finn had been right about one thing, though. Nothing he'd found out last night changed the fact that he loved her. And he needed to find her, needed to fix this. It was just a matter of getting vertical.

He opened his eyes again before he slowly rolled over and put his legs over the side of the bed. He glanced at the alarm clock and was shocked to see it was after noon. Apparently, this was what happened when you drank almost half a bottle of Jack Daniel's.

His head spun and his stomach churned as he got to his feet and walked into the bathroom. He needed a hot shower and a strong cup of coffee.

The first would have to wait. He'd just have to make do with brushing his teeth and splashing cold water on his face. The second he found when he headed out into the kitchen.

He poured a cup of coffee, downing half of it before he refilled it. He grabbed the bottle of Advil in one of the cabinets and dumped three into his hand, popping them into his mouth before he took a mouthful of coffee to wash them down.

He closed his eyes and leaned back against the counter, letting the coffee and medicine settle in before he went off In search of Hannah.

The downstairs was entirely empty, no sound coming from any of the rooms. He did a quick check out the window in the kitchen, seeing Hannah's car parked in front. He stepped out into the living room and glanced toward the back doors, but he didn't see her out there, either.

A loud thump echoed through the ceiling above him. He headed for the stairs, making his way up to the third floor. He had a feeling of where she was, and it was confirmed when he heard her voice drifting down the hallway from the partially open door at the very end.

It was the room she'd stayed in all those years ago. The room he'd snuck into more times than he could count. The room where hours of their relationship had played out.

The closer he got, the more he heard. He put his hand on the door and stilled right before he pushed it open, hearing the next words that came out of her mouth.

"No. I think the sooner I get it on the market the better. If you can get people looking at it now, then go for it. I just want it to sell. Get it over and done with. There's absolutely no reason for me to keep it. It isn't like I'll be visiting all that often. Or ever, really."

Her words hit him like a punch to the gut.

She's selling the inn? Without talking to me?

So what if things weren't exactly settled between them at the moment. All the more reason to not make a major decision that impacted both of them.

Shouldn't they talk before she sold the inn? Shouldn't they figure this out together?

And they wouldn't be visiting? They wouldn't be coming down here for vacations or holidays?

Or was there no *they*? She'd only said *I* during the entire conversation.

Had she changed her mind?

How had he been this wrong?

This... this wasn't right.

"I should be up in a few days," she continued.

No, we have until the end of the month before she has to be back.

"I'll pack up my stuff, tie up a few loose ends at work, and then I'll be back here. So whatever we can get started now would be best. I'm done with New York."

Wait...

"What?" Shep couldn't stop the word that came out of his mouth. He pushed the door open to find Hannah sitting on the floor. Her back was to the wall while she pet a purring Henry, who was in her lap.

She stopped talking into the phone for just a second as she looked up. "I have to go, Morrisey. Get the ball rolling for me, and I'll call you back in a little bit. Bye."

She ended the call, her eyes not leaving his. The wariness he found there was unsettling.

He didn't say anything as he crossed the room. He leaned back against the wall before he slid down and sat next to her on the floor. She set her phone up on the dresser next to her and turned to look at him.

"How's your head?" she asked.

"Throbbing. I think I'm hallucinating."

"Why's that?"

"Did I just hear you say you're moving down here?"

She took a deep breath and let it out in a frustrated huff. "Why is it that I can never tell you things how I want to tell you them?"

"Hannah?" He couldn't stop himself from reaching out and trailing his fingers down her cheek. She closed her eyes for just a second as she leaned in to his touch. When she opened her eyes slowly, he realized there was much more than wariness there. There was exhaustion and fear.

And determination.

She picked Henry up and placed him on the floor, where the cat quickly scampered out of the room. And then Hannah was moving, throwing her leg across Shep's and climbing up onto his lap.

She reached up and grabbed his face, leaning forward as she looked into his eyes. "Yes. I'm moving here. To Mirabelle. To the inn. To...you."

"What about your job?"

"Well, as I quit yesterday, I no longer have one."

"You quit *yesterday*...before...?"

"Everything went to hell? Yes. I called Allison before the wedding and told her I'd be resigning to pursue other endeavors."

"Other endeavors?" he asked as he placed his hands on her hips. He might be sitting down, but the more she talked, the more he needed something to ground him.

"You. I want a life with you. And I want it here." She dropped her hands and indicated the room around them. "This is home. My home with you. Tell me you want that, too. Tell me you want to make this work, because, Shep, I'm not giving up."

He grabbed her hands and pulled her against his chest, pressing his mouth to hers in a slow, gentle kiss. Her mouth was much more of a balm to his hangover than the coffee or medicine had been. "Yes, I want that. So damn much. But, Hannah, no more secrets."

"No more." She shook her head. "You know everything now."

"That's good, 'cause I don't know if I could survive another bomb." His hold on her hands loosened, and he skimmed his palms up her arms and to her shoulders

"I'm sorry, Shep." She pulled back, her hands gliding up his chest. "I tried to call you so many times, and I don't know if you will ever forgive me for how everything happened. But when I thought you'd moved on, when I thought you'd never really loved me—"

"Hannah—"

"No." She placed her fingers over his mouth and shook her head. "Let me finish. I know the truth now. I know that you never stopped loving me. But I didn't know it then. And I couldn't handle everything that was happening. I was eighteen, and terrified, and hurt, and confused, and about a hundred other emotions. I didn't have you, and it was…painful. I screwed up. I'm sorry that I hurt you. I'm sorry that I hurt *us*."

She dropped her hand from his mouth, and he took that as his cue that it was his turn to speak.

"We both screwed up, babe. And I think that I have a lot more to be sorry for than you do." He leaned down, resting his forehead against hers. "I was so mad at you for not telling me," he whispered. She tensed and started to pull away, but he grabbed her wrists again, holding her close. "But I was angrier at myself. I *am* angrier at myself."

"Why?"

"Because I wasn't there. If I'd fought for you thirteen years ago, I would've been. If I hadn't let you go, I would've been there and I could've...I could've done something." His throat constricted and his eyes burned.

"Shep, no." She shook her head, pulling one of her hands from his grasp and reaching up to his face. She ran her thumb under his eye, catching the tears that fell. "There was nothing that could've been done. You have to understand that. Nothing could've changed what happened."

"Maybe not with the baby. But there were a lot of things that I could've done differently. I'm the one who should be begging for your forgiveness. I failed you, Hannah. I hurt us more than you ever could. I knew that it was supposed to be us in the end thirteen years ago, but I didn't listen. I didn't fight for you. And I did it again last night. Instead of fighting for us when it got hard, I ran."

"Shep, battles aren't always won immediately. Sometimes you have to recuperate after a hard blow before you can fight. What do you think this is?" She traced his temple with her thumb before she moved her hand back and ran her fingers through his hair. "This doesn't look like running to me. This looks like fighting. We can't change the past. All we can do is learn from it, move on from here, and try again."

"Try again?" He swallowed thickly, hoping she was talking about what he thought she was talking about. "With...with what exactly?"

"Everything. Us and...a family."

"You want kids."

"Very much." She nodded. "When I took that pregnancy test, I didn't realize how much I wanted it to be positive until I saw that negative."

"This is what you want? We're really going to do this?" he asked, searching her face for doubt, but there wasn't any.

"Yes."

"No more running. Not ever."

"Never again." She shook her head. "It's you and me from here on out. No lies, no barriers, nothing between us."

"Nothing between us," he agreed before he pressed his mouth to hers. He reached up, his fingers spearing through her hair, and pulled back, looking into that face that he loved so much. "Gigi was a wise woman, getting you to come down here."

"Very wise," Hannah agreed. "I'm glad you didn't forget about me, Nathanial Shepherd." Her hand moved over his heart, and he felt her touch all the way to his bones.

"How many times do I have to tell you, Hannah Sterling? You're unforgettable."

Epilogue

Forever and for Always

One year later…

Hannah stretched out on the blanket, snuggling closer in to Shep's side as they both stared up at the stars. It was the same field he'd brought her out to all those years ago. The same field they'd made love in for the first time. It was actually fourteen years to the day it had happened.

A train rumbled by a few miles away, its horn drowning out the steady hum of the cicadas that surrounded them. The July air was humid, but the breeze off the ocean was constant, making the Saturday evening more than pleasant.

Hannah loved nights like this: Shep's arms wrapped around her body, her head on his chest, and the steady beat of his heart echoing in her ear.

It was perfection.

She didn't miss the life she'd left behind in Manhattan, didn't miss it one little bit. Didn't miss the stress, or the loneliness, or the constant ache. She wasn't done being a lawyer, but the inn had been her focus for the last year, and it had kept her plenty busy.

She'd spent months pouring over blueprints with Shep and Bennett, deciding to turn the bottom floor into a home for her and Shep and renovating the top two floors into little vacation rentals. It was still an inn in some ways, but they would get the privacy they needed when they rented out the new rooms.

The renovations had turned out to be an investment of time and money. With her lack of a job and the brownstone in Manhattan selling, she had a lot of both.

Shep's schedule had changed as well. He still worked at the Sleepy Sheep a few nights a week, but his new focus was the brewery that had been built right next to the bar. And since he spent most of his days running that, she got more of his nights. This was why she got slow, lazy evenings under the stars.

She loved these moments more than anything, and she appreciated every second of them.

Gigi buying the inn had been the catalyst to the best decision Hannah had ever made. She would be forever grateful for her grandmother. Even in death the woman was taking care of her, would forever be taking care of her.

There were no doubts in Hannah's mind that this was the life she'd been destined for, that this was the life she'd been meant to lead, that this was the man she was supposed to be with for the rest of her life.

He was hers just as much as she was his.

She turned slightly, snuggling in to his side, her left hand running across his chest and the diamond on her ring finger glinting in the moonlight.

He'd proposed two months after they'd moved all of their things into the inn, two months after she'd packed up her life in Manhattan and headed south permanently.

Her mind flashed to that day, the memory so clear it was like it had happened yesterday.

It was a Sunday afternoon and they'd just gotten home from riding. They'd showered—together, obviously—and were both getting dressed in their bedroom. She caught his reflection in the mirror above her dresser, watching as he pulled a T-shirt out of his drawer.

It was such a simple thing, both of them getting dressed in their bedroom, a bedroom that was the perfect mix of the two of them.

There was *their* bed, a bed that they'd slept in only together, with a painting of two horses running across the beach hanging above it. Paige had painted it for them, and it was stunning, with the water splashing up all around horses that looked a lot like Springsteen and Nigel.

Then there was the teal and emerald-green woven rug that was spread across the floor. A rug that they'd picked out together. A rug that they'd made love on many times.

It was home. *He* was home.

It was more than a little overwhelming, and she reached out to hold on to her dresser for balance, trying to breathe past the light-headed feeling in her head.

It was at that moment that Shep turned as he pulled his T-shirt on, and when his head cleared the fabric, his eyes met hers in the reflection of the mirror.

"You okay?" he asked as he crossed the room.

Hannah turned and leaned back against her dresser, looking up at him as he wrapped his arms around her. She was wearing only a simple pair of green cotton panties and a white cotton bra. His hands moved up and down her almost bare back, tracing her spine.

"Yeah." She nodded, stretching up and placing a soft kiss to his mouth. "I just... I'm happy, Shep, so much so that I can barely see straight."

"Well, that's good, 'cause you're kind of stuck with me."

"How stuck?"

"How stuck do you want to be?"

"Well, I was thinking," she said, running her hands up his chest, tracing the soft cotton with her fingertips. "A binding legal document would be nice."

"Is that lawyer talk for marriage?" He quirked his head to the side, his lips twisting into a grin.

"It just might be."

"I like that kind of talk." He moved back just slightly as he dropped his hands from her back and grabbed her hands. He pulled them from his chest and brought them to his mouth, kissing each of her palms. "Something to discuss over dinner, I think, when I can get you nice and full of food and wine. Easier to convince you that a quick engagement would be the best."

"You've thought about this?" she asked, her heart kicking up hard in her throat. That light-headed feeling returned in full force.

"Hannah, I think about marrying you on a daily basis." He let go of her hands and pulled back. "Now, get dressed so I don't get distracted with your lack of clothing and we can actually have that conversation."

"When are you going to stop telling me what to do?"

"Never." He shook his head and grinned as he left the room.

He wants to talk about marriage? Thank the good Lord.

The grin that spread across her face was huge as she dug a pair of shorts out of her dresser. She pulled them on before she went over to Shep's dresser, wanting to wear one of his T-shirts. She preferred the ones that he'd already worn, but as they'd gone riding, his shirt from this afternoon smelled more like horses than like him. She chose to go with a clean one.

She was distracted for just a second as she opened the drawer. The picture that sat on top of his dresser always caught her attention. It was the one Paige had taken at Trevor's birthday party. The one of Hannah and Shep staring at each other.

Even then their love for each other was evident. A future that neither of them could run from. A future that involved marriage and babies and growing old together.

She looked down and froze as she caught sight of the object that sat on top of the neatly folded stack of T-shirts.

A cushion cut diamond ring stood out plainly among the black fabric.

If she thought her heart was pounding earlier, she'd had no idea.

"Oh my God," she whispered as she reached for the ring with an unsteady hand.

"Marry me."

Hannah spun around to find Shep on his knee behind her. He looked up at her with so much love and adoration she couldn't breathe. He held out his hand, and she walked the few steps to him.

"I want to spend the rest of my life with you," he said as he pulled the ring from her fingers. "I've always wanted to spend my life with you, and I always *will* want to. You're it for me, Hannah. You were the first time I saw you. I love you more than anything."

Her eyes watered and her bottom lip trembled. "I love you, too."

"Then say yes." He reached for her hand and she gave it to him willingly. He slipped the ring onto her finger, staring at it for just a second before he brought her hand to his mouth and kissed the ring.

He looked up at her, waiting for her answer.

"Yes." She nodded, lucky she'd been able to get the word out past her constricted throat.

He pulled her forward, kissing her belly as he wrapped his arms around her and held her to him.

"You're mine, Hannah Sterling."

"As you're mine, Nathanial Shepherd." She buried her fingers in his hair as he continued to cover her belly with kisses.

The barefoot wedding on the beach by the inn had been a little more than a month later, the very last weekend in October. The weather had been perfect, with crystal-clear skies and a touch of autumn on the breeze.

Her dress had been simple yet elegant. An antique lace with an open back. The groomsmen wore khaki suits and the brides-maids, dresses made of champagne satin.

The fact that none of Hannah's immediate family was there stung only a little bit. The truth was, her real family was standing up there with her. Those girls had welcomed her into their fold immediately. Hannah was closer to them in the months she'd been in Mirabelle than she was with her sister in all the years they'd spent together.

And all of the guys, Shep's brothers by blood or not, who she knew would do anything for her. Do anything for them.

Yes, her real family surrounded her when she had walked down that aisle. Well, when she and Shep had walked down that aisle together.

Whenever that moment replayed in her mind, she couldn't help but grin. As she'd made her way down the steps, he'd been walking up through the crowd.

"I've waited for you long enough," he said as he stopped in front of her and grabbed her hands. And then he'd leaned down to kiss her, placing a soft kiss on her lips. "I'm done waiting. We do this together."

Together.

He said that word a lot. Like when he got the tattoo that now stretched up his left side, the counterpart to the broken angel wing on her hip.

"Not broken anymore," he'd told her. "We'll fly together."

She had no doubts about that. Would never doubt it again.

She was brought back to the present as Shep shifted underneath her. He moved, gently laying her flat on her back so that he could roll to his side and look down into her face. He smiled down at her as he ran his palm along her ever-growing belly.

The no-barriers promise they'd made became a reality in every way the night of the wedding. There had been more than a small amount of niggling fear when they'd watched that pregnancy test turn positive a few months later.

But she was seven months along now, and Nathanial Owen III was growing strong and healthy. Every time he kicked, or moved, or just got the hiccups, her fear shrank a little bit more.

"You still good here?" Shep asked as he pushed his hand under her shirt so that his palm was on her bare skin. "Or do you want to head home?"

"A little bit longer." She smiled as she reached up to his face.

"Okay," he said before he leaned down and kissed her.

His tongue dipped into her mouth, and she let him take full advantage of the situation, his lips moving over hers until she was good and breathless. He pulled back and looked down at her, his eyes filled with that adoration that she didn't think she'd ever get used to seeing. It still made her stomach flutter.

"I love you so damn much. Did you know that?" he asked.

"I did." She nodded. "Did you know that I love you so damn much, too?"

"I did." He grinned as he kissed her neck, his lips traveling down as he made a path down her body. When he got to her stomach, he pushed her shirt up and pressed his lips to her skin. "I love you, too," he whispered against her belly. "Forever and for always."

Forever and for always. Those words had been part of their vows. There was no doubt in her mind that this time neither of them was going to let go.

Not ever again.

Things Paige Morrison will never understand
about Mirabelle, Florida:

Why wearing red shoes makes a girl a harlot
Why a shop would ever sell something called "buck urine"
Why everywhere she goes, she runs into sexy—and
infuriating—Brendan King.

Please see the next page for an excerpt from

Undone,

the first book in Shannon Richard's Country Roads series.

Chapter 1

Short Fuses and a Whole Lot of Sparks

Bethelda Grimshaw was a snot-nosed wench. She was an evil, mean-spirited, vindictive, horrible human being.

Paige should've known. She should've known the instant she'd walked into that office and sat down. Bethelda Grimshaw had a malevolent stench radiating off her, kind of like roadkill in ninety-degree weather. The interview, if it could even be called that, had been a complete waste of time.

"She didn't even read my résumé," Paige said, slamming her hand against the steering wheel as she pulled out of the parking lot of the Mirabelle Information Center.

No, Bethelda had barely even looked at said résumé before she'd set it down on the desk and leaned back in her chair, appraising Paige over her cat's-eye glasses.

"So you're the *infamous* Paige Morrison," Bethelda had said, raising a perfectly plucked, bright red eyebrow. "You've caused *quite* a stir since you came to town."

Quite a stir?

Okay, so there had been that incident down at the Piggly Wiggly, but that hadn't been Paige's fault. Betty Whitehurst might seem like a sweet, little old lady, but in reality she was as blind as a bat and as vicious as a shrew. Betty drove her shopping cart like she was racing in the Indy 500, which was an accomplishment, as she barely cleared the handle. She'd slammed her cart into Paige, who in turn fell into a display of cans. Paige had been calm for all of about five seconds before Betty had started screeching at her about watching where she was going.

Paige wasn't one to take things lying down covered in cans of creamed corn, so she'd calmly explained to Betty that she *had* been watching where she was going. "Calmly" being that Paige had started yelling and the store manager had to get involved to quiet everyone down.

Yeah, Paige didn't deal very well with certain types of people. Certain types being evil, mean-spirited, vindictive, horrible human beings. And Bethelda Grimshaw was quickly climbing to the top of that list.

"As it turns out," Bethelda had said, pursing her lips in a patronizing pout, "we already filled the position. I'm afraid there was a mistake in having you come down here today."

"When?"

"Excuse me?" Bethelda had asked, her eyes sparkling with glee.

"When did you fill the position?" Paige had repeated, trying to stay calm.

"Last week."

Really? So the phone call Paige had gotten that morning to confirm the time of the interview had been a mistake?

This was the eleventh job interview she'd gone on in the last two months. And it had most definitely been the worst. It hadn't even been an interview. She'd been set up; she just didn't understand why. But she hadn't been about to ask that question out loud. So instead of flying off the handle and losing the last bit of restraint she had, Paige had calmly gotten up from the chair and left without making a scene. The whole thing was a freaking joke, which fit perfectly for the current theme of Paige's life.

Six months ago, Paige had been living in Philadelphia. She'd had a good job in the art department of an advertising agency. She'd shared a tiny two-bedroom apartment above a coffee shop with her best friend, Abby Fields. And she'd had Dylan, a man whom she'd been very much in love with.

And then the rug got pulled out from under her and she'd fallen flat on her ass.

First off, Abby got a job at an up-and-coming PR firm. Which was good news, and Paige had been very excited for her, except the job was in Washington, DC, which Paige was not excited about. Then, before Paige could find a new roommate, she'd lost her job. The advertising agency was bought out and she was in the first round of cuts. Without a job, she couldn't renew her lease, and was therefore homeless. So she'd moved in with Dylan. It was always supposed to be a temporary thing, just until Paige could find another job and get on her feet again.

But it never happened.

Paige had tried for two months and found nothing, and then the real bomb hit. She was either blind or just distracted by everything else that was going on, but either way, she never saw it coming.

Paige had been with Dylan for about a year and she'd really thought he'd been the one. Okay, he tended to be a bit of a snob when it came to certain things. For example, wine. Oh, was he ever a wine snob, rather obnoxious about it really. He would always swirl it around in his glass, take a sip, sniff, and then take another loud sip, smacking his lips together.

He was also a snob about books. Paige enjoyed reading the classics, but she also liked reading romance, mystery, and fantasy. Whenever she would curl up with one of her books, Dylan tended to give her a rather patronizing look and shake his head.

"Reading fluff again I see," he would always say.

Yeah, she didn't miss *that* at all. Or the way he would roll his eyes when she and Abby would quote movies and TV shows to each other. Or how he'd never liked her music and flat-out refused to dance with her. Which had always been frustrating because Paige loved to dance. But despite all of that, she'd loved him. Loved the way he would run his fingers through his hair when he was distracted, loved his big goofy grin, and loved the way his glasses would slide down his nose.

But the thing was, he hadn't loved her.

One night, he'd come back to his apartment and sat Paige down on the couch. Looking back on it, she'd been an idiot, because there was a small part of her that thought he was actually about to propose.

"Paige," he'd said, sitting down on the coffee table and grabbing her hands. "I know that this was supposed to be a temporary thing, but weeks have turned into months. Living with you has brought a lot of things to light."

It was wrong, everything about that moment was *all wrong*. She could tell by the look in his eyes, by the tone of his voice, by the way he said *Paige* and *light*. In that moment she'd known exactly where he was going, and it wasn't anywhere with her. He wasn't proposing. He was breaking up with her.

She'd pulled her hands out of his and shrank back into the couch.

"This," he'd said, gesturing between the two of them, "was never going to go further than where we are right now."

And that was the part where her ears had started ringing.

"At one point I thought I might love you, but I've realized I'm not *in* love with you," he'd said, shaking his head. "I feel like you've thought this was going to go further, but the truth is, I'm never going to marry you. Paige, you're not the one. I'm tired of pretending. I'm tired of putting in the effort for a relationship that isn't going anywhere else. It's not worth it to me."

"You mean I'm not worth it," she'd said, shocked.

"Paige, you deserve to be with someone who wants to make the effort, and I deserve to be with someone who I'm willing to make the effort for. It's better that we end this now, instead of delaying the inevitable."

He'd made it sound like he was doing her a favor, like he had her best interests at heart.

But all she'd heard was *You're not worth it* and *I'm not in love with you.* And those were the words that kept repeating in her head, over and over and over again.

Dylan had told her he was going to go stay with one of his friends for the week. She'd told him she'd be out before the end of the next day. She'd spent the entire night packing up her stuff. Well, packing and crying and drinking two entire bottles of the prick's wine.

Paige didn't have a lot of stuff. Most of the furniture from her and Abby's apartment had been Abby's. Everything that Paige owned had fit into the back of her Jeep and the U-Haul trailer that she'd rented first thing the following morning. She'd loaded up and gotten out of there before four o'clock in the afternoon.

She'd stayed the night in a hotel room just outside Philadelphia, where she'd promptly passed out. She'd been exhausted after her marathon packing, which was good because it was harder for a person to feel beyond pathetic in her sleep. No, that was what the eighteen-hour drive the following day had been reserved for.

Jobless, homeless, and brokenhearted, Paige had nowhere else to go but home to her parents. The problem was, there was no *home* anymore. The house in Philadelphia that Paige had grown up in was no longer her parents'. They'd sold it and retired to a little town in the South.

Mirabelle, Florida: population five thousand.

There were roughly the same amount of people in the six hundred square miles of Mirabelle as there were in half a square mile of Philadelphia. Well, unless the mosquitoes were counted as residents.

People who thought that Florida was all sunshine and sand were sorely mistaken. It did have its fair share of beautiful beaches. The entire southeast side of Mirabelle was the Gulf of Mexico. But about half of the town was made up of water. And all of that water, combined with the humidity that plagued the area, created the perfect breeding ground for mosquitoes. Otherwise known as tiny, blood-sucking villains that loved to bite the crap out of Paige's legs.

Paige had visited her parents a couple of times over the last couple of years, but she'd never been in love with Mirabelle like her parents were. And she still wasn't. She'd spent a month moping around her parents' house. Again, she was pathetic enough to believe that maybe, just maybe, Dylan would call her and tell her that he'd been wrong. That he missed her. That he loved her.

He'd never called, and Paige realized he was never going to. That was when Paige resigned herself to the fact that she had to move on with her life. So she'd started looking for a job.

Which had proved to be highly unsuccessful.

Paige had been living in Mirabelle for three months now.

Three long, miserable months when nothing had gone right. Not one single thing.

And as that delightful thought crossed her mind, she noticed that her engine was smoking. Great white plumes of steam escaped from the hood of her Jeep Cherokee.

"You've got to be kidding me," she said as she pulled off to the side of the road and turned the engine off. "Fan-freaking-tastic."

Paige grabbed her purse and started digging around in the infinite abyss, searching for her cell phone. She sifted through old receipts, a paperback book, her wallet, lip gloss, a nail file, gum… *ah*, cell phone. She pressed speed dial for her father. She held the phone against her ear while she leaned over and searched for her shoes, which she'd thrown on the floor of the passenger side. As her hand closed over one of her black wedges, the phone beeped in her ear and disconnected. She sat up and held her phone out, staring at the display screen in disbelief.

No service.

"This has to be some sick, twisted joke," she said, banging her head down on the steering wheel. No service on her cell phone shouldn't have been that surprising; there were plenty of dead zones around Mirabelle. Apparently there was a lack of cell phone towers in this little piece of purgatory.

Paige resigned herself to the fact that she was going to have to walk to find civilization, or at least a bar of service on her cell phone. She went in search of her other wedge, locating it under the passenger seat.

The air conditioner had been off for less than two minutes, and it was already starting to warm up inside the Jeep. It was going to be a long, hot walk. Paige grabbed a hair tie from the gearshift, put her long brown hair up into a messy bun, and opened the door to the sweltering heat.

I hate *this godforsaken place.*

Paige missed Philadelphia. She missed her friends, her apartment with its rafters and squeaky floors. She missed having a job, missed having a paycheck, missed buying shoes. And even though she hated it, she still missed Dylan. Missed his dark shaggy hair and the way he would nibble on her lower lip when they kissed. She even missed his humming when he cooked.

She shook her head and snapped back to the present. She might as well focus on the task at hand and stop thinking about what was no longer her life.

Paige walked for twenty minutes down the road to nowhere, not a single car passing her. By the time Paige got to Skeeter's Bait, Tackle, Guns, and Gas, she was sweating like nobody's business, her dress was sticking to her everywhere, and her feet were killing her. She had a nice blister on the back of her left heel.

She pushed the door open and was greeted with the smell of fish mixed with bleach, making her stomach turn. At least the air conditioner was cranked to full blast. There was a huge stuffed turkey sitting on the counter. The fleshy red thing on its neck looked like the stuff nightmares were made of, and the wall behind the register was covered in mounted fish. She really didn't get the whole "dead animal as a trophy" motif that the South had going on.

There was a display on the counter that had tiny little bottles that looked like energy drinks.

New and improved scent. Great for attracting the perfect game.

She picked up one of the tiny bottles and looked at it. It was doe urine.

She took a closer look at the display. They apparently also had the buck urine variety. She looked at the bottle in her hand, trying to grasp why people would cover themselves in this stuff. Was hunting really worth smelling like an animal's pee?

"Can I help you?"

The voice startled Paige, and she looked up into the face of a very large balding man, his apron covered in God only knew what. She dropped the tiny bottle she had in her hand. It fell to the ground. The cap smashed on the tile floor and liquid poured out everywhere.

It took a total of three seconds for the smell to punch her in the nose. It had to be the foulest scent she'd ever inhaled.

Oh crap. Oh crap, oh crap, oh crap.

She was just stellar at first impressions these days.

"I'm so sorry," she said, trying not to gag. She took a step back from the offending puddle and looked up at the man.

His arms were folded across his chest and he frowned at her, saying nothing.

"Do you, uh, have something I can clean this up with?" she asked nervously.

"You're not from around here," he said, looking at her with his deadpan stare. It wasn't a question. It was a statement, one that she got whenever she met someone new. One that she was so sick and tired of she could scream. Yeah, all of the remorse she'd felt over spilling that bottle drained from her.

In Philadelphia, Paige's bohemian style was normal, but in Mirabelle her big earrings, multiple rings, and loud clothing tended to get her noticed. Her parents' neighbor, Mrs. Forns, thought that Paige was trouble, which she complained about on an almost daily basis.

"You know that marijuana is still illegal," Mrs. Forns had said the other night, standing on her parents' porch and lecturing Paige's mother. "And I won't hesitate to call the authorities if I see your hippie daughter growing anything suspicious or doing any other illegal activities."

Denise Morrison, ever the queen of politeness, had just smiled. "You have nothing to be concerned about."

"But she's doing *something* in that shed of yours in the backyard."

The *something* that Paige did in the shed was paint. She'd converted it into her art studio, complete with ceiling fan.

"Don't worry, Mrs. Forns," Paige had said, sticking her head over her mother's shoulder. "I'll wait to have my orgies on your bingo nights. Is that on Tuesdays or Wednesdays?"

"Paige!" Denise had said as she'd shoved Paige back into the house and closed the door in her face.

Five minutes later, Denise had come into the kitchen shaking her head.

"Really, Paige? You had to tell her that you're having *orgies* in the backyard?"

Paige's father, Trevor Morrison, chuckled as he went through the mail at his desk.

"You need to control your temper and that smart mouth of yours," Denise had said.

"You know what you should start doing?" Trevor said, looking up with a big grin. "You should grow oregano in pots on the windowsill and then throw little dime bags into her yard."

"Trevor, don't encourage her harassing that woman. Paige, she's a little bit older, very set in her ways, and a tad bit nosy."

"She needs to learn to keep her nose on her side of the fence," Paige had said.

"Don't let her bother you."

"That's easier said than done."

"Well, then, maybe you should practice holding your tongue."

"Yes, Mother, I'll get right on that."

So, as Paige stared at the massive man in front of her, whom she assumed to be Skeeter, she pursed her lips and held back the smart-ass retort that was on the tip of her tongue.

Be polite, she heard her mother's voice in her head say. *You just spilled animal pee all over his store. And you need to use his phone.*

"No," Paige said, pushing her big sunglasses up her nose and into her hair. "My car broke down and I don't have any cell phone service. I was wondering if I could use your phone to call a tow truck."

"I'd call King's if I were you. They're the best," he said as he ripped a piece of receipt paper off the cash register and grabbed a pen with a broken plastic spoon taped to the top. He wrote something down and pushed the paper across the counter.

"Thank you. I can clean that up first," she said, pointing to the floor.

"I got it. I'd hate for you to get those hands of yours dirty," he said, moving the phone to her side of the counter.

She just couldn't win.

* * *

Brendan King leaned against the front bumper of Mr. Thame's minivan. He was switching out the old belt and replacing it with a new one when his grandfather stuck his head out of the office.

"Brendan," Oliver King said. "A car broke down on Buckland Road. It's Paige Morrison, Trevor and Denise Morrison's daughter. She said the engine was smoking. She had to walk to Skeeter's to use the phone. I told her you'd pick her up so she didn't have to walk back."

Oliver King didn't look his seventy years. His salt-and-pepper hair was still thick and growing only on the top of his head, and not out of his ears. He had a bit of a belly, but he'd had that for the last twenty years and it wasn't going anywhere. He'd opened King's Auto forty-three years ago, when he was twenty-seven. Now he mainly worked behind the front counter, due to the arthritis in his hands and back. But it was a good thing because King's Auto was one of only a handful of auto shops in the county. They were always busy, so they needed a constant presence running things out of the shop.

Including Brendan and his grandfather, there were four full-time mechanics and two part-time kids who were still in high school and who worked in the garage. Part of the service that King's provided was towing, and Brendan was the man on duty on Mondays. And oh was he ever so happy he was on duty today.

Paige Morrison was the new girl in town. Her parents had moved down from Pennsylvania when they'd retired about two years ago, and Paige had moved in with them three months ago. Brendan had yet to meet her, but he'd most definitely seen her. You couldn't really miss her as she jogged around town, with her very long legs, in a wide variety of the brightest and shortest shorts he'd ever seen in his life. His favorite pair had by far been the hot-pink pair, but the zebra-print ones came in a very close second.

He'd also heard about her. People had a lot to say about her more-than-*interesting* style. It was rumored that she had a bit of a temper and a pretty mouth that said whatever it wanted. Not that Brendan put a lot of stock in gossip. He'd wait to reserve his own judgment.

"Got it," Brendan said, pulling his gloves off and sticking them in his back pocket. "Tell Randall this still needs new spark plugs," he said, pointing to the minivan and walking into the office.

"I will." Oliver nodded and handed Brendan the keys to the tow truck.

Brendan grabbed two waters from the minifridge and his sunglasses from the desk and headed off into the scorching heat. It was a hot one, ninety-eight degrees, but the humidity made it feel like one hundred and three. He flipped his baseball cap so that the bill would actually give him some cover from the August sun, and when he got into the tow truck, he cranked the air as high as it would go.

It took him about fifteen minutes to get to Skeeter's, and when he pulled up into the gravel parking lot, the door to the little shop opened and Brendan couldn't help but smile.

Paige Morrison's mile-long legs were shooting out of the sexiest shoes he'd ever seen. She was also wearing a flowing yellow dress that didn't really cover her amazing legs but did hug her chest and waist, and besides the two skinny straps at her shoulders, her arms were completely bare. Massive sunglasses covered her eyes, and her dark brown hair was piled on top of her head.

There was no doubt about it; she was beautiful, all right.

Brendan put the truck in park and hopped out.

"Ms. Morrison?" he asked even though he already knew who she was.

"Paige," she corrected, stopping in front of him. She was probably five foot ten or so, but her shoes added about three inches, making her just as tall as him. If he weren't wearing his work boots she would've been taller than him.

"I'm Brendan King," he said, sticking his hand out to shake hers. Her hand was soft and warm. He liked how it felt in his. He also liked the freckles that were sprinkled across her high cheek-bones and straight, pert nose.

"I'm about a mile up the road," she said, letting go of his hand and pointing in the opposite direction from the way he'd come.

"Not the most sensible walking shoes," he said, eyeing her feet. The toes that peeked out of her shoes were bright red, and a thin band of silver wrapped around the second toe on her right foot. He looked back up to see her arched eyebrows come together for a second before she took a deep breath.

"Thanks for the observation," she said, walking past him and heading for the passenger door.

Well, this was going to be fun.

* * *

Stupid jerk.

Not the most sensible walking shoes, Paige repeated in her head. *Well, no shit, Sherlock.*

Paige sat in the cab of Brendan's tow truck, trying to keep her temper in check. Her feet were killing her, and she really wanted to kick off her shoes. But she couldn't do that in front of him because then he would *know* that her feet were killing her.

"I'm guessing the orange Jeep is yours?" Brendan asked as it came into view.

"Another outstanding observation," she mumbled under her breath.

"I'm sorry?"

"Yes, it's mine," she said, trying to hide her sarcasm.

"Well, at least the engine isn't smoking anymore," he said as he pulled in behind it and jumped out of the truck. Paige grabbed her keys from her purse and followed, closing the door behind her.

He stopped behind the back of her Jeep for a moment, studying the half a dozen stickers that covered her bumper and part of her back window.

She had one that said MAKE ART NOT WAR in big blue letters. Another said LOVE with a peace sign in the *O*. There was also a sea turtle, an owl with reading glasses, the Cat in the Hat, and her favorite, which said I LOVE BIG BOOKS AND I CANNOT LIE.

He shook his head and laughed, walking to the front of the Jeep.

"What's so funny?" she asked, catching up to his long stride and standing next to him.

"Keys?" he asked, holding out his hand.

She put them in his palm but didn't let go.

"What's so funny?" she repeated.

"Just that you're clearly not from around here." He smiled, closing his hand over hers.

Brendan had a Southern accent, not nearly as thick as some of the other people's in town, and a wide, cocky smile that she really hated, but only because she kind of liked it. She also kind of liked the five-o'clock shadow that covered his square jaw. She couldn't see anything above his chiseled nose, as half of his face was covered by his sunglasses and the shadow from his grease-stained baseball cap, but she could tell his smile reached all the way up to his eyes.

He was most definitely physically fit, filling out his shirt and pants with wide biceps and thighs. His navy blue button-up shirt had short sleeves, showing off his tanned arms, which were covered in tiny blond hairs.

God, he was attractive. But he was also pissing her off.

"I am so sick of everyone saying that," she said, ripping her hand out of his. "Is it such a bad thing to not be from around here?"

"No," he said, his mouth quirking. "It's just very obvious that you're not."

"Would I fit in more if I had a bumper sticker that said MY OTHER CAR IS A TRACTOR or one that said IF YOU'RE NOT CONSERVATIVE YOU JUST AREN'T WORTH IT, or what about WHO NEEDS LITERACY WHEN YOU CAN SHOOT THINGS? What if I had a gun rack mounted on the back window or if I used buck piss as perfume to attract a husband? Would those things make me fit in?" she finished, folding her arms across her chest.

"No. I'd say you could start with not being so judgmental though," he said with a sarcastic smirk.

"Excuse me?"

"Ma'am, you just called everyone around here gun-toting, illiterate rednecks who like to participate in bestiality. Insulting people really isn't a way to fit in," he said, shaking his head. "I would also refrain from spreading your liberal views to the masses, as politics are a bit of a hot-button topic around here. And if you want to attract a husband, you should stick with wearing doe urine, because that attracts only males. The buck urine attracts both males and females." He stopped and looked her up and down with a slow smile. "But maybe you're into that sort of thing."

"Yeah, well, everyone in this town thinks that I'm an amoral, promiscuous pothead. And you," she said, shoving her finger into his chest, "aren't any better. People make snap judgments about me before I even open my mouth. And just so you know, *I'm not even a liberal,*" she screamed as she jabbed her finger into his chest a couple of times. She took a deep breath and stepped back, composing herself. "So maybe I would be *nice* if people would be just a little bit *nice* to me."

"I'm quite capable of being nice to people who deserve it. Can I look at your car now, or would you like to yell at me some more?"

"Be my guest," she said, glaring at him as she moved out of his way.

He unlocked the Jeep and popped the hood. As he moved to the front, he pulled off his baseball cap and wiped the top of his head with his hand. Paige glimpsed his short, dirty-blond hair before he put the hat on backward. As he moved around in her engine, his shirt pulled tight across his back and shoulders. He twisted off the cap to something and stuck it in his pocket. Then he walked back to his truck and grabbed a jug from a metal box on the side. He came back and poured the liquid into something in the engine, and after a few seconds it gushed out of the bottom.

"Your radiator is cracked," he said, grabbing the cap out of his pocket and screwing it back on. "I'm going to have to tow this back to the shop to replace it."

"How much?"

"For everything? We're looking at four maybe five hundred."

"Just perfect," she mumbled.

"Would you like a ride? Or were you planning on showing those shoes more of the countryside?"

"I'll take the ride."

* * *

Paige was quiet the whole time Brendan loaded her Jeep onto the truck. Her arms were folded under her perfect breasts, and she stared at him with her full lips bunched in a scowl. Even pissed off she was stunning, and God, that mouth of hers. He really wanted to see it with an actual smile on it. He was pretty sure it would knock him on his ass.

Speaking of asses, seeing her smile probably wasn't likely at the moment. True, he had purposefully egged her on, but he couldn't resist going off on her when she'd let loose her colorful interpretations of the people from the area. A lot of them were true, but there was a difference between making fun of your own people and having an outsider make fun of them. But still, according to her, the people around here hadn't exactly been nice to her.

Twenty minutes later, with Paige's Jeep on the back of the tow truck, they were on their way to the shop. Brendan glanced over at her as he drove. She was looking out the window with her back to him. Her shoulders were stiff, and she looked like she'd probably had enough stress before her car had decided to die on her.

Brendan looked back at the road and cleared his throat.

"I'm sorry about what I said back there."

Out of the corner of his eye he saw her shift in her seat and he could feel her eyes on him.

"Thank you. I should have kept my mouth shut, too. I just haven't had the best day."

"Why?" he asked, glancing over at her again.

Her body was angled toward him, but her arms were still folded across her chest like a shield. He couldn't help but glance down and see that her dress was slowly riding up her thighs. She had nice thighs, soft but strong. They would be good for... well, a lot of things.

He quickly looked back at the road, thankful he was wearing sunglasses.

"I've been trying to get a job. Today I had an interview, except it wasn't much of an interview."

"What was it?" he asked.

"A setup."

"A setup for what?"

"That *is* the question," she said bitterly.

"Huh?" he asked, looking at her again.

"I'm assuming you know who Bethelda Grimshaw is?"

Brendan's blood pressure had a tendency to rise at the mere mention of that name. Knowing that Bethelda had a part in Paige's current mood had Brendan's temper flaring instantly.

"What did she do?" he asked darkly.

Paige's eyebrows raised a fraction at his tone. She stared at him for a second before she answered. "There was a job opening at the Mirabelle Information Center to take pictures for the brochures and the local businesses for their website. They filled the position last week, something that Mrs. Grimshaw failed to mention when she called this morning to confirm my interview."

"She's looking for her next story."

"What?"

"Bethelda Grimshaw is Mirabelle's resident gossip," Brendan said harshly as he looked back to the road. "She got fired from the newspaper a couple of years ago because of the trash she wrote. Now she has a blog to spread her crap around."

"And she wants to write about me? Why?"

"I can think of a few reasons."

"What's that supposed to mean?" she asked, her voice going up an octave or two.

"Your ability to fly off the handle. Did you give her something to write about?" he asked, raising an eyebrow as he spared a glance at her.

"No," she said, bunching her full lips together. "I saved my freak-out for you."

"I deserved it. I wasn't exactly nice to you," Brendan said, shifting his hands down the steering wheel.

"You were a jerk."

Brendan came to a stop at a stop sign and turned completely in his seat to face Paige. Her eyebrows rose high over her sunglasses and she held her breath.

"I was, and I'm sorry," he said, putting every ounce of sincerity into his words.

"It's...I forgive you," she said softly and nodded her head.

Brendan turned back to the intersection and made a right. Paige was silent for a few moments, but he could feel her gaze on him as if she wanted to say something.

"What?"

"Why does buck urine attract males and females?"

Brendan couldn't help but smile.

"Bucks like to fight each other," he said, looking at her.

"Oh." She nodded and leaned back in her seat, staring out the front window.

"You thirsty?" Brendan asked as he grabbed one of the waters in the cup holder and held it out to her.

"Yes, thank you," she said, grabbing it and downing half of the bottle.

"Who were the other interviews with?" Brendan asked, grabbing the other bottle for himself. He twisted the cap off and threw it into the cup holder.

"Landingham Printing and Design. Mrs. Landingham said I wouldn't be a good fit. Which is completely false because the program they use is one that I've used before."

Now he couldn't help but laugh.

"Uh, Paige, I can tell you right now why you didn't get that job. Mrs. Landingham didn't want you around Mr. Landingham."

"What?" she said, sitting up in her seat again. "What did she think I was going to do, steal her husband? I don't make plays on married men. Or men in their forties for that matter."

"Did you wear something like what you're wearing now to the interview?" he asked, looking at her and taking another eyeful of those long legs.

"I wore a black blazer with this. It's just so hot outside that I took it off."

"Maybe you should try wearing pants next time, and flats," he said before he took a sip of water.

"What's wrong with this dress?" she asked, looking down at herself. "It isn't that short."

"Sweetheart, with those legs, anything looks short."

"Don't call me sweetheart. And it isn't my fault I'm tall."

"No, it isn't, but people think the way they think."

"So Southern hospitality only goes so far when people think you're a whore."

"Hey, I didn't say that. I was just saying that your legs are long without those shoes that you're currently wearing. With them, you're pretty damn intimidating."

"Let's stop talking about my legs."

"Fine." He shrugged, looking back to the road. "But it is a rather visually stimulating conversation."

"Oh no. You are *not* allowed to flirt with me."

"Why not?"

"You were mean to me. I do *not* flirt with mean men."

"I can be nice," he said, turning to her and giving her a big smile.

"Stop it," she said, raising her eyebrows above her glasses in warning. "I mean it."

"So what about some of the other interviews? Who were they with?"

"Lindy's Frame Shop, that art gallery over on the beach—"

"Avenue Ocean?"

"Yeah, that one. And I also went to Picture Perfect. They all said I wasn't a good fit for one reason or another," she said, dejected.

"Look, I'm really not one to get involved in town gossip. I've been on the receiving end my fair share of times and it isn't fun. But this is a small town, and everybody knows one another's business. Since you're new, you have no idea. Cynthia Bowers at Picture Perfect would've never hired you. Her husband has monogamy issues. The owner of Avenue Ocean, Mindy Trist, doesn't like anyone that's competition."

"Competition?"

Mindy Trist was a man-eater. Brendan knew this to be a fact because Mindy had been trying to get into his bed for years. He wasn't even remotely interested.

"You're prettier than she is."

Understatement of the year.

Paige was suddenly silent on her side of the truck.

"And as for Hurst and Marlene Lindy," Brendan continued, "they, uh, tend to be a little more conservative."

"Look," she said, snapping out of her silence.

Brendan couldn't help himself; her sudden burst of vehemence made him look at her again. If he kept this up he was going to drive into a ditch.

"I know I might appear to be some free-spirited hippie, but I'm really not. I'm moderate when it comes to politics," she said, holding up one finger. "I eat meat like it's nobody's business." Two fingers. "And I've never done drugs in my life." Three fingers.

"You don't have to convince me," he said, shaking his head.

"So I'm sensing a pattern here with all of these jobs. Are you a photographer?"

"Yes, but I do graphic design and I paint."

"So a woman of many talents."

"I don't know about that," she said, shaking her head.

"Oh, I'm sure you have a lot of talent. It's probably proportional to the length of your legs."

"What did I tell you about flirting?" she asked seriously, but betrayed herself when the corners of her mouth quirked up.

"Look, Paige, don't let it get to you. Not everyone is all bad."

"So I've just been fortunate enough to meet everyone who's mean."

"You've met me."

"Yeah, well, the jury's still out on you."

"Then I guess I'll have to prove myself."

"I guess so," she said, leaning back in her seat. Her arms now rested in her lap, her shield coming down a little.

"I have a question," Brendan said, slowing down at another stop sign. "If you eat meat, why do you have such a problem with hunting?"

"It just seems a little barbaric. Hiding out in the woods to shoot Bambi and then mounting his head on a wall."

"Let me give you two scenarios."

"Okay."

"In scenario one, we have Bessie the cow. Bessie was born in a stall, taken away from her mother shortly after birth, when she was moved to a pasture for a couple of years, all the while being injected with hormones and then shoved into a semitruck, where she was shipped off to be slaughtered. And I don't think that you even want me to get started on that process.

"In scenario two, we have Bambi. Bambi was born in the

wilderness and wasn't taken away from his mother. He then found a mate, had babies, and one day was killed. He never saw it coming. Not only is Bambi's meat hormone free, but he also lived a happy life in the wild, with no fences.

"Now, you tell me, which scenario sounds better: being raised to be slaughtered, or living free where you might or might not be killed?"

She was silent for a few moments before she sighed.

"Fine, you win. The second sounds better."

"Yeah, that's what I thought," Brendan said as he pulled into the parking lot of King's Auto. "How are you getting home?" he asked as he put the truck into park.

"I called my dad after I called you. He's here actually," she said, pointing to a black Chevy Impala.

They both got out of the truck and headed toward the auto shop. Brendan held the door open for Paige, shoving his sunglasses into his shirt pocket. His grandfather and a man who Brendan recognized as Paige's father stood up from their chairs as Brendan and Paige walked in.

Trevor Morrison was a tall man, maybe six foot four or six foot five. He had light reddish-brown wispy hair on his head and large glasses perched on his nose. And like his daughter, his face and arms were covered in freckles.

"Hi, Daddy," Paige said, pushing her glasses up her nose and into her hair.

Brendan immediately noticed the change in her voice. Her cautious demeanor vanished and her shoulders relaxed. He'd caught a glimpse of this in the truck, but not to this extent.

"Mr. Morrison," Brendan said, taking a step forward and sticking his hand out.

Trevor grabbed Brendan's hand firmly. "Brendan," he said,

giving him a warm smile and nodding his head. Trevor let go of Brendan's hand and turned to his daughter. "Paige, this is Oliver King," he said, gesturing to Brendan's grandfather, who was standing behind his desk. "Oliver, this is my daughter, Paige."

"I haven't had the pleasure," Oliver said, moving out from behind his desk and sticking out his hand.

Paige moved forward past Brendan, her arm brushing his as she passed.

"It's nice to meet you, sir," she said, grabbing Oliver's hand.

Oliver nodded as he let go of Paige's hand and looked up at Brendan. "So what happened?"

Paige turned to look at Brendan, too. It was the first time he'd gotten a full look at her face without her sunglasses on. She had long dark eyelashes that framed her large gray irises. It took him a second to remember how to speak. He cleared his throat and looked past her to the other two men.

"It's the radiator. I'm going to have to order a new one, so it's going to take a few days."

"That's fine," she said, shrugging her shoulders. "It's not like I have anywhere to go."

Trevor's face fell. "The interview didn't go well?"

"Nope," Paige said, shaking her head. The tension in her shoulders came back, but she tried to mask it by pasting a smile on her face. He desperately wanted to see a genuine, full-on smile from her.

"Things haven't exactly gone Paige's way since she moved here," Trevor said.

"Oh, I think my bad luck started long before I moved here," she said, folding her arms across her chest. Every time she did that, it pushed her breasts up, and it took everything in Brendan not to stare.

"I don't think it was Paige's fault," Brendan said, and everyone turned to look at him. "It was with Bethelda Grimshaw," he said to Oliver.

"Oh," Oliver said, shaking his head ruefully. "Don't let anything she says get to you. She's a horrible hag."

Paige laughed and the sound of it did funny things to Brendan's stomach.

"Told you," Brendan said, looking at her. Paige turned to him, a small smile lingering on her lips and in her eyes.

God, she was beautiful.

"Things will turn around," Oliver said. "We'll call you with an estimate before we do anything to your car."

They said their good-byes, and as Paige walked out with her father, she gave Brendan one last look, her lips quirking up slightly before she shook her head and walked out the door.

"I don't believe any of that nonsense people are saying about her," Oliver said as they both watched Paige and her dad walk out. "She's lovely."

Lovely? Yeah, that wasn't exactly the word Brendan would have used to describe her.

Hot? Yes. *Fiery?* Absolutely.

"Yeah, she's something, all right."

"Oh, don't tell me you aren't a fan of hers. Son, you barely took your eyes off her."

"I'm not denying she's beautiful." How could he? "I bet she's a handful though and she's got a temper on her, along with a smart mouth." But he sure did like that smart mouth.

"That's a bit of the pot calling the kettle black," Oliver said, raising one bushy eyebrow. "If all of her experiences in this town have been similar to what Bethelda dishes out, I'm not surprised she's turned on the defense. You know what it's like to be the center of less than savory gossip in this town. To have a lot of the people turn their backs on you and turn you into a pariah," Oliver said, giving Brendan a knowing look.

"I know," Brendan conceded. "She deserves a break."

"You should help her find a job."

"With whom?"

"You'll think of something," Oliver said, patting Brendan on the shoulder before going back to his desk. "You always do."

Shannon Richard's sexy small-town series continues!

Jax has been protecting his best friend's kid sister, Grace, since they were young. Now that they're all grown up, they insist there's nothing between them—until one night changes everything...

Please turn this page for an excerpt of

Undeniable.

Prologue

The Princess

At six years old there were certain things Grace King didn't understand. She didn't understand where babies came from, how birds flew way up high in the sky, or where her father was. Grace had never met her dad; she didn't know what he looked like, she didn't even know his name, and for some reason this fact fascinated many people in Mirabelle.

"What's a girl bastard?"

Grace looked up from the picture she was coloring to see Hoyt Reynolds and Judson Coker looming over the other side of the picnic table where she was sitting.

Every day after the bell rang, Grace would wait outside on the playground for her brother, Brendan, to come and get her, and they'd walk home together. Today Brendan was running a little late.

"I don't know." Judson smirked. "I think bastard works for boys and girls."

"Yeah." Hoyt shrugged. "Trash is trash."

Brendan was always telling Grace to ignore bullies, advice he had a problem following himself. Half the time she didn't even know what they were saying. Today was no different. She had no idea what a bastard was, but she was pretty sure it wasn't anything nice.

Grace looked back down to her picture and started coloring the crown of the princess. She grabbed her pink crayon from the pile she'd dumped out on the table, and just before she started coloring the dress the picture disappeared out from under her hands.

"Hey," she protested, looking back up at the boys, "give that back."

"No, I don't think I will," Judson said before he slowly started to rip the picture.

"Stop it," Grace said, swinging her legs over the bench and getting quickly to her feet. She ran to the other side of the table and stood in front of Judson. "Give it back to me."

"Make me," he said, holding the picture up high over her head as he ripped it cleanly in half.

Grace took a step forward and stomped down hard on his foot.

"You little bitch!" Judson screamed, hopping up and down on his uninjured foot.

Grace had one second of satisfaction before she found herself sprawled out on her back, the wind knocked out of her.

"Don't ever touch her again!"

Grace looked up just in time to see a tall, freckled, red-haired boy punch Hoyt in the face. It was Jax, one of Brendan's best friends, who had come to her rescue. And boy did Jax know what he was doing, because Hoyt fell back onto his butt hard.

"And if you ever call her that word again, you'll get a lot more than a punch in the face, you stupid little scumbag," Jax said as he put himself in between Grace and Judson. "Now get out of here."

"I'm going to tell my father about this," Hoyt said. This was a legitimate threat, as Hoyt's father was the principal.

"You do that." Jax shrugged.

Apparently the two eight-year-olds didn't have anything else to say and they didn't want to take their chances against a big, bad eleven-year-old, because they scrambled away and ran around the side of the building and out of sight.

"You okay?" Jax asked, turning around to Grace.

It was then that Grace realized the back of her dress was covered in mud and her palms were scraped and bleeding.

"No," she sniffed before she started to bawl.

"Oh, Grace," Jax said, grabbing her under her arms and pulling her to her feet. "Come here." He pulled her in to his chest and rubbed her back. "It's okay, Gracie."

She looked up at him and bit her trembling lip. "They called me names." She hiccupped.

"They weren't true," he said, looking down at her.

"What's a bastard, Jax?"

Jax's hand stilled and his nose flared. "Nothing you need to worry about," he said. "Grace, sometimes dads aren't all they're cracked up to be."

She nodded once before she buried her head back in his chest. By the time she'd cried herself out, Jax's shirt was covered in her tears. She took a step back from him and wiped her fingers underneath her eyes. Jax reached down and grabbed the two halves of her picture from the ground.

"We can tape this back together," he said, looking down at the paper. He studied it for a second before he looked back to her. "This is what you are, Grace. A princess. Don't let anyone tell you different. You understand?" he asked, lightly tugging on her blond ponytail.

"Yes." She nodded.

"All right," he said, handing the papers back to her. "Get your stuff together and we'll go wait for Brendan."

"Where is he?" Grace asked as she gathered her crayons and put them back into the box.

"He got into trouble with Principal Reynolds again."

Grace looked up at Jax and frowned. She really didn't like the Reynolds family. Principal Reynolds wasn't any better than his son.

"No frowning, Princess. Let's go," Jax said, holding out his hand for her.

Grace shoved her crayons and drawing into her bag. She grabbed Jax's outstretched hand and let him lead her away.

Chapter 1

The Protector

The nightmares felt so real. They always started off the exact same way as the accident had, but then they morphed into something so much worse, something that haunted Jax even when he was awake.

As a deputy sheriff for Atticus County, Jaxson Anderson was no stranger to being the first person to arrive at the scene of an accident. What he wasn't used to was being the first to an accident that involved two people he cared about. That day it had been Grace and Paige King. Grace was the little sister of Brendan King, one of Jax's best friends. Paige was Brendan's wife.

It had happened more than six months ago. Violent storms had raged across Mirabelle for days, and the rains had flooded the river that ran through town, making the current swift and deadly. By some miracle Jax and been driving right behind Paige and Grace. Jax and his friend Bennett Hart had watched as the SUV the girls were in swerved off the road, crashed through a barrier, and disappeared down to Whiskey River. The only thing that had stopped the car from being swept under the water was a tree growing out of the bank. The tree was barely strong enough to hold the car back.

That day Jax had experienced a panic like no other. He'd gone into the river desperate to pull them out. And that was when the second miracle of the day happened. Brendan, along with Nathanial Shepherd and Baxter McCoy, had shown up. It took the efforts of all five men to pull the girls out of the car before it was swept under the water. It had been just a matter of seconds of getting them out before the tree gave way.

Jax went over those moments, over and over again, replaying everything from what he'd said to what he'd done. The one thing he was absolutely sure about was that getting those girls out of that river alive was miracle number three.

But Jax's nightmares didn't play out like the miracle. No, in his nightmares he watched as Grace died.

When the accident happened, they'd had to pull Grace out from the car before Paige. In the nightmare, it was Grace who was pulled out second. Paige was safe in Brendan's arms, and Jax would go to get Grace, but the tree would snap right before his hands touched hers. Jax would scream her name as the river dragged her away and she disappeared under the surface of the water.

Jax woke up, Grace's name still on his lips. He was breathing hard and drenched in sweat, the sheets sticking to his skin. He blinked, his eyes adjusting to the darkness as he slowly began to realize that what he'd seen wasn't real. That it was just another nightmare. That Grace wasn't lost. She'd walked away from the accident with a dislocated shoulder and minor scrapes and bruises.

Jax lay there, and when he got his breathing under control and his heart stopped pounding out of his chest, he turned to look at the alarm clock. It was ten to five in the morning. He didn't need to be up for another hour, but it was pointless for him to even attempt to go back to sleep. Whenever he had a nightmare about Grace, he was on edge until he saw her and knew she was okay.

So instead, Jax threw back the sheets that were tangled around his legs and sat on the edge of the bed. He rubbed his face with his hands before he got up and padded into the bathroom. He brushed his teeth and splashed his face with cold water. He looked into the mirror as water dripped off the end of his long, freckled nose. The hollows under his eyes were tinged a light purple.

Mirabelle had a whopping five thousand people in its six hundred square miles, half of which was water. The little beach town made up sixty percent of Atticus County's population, and boy did those five thousand sure know how to keep the sheriff's office busy. Deputies worked twelve-hour shifts. Two days on, then two days off; three days on, then two days off.

Jax had worked only the first day of his three-day shift, and he'd had to deal with plenty already: a kid who'd stolen his mom's car to go joy riding with his girlfriend, more drunken college kids on spring break than he could count, and three house calls for domestic disturbances, two of which had ended in arrests. He was also investigating a string of burglaries that had been going on in Mirabelle. Five alone in the last two months, and they all looked to be connected.

The day before had been a long one and he left work exhausted. For normal people that would mean sleep would come easier, but that wasn't the case for Jax. For Jax, deep sleep brought on his nightmares. He'd been having nightmares for as far back as he could remember, and at twenty-nine years old, that was a long time. It was hard not to have nightmares when you grew up in an environment that was less than friendly.

Haldon Anderson was one mean son of a bitch, and he took

great pleasure in making his son feel like shit as often as possible. When Haldon wasn't in jail, he was out on a fishing boat making money to drown himself in a bottle of liquor and whatever pills he could get his hands on. And when Haldon got on one of his benders, there was absolutely nothing that was going to stop him. Whether Haldon used his fists or his words, he knew how to make a person bleed.

Haldon had laughed when Jax became a deputy seven years ago. He'd thought it was one of the greatest jokes of his life.

"This is perfect," he'd said, wiping his fingers underneath his eyes. "A worthless boy doing a thankless job. Working for justice, my ass. You're not going to do anything to make this world a better place. The only thing you could've possibly done to achieve that was to have never been born."

Yup, Haldon Anderson, father of the *fucking* year.

As a child, Jax couldn't understand why his mother let his father get away with all the abuse. But Patricia Anderson wasn't a strong woman and her greatest weakness was Haldon. She hadn't protected her child like a mother should. Actually, she hadn't done anything that a mother should do.

Jax shook his head and pulled himself out of the past. That was the last thing he wanted to think about.

He put on a sweatshirt, a pair of gym shorts, and his sneakers before he headed out into the chilly April morning. He stretched for a minute before he hit the pavement and attempted to run from his demons.

* * *

Grace King inhaled deeply as she pulled out a fresh batch of Bananas Foster muffins. The rich smell filled her nose before it expanded her lungs. She smiled as she set them on the counter to cool. These muffins were going to sell out with the morning breakfast rush.

Grace didn't care if she was making cookies, pies, or cupcakes; she never got tired of it. One of her first memories was sitting in the kitchen at her grandparents' house while she watched her mother stir chocolate cake batter. Grace's fondest memories of her mother were the two of them baking together. Claire King had lost her battle to breast cancer almost fourteen years ago. But before she died, she'd passed on her love for baking to her daughter.

Grace had been working in her grandmother's café since she was eight years old. Now, at twenty-four, she helped her grandmother run Café Lula. The café was a small, brightly painted cottage out on Mirabelle Beach. The promise of freshly baked food kept customers from all over town and the county pouring in no matter the time of day or the season.

The day promised to be a busy one, as Grace had to fill up the dessert case with fresh goodies. She'd been experimenting with cupcake recipes the past couple of weeks. She'd wanted to make something amazing for her sister-in-law's baby shower. Grace had eaten dinner at Brendan and Paige's the night before, and she'd been the one in charge of dessert. For fear of disappointing a sassy pregnant woman, she'd brought her A-game and made two different types of cupcakes.

"I think my favorite is the Blueberry Lemonade," Paige had said as she'd rubbed her ever-growing belly. "But Trevor seems to like this Red Velvet Cheesecake one. I think he's dancing in there."

Trevor Oliver King was supposed to be gracing the world with his presence around the middle of May. Grace couldn't wait to meet her nephew. Paige was more than seven months pregnant, and she was one of those women who still looked beautiful even though she was growing another human being inside of her. If Grace didn't love her sister-in-law dearly, she would've been fifty shades of jealous. As it was, she was only about twenty shades.

But really, Grace couldn't be happier for her brother and sister-in-law. Brendan was going to be an amazing father. Much better than his or Grace's had been.

Neither Brendan nor Grace had ever had their fathers in their lives. Brendan's dad had gotten their mother pregnant when she was seventeen. When he'd found out, he promptly split town and never looked back. But while Brendan at least knew who his father was, Grace had no idea about hers. It was one of the great mysteries, and a constant source of gossip in Mirabelle.

There were many things in life that Grace was grateful for, her brother and Paige topping the list. They were a team and they worked together. They loved each other deeply. And Grace envied that stupid dopey look they always had on their faces. She wanted that. And she knew exactly whom she wanted it with. It was just too bad for her that the man in question was stubborn and refused to see her as anything besides his best friend's little sister.

Grace took a deep breath and shook her head, bringing herself back to the muffins that she had to take to the front of the café. There was no need to concern herself with frustrating men at the moment. So she loaded up a tray with an already cooled batch of muffins and went to load the display case before the eight-o'clock rush of customers filled the café. But when she pushed her way through the door, she found the frustrating man in question on the other side, staring at her with her favorite pair of deep green eyes.

* * *

Jax's whole body relaxed when he saw Grace push through the door from the kitchen. The moment she saw him, her blue eyes lit up and her Cupid's bow mouth split into a giant grin. She'd always looked at him that way. Like he was her favorite person in the whole world. God knew she was his.

"Heya, Deputy. Let me guess," she said as she put the tray down on the counter. "You came here for coffee?"

No. He'd come here to see her. He always came here to see her. But coffee was a legitimate enough excuse, especially since he hadn't gotten that much sleep and was at the beginning of another twelve-hour shift.

"Please," he said, drumming his long, freckled fingers on the counter.

"Did you eat breakfast?" she asked as she pulled a to-go cup off the stack and started pumping coffee into it.

"I'm fine."

"Hmm." She looked over her shoulder at him and pursed her lips. "You know that isn't going to fly for a second. I got just the thing to go with this." She put the steaming cup and a lid down on the counter. "Go fix your coffee while I bag up your breakfast."

Grace turned around and pushed through the door to the kitchen as Jax grabbed his cup and went over to the end of the counter where the sugar and milk was.

Since Jax was four years old, the King women had been feeding him. Between them and Shep's mom, theirs were the only home-cooked meals he'd gotten after his grandmother died. If it hadn't been for them, he would've gone to bed with an empty stomach more nights than most.

Patricia Anderson wasn't much of a Susie Homemaker.

Between her long hours working at the Piggly Wiggly, and drinking herself into a stupor and getting high when Haldon was on parole, she sometimes forgot to stock the freezer with corn dogs and mini pizzas for her son.

"Here you go."

Jax turned to find Grace by his side. She hadn't gotten the height gene like Brendan. She was about five feet four and came in just under Jax's chin. Her petite stature and soft heart-shaped face inspired an overwhelming urge in him to protect her. She'd always inspired that feeling in him, ever since her mother brought her home from the hospital all those years ago.

"They're Bananas Foster muffins and they're fresh out of the oven," she said, holding out a bag.

"Thanks, Princess," he said, grabbing the bag and letting his fingers brush the back of her hand.

God, he loved the way her skin felt against his.

"Anytime, Jax." She smiled widely at him. A second later she stepped in to him and grabbed his forearms for balance as she stretched up on her toes and kissed his jaw.

It was something Grace had done a thousand and one times before. She had no concept of personal boundaries with him, and she was wide open with her affection. And just like always, when her lips brushed his skin he had the overwhelming desire to turn in to her. To feel her lips against his. To grab her and hold her against him while he explored her mouth with his.

But instead of following that impulse, he let her pull back from him.

"Eat those while they're hot," she said, pointing to the bag.

"I will," he promised.

"Do you need something for lunch? I can get you a sandwich."

"I'm good," he said, shaking his head.

"Really?" she asked, putting her hands on her hips and narrowing her eyes at him.

He couldn't help but grin at her attempt to intimidate him.

There was no doubt about the fact that Grace King was tough. She'd had to grow a thick skin over the years. Even though Jax, along with Brendan and Shep, had done everything in their power to try to protect her, they couldn't be there to shield her from everything. So Grace had done everything to even up the score with whoever tried to put her down. She wasn't a shy little thing by any means, and she'd tell anybody what was up without a moment's hesitation.

"I'll stop somewhere and get something," he said.

"Or I can give you something now," she said, exasperated. "I'm getting you a sandwich." She turned on her heel and walked back into the kitchen.

"Grace, you don't have to do this," Jax said, following her.

"I know," she said, looking over her shoulder as she opened the refrigerator. "But I'm going to anyway."

Jax watched as Grace filled a bag with two sandwiches, a bag of chips, a cup of fruit salad, and his favorite, a butterscotch cookie.

"This should last you till dinner."

Jax didn't say anything as he pulled his wallet out to pay for everything.

"Oh, I don't think so," Grace said, shaking her head. "You are *not* paying."

Before Jax could respond, the side door in the kitchen opened and Lula Mae walked in.

To the casual observer, Grace and Brendan's grandmother wouldn't strike a person as someone to be feared. She had a kind face and bright blue eyes that, when paired with her ample stature and friendly disposition, inspired a feeling of warmth and openness. But Lula Mae was fiercely loyal, and those blue eyes could go as cold as ice when someone hurt anyone she loved. Lula Mae had declared Jax as one of hers more than twenty-five years ago, and she'd marched down to his parents' house more than once to give them a piece of her mind.

Jax had spent more nights sleeping at the Kings' house than he could count. It was one of the few places he'd actually felt safe growing up. And even now whenever he saw her or her husband, Oliver, he had that overwhelming feeling of being protected.

"Jaxson Lance Anderson," Lula Mae said, walking up to him, "what in the world is your wallet doing out? Your money is no good here."

"That's what I just told him."

Jax turned back to Grace, who was wearing a self-satisfied smile.

"Your granddaughter just gave me more than thirty dollars' worth of food," he said, indicating the stuffed bag on the counter before he turned back to Lula Mae.

"I don't care," she said, shaking her head. "Now give me some sugar before you go and keep the people of Mirabelle safe."

"Yes, ma'am," Jax said, leaning down and giving Lula Mae a peck on the check.

"And next time I see that wallet of yours make an appearance in this establishment, you are going to get a smack upside that handsome head of yours. You understand me?"

"Yes, ma'am," Jax repeated.

"Good boy." She nodded, patting his cheek.

"Thanks again," he said, reaching for the bag of food and his coffee. "I'll see you two later."

"Bye, sugar," Lula Mae said as she rounded the counter.

"See you later," Grace said, giving him another of her face-splitting grins.

Jax headed for the door, unable to stop his own smile from spreading across his face.

* * *

Grace stared at Jax's retreating form as he walked out of the kitchen, and she appreciated every inch of it. He had a lean, muscular body. His shoulders filled out the top of his forest-green deputy's shirt, and his strong back tapered down to his waist. His shirt was tucked into his green pants, which hung low from his narrow hips and covered his long, toned legs.

And oh, dear God, did Jaxson Anderson have a nice ass.

Though her appreciation of said ass had been going on for only about ten years, her appreciation of Jaxson Anderson had been discovered a long time ago. He was the boy who saved her from bullies on the playground. The boy who gave her his ice-cream cone when hers fell in the dirt. The boy who picked her up off the ground when she Rollerbladed into a tree. The boy who let her cry on his shoulder after her mom died.

Yes, Brendan and Shep had done all those things as well, but Jax was different. Jax was hers. She'd decided that eighteen years ago. She'd just been waiting for him to figure it out.

But the man was ridiculously slow on the uptake.

Grace had been in love with him since she was six years old. She loved his freckles and his reddish-brown hair. His hair that was always long enough to where someone could run their fingers through it and rumple it just a little. Not that she'd ever rumpled Jax's hair, but a girl always had her fantasies, and getting Jax all tousled was most definitely one of Grace's.

Jax was always so in control and self-contained, and so damn serious. More often than not, that boy had a frown on his face, which was probably why every time Grace saw his dimpled smile it made her go all warm and giddy.

God, she loved his smile. She just wanted to kiss it, to run her lips down from his mouth to his smooth, triangular jaw.

Grace sighed wistfully as the door shut behind him and turned to her grandmother.

"You get your young man all fed and caffeinated?" Lula Mae asked as she pulled containers out of the refrigerator.

"I don't know about 'my young man,' but I did get Jax something to soak up that coffee he came in for."

"Oh, sweetie," Lula Mae said, looking at Grace and shaking her head pityingly, "that boy did not come in here for coffee."

"Hmmm, well, he sure didn't ask for anything else," Grace said as she walked over to the stove and started plating the rest of her muffins.

"Just give it time."

"Time?" Grace spun around to look at her grandmother. "How much *time* does the man need? He's had years."

"Yes, well, he'll figure things out. Sooner than later, I think."

"I don't think so. To him, I'm just Brendan's little sister."

"There's no *just* about it," Lula Mae said, grabbing one last container before she closed the fridge and walked back to the counter where she'd piled everything else. "He doesn't have brotherly feelings for you, Gracie. I've never seen anyone fluster that boy the way you do."

"Oh, come on. Jaxson Anderson doesn't get flustered," Grace said, shaking her head.

"If you think that, then he isn't the only one who's blind."

"What's that supposed to mean?"

"You see, Gracie, you've never had the chance to observe him when you aren't around."

"And?" she prompted, gesturing with her hand for her grandmother to carry on.

"He changes when you're around. Smiles more."

"Really? Because he still frowns a whole lot around me."

"Well, that's usually when some other boy is trying to get your attention, and he's jealous."

"Jealous." Grace scoffed. "Jax doesn't get jealous."

"Oh, yes, he does. Grace, you need to open your eyes; that boy has been fighting his feelings for you for years."

And with that, Lula Mae went about fixing her menu for the day, leaving Grace even more frustrated than she had been the minute before.

* * *

"Holy hell, that girl can bake."

Jax bit into his second muffin and chewed slowly. He hadn't realized how hungry he'd been until he'd taken that first bite, and then he'd promptly inhaled the first muffin. This one he intended to savor. He let the warm richness of the bread rest on his tongue for a moment before he swallowed and took a swig of his steaming coffee.

It was amazing how much better he felt with food in his stomach, or maybe he just felt better because he'd seen Grace. He *always* felt better when he saw Grace. She made everything so much brighter, so much *more*. Like swallowing a warm liquid that settled in his stomach before it shot out to this fingers and toes and made him feel like he could take on anything.

The power of caffeine had nothing on Grace King.

She was loud and vibrant, and it was almost impossible to escape her enthusiasm. She'd always had the ability to draw whoever was around into her atmosphere and keep them there. She'd drawn Jax in when she was a baby, and he'd been hooked ever since.

Though how he was hooked had changed in recent years. It hadn't been a slow, gradual change, either. It had been about as subtle as Grace. Jax remembered the day vividly. She'd been eighteen years old; he'd been twenty-three.

He'd stopped by the Kings' house for dinner one night and Grace was out in the yard, washing her vintage yellow Bug. She had the radio blasting music, so she hadn't heard him pull up on the street. She was wearing short cutoff blue jeans and a bright blue bikini top, the strings tied around the middle of her back and around her neck. Her light blonde hair had been up in a ponytail, but a few strands had escaped and were sticking to the side of her neck. It was then, as Jax studied the slope of her neck, that he felt it. He'd wanted to come up behind her and put his mouth to that neck, taste her warm skin against his tongue.

He remembered stopping so suddenly at the thought that he'd almost tripped and landed on his face.

Grace was Brendan's little sister. Jax had watched her grow up, been there when they'd brought her home from the hospital, heard her first laugh as a baby, watched as she'd taken her first steps, sang happy birthday to her as she blew out candles on every single birthday. This was Grace, the girl he'd always thought of as his little sister. But damn if every single one of those brotherly feelings was gone.

Every. Last. One. Of. Them.

And then he'd watched, paralyzed from the revelation, as she turned to dunk the sponge in her hand in a bucket of soapy water, and he got a glimpse of her side.

"What the hell is that?"

Somehow he'd found his tongue and his voice had carried over the beat of the music.

Grace looked up and turned to him, her usual grin spreading across her face. But he'd had only a moment to register her smile because his eyes darted back down to her side, where a blue swallow about the size of his hand was tattooed on her upper ribs. It was diving down; one of its wings spanned her side, and the other wrapped around to cup under her right breast.

Jax had never thought much of Grace's breasts. They were small, not even a handful. But now? Now he wanted to know what those felt like, too. His fingers were itching to untie those straps.

What the hell is wrong with me?

"Why, Jaxson Anderson," Grace drawled, "are you staring at my chest?"

Jax looked up, and he could feel the flush coming to his cheeks. But he was determined to play this off, because he would go to the grave before he admitted to wanting the baby sister of one of his best friends.

"No, I'm looking at that tattoo on your side," he said, letting his anger boil over into his voice. "What the hell did you do? Does Brendan know about this?" he almost screamed at her.

Why the hell am I so pissed off?

Because that tattoo was sexy as hell and he didn't want anyone looking at it. Or God, touching it. Touching her.

Her smile disappeared in an instant and her blue eyes turned icy. "He was there when I got it a month ago," she said, narrowing her eyes at him.

"He let you?" Jax asked, incredulous.

"Brendan doesn't *let me* do anything," Grace said, crossing her arms under her chest. It made her small breasts more prominent.

How had he not noticed how amazing they were before that moment?

"In case you hadn't noticed, I'm not a child anymore, Jax."

And that had been precisely the problem, because he *had* finally noticed. And it had tortured him every single day for the last six years.

Jax sighed before he took another bite of his muffin, because boy did Grace ever like to torture him.

Grace's friendliness tended to come off as flirting, and nothing got under Jax's skin more than when he saw Grace flirting with some little schmuck. He'd had to watch as guy after guy paraded through her life. Okay, so there hadn't been that many guys who'd gotten past the flirting stage. But none of them had been good enough for her, not a single one.

Jax wasn't good enough, either, so he'd resigned himself to doing what he *was* good enough for, watching out for her. And man was watching hard.

About the Author

Shannon Richard grew up in the Florida Panhandle as the baby sister of two overly protective but loving brothers. She was raised by a more-than-somewhat-eccentric mother, a self-proclaimed vocabularist who showed her how to get lost in a book, and a father who passed on his love for coffee and really loud music. She graduated from Florida State University with a BA in English literature and still lives in Tallahassee, where she battles everyday life with writing, reading, and a rant every once in a while. Okay, so the rants might happen on a regular basis. She's still waiting for her Southern, scruffy Mr. Darcy, and in the meantime writes love stories to indulge her overactive imagination. Oh, and she's a pretty big fan of the whimsy.

Learn more at:
ShannonRichard.net
Twitter, @Shan_Richard
Facebook.com/ShannonNRichard

You Might Also Like...

FOREVER

Don't miss the rest of Shannon Richards's Country Roads novels!

Things Paige Morrison will never understand about Mirabelle, Florida:

Why wearing red shoes makes a girl a harlot

Why a shop would ever sell something called "buck urine"

Why everywhere she goes, she runs into sexy—and infuriating—Brendan King.

After losing her job, her apartment, and her boyfriend, Paige has no choice but to leave Philadelphia and move in with her retired parents. For an artsy outsider like Paige, finding her place in the tightly knit town isn't easy—until she meets Brendan, the hot mechanic who's interested in much more than Paige's car. In no time at all, Brendan helps Paige find a new job, new friends, and a happiness she wasn't sure she'd ever feel again. With Brendan by her side, Paige finally feels like she can call Mirabelle home. But when a new bombshell drops, will the couple survive, or will their love come undone?

THEIR LOVE WAS *UNDENIABLE*

Grace King knows two things for certain: she loves working at her grandmother's café and she loves the hunky town sheriff. She always has. As she bakes him sweet treats, Grace fantasizes about helping him work up an appetite all night long. But whenever she thinks she's finally getting somewhere, he whips out some excuse to escape. Growing up, he never looked twice at her. Now Grace won't rest until she has Jax's undivided attention.

Jaxson Anderson can't deny that his best friend's kid sister is the sexiest woman in Mirabelle, Florida. Unwilling to burden Grace with his painful past, Jax keeps the sassy blonde at arm's length. Yet one heated kiss crumbles all of his carefully built defenses. But when a town secret surfaces, threatening to destroy everything they believe in, can the man who defended Grace from bullies as a child protect her now?

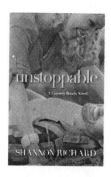

Some things you don't dare let go...

Melanie O'Bryan knows life is too short to be afraid of taking chances. And former air force sergeant Bennett Hart is certainly worth taking a chance on. He's agreed to help her students with a school project, but she's hoping the handsome handyman will offer her a whole lot more. Yet despite his heated glances and teasing touches, Mel senses there's something holding him back...

Bennett Hart is grateful to be alive and back home in Mirabelle, Florida. Peaceful and uncomplicated—that's all he's looking for. Until a spunky, sexy-as-hell teacher turns his life upside down. After one smoldering kiss, Bennett feels like he's falling without a parachute. But with memories of his past threatening to resurface, he'll have to decide whether to keep playing it safe, or take the biggest risk of all.

CPSIA information can be obtained at www.ICGtesting.com
Printed in the USA
LVOW07s1604190115

423455LV00001B/128/P